THE WORKS OF

WILKIE COLLINS

VOLUME ELEVEN

WITH NINE ILLUSTRATIONS

HIDE AND SEEK

NEW YORK
PETER FENELON COLLIER, PUBLISHER

37424

LIST OF ILLUSTRATIONS.

VOLUME ELEVEN.

HIDE AND SEEK.

PREFACE.

THIS novel ranks the third, in order of succession, of the works of fiction which I have produced. The history of its reception, on its first appearance, is soon told.

Unfortunately for me, "Hide-and-Seek" was originally published in the year eighteen hundred and fifty-four, at the outbreak of the Crimean war. All England felt the absorbing interest of watching that serious national event; and new books—some of them books of far higher pretensions than mine—found the minds of readers in general preoccupied or indifferent. My own little venture in fiction necessarily felt the adverse influence of the time. The demand among the book-sellers was just large enough to exhaust the first edition, and there the sale of this novel, in its original form, terminated.

Since that period, the book has been, in the technical phrase, "out of print." Proposals have reached me, at various times, for its republication; but I have resolutely abstained from availing myself of them for two reasons.

In the first place, I was anxious to wait until "Hide-and-Seek" could make its re-appearance on a footing of perfect equality with my other works. In the second place, I was resolved to keep it back until it might obtain the advantage of a careful revisal, guided by the light of the author's later experience. The period for the accomplishment of both these objects has now presented itself. "Hide-and-Seek," in this edition, forms one among the uniform series of my novels, which has begun with "Antonina," "The Dead Secret," and "The Woman in White;" and which will be continued with "Basil" and "The Queen of Hearts." My project of revisal has, at the same time, been carefully and rigidly executed. I have abridged, and in many cases omitted, several passages in the first edition, which made larger demands upon the reader's patience than I should now think it desirable to venture on if I were writing a new book; and I have, in one important respect, so altered the termination of the story, as to make it, I hope, more satisfactory and more complete than it was in its original form.

With such advantages, therefore, as my diligent revision can give it, "Hide-and-Seek" now appeals, after an interval of seven years, for another hearing. I cannot think it becoming—especially in this age of universal self-assertion—to state the grounds on which I believe my book to be worthy of gaining more attention than it obtained, through accidental circumstances, when it was first published. Neither can I con-

sent to shelter myself under the favorable opinions which many of my brother-writers—and
notably the great writer to whom "Hide-and-
Seek" is dedicated—expressed of these pages
when I originally wrote them. I leave it to the
reader to compare this novel—especially in reference to the conception and delineation of character—with the two novels ("Antonina" and
"Basil") which preceded it; and then to decide
whether my third attempt in fiction, with all its
faults, was, or was not, an advance in Art on
my earlier efforts. This is all the favor I ask
for a work which I once wrote with anxious care
—which I have since corrected with no sparing
hand—which I have now finally dismissed to
take its second journey through the world of letters as usefully and prosperously as it can.

HARLEY STREET, LONDON, *September*, 1861.

TO

CHARLES DICKENS,

THIS STORY IS INSCRIBED,

AS A

TOKEN OF ADMIRATION AND AFFECTION.

BY HIS FRIEND

THE AUTHOR.

HIDE-AND-SEEK.

OPENING CHAPTER.

A CHILD'S SUNDAY.

AT a quarter to one o'clock, on a wet Sunday afternoon, in November, 1837, Samuel Snoxell, page to Mr. Zachary Thorpe, of Baregrove Square, London, left the area gate with three umbrellas under his arm, to meet his master and mistress at the church door, on the conclusion of morning service. Snoxell had been specially directed by the house-maid to distribute his three umbrellas in the following manner: the new silk umbrella was to be given to Mr. and Mrs. Thorpe; the old silk umbrella was to be handed to Mr. Goodworth, Mrs. Thorpe's father; and the heavy gingham was to be kept by Snoxell himself, for the special protection of "Master Zack," aged six years, and the only child of Mr. Thorpe. Furnished with these instructions, the page set forth on his way to the church.

The morning had been fine for November; but before midday the clouds had gathered, the rain had begun, and the inveterate fog of the season had closed dingily over the wet streets, far and

near. The garden in the middle of Baregrove
Square—with its close-cut turf, its vacant beds,
its brand-new rustic seats, its withered young
trees that had not yet grown as high as the railings around them—seemed to be absolutely rotting away in yellow mist and softly-steady rain,
and was deserted even by the cats. All blinds
were drawn down for the most part over all windows; what light came from the sky came like
light seen through dusty glass; the grim brown
hue of the brick houses looked more dirtily
mournful than ever; the smoke from the chimney-pots was lost mysteriously in deepening superincumbent fog; the muddy gutters gurgled;
the heavy rain-drops dripped into empty areas
audibly. No object great or small, no out-of-
door litter whatever appeared anywhere to break
the dismal uniformity of line and substance in
the perspective of the square. No living being
moved over the watery pavement, save the solitary Snoxell. He plodded on into a Crescent,
and still the awful Sunday solitude spread grimly
humid all around him. He next entered a street
with some closed shops in it; and here, at last,
some consoling signs of human life attracted his
attention. He now saw the crossing-sweeper of
the district (off duty till church came out) smoking a pipe under the covered way that led to a
mews. He detected, through half-closed shutters, a chemist's apprentice yawning over a large
book. He passed a navigator, a hostler, and two
costermongers wandering wearily backward and
forward before a closed public-house door. He

heard the heavy *clop clop* of thickly-booted feet advancing behind him, and a stern voice growling, "Now then! be off with you, or you'll get locked up!"—and, looking round, saw an orange-girl, guilty of having obstructed an empty pavement by sitting on the curb-stone, driven along before a policeman, who was followed admiringly by a ragged boy gnawing a piece of orange-peel. Having delayed a moment to watch this Sunday procession of three with melancholy curiosity as it moved by him, Snoxell was about to turn the corner of a street which led directly to the church, when a shrill series of cries in a child's voice struck on his ear and stopped his progress immediately.

The page stood stock-still in astonishment for an instant—then pulled the new silk umbrella from under his arm, and turned the corner in a violent hurry. His suspicions had not deceived him. There was Mr. Thorpe himself walking sternly homeward through the rain, before church was over. He led by the hand "Master Zack," who was trotting along under protest, with his hat half off his head, hanging as far back from his father's side as he possibly could, and howling all the time at the utmost pitch of a very powerful pair of lungs.

Mr. Thorpe stopped as he passed the page, and, snatching the umbrella out of Snoxell's hand with unaccustomed impetuosity, said sharply, "Go to your mistress, go on to the church;" and then resumed his road home, dragging his son after him faster than ever.

"Snoxy! Snoxy!" screamed Master Zack, turning round toward the page, so that he tripped himself up and fell against his father's legs at every third step, "I've been a naughty boy at church!"

"Ah! you look like it, you do," muttered Snoxell to himself, sarcastically, as he went on. With that expression of opinion, the page approached the church portico, and waited sulkily among his fellow-servants and their umbrellas for the congregation to come out.

When Mr. Goodworth and Mrs. Thorpe left the church, the old gentleman, regardless of appearances, seized eagerly on the despised gingham umbrella, because it was the largest he could get, and took his daughter home under it in triumph. Mrs. Thorpe was very silent, and sighed dolefully once or twice, when her father's attention wandered from her to the people passing along the street.

"You're fretting about Zack," said the old gentleman, looking round suddenly at his daughter. "Never mind! leave it to me. I'll undertake to beg him off this time."

"It's very disheartening and shocking to find him behaving so," said Mrs. Thorpe, "after the careful way we've brought him up in, too!"

"Nonsense, my love! No, I don't mean that —I beg your pardon. But who can be surprised that a child of six years old should be tired of a sermon forty minutes long by my watch? I was tired of it myself, I know, though I wasn't candid enough to show it as the boy did. There!

HE LED BY THE HAND "MASTER ZACK," WHO WAS TROTTING ALONG
UNDER PROTEST.—HIDE-AND-SEEK, Vol. XI., page 9.

there! we won't begin to argue: I'll beg Zack
off this time, and we'll say no more about it."

Mr. Goodworth's announcement of his benevolent intentions toward Zack seemed to have very
little effect on Mrs. Thorpe; but she said nothing
on that subject or any other during the rest of
the dreary walk home, through rain, fog, and
mud, to Baregrove Square.

Rooms have their mysterious peculiarities of
physiognomy as well as men. There are plenty
of rooms, all of much the same size, all furnished
in much the same manner, which, nevertheless,
differ completely in expression (if such a term
may be allowed) one from the other; reflecting
the various characters of their inhabitants by
such fine varieties of effect in the furniture-fea-
tures generally common to all, as are often, like
the infinitesimal varieties of eyes, noses, and
mouths, too intricately minute to be traceable.
Now, the parlor of Mr. Thorpe's house was neat,
clean, comfortably and sensibly furnished. It
was of the average size. It had the usual side-
board, dining-table, looking-glass, scroll fender,
marble chimney-piece with a clock on it, carpet
with a drugget over it, and wire window-blinds
to keep people from looking in, characteristic of
all respectable London parlors of the middle class.
And yet it was an inveterately severe-looking
room—a room that seemed as if it had never
been convivial, never uproarious, never anything but sternly· comfortable and serenely dull
—a room which appeared to be as unconscious of
acts of mercy, and easy unreasoning over-affec-

tionate forgiveness to offenders of any kind—
juvenile or otherwise—as if it had been a cell in
Newgate, or a private torturing chamber in the
Inquisition.   Perhaps Mr. Goodworth felt thus
affected by the parlor (especially in November
weather) as soon as he entered it—for, although
he had promised to beg Zack off, although Mr.
Thorpe was sitting alone by the table and acces-
sible to petitions, with a book in his hand, the
old gentleman hesitated uneasily for a minute or
two, and suffered his daughter to speak first.

"Where is Zack?" asked Mrs. Thorpe, glancing quickly and nervously all round her.

"He is locked up in my dressing-room," answered her husband, without taking his eyes off
the book.

"In your dressing-room!" echoed Mrs. Thorpe,
looking as startled and horrified as if she had received a blow instead of an answer; "in your
dressing-room!   Good heavens! Zachary! how do
you know the child hasn't got at your razors?"

"They are locked up," rejoined Mr. Thorpe,
with the mildest reproof in his voice, and the
mournfullest self-possession in his manner.   "I
took care, before I left the boy, that he should
get at nothing which could do him any injury.
He is locked up, and will remain locked up, because—"

"I say, Thorpe! won't you let him off this
time?" interrupted Mr. Goodworth, boldly
plunging headforemost, with his petition for
mercy, into the conversation.

"If you had allowed me to proceed, sir," said

Mr. Thorpe, who always called his father-in-law
Sir, "I should have simply remarked that, after
having enlarged to my son (in such terms, you
will observe, as I thought best fitted to his comprehension) on the disgrace to his parents and
himself of his behavior this morning, I set him
as a task three verses to learn out of the 'Select
Bible Texts for Children'; choosing the verses
which seemed most likely, if I may trust my
own judgment on the point, to impress on him
what his behavior ought to be for the future in
church. He flatly refused to learn what I told
him. It was, of course, quite impossible to allow
my authority to be set at defiance by my own
child (whose disobedient disposition has always,
God knows, been a source of constant trouble
and anxiety to me); so I locked him up, and
locked up he will remain until he has obeyed me.
My dear" (turning to his wife and handing her
a key), "I have no objection, if you wish, to
your going and trying what *you* can do toward
overcoming the obstinacy of this unhappy child."

Mrs. Thorpe took the key, and went upstairs
immediately—went up to do what all women
have done, from the time of the first mother; to
do what Eve did when Cain was wayward in
his infancy, and cried at her breast—in short,
went up to coax her child.

Mr. Thorpe, when his wife closed the door,
carefully looked down the open page on his knee
for the place where he had left off—found it—
referred back a moment to the last lines of the
preceding leaf—and then went on with his book,

not taking the smallest notice of Mr. Good-worth.

"Thorpe!" cried the old gentleman, plunging headforemost again into his son-in-law's reading this time instead of his talk, "you may say what you please; but your notion of bringing up Zack is a wrong one altogether."

With the calmest imaginable expression of face, Mr. Thorpe looked up from his book; and, first carefully putting a paper-knife between the leaves, placed it on the table. He then crossed one of his legs over the other, rested an elbow on each arm of his chair, and clasped his hands in front of him. On the wall opposite hung several lithographed portraits of distinguished preachers, in and out of the Establishment—mostly represented as very sturdily-constructed men with bristly hair, fronting the spectator interrogatively, and holding thick books in their hands. Upon one of these portraits—the name of the original of which was stated at the foot of the print to be the Reverend Aaron Yollop—Mr. Thorpe now fixed his eyes, with a faint approach to a smile on his face (he never was known to laugh), and with a look and manner which said as plainly as if he had spoken it: "This old man is about to say something improper or absurd to me; but he is my wife's father, it is my duty to bear with him, and therefore I am perfectly resigned."

"It's no use looking in that way, Thorpe," growled the old gentleman; "I'm not to be put down by looks at my time of life. I may have my own opinions, I suppose, like other people; and I don't see why I shouldn't express them, especially when they relate to my own daughter's boy. It's very unreasonable of me, I dare say, but I think I ought to have a voice now and then in Zack's bringing up."

Mr. Thorpe bowed respectfully—partly to Mr. Goodworth, partly to the Reverend Aaron Yollop. "I shall always be happy, sir, to listen to any expression of your opinion—"

"My opinion's this," burst out Mr. Goodworth; "you've no business to take Zack to church at all till he's some years older than he is now. I don't deny that there may be a few children, here and there, at six years old, who are so very patient, and so very—(what's the word for a child that knows a deal more than he has any business to know at his age? Stop! I've got it!—*precocious*—that's the word)—so very patient and so very precocious that they will sit quiet in the same place for two hours; making believe all the time that they understand every word of the service, whether they really do or not. I don't deny that there may be such children, though I never met with them myself, and should think them all impudent little hypocrites if I did! But Zack isn't one of that sort: Zack's a genuine child (God bless him!); Zack—"

"Do I understand you, my dear sir," interposed Mr. Thorpe, sorrowfully sarcastic, "to be praising the conduct of my son in disturbing the congregation, and obliging me to take him out of church?"

"Nothing of the sort," retorted the old gentleman; "I'm not praising Zack's conduct, but I *am* blaming yours. Here it is in plain words: *You* keep on cramming church down his throat; and *he* keeps on puking at it as if it was physic, because he don't know any better, and can't know any better at his age. Is that the way to make him take kindly to religious teaching? I know as well as you do, that he roared like a young Turk at the sermon. And pray what was the subject of the sermon? Justification by Faith. Do you mean to tell me that he, or any other child at his time of life, could understand anything of such a subject as that; or get an atom of good out of it? You can't—you know you can't! I say again, it's no use taking him to church yet; and what's more, it's worse than no use, for you only associate his first ideas of religious instruction with everything in the way of restraint and discipline and punishment that can be most irksome to him. There! that's my opinion, and I should like to hear what you've got to say against it?"

"Latitudinarianism," said Mr. Thorpe, looking and speaking straight at the portrait of the Reverend Aaron Yollop.

"You can't fob me off with long words which I don't understand, and which I don't believe you can find in Johnson's Dictionary," continued Mr. Goodworth, doggedly. "You would do much better to take my advice, and let Zack go to church, for the present, at his mother's knees. Let his Morning Service be about ten minutes long; let your wife tell him, out of the New Testament, about Our Saviour's goodness and gentleness to little children; and then let her teach him, from the Sermon on the Mount, to be loving and truthful and forbearing and forgiving, for our Saviour's sake. If such precepts as those are enforced—as they may be in one way or another—by examples drawn from his own daily life; from people around him; from what he meets with and notices and asks about, out-of-doors and in—mark my words, he'll take kindly to his religious instruction. I've seen that in other children: I've seen it in my own children, who were all brought up so. Of course, you don't agree with me! Of course, you've got another objection all ready to bowl me down with?"

"Rationalism," said Mr. Thorpe, still looking steadily at the lithographed portrait of the Reverend Aaron Yollop.

"Well, your objection's a short one this time, at any rate; and that's a blessing!" said the old gentleman, rather irritably. "Rationalism—eh? I understand that *ism*, I rather suspect, better than the other. It means, in plain English, that you think I'm wrong in only wanting to give religious instruction the same chance with Zack which you let all other kinds of instruction have —the chance of becoming useful by being first made attractive. You can't get him to learn to read by telling him that it will improve his mind —but you can by getting him to look at a picture-book. You can't get him to drink senna

and salts by reasoning with him about its doing
him good—but you can by promising him a
lump of sugar to take after it. You admit this
sort of principle so far, because you're obliged;
but the moment anybody wants (in a spirit of
perfect reverence and desire to do good) to extend it to higher things, you purse up your lips,
shake your head, and talk about Rationalism—
as if that was an answer! Well! well! it's no
use talking—go your own way—I wash my
hands of the business altogether. But now I *am*
at it, I'll just say this one thing more before I've
done—your way of punishing the boy for his behavior in church is, in my opinion, about as bad
and dangerous a one as could possibly be devised. Why not give him a thrashing, if you
must punish the miserable little urchin for what's
his misfortune as much as his fault? Why not
stop his pudding, or something of that sort?
Here you are associating verses in the Bible, in
his mind, with the idea of punishment and being locked up in the cold! You may make him
get his text by heart, I dare say, by fairly tiring
him out; but I tell you what, I'm afraid you'll
make him learn too, if you don't mind—you'll
make him learn to dislike the Bible as much as
other boys dislike the birch-rod!"

"Sir," cried Mr. Thorpe, turning suddenly
round, and severely confronting Mr. Goodworth, "once for all, I must most respectfully
insist on being spared for the future any open
profanities in conversation, even from your lips.
All my regard and affection for you, as Mrs.

Thorpe's father, shall not prevent me from solemnly recording my abhorrence of such awful infidelity as I believe to be involved in the words you have just spoken! My religious convictions recoil—"

"Stop, sir!" said Mr. Goodworth, seriously and sternly.

Mr. Thorpe obeyed at once. The old gentleman's manner was generally much more remarkable for heartiness than for dignity; but it altered completely while he now spoke. As he struck his hand on the table, and rose from his chair, there was something in his look which it was not wise to disregard.

"Mr. Thorpe," he went on, more calmly, but very decidedly, "I refrain from telling you what my opinion is of the 'respect' and 'affection' which have allowed *you* to rebuke *me* in such terms as you have chosen. I merely desire to say that I shall never need a second reproof of the same kind at your hands; for I shall never again speak to you on the subject of my grandson's education. If, in consideration of this assurance, you will now permit me, in my turn, not to rebuke, but to offer you one word of advice, I would recommend you not to be too ready, in future, lightly and cruelly to accuse a man of infidelity because his religious opinions happen to differ on some subjects from yours. To infer a serious motive for your opponent's convictions, however wrong you may think them, can do *you* no harm: to infer a scoffing motive can do *him* no good. We will say noth-

ing more about this, if you please. Let us
shake hands, and never again revive a subject
about which we disagree too widely ever to dis-
cuss it with advantage.''

At this moment the servant came in with
lunch. Mr. Goodworth poured himself out a
glass of sherry, made a remark on the weather,
and soon resumed his cheerful, everyday manner. But he did not forget the pledge that he
had given to Mr. Thorpe. From that time forth,
he never by word or deed interfered again in his
grandson's education.

WHILE the theory of Mr. Thorpe's system of
juvenile instruction was being discussed in the
free air of the parlor, the practical working of
that theory, so far as regarded the case of Master Zack, was being exemplified in anything but
a satisfactory manner in the prison-region of the
dressing-room.

While she ascended the first flight of stairs,
Mrs. Thorpe's ears informed her that her son
was firing off one uninterrupted volley of kicks
against the door of his place of confinement. As
this was by no means an unusual circumstance,
whenever the boy happened to be locked up for
bad behavior, she felt distressed, but not at all
surprised at what she heard; and went into the
drawing-room, on her way upstairs, to deposit
her Bible and Prayer-book (kept in a morocco
case, with gold clasps) on the little side-table,

upon which they were always placed during
week-days. Possibly, she was so much agitated
that her hand trembled; possibly, she was in too
great a hurry; possibly, the household imp who
rules the brittle destinies of domestic glass and
china, had marked her out as his destroying
angel for that day; but however it was, in placing the morocco case on the table, she knocked
down and broke an ornament standing near it—
a little ivory model of a church-steeple in the
florid style, enshrined in a glass case. Picking
up the fragments, and mourning over the catas-
trophe, occupied some little time, more than she
was aware of, before she at last left the drawing-
room, to proceed on her way to the upper regions.

As she laid her hand on the banisters, it struck
her suddenly and significantly that the noises in
the dressing-room above had entirely ceased.

The instant she satisfied herself of this, her
maternal imagination, uninfluenced by what
Mr. Thorpe had said below stairs, conjured up
an appalling vision of Zack before his father's
looking-glass, with his chin well lathered, and a
bare razor at his naked throat. The child had
indeed a singular aptitude for amusing himself
with purely adult occupations. Having once
been incautiously taken into church by his nurse
to see a female friend of hers married, Zack had,
the very next day, insisted on solemnizing the
nuptial ceremony from recollection, before a
bride and bridegroom of his own age, selected
from his playfellows in the garden of the square.
Another time, when the gardener had incau-

tiously left his lighted pipe on a bench while he
went to gather a flower for one of the local
nursery-maids, whom he was accustomed to favor horticulturally in this way, Zack contrived,
undetected, to take three greedy whiffs of pigtail
in close succession; was discovered reeling about
the grass like a little drunkard; and had to be
smuggled home (deadly pale, and bathed in cold
perspiration) to recover, out of his mother's sight,
in the congenial gloom of the back kitchen.   Although the precise infantine achievements here
cited were unknown to Mrs. Thorpe, there were
plenty more, like them, which she had discovered; and the warning remembrance of which
now hurried the poor lady up the second flight of
stairs in a state of breathless agitation and alarm.

Zack, however, had not got at the razors; for
they were all locked up, as Mr. Thorpe had declared. But he had nevertheless discovered in
the dressing-room a means of perpetrating domestic mischief which his father had never
thought of providing against. Finding that
kicking, screaming, stamping, sobbing, and
knocking down chairs, were quite powerless as
methods of enforcing his liberation, he suddenly
suspended his proceedings, looked all round the
room, observed the cock which supplied his father's bath with water, and instantly resolved to
flood the house. He had set the water going in
the bath, had filled it to the brim, and was anxiously waiting, perched up on a chair, to see it
overflow—when his mother unlocked the dress-
·ing-room door and entered the room.

"Oh, you naughty, wicked, shocking child!" cried Mrs. Thorpe, horrified at what she beheld, but instantly stopping the threatened deluge from motives of precaution connected with the drawing-room ceiling. "Oh, Zack! Zack! what *will* you do next? What *would* your papa say if he heard of this? You wicked, wicked, wicked child, I'm ashamed to look at you!"

And, in very truth, Zack offered at that moment a sufficiently disheartening spectacle for a mother's eyes to dwell on. There stood the young imp, sturdy and upright in his chair, wriggling his shoulders in and out of his frock, and holding his hands behind him in unconscious imitation of the favorite action of Napoleon the Great. His light hair was all rumpled down over his forehead; his lips were swelled; his nose was red; and from his bright blue eyes Rebellion looked out frankly mischievous, amid a surrounding halo of dirt and tears, rubbed circular by his knuckles. After gazing on her son in mute despair for a minute or so, Mrs. Thorpe took the only course that was immediately open to her—or, in other words, took the child off the chair.

"Have you learned your lesson, you wicked boy?" she asked.

"No, I haven't," answered Zack, resolutely.

"Then come to the table with me; your papa's waiting to hear you. Come here and learn your lesson directly," said Mrs. Thorpe, leading the way to the table.

"I won't!" rejoined Zack, emphasizing the

refusal by laying tight hold of the wet sides of the bath with both hands.

It was lucky for this rebel of six years old that he addressed those two words to his mother only. If his nurse had heard them, she would instantly have employed that old-established resource in all educational difficulties, familiarly known to persons of her condition under the appellation of "a smack on the head"; if Mr. Thorpe had heard them, the boy would have been sternly torn away, bound to the back of a chair, and placed ignominiously with his chin against the table; if Mr. Goodworth had heard them, the probability is that he would instantly have lost his temper, and soused his grandson head over ears in the bath. Not one of these ideas occurred to Mrs. Thorpe, who possessed no ideas. But she had certain substitutes which were infinitely more useful in the present emergency: she had instincts.

"Look up at me, Zack," she said, returning to the bath, and sitting in the chair by its side; "I want to say something to you."

The boy obeyed directly. His mother opened her lips, stopped suddenly, said a few words, stopped again, hesitated—and then ended her first sentence of admonition in the most ridiculous manner, by snatching at the nearest towel, and bearing Zack off to the wash-hand basin.

The plain fact was, that Mrs. Thorpe was secretly vain of her child. She had long since, poor woman, forced down the strong strait-waistcoats of prudery and restraint over every other moral weakness but this—of all vanities the most beautiful; of all human failings surely the most pure! Yes, she was proud of Zack! The dear, naughty, handsome, church-disturbing, door-kicking, house-flooding Zack! If he had been a plain-featured boy, she could have gone on more sternly with her admonition; but to look coolly on his handsome face, made ugly by dirt, tears, and rumpled hair; to speak to him in that state while soap, water, brush, and towel were all within reach, was more than the mother (or the woman either, for that matter) had the self-denial to do! So, before it had well begun, the maternal lecture ended impotently in the wash-hand basin.

When the boy had been smartened and brushed up, Mrs. Thorpe took him on her lap, and suppressing a strong desire to kiss him on both his round, shining cheeks, said these words:

"I want you to learn your lesson, because you will please *me* by obeying your papa. I have always been kind to *you*, now I want you to be kind to *me*."

For the first time Zack hung down his head, and seemed unprepared with an answer. Mrs. Thorpe knew by experience what this symptom meant. "I think you are beginning to be sorry for what you have done, and are going to be a good boy," she said. "If you are, I know you will give me a kiss." Zack hesitated again—then suddenly reached up, and gave his mother a hearty and loud-sounding kiss on the tip of her chin. "And now you will learn your lesson?"

continued Mrs. Thorpe. "I have always tried to make *you* happy, and I am sure you are ready by this time to try and make *me* happy—are you not, Zack?"

"Yes, I am," said Zack, manfully. His mother took him at once to the table, on which the "Select Bible Texts for Children" lay open, and tried to lift him into a chair. "No!" said the boy, resisting and shaking his head resolutely; "I want to learn my lesson on your lap."

Mrs. Thorpe humored him immediately. She was not a handsome, not even a pretty woman; and the cold atmosphere of the dressing-room by no means improved her personal appearance. But notwithstanding this, she looked absolutely attractive and interesting at the present moment, as she sat with Zack in her arms, bending over him while he studied his three verses in the "Bible Texts." Women who have been ill-used by Nature have this great advantage over men in the same predicament—wherever there is a child present, they have a means ready at hand, which they can all employ alike, for hiding their personal deficiencies. Who ever saw an awkward woman look awkward with a baby in her arms? Who ever saw an ugly woman look ugly when she was kissing a child?

Zack, who was a remarkably quick boy when he chose to exert himself, got his lesson by heart in so short a time that his mother insisted on hearing him twice over, before she could satisfy herself that he was really perfect enough to appear in his father's presence. The second trial decided her doubts, and she took him in triumph downstairs.

Mr. Thorpe was reading intently, Mr. Good-worth was thinking profoundly, the rain was falling inveterately, the fog was thickening dirtily, and the austerity of the severe-looking parlor was hardening apace into its most ada-mantine Sunday grimness, as Zack was brought to say his lesson at his father's knees. He got through it perfectly again; but his childish man-ner, during this third trial, altered from frank-ness to distrustfulness; and he looked much oftener, while he said his task, at Mr. Good-worth than at his father.   When the texts had been repeated, Mr. Thorpe just said to his wife, before resuming his book, "You may tell the nurse, my dear, to get Zachary's dinner ready for him—though he doesn't deserve it for behav-ing so badly about learning his lesson."

"Please, grandpapa, may I look at the picture-book you brought for me last night after I was in bed?" said Zack, addressing Mr. Goodworth, and evidently feeling that he was entitled to his reward, now he had suffered his punish-ment.

"Certainly not on a Sunday," interposed Mr. Thorpe; "your grandpapa's book is not a book for Sundays."

Mr. Goodworth started, and seemed about to speak; but recollecting what he had said to Mr. Thorpe, contented himself with poking the fire. The book in question was a certain romance, en-titled "Jack and the Bean Stalk," adorned with

illustrations in the freest style of water-color
art.

"If you want to look at picture-books, you
know what books you may have to-day; and
your mamma will get them for you when she
comes in again," continued Mr. Thorpe.

The works now referred to were, an old copy
of the "Pilgrim's Progress," containing four
small prints of the period of the last century,
and a "Life of Moses," illustrated by severe
German outlines in the manner of the modern
school. Zack knew well enough what books his
father meant, and exhibited his appreciation of
them by again beginning to wriggle his shoulders in and out of his frock. He had evidently
had more than enough already of the "Pilgrim's
Progress" and the "Life of Moses."

Mr. Thorpe said nothing more, and returned
to his reading. Mr. Goodworth put his hands
in his pockets, yawned disconsolately, and
looked, with a languidly satirical expression in
his eyes, to see what his grandson would do
next. If the thought passing through the old
gentleman's mind at that moment had been put
into words, it would have been exactly expressed
in the following sentence: "You miserable little
boy! When I was your age, how I should have
kicked at all this!"

Zack was not long in finding a new resource.
He spied Mr. Goodworth's cane standing in a
corner; and, instantly getting astride of it, prepared to amuse himself with a little imaginary
horse-exercise up and down the room. He had

just started at a gentle canter, when his father
called out, "Zachary!" and brought the boy to
a stand-still directly.

"Put back the stick where you took it from,"
said Mr. Thorpe; "you mustn't do that on Sunday.   If you want to move about, you can walk
up and down the room."

· Zack paused, debating for an instant whether
he should disobey or burst out crying.

"Put back the stick," repeated Mr. Thorpe.

Zack remembered the dressing-room and the
"Select Bible Texts for Children," and wisely
obeyed.   He was by this time completely crushed
down into as rigid a state of Sunday discipline
as his father could desire.   After depositing the ·
stick in the corner, he slowly walked up to Mr.
Goodworth, with a comical expression of amazement and disgust in his chubby face, and meekly
laid down his head on his grandfather's knee.

"Never say die, Zack," said the kind old gentleman, rising and taking the boy in his arms.
"While nurse is getting your dinner ready, let's
look out of window, and see if it's going to clear
up."

Mr. Thorpe raised his head disapprovingly
from his book, but said nothing this time.

"Ah, rain! rain! rain!" muttered Mr. Goodworth, staring desperately out at the miserable
prospect, while Zack amused himself by rubbing
his nose vacantly backward and forward against
a pane of glass.   "Rain! rain! Nothing but
rain and fog in November. · Hold up, Zack!
Ding-dong, ding-dong; there go the bells for

afternoon church! I wonder whether it will be fine to-morrow? Think of the pudding, my boy!'' whispered the old gentleman, with a benevolent remembrance of the consolation which that thought had often afforded to him when he was a child himself.

"Yes," said Zack, acknowledging the pudding suggestion, but declining to profit by it. "And, please, when I've had my dinner, will somebody put me to bed?"

"Put you to bed!" exclaimed Mr. Goodworth. "Why, bless the boy! what's come to him now? He used always to be wanting to stop up."

"I want to go to bed, and get to to-morrow, and have my picture-book," was the weary and whimpering answer.

"I'll be hanged, if I don't want to go to bed too!" soliloquized the old gentleman under his breath, "and get to to-morrow, and have my *Times* at breakfast. I'm as bad as Zack, every bit!"

"Grandpapa," continued the child, more wearily than before, "I want to whisper something in your ear."

Mr. Goodworth bent down a little. Zack looked round cunningly toward his father, then putting his mouth close to his grandfather's ear, communicated the conclusion at which he had arrived, after the events of the day, in these words:

"*I say, grandpapa, I hate Sunday!*"

BOOK I.—THE HIDING.

CHAPTER I.

A NEW NEIGHBORHOOD, AND A STRANGE CHARACTER.

At the period when the episode just related occurred in the life of Mr. Zachary Thorpe the younger—that is to say, in the year 1837—Baregrove Square was the furthest square from the city, and the nearest to the country, of any then existing in the north-western suburb of London. But, by the time fourteen years more had elapsed —that is to say, in the year 1851—Baregrove Square had lost its distinctive character altogether; other squares had filched from it those last remnants of healthy rustic flavor from which its good name had been derived; other streets, crescents, rows, and villa residences had forced themselves pitilessly between the old suburb and the country, and had suspended forever the once neighborly relations between the pavement of Baregrove Square and the pathways of the pleasant fields.

Alexander's armies were great makers of conquests; and Napoleon's armies were great makers of conquests; but the modern Guerilla regiments of the hod, the trowel, and the brick-kiln are the greatest conquerors of all; for they hold the longest the soil that they have once possessed. How mighty the devastation which follows in the wake of these tremendous aggressors, as they march through the kingdom of nature, triumphantly bricklaying beauty wherever they go! Whatever dismantled castle, with the enemy's flag flying over its crumbling walls, ever looked so utterly forlorn as a poor field-fortress of nature, imprisoned on all sides by the walled camp of the enemy, and degraded by a hostile banner of pole and board, with the conqueror's device inscribed on it—"THIS GROUND TO BE LET ON BUILDING LEASES?" What is the historical spectacle of Marius sitting among the ruins of Carthage, but a trumpery theatrical set-scene, compared with the mournful modern sight of the last tree left standing, on the last few feet of grass left growing, amid the greenly-festering stucco of a finished Paradise Row, or the naked scaffolding poles of a half-completed Prospect Place? Oh, gritty-natured Guerilla regiments of the hod, the trowel, and the brick-kiln! the town-pilgrim of nature, when he wanders out at fall of day into the domains which you have spared for a little while, hears strange things said of you in secret, as he duteously interprets the old, primeval language of the leaves; as he listens to the death-doomed trees, still whispering mournfully around him the last notes of their ancient even-song!

But what avails the voice of lamentation? What new neighborhood ever stopped on its way

into the country, to hearken to the passive remonstrance of the fields, or to bow to the indignation of outraged admirers of the picturesque.
Never was suburb more impervious to any faint
influences of this sort, than that especial suburb
which grew up between Baregrove Square and
the country; removing a walk among the hedge-
rows a mile off from the resident families, with
a ruthless rapidity at which sufferers on all sides
stared aghast. First stories were built, and
mortgaged by the enterprising proprietors to get
money enough to go on with the second; old
speculators failed and were succeeded by new;
foundations sank from bad digging; walls were
blown down in high winds from hasty building;
bricks were called for in such quantities, and
seized on in such haste, half-baked from the
kilns, that they set the carts on fire, and had to
be cooled in pails of water before they could be
erected into walls—and still the new suburb defied all accidents, and grew irrepressibly into a
little town of houses, ready to be let and lived
in, from the one end to the other.

The new neighborhood offered house-accom-
modation—accepted at the higher prices as yet
only to a small extent—to three distinct subdi-
visions of the great middle class of our British
population. Rents and premises were adapted,
in a steeply descending scale, to the means of the
middle classes with large incomes, of the middle
classes with moderate incomes, and of the middle
classes with small incomes. The abodes for the
large incomes were called "mansions," and were

fortified strongly against the rest of the suburb by being all built in one wide row, shut in at either end by ornamental gates, and called a "park." The unspeakable desolation of aspect common to the whole suburb was in a high state of perfection in this part of it. Irreverent street noises fainted dead away on the threshold of the ornamental gates, at the sight of the hermit lodge-keeper. The cry of the costermonger and the screech of the vagabond London boy were banished out of hearing. Even the regular tradesman's time-honored business noises at customers' doors seemed as if they ought to have been relinquished here. The frantic falsetto of the milkman, the crash of the furious butcher's cart over the never-to-be pulverized stones of the new road through the "park," always sounded profanely to the passing stranger, in the spick-and-span stillness of this Paradise of the large incomes.

The hapless small incomes had the very worst end of the whole locality entirely to themselves, and absorbed all the noises and nuisances, just as the large incomes absorbed all the tranquillities and luxuries of suburban existence. Here were the dreary limits at which architectural invention stopped in despair. Each house in this poor man's purgatory was, indeed, and in awful literalness, a brick box with a slate top to it. Every hole drilled in these boxes, whether door-hole or window-hole, was always overflowing with children. They often mustered by forties and fifties in one street, and were the great per-

vading feature of the quarter. In the world of
the large incomes, young life sprang up like a
garden fountain, artificially playing only at
stated periods in the sunshine. In the world of
the small incomes, young life flowed out turbu-
lently into the street, like an exhaustless kennel-
deluge, in all weathers. Next to the children of
the inhabitants, in visible numerical importance,
came the shirts and petticoats, and miscellaneous
linen of the inhabitants; fluttering out to dry
publicly on certain days of the week, and en-
livening the treeless little gardens where they
hung, with lightsome avenues of pinafores, and
solemn-spreading foliage of stout Welsh flannel.
Here that absorbing passion for oranges (especially active when the fruit is half ripe, and the
weather is bitter cold), which distinguishes the
city English girl of the lower orders, flourished
in its finest development; and here, also, the
poisonous fumes of the holiday shopboy's bad
cigar told all resident nostrils when it was Sunday, as plainly as the church-bells could tell it to
all resident ears. The one permanent rarity in
this neighborhood, on week days, was to discover
a male inhabitant in any part of it, between the
hours of nine in the morning and six in the
evening; the one sorrowful sight which never
varied, was to see that every woman, even to the
youngest, looked more or less unhappy, often
care-stricken, while youth was still in the first
bud; oftener child-stricken before maturity was
yet in the full bloom.

As for the great central portion of the suburb

—or, in other words, the locality of the moderate incomes—it reflected exactly the lives of those who inhabited it, by presenting no distinctive character of its own at all.

In one part, the better order of houses imitated as pompously as they could the architectural grandeur of the mansions owned by the large incomes; in another, the worst order of houses respectably, but narrowly, escaped a general resemblance to the brick boxes of the small incomes. In some places, the "park" influences vindicated their existence superbly in the persons of isolated ladies who, not having a carriage to go out in for an airing, exhibited the next best thing, a footman to walk behind them: and so got a pedestrian airing genteelly in that way. In other places, the obtrusive spirit of the brick boxes rode about, thinly disguised, in children's carriages, drawn by nursery-maids; or fluttered aloft, delicately discernible at angles of view, in the shape of a lace pocket-handkerchief, or a fine worked chemisette, dying modestly at home in retired corners of back gardens. Generally, however, the hostile influences of the large incomes and the small mingled together on the neutral ground of the moderate incomes; turning it into the dullest, the dreariest, the most oppressively conventional division of the whole suburb. It was just that sort of place where the thoughtful man, looking about him mournfully at the locality, and physiologically observing the inhabitants, would be prone to stop suddenly, and ask himself one plain but

terrible question: "Do these people ever manage
to get any real enjoyment out of their lives from
one year's end to another?"

To the looker-on at the system of life prevail-
ing among the moderate incomes in England, the
sort of existence which that system embodies
seems in some aspects to be without a parallel in
any other part of the civilized world. Is it not
obviously true that, while the upper classes and
the lower classes of English society have each
their own characteristic recreations for leisure
hours, adapted equally to their means and to
their tastes, the middle classes, in general, have
(to expose the sad reality) nothing of the sort?
To take an example from those eating and drinking recreations which absorb so large a portion
of existence: If the rich proprietors of the "mansions" in the "park" could give their grand dinners, and be as prodigal as they pleased with
their first-rate Champagne, and their rare gas-
tronomic delicacies; the poor tenants of the brick
boxes could just as easily enjoy their tea-garden
conversazione, and be just as happily and hospitably prodigal, in turn, with their porter-pot,
their tea-pot, their plate of bread-and-butter, and
their dish of shrimps. On either side, these rep-
resentatives of two pecuniary extremes in society
looked for what recreations they wanted with
their own eyes, pursued those recreations within
their own limits, and enjoyed themselves unreservedly in consequence. Not so with the moderate incomes: they, in their social moments,
shrank absurdly far from the poor people's porter

and shrimps; crawled contemptibly near to the rich people's rare wines and luxurious dishes; exposed their poverty in imitation by chemical Champagne from second-rate wine-merchants, by flabby salads and fetid oyster-patties from second-rate pastry-cooks; were, in no one of their festive arrangements, true to their incomes, to their order, or to themselves; and, in very truth, for all these reasons and many more, got no real enjoyment out of their lives, from one year's end to another.

On the outskirts of that part of the new suburb appropriated to these unhappy middle classes with moderate incomes, there lived a gentleman (by name Mr. Valentine Blyth) whose life offered as strong a practical contradiction as it is possible to imagine to the lives of his neighbors.

He was by profession an artist—an artist in spite of circumstances. Neither his father, nor his mother, nor any relation of theirs on either side, had ever practiced the art of painting, or had ever derived any special pleasure from the contemplation of pictures. They were all respectable commercial people of the steady fund-holding old school, who lived exclusively within their own circle, and had never so much as spoken to a live artist or author in the whole course of their lives. The City-world in which Valentine's boyhood was passed was as destitute of art influences of any kind as if it had been situated on the coast of Greenland; and yet, to the astonishment of everybody, he was always drawing and painting, in his own rude way, at every leisure hour. His father was, as might be expected, seriously disappointed and amazed at the strange direction taken by the boy's inclinations. No one (including Valentine himself) could ever trace them back to any recognizable source; but every one could observe plainly enough that there was no hope of successfully opposing them by fair means of any kind. Seeing this, old Mr. Blyth, like a wise man, at last made a virtue of necessity; and, giving way to his son, entered him, under strong commercial protest, as a student in the Schools of the Royal Academy.

Here Valentine remained, working industriously, until his twenty-first birthday. On that occasion, Mr. Blyth had a little serious talk with him about his prospects in life. In the course of this conversation, the young man was informed that a rich merchant-uncle was ready to take him into partnership; and that his father was equally ready to start him in business with his whole share, as one of three children, in the comfortable inheritance acquired for the family by the well-known City house of Blyth and Company. If Valentine consented to this arrangement, his fortune was secured, and he might ride in his carriage before he was thirty. If, on the other hand, he really chose to fling away a fortune, he should not be pinched for means to carry on his studies as a painter. The interest of his inheritance on his father's death should be paid quarterly to him during his father's lifetime: the annual independence thus secured to the young artist, under any circumstances, being calculated as amounting to a little over four hundred pounds a year.

Valentine was not deficient in gratitude. He took a day to consider what he should do, though his mind was quite made up about his choice beforehand; and then persisted in his first determination; throwing away the present certainty of becoming a wealthy man, for the sake of the future chance of turning out a great painter.

If he had really possessed genius, there would have been nothing very remarkable in this part of his history, so far; but having nothing of the kind, holding not the smallest spark of the great creative fire in his whole mental composition, surely there was something very discouraging to contemplate, in the spectacle of a man resolutely determining, in spite of adverse home circumstances and strong home temptation, to abandon all those paths in life along which he might have walked fairly abreast with his fellows, for the one path in which he was predestinated by Nature to be always left behind by the way. Do the announcing angels, whose mission it is to whisper of greatness to great spirits, ever catch the infection of fallibility from their intercourse with mortals? Do the voices which said truly to Shakespeare, to Raphael, and to Mozart, in their youth-time, You are chosen to be gods in this world, ever speak wrongly to souls which they are not ordained to approach? It may be so. There are men enough in all countries whose lives would seem to prove it — whose deaths have not contradicted it.

But even to victims such as these, there are pleasant resting-places on the thorny way, and flashes of sunlight now and then, to make the cloudy prospect beautiful, though only for a little while. It is not all misfortune and disappointment to the man who is mentally unworthy of a great intellectual vocation, so long as he is morally worthy of it; so long as he can pursue it honestly, patiently, and affectionately, for its own dear sake. Let him work, though ever so obscurely, in this spirit toward his labor, and he shall find the labor itself its own exceeding great reward. In that reward lives the divine consolation, which, though Fame turn her back on him contemptuously, and Affluence pass over unpitying to the other side of the way, shall still pour oil upon all his wounds, and take him quietly and tenderly to the hard journey's end. To this one exhaustless solace, which the work, no matter of what degree, can yield always to earnest workers, the man who has succeeded, and the man who has failed, can turn alike, as to a common mother—the one, for refuge from mean envy and slanderous hatred, from all the sorest evils which even the thriving child of Fame is heir· to; the other, from neglect, from ridicule, from defeat, from all the petty tyrannies which the pining bondman of Obscurity is fated to undergo.

Thus it was with Valentine. He had sacrificed a fortune to his art; and his art—in the world's eye at least—had given to him nothing in return. Friends and relatives who had not scrupled, on being made acquainted with his choice of a vocation, to call it in question, and thereby to commit that worst and most universal of all human impertinences, which consists of telling a man to his face, by the plainest possible inference, that others are better able than he is himself to judge what calling in life is fittest and worthiest for him—friends and relatives who thus upbraided Valentine for his refusal to accept the partnership in his uncle's house, affected, on discovering that he made no public progress whatever in art, to believe that he was simply an idle fellow, who knew that his father's liberality placed him beyond the necessity of working for his bread, and who had taken up the pursuit of painting as a mere amateur amusement to occupy his leisure hours.   To a man who labored like poor Blyth, with the steadiest industry and the highest aspirations, such whispered calumnies as these were of all mortifications the most cruel, of all earthly insults the hardest to bear.

Still he worked on patiently, never losing faith or hope, because he never lost the love of his art, or the enjoyment of pursuing it, irrespective of results, however disheartening.   Like most other men of his slight intellectual caliber, the works he produced were various, if nothing else.   He tried the florid style, and the severe style; he was by turns devotional, allegorical, historical, sentimental, humorous.   At one time, he aban-

doned figure-painting altogether, and took to
landscape; now producing conventional studies
from Nature—and now, again, reveling in poetical compositions, which might have hung undetected in many a collection as doubtful specimens of Berghem or Claude.

But whatever department of painting Valentine tried to excel in, the same unhappy destiny
seemed always in reserve for each completed
effort.   For years and years his pictures pleaded
hard for admission at the Academy doors, and
were invariably (and not unfairly, it must be
confessed) refused even the worst places on the
walls of the Exhibition rooms.   Season after
season he still bravely struggled on, never de-
pressed, never hopeless while he was before his
easel, until at last the day of reward—how long
and painfully wrought for!—actually arrived.
A small picture of a very insignificant subject—
being only a kitchen "interior," with a sleek cat
on a dresser, stealing milk from the tea-tray
during the servant's absence—was benevolently
marked "doubtful" by the Hanging Committee;
was thereupon kept in reserve, in case it might
happen to fit any forgotten place near the floor—
did fit such a place—and was really hung up, as
Mr. Blyth's little unit of a contribution to the
one thousand and odd works exhibited to the
public that year by the Royal Academy.

But Valentine's triumph did not end here.
His picture of the treacherous cat stealing the
household milk—entitled, by way of appealing
jocosely to the strong Protestant interest, "The

Jesuit in the Family"—was really sold to an Art-Union prize-holder for ten pounds. Once furnished with a bank-note won by his own brush, Valentine indulged in the most extravagant anticipations of future celebrity and future wealth; and proved, recklessly enough, that he believed as firmly as any other visionary in the wildest dreams of his own imagination, by marrying, and setting up an establishment, on the strength of the success which had been achieved by "The Jesuit in the Family."

He had been for some time past engaged to the lady who had now become Mrs. Valentine Blyth. She was the youngest of eight sisters, who formed part of the family of a poor engraver, and who, in the absence of any mere money qualifications, were all rich alike in the ownership of most magnificent Christian names. Mrs. Blyth was called Lavinia-Ada; and hers was by far the humblest name to be found among the whole sisterhood. Valentine's relations all objected strongly to this match, not only on account of the bride's poverty, but for another and a very serious reason, which events soon proved to be but too well founded.

Lavinia had suffered long and severely, as a child, from a bad spinal malady. Constant attention, and such medical assistance as her father could afford to employ, had, it was said, successfully combated the disorder; and the girl grew up, prettier than any of her sisters, and apparently almost as strong as the healthiest of them. Old Mr. Blyth, however, on hearing that

his son was now just as determined to become a
married man as he had formerly been to become
a painter, thought it advisable to make certain
inquiries about the young lady's constitution,
and addressed them, with characteristic caution,
to the family doctor, at a private interview.

The result of this conference was far from being satisfactory. The doctor was suspiciously
careful not to commit himself: he said that he
hoped the spine was no longer in danger of being affected, but that he could not conscientiously
express himself as feeling quite sure about it.
Having repeated these discouraging words to his
son, old Mr. Blyth delicately and considerately,
but very plainly, asked Valentine whether, after
what he had heard, he still honestly thought that
he would be consulting his own happiness, or the
lady's happiness either, by marrying her at all?
or, at least, by marrying her at a time when the
doctor could not venture to say that the poor girl
might not be even yet in danger of becoming an
invalid for life?

Valentine, as usual, persisted at first in looking exclusively at the bright side of the question, and made light of the doctor's authority
accordingly.

"Lavvie and I love each other dearly," he
said, with a little trembling in his voice, but
with perfect firmness of manner. "I hope in
God that what you seem to fear will never happen; but even if it should, I shall never repent
having married her, for I know that I am just
as ready to be her nurse as to be her husband. I

am willing to take her in sickness and in health, as the Prayer-book says. In my home she would have such constant attention paid to her wants and comforts as she could not have at her father's, with his large family and his poverty, poor fellow! And this is reason enough, I think, for my marrying her, even if the worst should take place. But I always have hoped for the best, as you know, father: and I mean to go on hoping for poor Lavvie just the same as ever!''

What could old Mr. Blyth, what could any man of heart and honor, oppose to such an answer as this? Nothing. The marriage took place; and Valentine's father tried hard, and not altogether vainly, to feel as sanguine about future results as Valentine himself.

For several months — how short the time seemed, when they looked back on it in after-years!—the happiness of the painter and his wife more than fulfilled the brightest hopes which they had formed as lovers. As for the doctor's cautious words, they were hardly remembered now; or, if recalled, were recalled only to be laughed over. But the time of bitter grief, which had been appointed, though they knew it not, came inexorably, even while they were still lightly jesting at all medical authority round the painter's fireside. Lavinia caught a severe cold. The cold turned to rheumatism, to fever, then to general debility, then to nervous attacks—each one of these disorders being really but so many false appearances, under which the horrible spinal malady was treacherously and slowly advancing in disguise.

When the first positive symptoms appeared, old Mr. Blyth acted with all his accustomed generosity toward his son. "My purse is yours, Valentine," said he; "open it when you like; and let Lavinia, while there is a chance for her, have the same advice and the same remedies as if she was the greatest duchess in the land." The old man's affectionate advice was affectionately followed. The most renowned doctors in England prescribed for Lavinia; everything that science and incessant attention could do, was done; but the terrible disease still baffled remedy after remedy, advancing surely and irresistibly, until at last the doctors themselves lost all hope. So far as human science could foretell events, Mrs. Blyth, in the opinion of all her medical advisers, was doomed for the rest of her life never to rise again from the bed on which she lay; except, perhaps, to be sometimes moved to the sofa, or, in the event of some favorable reaction, to be wheeled about occasionally in an invalid chair.

What the shock of this intelligence was, both to husband and wife, no one ever knew; they nobly kept it a secret even from each other. Mrs. Blyth was the first to recover courage and calmness. She begged, as an especial favor, that Valentine would seek consolation, where she knew he must find it sooner or later, by going back to his studio, and resuming his old familiar labors, which had been suspended from the time when her illness had originally declared itself.

On the first day when, in obedience to her wishes, he sat before his picture again—the half-finished picture from which he had been separated for so many months on that first day, when the friendly occupation of his life seemed suddenly to have grown strange to him; when his brush wandered idly among the colors, when his tears dropped fast on the palette every time he looked down on it; when he tried hard to work as usual, though only for half an hour, only on simple background places in the composition; and still the brush made false touches, and still the tints would not mingle as they should, and still the same words, repeated over and over again, would burst from his lips: "Oh, poor Lavvie! oh, poor, dear, dear Lavvie!"—even then, the spirit of that beloved art, which he had always followed so humbly and so faithfully, was true to its divine mission, and comforted and upheld him at the last bitterest moment when he laid down his palette in despair.

While he was still hiding his face before the very picture which he and his wife had once innocently and secretly glorified together, in those happy days of its beginning that were never to come again, the sudden thought of consolation shone out on his heart, and showed him how he might adorn all his after-life with the deathless beauty of a pure and noble purpose. Thenceforth his vague dreams of fame, and of rich men wrangling with each other for the possession of his pictures, took the second place in his mind; and in their stead sprang up the new resolution that he would win independently, with his own brush, no matter at what sacrifice of pride and ambition, the means of surrounding his sick wife with all those luxuries and refinements which his own little income did not enable him to obtain, and which he shrank with instinctive delicacy from accepting as presents bestowed by his father's generosity. Here was the consoling purpose which robbed affliction of half its bitterness already, and bound him and his art together by a bond more sacred than any that had united them before. In the very hour when this thought came to him, he rose without a pang to turn the great historical composition, from which he had once hoped so much, with its face to the wall, and set himself to finish an unpretending little "Study" of a cottage court-yard, which he was certain of selling to a picture-dealing friend. The first approach to happiness which he had known for a long, long time past, was on the evening of that day when he went upstairs to sit with Lavinia; and, keeping secret his purpose of the morning, made the sick woman smile in spite of her sufferings, by asking her how she should like to have her room furnished, if she were the lady of a great lord, instead of being only the wife of Valentine Blyth.

Then came the happy day when the secret was revealed, and afterward the pleasant years when poor Mrs. Blyth's most splendid visions of luxury were all gradually realized through her husband's exertions in his profession. But for his wife's influence, Valentine would have been in danger of abandoning High Art and Classical Landscape altogether, for cheap portrait-painting, cheap copying, and cheap studies of Still Life. But Mrs. Blyth, bedridden as she was, contrived to preserve all her old influence over the labors of the studio, and would ask for nothing new, and receive nothing new, in her room, except on condition that her husband was to paint at least one picture of High Art every year, for the sake (as she proudly said) of "asserting his intellect and his reputation in the eyes of the public." Accordingly, Mr. Blyth's time was pretty equally divided between the production of great unsalable "compositions," which were always hung near the ceiling in the Exhibition, and of small marketable commodities, which were as invariably hung near the floor.

Valentine's average earnings from his art, though humble enough in amount, amply sufficed to fulfill the affectionate purpose for which, to the last farthing, they were rigorously set aside. "Lavvie's Drawing-room" (this was Mr. Blyth's name for his wife's bedroom) really looked as bright and beautiful as any royal chamber in the universe. The rarest flowers, the prettiest gardens under glass, bowls with gold and silver fish in them, a small aviary of birds, an Æolian harp to put on the window-sill in summer-time, some of Valentine's best drawings from the old masters, prettily framed proof-impressions of engravings done by Mrs. Blyth's fa-

ther, curtains and hangings of the tenderest color
and texture, inlaid tables, and delicately-carved
book-cases, were among the different objects of
refinement and beauty which, in the course of
years, Mr. Blyth's industry had enabled him to
accumulate for his wife's pleasure. No one but
himself ever knew what he had sacrificed in la-
boring to gain these things. The heartless people whose portraits he had painted, and whose
impertinences he had patiently submitted to; the
mean bargainers who had treated him like a
tradesman; the dastardly men of business who
had disgraced their order by taking advantage of
his simplicity—how hardly and cruelly such in-
sect natures of this world had often dealt with
that noble heart! how despicably they had
planted their small gadfly stings in the high
soul which it was never permitted to them to
subdue!

No! not once to subdue, not once to tarnish!
All petty humiliations were forgotten in one look
at "Lavvie's Drawing-room"; all stain of insolent words vanished from Valentine's memory
in the atmosphere of the studio. Never was a
more superficial judgment pronounced than
when his friends said that he had thrown away
his whole life, because he had chosen a vocation
in which he could win no public success. The
lad's earliest instincts had indeed led him truly,
after all. The art to which he had devoted himself was the only earthly pursuit that could har-
monize as perfectly with all the eccentricities as
with all the graces of his character, that could

mingle happily with every joy, tenderly with every grief, belonging to the quiet, simple, and innocent life which, employ him anyhow, it was in his original nature to lead. But for this protecting art, under what prim disguises, amid what foggy social climates of class conventionality, would the worlds clerical, legal, mercantile, military, naval, or dandy, have extinguished this man, if any one of them had caught him in its snares! Where would then have been his frolicsome enthusiasm that nothing could dispirit; his inveterate oddities of thought, speech, and action, which made all his friends laugh at him and bless him in the same breath; his affections, so manly in their firmness, so womanly in their tenderness, so child-like in their frank, fearless confidence, that dreaded neither ridicule on the one side, nor deception on the other? Where and how would all these characteristics have vanished, but for his art—but for the abiding spirit, ever present to preserve their vital warmth against the outer and earthly cold? The wisest of Valentine's friends, who shook their heads disparagingly whenever his name was mentioned, were at least wise enough in *their* generation never to ask themselves such embarrassing questions as these.

Thus much for the history of the painter's past life. We may now make his acquaintance in the appropriate atmosphere of his own studio.

CHAPTER II.

MR. BLYTH IN HIS STUDIO.

IT was wintry weather—not such a November winter's day as some of us may remember looking at fourteen years ago, in Baregrove Square, but a brisk frosty morning in January. The country view visible from the back windows of Mr. Blyth's house, which stood on the extreme limit of the new suburb, was thinly and brightly dressed out for the sun's morning levee, in its finest raiment of pure snow. The cold blue sky was cloudless; every sound out-of-doors fell on the ear with a hearty and jocund ring; all newly-lighted fires burned up brightly and willingly without coaxing; and robin-redbreasts hopped about expectantly on balconies and window-sills, as if they only waited for an invitation to walk in and warm themselves, along with their larger fellow-creatures, round the kindly hearth.

The studio was a large and lofty room, lighted by a skylight, and running along the side of the house throughout its whole depth. Its walls were covered with plain brown paper, and its floor was only carpeted in the middle. The most prominent pieces of furniture were two large easels placed at either extremity of the room; each supporting a picture of considerable size, covered over for the present with a pair of

sheets which looked wofully in want of washing. There was a painting-stand with quantities of shallow little drawers, some too full to
open, others, again, too full to shut; there was a
movable platform to put sitters on, covered with
red cloth much disguised in dust; there was a
small square table of new deal, and a large round
table of dilapidated rosewood, both laden with
sketch-books, portfolios, dog's-eared sheets of
drawing-paper, tin pots, scattered brushes, pa-
lette-knives, rags variously defiled by paint and
oil, pencils, chalks, port-crayons — the whole
smelling powerfully at all points of turpentine.

Finally, there were chairs in plenty, no one of
which, however, at all resembled the other. In
one corner stood a mouldy antique chair with
a high back, and a basin of dirty water on the
seat. By the side of the fireplace a cheap straw
chair of the bee-hive pattern was tilted over
against a dining-room chair, with a horse-hair
cushion. Before the largest of the two pictures,
and hard by a portable flight of steps, stood a
rickety office-stool. On the platform for sitters
a modern easy-chair, with the cover in tatters,
invited all models to picturesque repose. Close
to the rose-wood table was placed a rocking-
chair, and between the legs of the deal table
were huddled together a camp-stool and a has-
sock. In short, every remarkable variety of the
illustrious family of Seats was represented in one
corner or another of Mr. Blyth's painting-room.

All the surplus small articles which shelves,
tables, and chairs were unable to accommodate,

reposed in comfortable confusion on the floor.
One half at least of a pack of cards seemed to be
scattered about in this way. A shirt-collar,
three gloves, a boot, a shoe, and half a slipper;
a silk stocking, and a pair of worsted muffetees;
three old playbills rolled into a ball; a pencil-
case, a paper-knife, a tooth-powder-box without
a lid, and a superannuated black beetle trap
turned bottom upward, assisted in forming part
of the heterogeneous collection of rubbish strewed
about the studio floor. And worse than all—as
tending to show that the painter absolutely enjoyed his own disorderly habits—Mr. Blyth had
jocosely desecrated his art, by making it imitate
litter where, in all conscience, there was real
litter enough already. Just in the way of anybody entering the room, he had painted, on the
bare floor, exact representations of a new quill
pen and a very expensive-looking sable brush,
lying all ready to be trodden upon by entering
feet. Fresh visitors constantly attested the skill-
fulness of these imitations by involuntarily stoop-
ing to pick up the illusive pen and brush; Mr.
Blyth always enjoying the discomfiture and astonishment of every new victim as thoroughly
as if the practical joke had been a perfectly new
one on each successive occasion.

Such was the interior condition of the painting-room, after the owner had inhabited it for a
period of little more than two months!

The church-clock of the suburb had just struck
ten, when quick, light steps approach the studio
door. A gentleman enters—trips gayly over the

imitative pen and brush—and, walking up to the
fire, begins to warm his back at it, looking about
him rather absently, and whistling "Drops of
Brandy" in a minor key. This gentleman is
Mr. Valentine Blyth.

He looks under forty, but is really a little over
fifty. His face is round and rosy, and not
marked by a single wrinkle in any part of it.
He has large, sparkling black eyes; wears
neither whiskers, beard, nor mustache; keeps
his thick curly black hair rather too closely cut;
and has a briskly-comical kindness of expression
in his face, which it is not easy to contemplate
for the first time without smiling at him. He is
tall and stout, always wears very tight trousers,
and generally keeps his wristbands turned up
over the cuffs of his coat. All his movements
are quick and fidgety. He appears to walk
principally on his toes, and seems always on the
point of beginning to dance, or jump, or run
whenever he moves about, either in or out of
doors. When he speaks he has an odd habit of
ducking his head suddenly, and looking at the
person whom he addresses over his shoulder.
These, and other little personal peculiarities of
the same undignified nature, all contribute to
make him exactly that sort of person whom
everybody shakes hands with, and nobody bows
to, on a first introduction. Men instinctively
choose him to be the recipient of a joke, girls to
be the male confidant of all flirtations which
they like to talk about, children to be their peti-
tioner for the pardon of a fault, or the reward of

a half-holiday. On the other hand, he is decidedly unpopular among that large class of Englishmen, whose only topics of conversation are public nuisances and political abuses; for he resolutely looks at everything on the bright side, and has never read a leading article or a parliamentary debate in his life. In brief, men of business habits think him a fool, and intellectual women with independent views cite him triumphantly as an excellent specimen of the inferior male sex.

Still whistling, Mr. Blyth walks toward an earthen pipkin in one corner of the studio, and takes from it a little china palette which he has neglected to clean since he last used it. Looking round the room for some waste paper, on which he can deposit the half-dried old paint that has been scraped off with the palette-knife, Mr. Blyth's eyes happen to light first on the deal table, and on four or five notes which lie scattered over it.

These he thinks will suit his purpose as well as anything else, so he takes up the notes, but before making use of them, reads their contents over for the second time—partly by way of caution, partly through a dawdling habit, which men of his absent disposition are always too ready to contract. Three of these letters happen to be in the same scrambling, blotted handwriting. They are none of them very long, and are the production of a former acquaintance of the reader's, who has somewhat altered in height and personal appearance during the course of the last fourteen years. Here is the first of the notes, which Valentine is now reading:

"DEAR BLYTH—My father says Theaters are the Devil's Houses, and I must be home by eleven o'clock. I'm sure I never did anything wrong at a Theater which I might not have done just the same anywhere else, unless laughing over a good play is one of the *national sins* he's always talking about. I can't stand it much longer, even for my mother's sake! You are my only friend. I shall come and see you to-morrow, so mind and be at home. How I wish I was an artist! Yours ever,

"Z. THORPE, Jun."

Shaking his head and smiling at the same time, Mr. Blyth finishes this letter—drops a perfect puddle of dirty paint and turpentine in the middle, over the words "national sins," throws the paper into the fire—and goes on to note number two:

"DEAR BLYTH—I couldn't come yesterday, because of another quarrel at home, and my mother crying about it, of course. My father smelled tobacco-smoke at morning prayers. It was my coat, which I forgot to air at the fire the night before; and he found it out, and said he wouldn't have me smoke, because it led to dissipation—but I told him (which is true) that lots of parsons smoked. I wish you visited at our house, and could come and say a word on my

side.   Dear Blyth, I am perfectly wretched; for
I have had all my cigars taken from me; and I
am, yours truly,   Z. THORPE, Jun.''

A third note is required before the palette can
be scraped clean.   Mr. Blyth reads the contents
rather gravely on this occasion; rapidly plaster-
ing his last morsels of waste paint upon the paper
as he goes on, until at length it looks as if it had
been well peppered with all the colors of the
rainbow.

Zack's third letter of complaint certainly promised serious domestic tribulation for the ruling
power at Baregrove Square:

"DEAR BLYTH—I have given in—at least for
the present.   I told my father about my wanting
to be an artist, and about your saying that I had
a good notion of drawing, and an eye for a likeness; but I might just as well have talked to one
of your easels.   He means to make a man of
business of me.   And here I have been, for the
last three weeks, at a Tea-Broker's office in the
City, in consequence.   They all say it's a good
opening for me, and talk about the respectability
of commercial pursuits.   I don't want to be respectable, and I hate commercial pursuits.   What
is the good of forcing me into a merchant's office,
when I can't say my Multiplication table?   Ask
my mother about that: *she'll* tell you!   Only
fancy me going round tea-warehouses in filthy
Jewish places like St. Mary-Axe, to take sam-
ples, with a blue bag to carry them about in;

and a dirty junior clerk, who cleans his pen in his hair, to teach me how to fold up parcels! Isn't it enough to make my blood boil to think of it? I can't go on, and I won't go on in this way! Mind you're at home to-morrow; I'm coming to speak to you about how I'm to begin learning to be an artist. The junior clerk is going to do all my sampling work for me in the morning; and we are to meet in the afternoon, after I have come away from you, at a chop-house; and then go back to the office as if we had been together all day, just as usual. Ever yours, Z. THORPE, Jun.

"P. S.—My mind's made up: if the worst comes to the worst, I shall leave home."

"Oh, dear me! oh, dear! dear me!" says Valentine, mournfully rubbing his palette clean with a bit of rag. "What will it all end in, I wonder. Old Thorpe's going just the way, with his obstinate severity, to drive Zack to something desperate. Coming here to-morrow, he says?" continues Mr. Blyth, approaching the smallest of the two pictures, placed on easels at opposite extremities of the room. "Coming to-morrow! He never dates his notes; but I suppose, as this one came last night, to-morrow means to-day."

Saying these words with eyes absently fixed on his picture, Valentine withdraws the sheet stretched over the canvas, and discloses a Classical Landscape of his own composition.

If Mr. Blyth had done nothing else in producing the picture which now confronted him, he

had at least achieved one great end of all Classic
Art, by reminding nobody of anything simple,
familiar, or pleasing to them in nature. In the
foreground of his composition were the three
lanky ruined columns, the dancing Bacchantes,
the musing philosopher, the mahogany-colored
vegetation, and the bosky and branchless trees,
with which we have all been familiar, from our
youth upward, in "classical compositions."
Down the middle of the scene ran that wonderful river, which is always rippling with the
same regular waves; and always bearing on-
ward the same capsizable galleys, with the same
vermilion and blue revelers striking lyres on the
deck. On the bank where there was most room
for it, appeared our old, old friend, the architectural City, which nobody could possibly live in;
and which is composed of nothing but temples,
towers, monuments, flights of steps, and bewildering rows of pillars. In the distance, our favorite blue mountains were as blue and as peaky
as ever, on Valentine's canvas; and our gen-
erally-approved pale yellow sun was still disfigured by the same attack of aerial jaundice, from
which he has suffered ever since classical compositions first forbade him to take refuge from
the sight behind a friendly cloud.

After standing before his picture in affectionate contemplation of its beauties for a minute or
so, Valentine resumes the business of preparing
his palette.

As the bee comes and goes irregularly from
flower to flower; as the butterfly flutters in a

zigzag course from one sunny place on the garden wall to another—or, as an old woman runs from wrong omnibus to wrong omnibus, at the Elephant and Castle, before she can discover the right one; as a countryman blunders up one street, and down another, before he can find the way to his place of destination in London—so does Mr. Blyth now come and go, flutter, run, and blunder in a mighty hurry about his studio, in search of missing colors which ought to be in his painting-box, but which are not to be found there. While he is still hunting through the room, his legs come into collision with a large drawing-board on which there is a blank sheet of paper stretched. This board seems to remind Mr. Blyth of some duty connected with it. He places it against two chairs in a good light; then approaching a shelf on which some plaster-casts are arranged, takes down from it a bust of the Venus de Medici—which bust he next places on his old office-stool, opposite to the two chairs and the drawing-board. Just as these preparations are completed, the door of the studio opens, and a very important member of the painter's household—who has not yet been introduced to the reader, and who is in no way related either to Valentine or his wife—enters the room.

This mysterious resident under Mr. Blyth's roof is a Young Lady.

She is dressed in very pretty, simple, Quaker-like attire. Her gown is of a light-gray color, covered by a neat little black apron in front, and fastened round the throat over a frill collar.

The sleeves of this dress are worn tight to the arm, and are terminated at the wrists by quaint-looking cuffs of antique lace, the only ornamental morsels of costume which she has on. It is impossible to describe how deliciously soft, bright, fresh, pure, and delicate this young lady is, merely as an object to look at, contrasted with the dingy disorder of the studio-sphere through which she now moves. The keenest observers, beholding her as she at present appears, would detect nothing in her face or figure, her manner or her costume, in the slightest degree suggestive of impenetrable mystery or incurable misfortune. And yet she happens to be the only person in Mr. Blyth's household at whom prying glances are directed whenever she walks out; whose very existence is referred to by the painter's neighbors with an invariable accompaniment of shrugs, sighs, and lamenting looks; and whose "case" is always compassionately designated as "a sad one," whenever it is brought forward, in the course of conversation, at dinner-tables and tea-tables in the new suburb.

Socially, we may be all easily divided into two classes in this world—at least in the civilized part of it. If we are not the people whom others talk about, then we are sure to be the people who talk about others. The young lady who had just entered Mr. Blyth's painting-room belonged to the former order of human beings.

She seemed fated to be used as a constant subject of conversation by her fellow-creatures. Even her face alone—simply *as* a face—could not escape perpetual discussion; and that, too, among Valentine's friends, who all knew her well, and loved her dearly. It was the oddest thing in the world, but no one of them could ever agree with another (except on a certain point, to be presently mentioned) as to which of her personal attractions ought to be first selected for approval, or quoted as particularly asserting her claims to the admiration of all worshipers of beauty.

To take three or four instances of this. There was Mr. Gimble, the civil little picture-dealer, and a very good friend in every way to Valentine: there was Mr. Gimble, who declared that her principal charm was in her complexion—her fair, clear, wonderful complexion — which he would defy any artist alive to paint, let him try ever so hard, or be ever so great a man. Then came the Dowager Countess of Brambledown, the frolicsome old aristocrat, who was generally believed to be "a little cracked"; who haunted Mr. Blyth's studio, after having once given him an order to paint her rare China tea-service, and her favorite muff, in one group; and who differed entirely from the little picture-dealer. "Fiddle-de-dee!" cried her ladyship, scornfully, on hearing Mr. Gimble's opinion quoted one day. "The man may know something about pictures, but he is an idiot about women. Her complexion, indeed! I could make as good a complexion for myself (we old women are painters too, in our way, Blyth). Don't tell me about her complexion—it's her eyes! her incomparable blue eyes, which would have driven the young men of *my* time mad—mad, I give you my word of honor! Not a gentleman, sir, in my youthful days—and they *were* gentlemen then— but would have been too happy to run away with her for her eyes alone; and what's more, to have shot any man who said as much as 'Stop him!' Complexion, indeed, Mr. Gimble? I'll complexion you, next time I find my way into your picture-gallery! Take a pinch of snuff, Blyth; and never repeat nonsense in my hearing again.''

There was Mr. Bullivant, the enthusiastic young sculptor, with the mangy flow of flaxen hair, and the plump, waxy face; who wrote poetry, and showed, by various sonnets, that he again differed completely about the young lady from the Dowager Countess of Brambledown and Mr. Gimble. This gentleman sang fluently, on paper—using, by-the-way, a professional epithet—about her "chiseled mouth,''

"Which breathed of rapture and the balmy South.''

He expatiated on

"Her sweet lips smiling at her dimpled chin,
    Whose wealth of kisses gods might long to win—''

and much more to the same maudlin effect. In plain prose, the ardent Bullivant was all for the lower part of the young lady's face, and actually worried her, and Mr. Blyth, and everybody in the house, until he got leave to take a cast of it.

Lastly, there was Mrs. Blyth's father, a meek old gentleman, with a continual cold in the head; who lived on marvelously to the utmost verge of human existence—as very poor men, with very large families, who would be much better out of this world than in it, very often do. There was this low-speaking, mildly-infirm, and perpetually-snuffling engraver, who, on being asked to mention what he most admired in her, answered that he thought it was her hair, "which was of such a nice light brown color; or, perhaps, it might be the pleasant way in which she carried her head, or, perhaps, her shoulders—or, perhaps, her head *and* shoulders, both together. Not that his opinion was good for much in tasty matters of this kind, for which reason he begged to apologize for expressing it at all." In speaking thus of his opinion, the worthy engraver surely depreciated himself most unjustly; for, if the father of eight daughters cannot succeed in learning (philoprogenitively speaking) to be a good judge of women, what man can?

However, there was one point on which Mr. Gimble, Lady Brambledown, Mr. Bullivant, Mrs. Blyth's father, and hosts of friends besides, were all agreed, without one discordant exception.

They unanimously asserted that the young lady's face was the nearest living approach they had ever seen to that immortal "Madonna" face, which has forever associated the idea of beauty with the name of RAPHAEL. The resemblance struck everybody alike, even those who were but slightly conversant with pictures, the moment they saw her. Taken in detail, her features might be easily found fault with. Her eyes might be pronounced too large, her mouth too small, her nose not Grecian enough for some people's tastes. But the general effect of these features, the shape of her head and face, and especially her habitual expression, reminded all beholders at once, and irresistibly, of that image of softness, purity, and feminine gentleness which has been engraven on all civilized memories by the "Madonnas" of Raphael.

It was in consequence of this extraordinary resemblance that her own English name of Mary had been, from the first, altered and Italianized by Mr. and Mrs. Blyth, and by all intimate friends, into "Madonna." One or two extremely strict and extremely foolish people objected to any such familiar application of this name, as being open, in certain directions, to an imputation of irreverence. Mr. Blyth was not generally very quick at an answer; but, on this occasion, he had three answers ready before the objections were quite out of his friends' mouths.

In the first place, he said that he and his friends used the name only in an artist-sense, and only with reference to Raphael's pictures. In the next place, he produced an Italian dictionary, and showed that "Madonna" had a second meaning in the language, signifying simply and literally, "My lady." And, in conclusion, he proved historically, that "Madonna" had been used in the old times as a prefix to the names of Italian women; quoting, for example, "Madonna Pia," whom he happened to remember just at that moment, from having once painted a picture from one of the scenes of her terrible story.   These statements silenced all objections; and the young lady was accordingly much better known in the painter's house as "Madonna" than as "Mary."

On now entering the studio, she walked up to Valentine, laid a hand lightly on each of his shoulders, and so lifted herself to be kissed on the forehead.   Then she looked down on his palette, and observing that some colors were still missing from it, began to search for them directly in the painting-box.   She found them in a moment, and appealed to Mr. Blyth with an arch look of inquiry and triumph.   He nodded, smiled, and held out his palette for her to put the colors on it herself.   Having done this very neatly and delicately, she next looked round the room, and at once observed the bust of Venus placed on the office-stool.

At the same time, Mr. Blyth, who saw the direction taken by her eyes, handed to her a port-crayon with some black chalk, which he had been carefully cutting to a point for the last minute or two.   She took it with a little mock courtesy, pouting her lip slightly, as if drawing the Venus was work not much to her taste—smiled when she saw Valentine shaking his head, and frowning comically at her—then went away at once to the drawing-board, and sat down opposite Venus, in which position she offered as decided a living contradiction as ever was seen to the assertion of the classical idea of beauty, as expressed in the cast that she was about to copy.

Mr. Blyth, on his side, set to work at last on the Landscape; painting upon the dancing Bacchantes in the foreground of his picture, whose scanty dresses stood sadly in need of a little brightening up. While the painter and the young lady are thus industriously occupied with the business of the studio, there is leisure to remark on one rather perplexing characteristic of their intercourse, so far as it has yet proceeded on this particular winter's morning.

Ever since Madonna has been in the room, not one word has she spoken to Valentine; and not one word has Valentine (who can talk glibly enough to himself) spoken to her. He never said "Good-morning," when he kissed her—or, "Thank you for finding my lost colors"—or, "I have set the Venus, my dear, for your drawing-lesson to-day." And she, woman as she is, has actually not asked him a single question since she entered the studio! What can this absolute and remarkable silence mean between two people who look as affectionately on each other as these two look, every time their eyes meet!

Is this one of the Mysteries of the painter's fireside?

Who is Madonna?

What is her real name besides Mary?

Is it Mary Blyth?

Some years ago, an extraordinary adventure happened to Valentine in the circus of an itinerant Equestrian Company. In that adventure, and in the strange results attending it, the clew lies hidden, which leads to the Mystery of the painter's fireside, and reveals the story of this book.

CHAPTER III.

MADONNA'S CHILDHOOD.

IN the autumn of 1838, Mrs. Blyth's malady had for some time past assumed the permanent form from which it seldom afterward varied. She now suffered little actual pain, except when she quitted a recumbent posture. But the general disorganization produced by almost exclusive confinement to one position had, even at this early period, begun to work sad changes in her personal appearance. She suffered that mortifying misfortune just as bravely and resignedly as she had suffered the first great calamity of her incurable disorder. Valentine never showed that he thought her altered; Valentine's kindness was just as affectionate and as constant as it had ever been in the happier days of their marriage. So encouraged, Lavinia had the heart to bear all burdens patiently; and could find sources of happiness for herself, where others could discover nothing but causes for grief.

The room she inhabited was already, through Valentine's self-denying industry, better furnished than any other room in the house; but was far from presenting the same appearance of luxury and completeness to which it attained in the course of after-years.

The charming maple-wood and ivory book-case, with the prettily-bound volumes ranged in such bright regularity along its shelves, was there certainly as early as the autumn of 1838. It would not, however, at that time have formed part of the furniture of Mrs. Blyth's room, if her husband had not provided himself with the means of paying for it, by accepting a certain professional invitation to the country, which he knew before, and would enable him to face the terrors of the upholsterer's bill.

The invitation in question had been sent to him by a clerical friend, the Reverend Doctor Joyce, Rector of St. Judy's, in the large agricultural town of Rubbleford. Valentine had produced a water-color drawing of one of the Doctor's babies, when the family at the Rectory were in London for a season, and this drawing had been shown to all the neighbors by the worthy clergyman on his return. Now, although Mr. Blyth was not over-successful in the adult department of portrait-art, he was invariably victorious in the infant department. He painted all babies on one ingenious plan—giving them the roundest eyes, the chubbiest red cheeks, the most serenely good-humored smiles, and the neatest and whitest caps ever seen on paper. If fathers and their male friends rarely appreciated the fidelity of his likenesses, mothers and nurses invariably made amends for their want of taste. It followed, therefore, almost as a matter of course, that the local exhibition of the Doctor's drawing must bring offers of long-clothes-portrait employment to Valentine. Three resident families decided immediately to have portraits of their babies, if the painter would only travel to their houses to take the likenesses. A bachelor sporting squire in the neighborhood also volunteered a commission of another sort. This gentleman arrived (by a logical process which it is hopeless to think of tracing) at the conclusion that a man who was great at babies must necessarily be marvelous at horses; and determined, in consequence, that Valentine should paint his celebrated cover-hack. In writing to inform his friend of these offers, Doctor Joyce added another professional order on his own account, by way of appropriate conclusion to his letter. Here, then, were five commissions, which would produce enough—cheaply as Valentine worked— to pay, not only for the new bookcase, but for the books to put in it when it came home.

Having left his wife in charge of two of her sisters, who were forbidden to leave the house till his return, Mr. Blyth started for the Rectory; and once there, set to work on the babies with a zeal and good-humor which straightway won the hearts of mothers and nurses, and made him a great Rubbleford reputation in the course of a few days. Having done the babies to admiration, he next undertook the bachelor squire's hack. Here he had some trouble. The sporting gentleman would look over him while he painted; would bewilder him with the pedigree of the

horse; would have the animal done in the most
unpicturesque view; and sternly forbade all introduction of "tone," "light and shade," or
purely artistic embellishment of any kind, in
any part of the canvas. In short, the squire
wanted a sign-board instead of a picture, and he
at last got what he wanted to his heart's content.

One evening, while Valentine—still deeply im-
mersed in the difficulties of depicting the cover-
hack—was returning to the Rectory, after a
day's work at the squire's house, his attention
was suddenly attracted in the high-street of
Rubbleford, by a flaming placard pasted up on
a dead wall opposite the market-house.

He immediately joined the crowd of rustics
congregated around the many-colored and magnificent sheet of paper, and read at the top of it,
in huge blue letters: "JUBBER'S CIRCUS. THE
EIGHTH WONDER OF THE WORLD." After
this came some small print, which nobody lost
any time in noticing. But below the small print
appeared a perfect galaxy of fancifully shaped
scarlet letters, which fascinated all eyes, and informed the public that the equestrian company
included "MISS FLORINDA BEVERLEY, known"
(here the letters turned suddenly green), "where-
ever the English language was known, as The
Amazonian Empress of Equitation." This announcement was followed by the names of inferior members of the company; by a programme
of the evening's entertainments; by testimonials
extracted from the provincial press; by illustrations of gentlemen with lusty calves and spangled

drawers, and of ladies with smiling faces, shameless petticoats, and pirouetting legs. These illustrations, and the particulars which preceded them, were carefully digested by all Mr. Blyth's neighbors; but Mr. Blyth himself passed them over unnoticed. His eye had been caught by something at the bottom of the placard, which instantly absorbed his whole attention.

In this place the red letters appeared again, and formed the following words and marks of admiration:

THE MYSTERIOUS FOUNDLING!

AGED TEN YEARS!!

TOTALLY DEAF AND DUMB!!!

Underneath came an explanation of what the red letters referred to, occupying no less than three paragraphs of stumpy small print, every word of which Valentine eagerly devoured. This is what he read:

"Mr. Jubber, as proprietor of the renowned Circus, has the honor of informing the nobility, gentry, and public, that the above wonderful Deaf and Dumb Female Child will appear between the first and second parts of the evening's performances. Mr. J. has taken the liberty of entitling this Marvel of Nature, The Mysterious Foundling; no one knowing who her father is, and her mother having died soon after her birth, leaving her in charge of the Equestrian Company, who have been fond parents and careful guardians to her ever since.

"She was originally celebrated in the annals

of Jubber's Circus, or Eighth Wonder of the World, as The Hurricane Child of the Desert; having appeared in that character, whirled aloft at the age of seven years in the hand of Muley Ben Hassan, the renowned Scourer of Sahara, in his daring act of Equitation, as exhibited to the terror of all England, in Jubber's Circus. At that time she had her hearing and speech quite perfect. But Mr. J. deeply regrets to state that a terrific accident happened to her soon afterward. Through no fault on the part of The Scourer (who, overcome by his feelings at the result of the above-mentioned frightful accident, has gone back to his native wilds a moody and broken-hearted man), she slipped from his hand while the three horses bestrode by the fiery but humane Arab were going at a gallop, and fell, shocking to relate, outside the Ring, on the boarded floor of the circus. She was supposed to be dead. Mr. Jubber instantly secured the inestimable assistance of the Faculty, who found that she was still alive, and set her arm, which had been broken. It was only afterward discovered that she had utterly lost her sense of hearing. To use the emphatic language of the medical gentlemen (who all spoke with tears in their eyes), she had been struck stone deaf by the shock. Under these melancholy circumstances, it was found that the faculty of speech soon failed her altogether; and she is now, therefore, Totally Deaf AND Dumb—but Mr. J. rejoices to say, quite cheerful and in good health notwithstanding.

"Mr. Jubber being himself the father of a family, ventures to think that these little particulars may prove of some interest to an Intelligent, a Sympathetic, and a Benevolent Public. He will simply allude, in conclusion, to the performances of the Mysterious Foundling, as exhibiting perfection hitherto unparalleled in the Art of Legerdemain, with wonders of untraceable intricacy on the cards, originally the result of abstruse calculations made by that renowned Algebraist, Mohammed Engedi, extending over a period of ten years, dating from the year 1215 of the Arab Chronology. More than this Mr. Jubber will not venture to mention, for 'Seeing is Believing,' and the Mysterious Foundling must be seen to be believed. For prices of admission consult bottom of bill."

Mr. Blyth read this grotesquely shocking narrative with sentiments which were anything rather than complimentary to the taste, the delicacy, and the humanity of the fluent Mr. Jubber. He consulted the bottom of the bill, however, as requested; and ascertained what were the prices of admission—then glanced at the top, and observed that the first performance was fixed for that very evening—looked about him absently for a minute or two—and resolved to be present at it.

Most assuredly, Valentine's resolution did not proceed from that dastard insensibility to all decent respect for human suffering which could feast itself on the spectacle of calamity paraded for hire, in the person of a deaf and dumb child of ten years old. His motives for going to the circus were stained by no trace of such degradation as this. But what were they then? That question he himself could not have answered: it was a common predicament with him not to know his own motives, generally from not inquiring into them. There are men who run breathlessly—men who walk cautiously—and men who saunter easily through the journey of life. Valentine belonged to the latter class; and, like the rest of his order, often strayed down a new turning, without being able to realize at the time what purpose it was which first took him that way. Our destinies shape the future for us out of strange materials; a traveling circus sufficed them, in the first instance, to shape a new future for Mr. Blyth.

He first went on to the Rectory, to tell them where he was going and to get a cup of tea, and then hurried off to the circus, in a field outside the town.

The performance had begun some time when he got in. The Amazonian Empress (known otherwise as Miss Florinda Beverley) was dancing voluptuously on the back of a cantering piebald horse with a Roman nose. Round and round careered the Empress, beating time on the saddle with her imperial legs to the tune of "Let the Toast be Dear Woman," played with intense feeling by the band. Suddenly the melody changed to "See the Conquering Hero Comes;" the piebald horse increased his speed; the Empress raised a flag in one hand, and a javelin in the other, and began slaying invisible enemies in the empty air at full (circus) gallop. The result on the audience was prodigious; Mr. Blyth alone sat unmoved. Miss Florinda Beverley was not even a good model to draw legs from, in the estimation of this anti-Amazonian painter!

When the Empress was succeeded by a Spanish Guerrilla, who robbed, murdered, danced, caroused, and made love on the back of a cream-colored horse—and when the Guerrilla was followed by a clown who performed superhuman contortions, and made jokes by the yard, without the slightest appearance of intellectual effort —still Mr. Blyth exhibited no demonstration of astonishment or pleasure. It was only when a bell rang between the first and second parts of the performance, and the band struck up "Gentle Zitella," that he showed any symptoms of animation. Then he suddenly rose; and, moving down to a bench close against the low partition which separated the ring from the audience, fixed his eyes intently on a doorway opposite to him, overhung by a frozy red curtain with a tinsel border.

From this doorway there now appeared Mr. Jubber himself, clothed in white trousers with a gold stripe, and a green jacket with military epaulets. He had big, bold eyes, a dyed mustache, great fat flabby cheeks, long hair parted in the middle, a turn-down collar with a rose-colored handkerchief; and was, in every respect, the most atrocious-looking stage vagabond that ever painted a blackguard face. He led with him, holding her hand, the little deaf and dumb girl, whose misfortune he had advertised to the whole population of Rubbleford.

The face and manner of the child, as she walked into the center of the circus, and made her innocent courtesy and kissed her hand, went to the hearts of the whole audience in an instant. They greeted her with such a burst of applause as might have frightened a grown actress. But not a note from those cheering voices, not a breath of sound from those loudly clapping hands could reach her; she could *see* that they were welcoming her kindly, and that was all!

When the applause had subsided, Mr. Jubber asked for the loan of a handkerchief from one of the ladies present, and ostentatiously bandaged the child's eyes. He then lifted her upon the broad low wall which encircled the ring, and walked her round a little way (beginning from the door through which he had entered), inviting the spectators to test her total deafness by clapping their hands, shouting, or making any loud noise they pleased close at her ear. "You might fire off a cannon, ladies and gentlemen," said Mr. Jubber, "and it wouldn't make her start till after she'd smelled the smoke!"

To the credit of the Rubbleford audience, the majority of them declined making any practical experiments to test the poor child's utter deafness. The women set the example of forbearance, by entreating that the handkerchief might be taken off, so that they might see her pretty eyes again. This was done at once, and she

HE LED WITH HIM, HOLDING HER HAND, THE LITTLE DEAF AND
DUMB GIRL WHOSE MISFORTUNE HE HAD ADVERTISED TO THE WHOLE
POPULATION OF RUBBLEFORD.—HIDE-AND-SEEK, Vol. XI., page 80.

began to perform her conjuring tricks, with Mr. Jubber and one of the ring-keepers on either side of her officiating as assistants. These tricks, in themselves, were of the simplest and commonest kind; and derived all their attraction from the child's innocently earnest manner of exhibiting them, and from the novelty to the audience of communicating with her only by writing on a slate. They never tired of scrawling questions, of saying "poor little thing!" and of kissing her whenever they could get the opportunity, while she slowly went round the circus. "Deaf and dumb! ah, dear, dear, deaf and dumb!" was the general murmur of sympathy which greeted her from each new group as she advanced; Mr. Jubber invariably adding with a smile: "And as you see, ladies and gentlemen, in excellent health and spirits, notwithstanding; as hearty and happy, I pledge you my sacred word of honor, as the very best of us!"

While she was thus delighting the spectators on one side of the circus, how were the spectators on the other side, whose places she had not yet reached, contriving to amuse themselves?

From the moment of the little girl's first appearance, ample recreation had been unconsciously provided for them by a tall, stout and florid stranger, who appeared suddenly to lose his senses the moment he set eyes on the deaf and dumb child. This gentleman jumped up and sat down again excitably a dozen times in a minute; constantly apologizing on being called to order, and constantly repeating the offense the

moment afterward.   Mad and mysterious words,
never heard before in Rubbleford, poured from
his lips.   "Devotional beauty," "Fra Angelico's
angels," "Giotto and the cherubs," "Enough to
bring the divine Raphael down from heaven to
paint her."   Such were a few fragments of the
mad gentleman's incoherent mutterings, as they
reached his neighbors' ears.   The amusement
they yielded was soon wrought to its climax by
a joke from an attorney's clerk, who suggested
that this queer man, with the rosy face, must
certainly be the long-lost father of the "Mysterious Foundling."   Great gratification was
consequently anticipated from what might take
place when the child arrived opposite the bench
occupied by the excitable stranger.

Slowly, slowly, the little light figure went
round upon the broad partition wall of the ring,
until it came near, very near, to the place where
Valentine was sitting.

Ah, woful sight! so lovely, yet so piteous to
look on!   Shall she never hear kindly human
voices, the song of birds, the pleasant murmur
of the trees again?   Are all the sweet sounds
that sing of happiness to childhood, silent forever to *her?*   From those fresh, rosy lips shall
no glad words pour forth, when she runs and
plays in the sunshine?   Shall the clear, laughing
tones be hushed always?   the young, tender life
be forever a speechless thing, shut up in dumbness from the free world of voices?   Oh! Angel
of judgment! hast thou snatched her hearing
and her speech from this little child, to abandon

her in helpless affliction to such profanation as she now undergoes? Oh, Spirit of mercy! how long thy white-winged feet have tarried on their way to this innocent sufferer, to this lost lamb that cannot cry to the fold for help! Lead, ah, lead her tenderly to such shelter as she has never yet found for herself! Guide her, pure as she is now, from this tainted place to pleasant pastures, where the sunshine of human kindness shall be clouded no more, and Love and Pity shall temper every wind that blows over her with the gentleness of perpetual spring!

Slowly, slowly, the light figure went round the great circle of gazers, ministering obediently to their pleasure, waiting patiently till their curiosity was satisfied. And now her weary pilgrimage was wellnigh over for the night. She had arrived at the last group of spectators who had yet to see what she looked like close, and what tricks she could exhibit with her cards.

She stopped exactly opposite to Valentine; and when she looked up, she looked on him alone.

Was there something in the eager sympathy of his eyes as they met hers, which spoke to the little lonely heart in the sole language that could ever reach it? Did the child, with the quick instinct of the deaf and dumb, read his compassionate disposition, his pity and longing to help her, in his expression at that moment? It might have been so. Her pretty lips smiled on him as they had smiled on no one else that night; and when she held out some cards to be chosen from, she left unnoticed the eager hands extended on either side of her and presented them to Valentine only.

He saw the small fingers trembling as they held the cards; he saw the delicate little shoulders and the poor frail neck and chest bedizened with tawdry mock jewelry and spangles; he saw the innocent young face, whose pure beauty no soil of stage paint could disfigure, with the smile still on the parted lips, but with a patient forlornness in the sad blue eyes, as if the seeing sense that was left mourned always for the hearing and speaking senses that were gone—he marked all these things in an instant, and felt that his heart was sinking as he looked. A dimness stole over his sight; a suffocating sensation oppressed his breathing; the lights in the circus danced and mingled together; he bent down over the child's hand, and took it in his own; twice kissed it fervently; then, to the utter amazement of the laughing crowd about him, rose up suddenly, and forced his way out as if he had been flying for his life.

There was a momentary confusion among the audience. But Mr. Jubber was too old an adept in stage-business of all kinds not to know how to stop the growing tumult directly, and turn it into universal applause.

"Ladies and gentlemen," he cried, with a deep theatrical quiver in his voice, "I implore you to be seated, and to excuse the conduct of the party who has just absented himself. The talent of the Mysterious Foundling has overcome people in that way in every town of England.

Do I err in believing that a Rubbleford audience can make kind allowances for their weaker fellow-creatures? Thanks, a thousand thanks in the name of this darling and talented child, for your cordial, your generous, your affectionate, your inestimable reception of her exertions to-night!" With this peroration Mr. Jubber took his pupil out of the ring amid the most vehement cheering and waving of hats and handkerchiefs. He was too much excited by his triumph to notice that the child, as she walked after him, looked wistfully to the last in the direction by which Valentine had gone out.

"The public like excitement," soliloquized Mr. Jubber, as he disappeared behind the red curtain. "I must have all this in the bills to-morrow. It's safe to draw at least thirty shillings extra into the house at night."

In the meantime, Valentine, after some blundering at wrong doors, at last found his way out of the circus, and stood alone on the cool grass, in the cloudless autumn moonlight. He struck his stick violently on the ground, which at that moment represented to him the head of Mr. Jubber; and was about to return straight to the Rectory, when he heard a breathless voice behind him calling: "Stop, sir! oh, do please stop for one minute!"

He turned round. A buxom woman in a tawdry and tattered gown was running toward him as fast as her natural impediments to quick progression would permit.

"Please, sir," she cried—"please, sir, wasn't

you the gentleman that was taken queer at seeing our little Foundling? I was peeping through the red curtains, sir, just at the time."

Instead of answering the question, Valentine instantly began to rhapsodize about the child's face.

"Oh, sir! if you know anything about her," interposed the woman, "for God's sake, don't scruple to tell it to me! I'm only Mrs. Peckover, sir, the wife of Jemmy Peckover, the clown, that you saw in the circus to-night. But I took and nursed the little thing by her poor mother's own wish; and ever since that time—"

"My dear, good soul," said Mr. Blyth, "I know nothing of the poor little creature. I only wish from the bottom of my heart that I could do something to help her and make her happy. If Lavvie and I had had such an angel of a child as that," continued Valentine, clasping his hands together fervently, "deaf and dumb as she is, we should have thanked God for her every day of our lives!"

Mrs. Peckover was apparently not much used to hear such sentiments as these from strangers. She stared up at Mr. Blyth with two big tears rolling over her plump cheeks.

"Mrs. Peckover! Halloo there, Peck! where are you?" roared a stern voice from the stable department of the circus, just as the clown's wife seemed about to speak again.

Mrs. Peckover started, courtesied, and, without uttering another word, went back even faster than she had come out. Valentine looked after her intently, but made no attempt to follow: he was thinking too much of the child to think of that. When he moved again, it was to return to the Rectory.

He penetrated at once into the library, where Doctor Joyce was spelling over the *Rubbleford Mercury*, while Mrs. Joyce sat opposite to him, knitting a fancy jacket for her youngest but one. He was hardly inside the door before he began to expatiate in the wildest manner on the subject of the beautiful deaf and dumb girl. If ever man was in love with a child at first sight, he was that man. As an artist, as a gentleman of refined tastes, and as the softest-hearted of male human beings, in all three capacities, he was enslaved by that little innocent, sad face. He made the Doctor's head whirl again; he fairly stopped Mrs. Joyce's progress with the fancy jacket, as he sang the child's praises, and compared her face to every angel's face that had ever been painted, from the days of Giotto to the present time. At last, when he had fairly exhausted his hearers and himself, he dashed abruptly out of the room, to cool down his excitement by a moonlight walk in the Rectory garden.

"What a very odd man he is!" said Mrs. Joyce, taking up a dropped stitch in the fancy jacket.

"Valentine, my love, is the best creature in the world," rejoined the Doctor, folding up the *Rubbleford Mercury*, and directing it for the post; "but, as I often used to tell his poor father (who never would believe me), a little cracked.

I've known him go on in this way about children before—though, I must own, not quite so wildly, perhaps, as he talked just now."

"Do you think he'll do anything imprudent about the child? Poor thing! I'm sure I pity her as heartily as anybody can."

"I don't presume to think," answered the Doctor, calmly pressing the blotting-paper over the address he had just written. "Valentine is one of those people who defy all conjecture. No one can say what he will do or what he won't. A man who cannot resist an application for shelter and supper from any stray cur who wags his tail at him in the street; a man who blindly believes in the troubles of begging-letter impostors; a man whom I myself caught, last time he was down here, playing at marbles with three of my charity-boys in the street, and promising to treat them to hard-bake and ginger-beer afterward, is —in short, is not a man whose actions it is possible to speculate on."

Here the door opened, and Mr. Blyth's head was popped in, surmounted by a ragged straw hat with a sky-blue ribbon round it. "Doctor," said Valentine, "may I ask an excellent woman, with whom I have made acquaintance, to bring the child here to-morrow morning for you and Mrs. Joyce to see?"

"Certainly," said the good-humored rector, laughing. "The child by all means, and the excellent woman, too."

"Not if it's Miss Florinda Beverley!" interposed Mrs. Joyce (who had read the circus placard). "Florinda, indeed! Jezebel would be a better name for her!"

"My dear madam, it isn't Florinda," cried Valentine, eagerly. "I quite agree with you; her name ought to be Jezebel. And, what's worse, her legs are out of drawing."

"Mr. Blyth!!!" exclaimed Mrs. Joyce, indignant at this professional criticism on Jezebel's legs.

"Why don't you tell us at once who the excellent woman is!" cried the Doctor, secretly tickled by the allusion which had shocked his wife.

"Her name's Peckover," said Valentine; "she's a respectable married woman; she doesn't ride in the circus at all; and she nursed the poor child by her mother's own wish."

"We shall be delighted to see her to-morrow," said the warm-hearted rector — "or, no—stop! Not to-morrow; I shall be out. The day after. Cake and cowslip-wine for the deaf and dumb child at twelve o'clock—eh, my dear?"

"That's right! God bless you! you're always kindness itself," cried Valentine; "I'll find out Mrs. Peckover, and let her know. Not a wink of sleep for me to-night—never mind!" Here Valentine suddenly shut the door, then as suddenly opened it again, and added: "I mean to finish that infernal horse-picture to-morrow, and go to the circus again in the evening." With these words he vanished, and they heard him soon afterward whistling his favorite "Drops of Brandy" in the Rectory garden.

"Cracked! cracked!" cried the Doctor. "Dear old Valentine!"

"I'm afraid his principles are very loose," said Mrs. Joyce, whose thoughts still ran on the unlucky professional allusion to Jezebel's legs.

The next morning, when Mr. Blyth presented himself at the stables, and went on with the portrait of the cover-hack, the squire had no longer the slightest reason to complain of the painter's desire to combine in his work picturesqueness of effect with accuracy of resemblance. Valentine argued no longer about introducing "light and shade," or "keeping the background subdued in tone." His thoughts were all with the deaf and dumb child and Mrs. Peckover; and he smudged away recklessly, just as he was told, without once uttering so much as a word of protest. By the evening he had concluded his labor. The squire said it was one of the best portraits of a horse that had ever been taken: to which piece of criticism the writer of the present narrative is bound in common candor to add, that it was also the very worst picture that Mr. Blyth had ever painted.

On returning to Rubbleford, Valentine proceeded at once to the circus; placing himself, as nearly as he could, in the same position which he had occupied the night before.

The child was again applauded by the whole audience, and again went through her performance intelligently and gracefully, until she approached the place where Valentine was standing. She started as she recognized his face, and made a step forward to get nearer to him; but was stopped by Mr. Jubber, who saw that the people immediately in front of her were holding out their hands to write on her slate, and have her cards dealt round to them in their turn. The child's attention appeared to be distracted by seeing the stranger again who had kissed her hand so fervently—she began to look confused—and ended by committing an open and most palpable blunder in the very first trick that she performed.

The spectators good-naturedly laughed, and some of them wrote on her slate: "Try again, little girl." Mr. Jubber made an apology, saying that the extreme enthusiasm of the reception accorded to his pupil had shaken her nerves; and then signed to her, with a benevolent smile, but with a very sinister expression in his eyes, to try another trick. She succeeded in this; but still showed so much hesitation that Mr. Jubber, fearing another failure, took her away with him while there was a chance of making a creditable exit.

As she was led across the ring, the child looked intently at Valentine.

There was terror in her eyes—terror palpable enough to be remarked by some of the careless people near Mr. Blyth. "Poor little thing! she seems frightened at the man in the fine green jacket," said one. "And not without cause, I dare say," added another. "You don't mean that he could ever be brute enough to ill-use a child like that?—it's impossible!" cried a third.

At this moment the clown entered the ring. The instant before he shouted the well-known "Here we are!" Valentine thought he heard a strange cry behind the red curtain. He was not certain about it, but the mere doubt made his blood run chill. He listened for a minute anxiously. There was no chance now, however, for testing the correctness of his suspicion. The band had struck up a noisy jig tune, and the clown was capering and tumbling wonderfully, amid roars of laughter.

"This may be my fault," thought Valentine. "*This!* What?" He was afraid to pursue that inquiry. His ruddy face suddenly turned pale; and he left the circus, determined to find out what was really going on behind the red curtain. He walked round the outside of the building, wasting some time before he found a door to apply at for admission. At last he came to a sort of a passage, with some tattered horse-cloths hanging over its outer entrance.

"You can't come in here," said a shabby lad, suddenly appearing from the inside in his shirt-sleeves.

Mr. Blyth took out half a crown. "I want to see the deaf and dumb child directly!"

"Oh, all right! go in," muttered the lad, pocketing the money greedily.

Valentine hastily entered the passage. As soon as he was inside a sound reached his ears at which his heart sickened and turned faint. No words can describe it in all the horror of its helplessness—it was the moan of pain from a dumb human creature.

He thrust aside a curtain, and stood in a filthy place, partitioned off from the stables on one side,

and the circus on the other, with canvas and old
boards. There, on a wooden stool, sat the woman who had accosted him the night before, crying and soothing the child, who lay shuddering
on her bosom. The sobs of the clown's wife
mingled with the inarticulate wailing, so low,
yet so awful to hear; and both sounds were audible with a fearful, unnatural distinctness, through
the merry melody of the jig. and the peals of
hearty laughter from the audience in the circus.

"Oh, my God!" cried Valentine, horrorstruck
at what he heard, "stop her! don't let her moan
in that way!"

The woman started from her seat and put the
child down, then recognized Mr. Blyth and
rushed up to him.

"Hush!" she whispered, eagerly; "don't call
out like that. The villain, the brutal, heartless
villain is somewhere about the stables. If he
hears you, he'll come in and beat her again.
Oh, hush! hush, for God's sake! It's true he
beat her—the cowardly, hellish brute!—only for
making that one little mistake with the cards.
No! no! no! don't speak out so loud, or you'll
ruin us. How did you ever get in here? Oh!
you *must* be quiet! There, sit down. Hark!
I'm sure he's coming! Oh! go away—go away!"

She tried to pull Valentine out of the chair
into which she had thrust him but the instant
before. He seized tight hold of her hand and refused to move. If Mr. Jubber had come in at
that moment, he would have been thrashed
within an inch of his life.

The child had ceased moaning when she saw Valentine. She anxiously looked at him through her tears—then turned away quickly—took out her little handkerchief—and began to dry her eyes.

"I can't go yet—I'll promise only to whisper —you *must* listen to me," said Mr. Blyth, pale and panting for breath; "I mean to prevent this from happening again—don't speak!—I'll take that injured, beautiful, patient little angel away from this villainous place: I will, if I go before a magistrate!"

The woman stopped him by pointing suddenly to the child.

She had put back the handkerchief, and was approaching him. She came close and laid one hand on his knee, and timidly raised the other as high as she could toward his neck. Standing so, she looked up quietly into his face. The pretty lips tried hard to smile once more; but they only trembled for an instant, and then closed again. The clear, soft eyes, still dim with tears, sought his with an innocent gaze of inquiry and wonder. At that moment the expression of the sad and lovely little face seemed to say: "You look as if you wanted to be kind to me; I wish you could find out some way of telling me of it."

Valentine's heart told him what was the only way. He caught her up in his arms and half smothered her with kisses. The frail, childish hands rose trembling, and clasped themselves gently round his neck, and the fair head drooped lower and lower, wearily, until it lay on his shoulder.

The clown's wife turned away her face, desperately stifling with both hands the sobs that were beginning to burst from her afresh. She whispered: "Oh, go, sir—pray go! Some of the riders will be in here directly; you'll get us into dreadful trouble!"

Valentine rose, still holding the child in his arms. "I'll go if you promise me—"

"I'll promise you anything, sir!"

"You know the Rectory! Doctor Joyce's—the clergyman—my kind friend—"

"Yes, sir; I know it. Do please, for little Mary's sake, be as quick as you can!"

"Mary! Her name's Mary!" Valentine drew back into a corner, and began kissing the child again.

"You must be out of your senses to keep on in that way after what I've told you!" cried the clown's wife, wringing her hands in despair and trying to drag him out of the corner. "Jubber will be here in another minute. She'll be beaten again, if you're caught with her; oh Lord! oh Lord! will nothing make you understand that?"

He understood it only too well, and put the child down instantly, his face turning pale again; his agitation becoming so violent that he never noticed the hand which she held out toward him, or the appealing look that said so plainly and pathetically: "I want to bid you good-by; but I can't say it as other children can." He never observed this; for he had taken Mrs. Peckover by the arm, and had drawn her away hurriedly after him into the passage.

The child made no attempt to follow them: she turned aside, and, sitting down in the darkest corner of the miserable place, rested her head against the rough partition which was all that divided her from the laughing audience. Her lips began to tremble again: she took out the handkerchief once more, and hid her face in it.

"Now, recollect your promise," whispered Valentine to the clown's wife, who was slowly pushing him out all the time he was speaking to her. "You must bring little Mary to the Rectory to-morrow morning at twelve o'clock exactly—you must! or I'll come and fetch her myself—"

"I'll bring her, sir, if you'll only go now. I'll bring her—I will, as true as I stand here!"

"If you don't!" cried Valentine, still distrustful, and trembling all over with agitation—"if you don't—!"

He stopped; for he suddenly felt the open air blowing on his face. The clown's wife was gone, and nothing remained for him to threaten but the tattered horse-cloths that hung over the empty doorway.

CHAPTER IV.

MADONNA'S MOTHER.

It is a quarter to twelve by the hall clock at the Rectory, and one of the finest autumn mornings of the whole season. Vance, Doctor Joyce's middle-aged man-servant, or "Bishop" Vance, as the small wits of Rubbleford call him, in allusion to his sleek and solemn appearance, his respectable manner, his clerical cravat, and speckless black garments, is placing the cake and cowslip-wine on the dining-table, with as much formality and precision as if his master expected an archbishop to lunch, instead of a clown's wife and a little child of ten years old. It is quite a sight to see Vance retiring and looking at the general effect of each knife and fork as he lays it down; or solemnly strutting about the room, with a spotless napkin waving gently in his hand; or patronizingly confronting the pretty house-maid at the door, and taking plates and dishes from her with the air of a kitchen Sultan who can never afford to lose his dignity for a moment in the presence of the female slaves.

The dining-room window opens into the Rectory garden. The morning shadows cast by the noble old elm-trees that grow all round are fading from the bright lawn. The rich flower-beds gleam like beds of jewels in the radiant sunshine. The rookery is almost deserted, a solitary sleepy *caw* being only heard now and then at long intervals. The singing of birds, and the buzzing of busy insects sound faint, distant and musical. On a shady seat, among the trees, Mrs. Joyce is just visible, working in the open air. One of her daughters sits reading on the turf at her feet. The other is giving the younger children a ride by turns on the back of a large

Newfoundland dog, who walks along slowly with his tongue hanging out, and his great bushy tail wagging gently. A prettier scene of garden beauty and family repose could not be found in all England than the scene which the view through the Rectory window now presents.

The household tranquillity, however, is not entirely uninterrupted. Across the picture, of which Vance and the luncheon-table form the foreground, and the garden with Mrs. Joyce and the young ladies the middle-distance and background, there flits from time to time an unquiet figure. This personage is always greeted by Leo, the Newfoundland dog, with an extra wag of the tail; and is apostrophized laughingly by the young ladies, under the appellation of "funny Mr. Blyth."

Valentine has in truth let nobody have any rest, either in the house or the garden, since the first thing in the morning. The rector having some letters to write, has bolted himself into his study in despair, and defies his excitable friend from that stronghold, until the arrival of Mrs. Peckover with the deaf and dumb child has quieted the painter's fidgety impatience for the striking of twelve o'clock, and the presence of the visitors from the circus. As for the miserable Vance, Mr. Blyth has discomposed, worried, and put him out, till he looks suffocated with suppressed indignation. Mr. Blyth has invaded his sanctuary to ask whether the hall clock is right, and has caught him "cleaning himself" in his shirt-sleeves. Mr. Blyth has broken one of his tumblers, and has mutinously insisted on showing him how to draw the cork of the cowslip - wine - bottle. Mr. Blyth has knocked down a fork and two spoons, just as they were laid straight, by whisking past the table like a madman on his way into the garden. Mr. Blyth has bumped up against the house-maid in returning to the dining-room, and has apologized to Susan by a joke which makes her giggle ecstatically in Vance's own face. If this sort of thing is to go on for a day or two longer, though he has been twenty years at the Rectory, Vance will be goaded into giving the doctor warning.

It is five minutes to twelve. Valentine has skipped into the garden for the thirtieth time at least, to beg that Mrs. Joyce and the young ladies will repair to the dining-room, and be ready to set Mrs. Peckover and her little charge quite at their ease the moment they come in. Mrs. Joyce consents to this proposal at last, and takes his offered arm; touching it, however, very gingerly, and looking straight before her, while he talks, with an air of matronly dignity and virtuous reserve. She is still convinced that Mr. Blyth's principles are extremely loose, and treats him as she might have treated Don Juan himself under similar circumstances.

They all go into the dining-room. Mrs. Joyce and her daughters take their places, looking de-liciously cool and neat in their bright morning dresses. Leo drops down lazily on the rug in-side the window, with a thump of his great heavy body that makes the glasses ring. The doctor comes in with his letters for the post, and apostrophizes Valentine with a harmless clerical joke. Vance solemnly touches up the already perfect arrangement of the luncheon-table. The clock strikes twelve. A faint, meek ring is heard at the Rectory bell.

Vance struts slowly to the door, when— Heaven and earth! are no conventions held sacred by these painters of pictures?—Mr. Blyth dashes past him with a shout of "Here they are!" and flies into the hall to answer the gate himself. Vance turns solemnly round toward his master, trembling and purple in the face, with an appealing expression, which says plainly enough: "If *you* mean to stand this sort of outrage, sir, I beg most respectfully to inform you that *I* don't." The rector bursts out laughing; the young ladies follow his example; the Newfoundland dog jumps up, and joins in with his mighty bark. Mrs. Joyce sits silent, and looks at Vance, and sympathizes with him.

Mr. Blyth is soon heard again in the hall, talking at a prodigious rate, without one audible word of answer proceeding from any other voice. The door of the dining-room, which has swung to, is suddenly pushed open, jostling the outraged Vance, who stands near it, into such a miserably undignified position flat against the wall, that the young ladies begin to titter behind their handkerchiefs as they look at him. Valentine enters, leading in Mrs. Peckover and the deaf and dumb child, with such an air of supreme happiness, that he looks absolutely handsome for the moment. The rector, who is, in the best and noblest sense of the word, a gentleman, receives Mrs. Peckover as politely and cordially as he would have received the best lady in Rubbleford. Mrs. Joyce comes forward with him, very kind, too, but a little reserved in her manner, nevertheless; being possibly apprehensive that any woman connected with the circus must be tainted with some slight flavor of Miss Florinda Beverley. The young ladies drop down into the most charming positions on either side of the child, and fall straightway into fits of ecstasy over her beauty. The dog walks up, and pokes his great honest muzzle among them companionably. Vance stands rigid against the wall, and disapproves strongly of the whole proceeding.

Poor Mrs. Peckover! She had never been in such a house as the Rectory, she had never spoken to a doctor of divinity before in her life. She was very hot and red and trembling, and made fearful mistakes in grammar, and clung as shyly to Mr. Blyth as if she had been a little girl. The rector soon contrived, however, to settle her comfortably in a seat by the table. She courtesied reverentially to Vance, as she passed by him; doubtless under the impression that he was a second doctor of divinity, even greater and more learned than the first. He stared in return straight over her head, with small unwinking eyes, his cheeks turning slowly from deep red to dense purple. Mrs. Peckover

shuddered inwardly, under the conviction that
she had insulted a dignitary, who was hoisted
up on some clerical elevation, too tremendous to
be courtesied to by such a social atom as a
clown's wife.

Mrs. Joyce had to call three times to her
daughters before she could get them to the
luncheon-table. If she had possessed Valentine's eye for the picturesque and beautiful, she
would certainly have been incapable of disturbing the group which her third summons broke
up.

In the center stood the deaf and dumb child,
dressed in a white frock, with a little silk man-
tilla over it, made from a cast-off garment belonging to one of the ladies of the circus. She
wore a plain straw hat, ornamented with a morsel of narrow white ribbon, and tied under the
chin with the same material. Her clear, delicate complexion was overspread by a slight rosy
tinge—the tender coloring of Nature, instead of
the coarsely glaring rouge with which they disfigured her when she appeared before the public.
Her wondering blue eyes, that looked so sad in
the piercing gas-light, appeared to have lost that
sadness in the mellow atmosphere of the Rectory
dining-room. The tender and touching stillness
which her affliction had cast over her face seemed
a little at variance with its childish immaturity
of feature and roundness of form, but harmonized
exquisitely with the quiet smile which seemed
habitual to her when she was happy—gratefully
and unrestrainedly happy, as she now felt among

the new friends who were receiving her, not like
a stranger and an inferior, but like a younger
sister who had been long absent from them.

She stood near the window, the center figure
of the group, offering a little slate that hung by
her side, with a pencil attached to it, to the rector's eldest daughter, who was sitting at her
right hand on a stool. The second of the young
ladies knelt on the other side, with both her arms
round the dog's neck; holding him back as he
stood in front of the child, so as to prevent him
from licking her face, which he had made several resolute attempts to do, from the moment
when she first entered the room. Both the Doctor's daughters were healthy, rosy English beauties in the first bloom of girlhood; and both were
attired in the simplest and prettiest muslin
dresses, very delicate in color and pattern. Pity
and admiration, mixed with some little perplexity and confusion, gave an unusual animation to
their expressions; for they could hardly accustom
themselves as yet to the idea of the poor child's
calamity. They talked to her eagerly, as if she
could hear and answer them—while she, on her
part, stood looking alternately from one to the
other, watching their lips and eyes intently, and
still holding out the slate, with her innocent
gesture of invitation and gentle look of apology,
for the eldest girl to write on. The varying
expressions of the three; the difference in their
positions; the charming contrast between their
light, graceful figures and the bulky strength
and grand solidity of form in the noble New-

foundland dog who stood among them; the lustrous background of lawn and flowers and trees, seen through the open window; the sparkling purity of the sunshine which fell brightly over one part of the group; the transparency of the warm shadows that lay so caressingly, sometimes on a round smooth cheek, sometimes over ringlets of glistening hair, sometimes on the crisp folds of a muslin dress—all these accidental combinations of the moment, these natural and elegant positions of Nature's setting, these accessories of light and shade and background garden objects beautifully and tenderly filling up the scene, presented together a picture which it was a luxury to be able to look on, which it seemed little short of absolute profanation to disturb.

Mrs. Joyce, nevertheless, pitilessly disarranged it. In a moment the living picture was destroyed; the young ladies were called to their mother's side; the child was placed between Valentine and Mrs. Peckover, and the important business of luncheon began in earnest.

It was wonderful to hear how Mr. Blyth talked; how he alternately glorified the clown's wife for the punctual performance of her promise, and appealed triumphantly to the rector to say whether he had not underrated rather than exaggerated little Mary's beauty. It was also wonderful to see Mrs. Peckover's blank look of astonishment when she found the rigid doctor of divinity, who would not so much as notice her courtesy, suddenly relax into blandly supplying her with everything she wanted to eat or drink. But a very much more remarkable study of human nature than either of these, was afforded by the grimly patronizing and profoundly puzzled aspect of Vance, as he waited, under protest, upon a woman from a traveling circus. It is something to see the Pope serving the Pilgrims their dinner, during the Holy Week at Rome. Even that astounding sight, however, fades into nothing, as compared with the sublimer spectacle of Mr. Vance waiting upon Mrs. Peckover.

The rector, who was a sharp observer in his own quiet, unobtrusive way, was struck by two peculiarities in little Mary's behavior during lunch. In the first place, he remarked, with some interest and astonishment, that while the clown's wife was, not unnaturally, very shy and embarrassed in her present position, among strangers who were greatly her social superiors, little Mary had maintained her self-possession, and had unconsciously adapted herself to her new sphere from the moment when she first entered the dining-room. In the second place, he observed that she constantly nestled close to Valentine; looked at him oftener than she looked at any one else; and seemed to be always trying, sometimes not unsuccessfully, to guess what he was saying to others by watching his expression, his manner, and the action of his lips. "That child's character is no common one," thought Doctor Joyce; "she is older at heart than she looks; and is almost as fond of Blyth already as he is of her."

When lunch was over, the eldest Miss Joyce whispered a petition in her mother's ear: "May Carry and I take the dear little girl out with us to see our gardens, mamma?"

"Certainly, my love, if she likes to go. You had better ask her— Ah, dear! dear! I forgot —I mean, write on her slate. It's so hard to remember she's deaf and dumb when one sees her sitting there looking so pretty and happy. She seems to like the cake. Remind me, Emmy, to tie some up for her in paper before she goes away."

Miss Emily and Miss Caroline went round to the child directly, and made signs for the slate. They alternately wrote on it with immense enthusiasm, until they had filled one side; signing their initials in the most business-like manner at the end of each line, thus:

"Oh, do come and see my gardens. E. J."— "We will gather you such a nice nosegay. C. J."—"I have got some lovely little guinea-pigs. E. J."—"And Mark, our gardener, has made me a summer-house, with such funny chairs in it. C. J."—"You shall have my parasol to keep the sun off. E. J."—"And we will send Leo into the water as often as you like him to go. C. J."—Thus they went on till they got to the bottom of the slate.

The child, after nodding her head and smiling as she read each fresh invitation, turned the slate over, and, with some little triumph at showing that she could write too, began slowly to trace some large text letters in extremely crooked lines. It took her a long time—especially as Mr. Blyth was breathlessly looking over her shoulder all the while—to get through these words: "Thank you for being so kind to me. I will go with you anywhere you like."

In a few minutes more the two young ladies and little Mary were walking over the bright lawn, with Leo in close attendance, carrying a stick in his mouth.

Valentine started up to follow them; then appeared suddenly to remember something, and sat down again with a very anxious expression on his face. He and Doctor Joyce looked at one another significantly. Before breakfast, that morning, they had been closeted at a private interview. Throughout the conversation which then took place, Mr. Blyth had been unusually quiet, and very much in earnest. The Doctor had begun by being incredulous and sarcastic in a good-humored way; but had ended by speaking seriously, and making a promise under certain conditions. The time for the performance of that promise had now arrived.

"You needn't wait, Vance," said the rector. "Never mind about taking the things away. I'll ring when you're wanted."

Vance gloomily departed.

"Now the young people have left us, Mrs. Peckover," said Doctor Joyce, turning to the clown's wife, "there is a good opportunity for my making a proposition to you on behalf of my old and dear friend here, Mr. Blyth, who, as you must have noticed, feels great sympathy and fondness for your little Mary. But, before I mention this proposal (which I am sure you will receive in the best spirit, however it may surprise you), I should wish—we should all wish, if you have no objection—to hear any particulars you can give us on the subject of this poor child. Do you feel any reluctance to tell us in confidence whatever you know about her?"

"Oh dear no, sir!" exclaimed Mrs. Peckover, very much amazed. "I should be ashamed of myself if I went making any objections to anything you wanted to know about little Mary. But it's strange to me to be in a beautiful place like this, drinking wine with gentlefolks—and I'm almost afraid—"

"Not afraid, I hope, that you can't tell us what we are so anxious to know, quite at your ease, and in your own way?" said the rector, pleasantly. "Pray, Mrs. Peckover, believe I am sincere in saying that we meet on equal terms here. I have heard from Mr. Blyth of your motherly kindness to that poor helpless child; and I am indeed proud to take your hand, and happy to see you here, as one who should always be an honored guest in a clergyman's house—the doer of a good and charitable deed. I have always, I hope, valued the station to which it has pleased God to call me, because it especially offers me the privilege of being the friend of all my fellow-Christians, whether richer or poorer, higher or lower in worldly rank, than I am myself."

Mrs. Peckover's eyes began to fill. She could have worshiped Doctor Joyce at that moment.

"Mr. Blyth!" exclaimed Mrs. Joyce, sharply, before another word could be spoken—"excuse me, Mr. Blyth; but really—"

Valentine was trying to pour out a glass of sherry for Mrs. Peckover. His admiration of the doctor's last speech, and his extreme anxiety to re-assure the clown's wife, must have interfered with his precision of eye and hand; for one-half of the wine, as he held the decanter, was dropping into the glass, and the other half was dribbling into a little river on the cloth. Mrs. Joyce thought of the walnut-wood table underneath, and felt half distracted as she spoke. Mrs. Peckover, delighted to be of some use, forgot her company manners in an instant, pulled out her red cotton pocket-handkerchief, and darted at the spilled sherry. But the rector was even quicker with his napkin. Mrs. Peckover's cheeks turned the color of her handkerchief, as she put it back in her pocket, and sat down again.

"Much obliged—no harm done—much obliged, ma'am," said Doctor Joyce. "Now, Valentine, if you don't leave off apologizing, and sit down directly in that arm-chair against the wall, I shall take Mrs. Peckover into my study, and hear everything she has to say, at a private interview. There! we are all comfortable and composed again at last, and ready to be told how little Mary and the good friend who has been like a mother to her first met."

Thus appealed to, Mrs. Peckover began her narrative; sometimes addressing it to the Doc-

tor, sometimes to Mrs. Joyce, and sometimes to
Valentine. From beginning to end, she was
only interrupted at rare intervals by a word of
encouragement, or sympathy, or surprise, from
her audience. Even Mr. Blyth sat most uncharacteristically still and silent; his expression
alone showing the varying influences of the story
on him, from its strange commencement to its
melancholy close.

"It's better than ten years ago, sir," began
the clown's wife, speaking first to Doctor Joyce,
"since my little Tommy was born; he being
now, if you please, at school and costing nothing, through a presentation, as they call it, I
think, which was given us by a kind patron to
my husband. Some time after I had got well
over my confinement, I was out one afternoon
taking a walk with baby and Jemmy; which
last is my husband, ma'am. We were at Bangbury, then, just putting up the circus; it was a
fine large neighborhood, and we hoped to do
good business there. Jemmy and me and the
baby went out into the fields, and enjoyed ourselves very much; it being such nice warm
spring weather, though it was March at the
time. We came back to Bangbury by the road;
and just as we got near the town, we see a
young woman sitting on the bank, and holding
her baby in her arms, just as I had got my baby
in mine.

"'How dreadful ill and weak she do look,
don't she?' says Jemmy. Before I could say as

much as 'Yes,' she stares up at us, and asks in a wild voice, though it wasn't very loud, either, if we can tell her the way to Bangbury work-house. Having pretty sharp eyes of our own, we both of us knew that a workhouse was no fit place for her. Her gown was very dusty, and one of her boots was burst, and her hair was draggled all over her face, and her eyes was sunk in her head, like; but we saw somehow that she was a lady—or, if she wasn't exactly a lady, that no workhouse was proper for her, at any rate. I stooped down to speak to her; but her baby was crying so dreadful she could hardly hear me. 'Is the poor thing ill?' says I. 'Starving,' says she, in such a desperate, fierce way, that it gave me a turn. 'Is that your child?' says I, a bit frightened about how she'd answer me. 'Yes,' she says, in quite a new voice, very soft and sorrowful, and bending her face away from me over the child. 'Then why don't you suckle it?' says I. She looks up at me, and then at Jemmy, and shakes her head, and says nothing. I give my baby to Jemmy to hold, and went and sat down by her. He walked away a little; and I whispered to her again: 'Why don't you suckle it?' and she whispered to me: 'My milk's all dried up.' I couldn't wait to hear no more till I'd got her baby at my own breast.

"That was the first time I suckled little Mary, ma'am. She wasn't a month old then, and oh, so weak and small! such a mite of a baby compared to mine!

"You may be sure, sir, that I asked the young woman lots of questions while I was sitting side by side with her. She stared at me with a dazed look in her face, seemingly quite stupefied by weariness or grief, or both together. Sometimes she give me an answer and sometimes she wouldn't. She was very secret. She wouldn't say where she come from, or who her friends were, or what her name was. She said she should never have name or home or friends again. I just quietly stole a look down at her left hand, and saw that there was no wedding-ring on her finger, and guessed what she meant. 'Does the father know you are wandering about in this way?' says I. She flushes up directly. 'No,' says she, 'he doesn't know where I am. He never had any love for me, and he has no pity for me now. God's curse on him wherever he goes!'—'Oh, hush! hush!' says I, 'don't talk like that!' 'Why do you ask me questions?' says she, more fiercely than ever. 'What business have you to ask me questions that make me mad?' 'I've only got one more to bother you with,' says I, quite cool; 'and that is, haven't you got any money at all with you?' You see, ma'am, now I'd got her child at my own bosom, I didn't care for what she said, or fear for what she might do to me. The poor mite of a baby was sure to be a peace-maker between us, sooner or later.

"It turned out she'd got sixpence and a few half-pence—not a farthing more, and too proud to ask help from any one of her friends. I managed to worm out of her that she had run away from home before her confinement, and had gone to some strange place to be confined, where they'd ill-treated and robbed her. She hadn't long got away from the wretches who'd done it. By the time I'd found out all this, her baby was quite quiet, and ready to go to sleep. I gave it her back. She said nothing, but took and kissed my hand, her lips feeling like burning coals on my flesh. 'You're kindly welcome,' says I, a little flustered at such a queer way of thanking me. 'Just wait a bit while I speak to my husband.' Though she'd been and done wrong, I couldn't for the life of me help pitying her, for all her fierce ways. She was so young, and so forlorn and ill, and had such a beautiful face (little Mary's is the image of it, 'specially about the eyes), and seemed so like a lady, that it was almost a sin, as I thought, to send her to such a place as a workhouse.

"Well, I went and told Jemmy all I had got out of her—my own baby kicking and crowing in my arms again, as happy as a king, all the time I was speaking. 'It seems shocking,' says I, 'to let such as her go into a workhouse. What had we better do?'—Says Jemmy, 'Let's take her with us to the circus and ask Peggy Burke.'

"Peggy Burke, if you please, sir, was the finest rider that ever stepped on a horse's back. We've had nothing in our circus to come near her, since she went to Astley's. She was the wildest devil of an Irish girl—oh! I humbly beg

your pardon, sir, for saying such a word; but
she really *was* so wild, I hope you'll excuse it.
She'd go through fire and water, as they say,
to serve people she liked; but as for them she
didn't, she'd often use her riding-whip among
'em as free as her tongue. That cowardly brute
Jubber would never have beaten my little Mary,
if Peggy had been with us still! He was so
frightened of her that she could twist him round
her finger; and she did, for he dursn't quarrel
with the best rider in England, and let other cir-
cuses get hold of her. Peggy was a wonderful
sharp girl besides, and was always fond of me,
and took my part; so when Jemmy said he
thought it best to ask her what we had better do,
you may be sure that I thought it best, too. We
took the young woman and the baby with us to
the circus at once. She never asked any questions; she didn't seem to care where she went, or
what she did; she was dazed and desperate—a
sight, ma'am, to make your heart ache.

"They were just getting tea in the circus,
which was nearly finished. We mostly have tea
and dinner there, sir; finding it come cheaper in
the end to mess together when we can. Peggy
Burke, I remember, was walking about on the
grass outside, whistling (that was one of her
queer ways) 'The Girl I Left Behind Me.' 'Ah!
Peck,' says she, 'what have you been after now?
Who's the company lady ye've brought to tea
with us?' I told her, sir, all I have told you;
while Jemmy set the young woman down on one
of our trunks, and got her a cup of tea. 'It

seems dreadful,' says I, when I'd done, 'to send such as her to the workhouse, don't it?' 'Workhouse!' says Peggy, firing up directly; 'I only wish we could catch the man who's got her in that scrape, and put him in there on water-gruel for the rest of his life. I'd give a shillin' a wheal out of my own pocket for the blessed privilege of scoring the thief's face with my whip, till his own mother wouldn't know him!' And then she went on, sir, abusing all the men in her Irish way, which I can't repeat. At last she stops, and claps me on the back. 'You're a darlin' old girl, Peck!' says she, 'and your friends are my friends. Stop where you are, and let me speak a word to the young woman on the trunk.'

"After a little while she comes back, and says: 'I've done it, Peck! She's mighty close, and as proud as Lucifer; but she's only a dressmaker for all that.' 'A dressmaker!' says I; 'how did you find out she was a dressmaker?' 'Why, I looked at her forefinger, in course,' says Peggy, 'and saw the pricks of the needle on it, and soon made her talk a bit after that. She knows fancy-work and cuttin' out—would ye ever have thought it? And I'll show her how to give the workhouse the go-by to-morrow, if she only holds out and keeps in her senses. Stop where you are, Peck! I'm going to make Jubber put his dirty hand into his pocket and pull out some money; and that's a sight worth stoppin' to see any day in the week.'

"I waited as she told me; and she called for Jubber, just as if he'd been her servant; and he

come out of the circus. 'I want ten shillings
advance of wages for that lady on the trunk,'
says Peggy. He laughed at her. 'Show your
ugly teeth at me again,' says she, 'and I'll box
your ears. I've my light hand for a horse's
mouth, and my heavy hand for a man's cheek;
you ought to know that by this time! Pull out
the ten shillings.' 'What for?' said he, frowning at her. 'Just this,' says she. 'I mean to
leave your circus, unless I get those six charac-
ter-dresses you promised me; and the lady there
can do them up beautiful. Pull out the ten
shillings! for I've made up my mind to appear
before the Bangbury public on Garryowen's
back, as six women at once.'

"What she meant by this, sir, was that she
was to have six different dresses on, one over
another; and was to go galloping round the ring
on Garryowen (which was a horse), beginning, I
think it was, as Empress of Roossia; and then
throwing off the top dress without the horse
stopping, and showing next as some famous
Frenchwoman, in the dress underneath; and
keeping on so with different nations, till she got
down to the last dress, which was to be Britannia and the Union-jack. We'd got bits of remnants, and old dresses and things to make and
alter, but hadn't anybody clever enough at cutting out, and what they called 'Costoom,' to do
what Peggy wanted—Jubber being too stingy
to pay the regular people who understand such
things. The young woman, knowing as she did
about fancy work, was just what was wanted, if

she could only get well enough to use her needle. 'I'll see she works the money out,' says Peggy; 'but she's dead beat to-night, and must have her rest and bit o' supper before she begins to-morrow.' Jubber wanted to give less than ten shillings; but between threatening and saying it should buy twenty shillings' worth of tailor's work, she got the better of him. And ne gave the money, sulky enough.

" 'Now,' says Peggy, 'you take her away, and get her a lodging in the place where you're staying; and I'll come to-morrow with some of the things to make up.' But, ah dear me! sir, she was never to work as much as sixpence of that ten shillings out. She was took bad in the night, and got so much worse in the morning that we had to send for the doctor.

"As soon as he'd seen her, he takes me into the passage, and says he to me: 'Do you know who her friends are?' 'No, sir,' says I; 'I can't get her to tell me. I only met her by accident yesterday.' 'Try and find out again,' says he; 'for I'm afraid she won't live over the night. I'll come back in the evening and see if there is any change.'

"Peggy and me went into her room together; but we couldn't even get her to speak to us for ever so long a time. All at once she cries out, 'I can't see things as I ought. Where's the woman who suckled my baby when I was alone by the road-side?' 'Here,' says I—'here; I've got hold of your hand. Do tell us where we can write to about you.' 'Will you promise to take care of my baby and not let it go into the work-house?' says she. 'Yes, I promise,' says I; 'I do indeed promise with my whole heart.' 'We'll all take care of the baby,' says Peggy; 'only you try and cheer up, and you'll get well enough to see me on Garryowen's back before we leave Bangbury—you will for certain, if you cheer up a bit.' 'I give my baby,' she says, clutching tight at my hand, 'to the woman who suckled it by the road-side; and I pray God to bless *her* and forgive *me*, for Jesus Christ's sake.' After that she lay quiet for a minute or two. Then she says faintly: 'It's name's to be Mary. Put it into bed to me again; I should like to touch its cheek, and feel how soft and warm it is once more.' And I took the baby out of its crib, and lifted it, asleep as it was, into the bed by her side, and guided her hand up to its cheek. I saw her lips move a little, and bent down over her. 'Give me one kiss,' she whispered, 'before I die.' And I kissed her, and tried to stop crying as I did it. Then I says to Peggy: 'You wait here while I run and fetch the doctor back; for I'm afraid she's going fast.' He wasn't at home when I got to his house. I didn't know what to do next, when I see a gentleman in the street who looked like a clergyman, and I asked him if he was one; and he said 'Yes'; and he went back with me. I heard a low wailing and crying in the room, and saw Peggy sitting on the bundle of dresses she'd brought in the morn-ing, rocking herself backward and forward as Irish people always do when they're crying. I

went to the bed and looked through the curtains.
The baby was still sleeping as pretty as ever,
and its mother's hand was touching one of its
arms. I was just going to speak to her again,
when the clergyman said 'Hush,' and took a bit
of looking-glass that was set up on the chimney-
piece, and held it over her lips. She was gone.
Her poor white wasted hand lay dead on the living baby's arm.

"I answered all the clergyman's questions
quite straightforward, telling him everything I
knew from beginning to end. When I'd done,
Peggy starts up from the bundle and says:
'Mind, sir, whatever you do, the child's not to
be took away from this person here and sent to
the workhouse. The mother give it to her on
that very bed, and I'm a witness of it.' 'And I
promised to be a mother to the baby, sir,' says I.
He turns round to me, and praises me for what I
done, and says nobody shall take it away from
me, unless them as can show their right comes
forward to claim it. 'But now,' says he, 'we
must think of other things. We must try and
find out something about this poor woman who
has died in such a melancholy way.'

"It was easier to say that than to do it. The
poor thing had nothing with her but a change of
linen for herself and the child, and that gave us
no clew. Then we searched her pocket. There
was a cambric handkerchief in it, marked 'M.
G.'; and some bits of rusks to sop for the child;
and the sixpence and half-pence which she had
when I met her; and beneath all, in a corner, as

if it had been forgotten there, a small hair bracelet. It was made of two kinds of hair—very little of one kind, and a good deal of the other.
And on the flat clasp of the bracelet there was
cut in tiny letters: '*In memory of S. G.*' I
remember all this, sir, for I've often and often
looked at the bracelet since that time.

"We found nothing more—no letters, or cards,
or anything. The clergyman said that the 'M.
G.' on the handkerchief must be the initials of
her name; and the 'S. G.' on the bracelet must
mean, he thought, some relation whose hair she
wore as a sort of keepsake. I remember Peggy
and me wondering which was S. G.'s hair; and
who the other person might be, whose hair was
wove into the bracelet. But the clergyman he
soon cut us short by asking for pen, ink, and
paper directly. 'I'm going to write out an advertisement,' says he, 'saying how you met with
the young woman, and what she was like, and
how she was dressed.' 'Do you mean to say
anything about the baby, sir?' says I. 'Certainly,' says he; 'it's only right, if we get at her
friends by advertising, to give them the chance
of doing something for the child. And if they
live anywhere in this county, I believe we shall
find them out; for the *Bangbury Chronicle*,
into which I mean to put the advertisement, goes
everywhere in our part of England.'

"So he sits down and writes what he said he
would, and takes it away to be printed in the
next day's number of the newspaper. 'If nothing comes of this,' says he, 'I think I can man-

age about the burial with a charitable society here. I'll take care and inform you the moment the advertisement's answered.' I hardly knew how it was, sir; but I almost hoped they wouldn't answer it. Having suckled the baby myself, and kissed its mother before she died, I couldn't make up my mind to the chance of its being took away from me just then. I ought to have thought how poor we were, and how hard it would be for us to bring the child up. But, somehow, I never did think of that—no more did Peggy—no more did Jemmy; not even when we put the baby to bed that night along with our own.

"Well, sir, sure enough, two days after the advertisement come out, it was answered in the cruelest letter I ever set eyes on. The clergyman he come to me with it. 'It was left this evening,' says he, 'by a strange messenger, who went away directly. I told my servant to follow him; but it was too late—he was out of sight.' The letter was very short, and we thought it was in a woman's handwriting—a feigned handwriting, the clergyman said. There was no name signed and no date at top or bottom. Inside it there was a ten-pound bank-note; and the person as sent it wrote that it was inclosed to bury the young woman decently. 'She was better dead than alive'—the letter went on—'after having disgraced her father and her relations. As for the child, it was the child of sin, and had no claim on people who desired to preserve all that was left of their good name, and to set a moral example to others. The parish must support it if nobody else would. It would be useless to attempt to trace them, or to advertise again. The baby's father had disappeared, they didn't know where; and they could hold no communication now with such a monster of wickedness, even if he was found. She was dead in her shame and her sin, and her name should never be mentioned among them she belonged to henceforth forever.'

"This was what I remember in the letter, sir. A shocking and unchristian letter I said; and the clergyman he said so, too.

"She was buried in the poor corner of the churchyard. They marked out the place, in case anybody should ever want to see it, by cutting the two letters M. G., and the date of when she died, upon a board of wood at the head of the grave. The clergyman then gave me the hair bracelet and the handkerchief, and said: 'You keep these as careful as you keep the child; for they may be of great importance one of these days. I shall seal up the letter (which is addressed to me) and put it in my strong-box.' He'd asked me, before this, if I'd thought of what a responsibility it was for such as me to provide for the baby. And I told him I'd promised, and would keep my promise, and trust to God's providence for the rest. The clergyman was a very kind gentleman, and got up a subscription for the poor babe; and Peggy Burke, when she had her benefit before the circus left Bangbury, give half of what she got as *her* subscription. I never heard nothing about the child's friends from that time to this; and I know no more who its father is now than I did then. And glad I am that he's never come forward—though, perhaps, I oughtn't to say so. I keep the hair bracelet and the handkerchief as careful as the clergyman told me, for the mother's sake as well as the child's. I've known some sorrow with her since I took her as my own; but I love her only the dearer for it, and still think the day a happy day for both of us, when I first stopped and suckled her by the road-side.

"This is all I have to say, if you please, sir, about how I first met with little Mary; and I wish I could have told it in a way that was more fit for such as you to hear."

CHAPTER V.

MADONNA'S MISFORTUNE.

As the clown's wife ended her narrative, but little was said in the way of comment on it by those who had listened to her. They were too much affected by what they had heard to speak, as yet, except briefly and in low voices. Mrs. Joyce more than once raised her handkerchief to her eyes. Her husband murmured some cordial words of sympathy and thanks—in an unusually subdued manner, however. Valentine said nothing; but he drew his chair close to Mrs. Peck-

over, and turning his face away as if he did not
wish it to be seen, took her hand in one of his
and patted it gently with the other. There was
now perfect silence in the room for a few minutes. Then they all looked out with one accord,
and as it seemed with one feeling, toward the
garden.

In a shady place, just visible among the trees,
the rector's daughters, and little Mary, and the
great Newfoundland do~, were all sitting together on the grass. The two young ladies appeared to be fastening a garland of flowers round
the child's neck, while she was playfully offering a nosegay for Leo to smell at. The sight
was homely and simple enough; but it was full
of the tenderest interest—after the narrative
which had just engaged them—to those who
now witnessed it. They looked out on the garden scene silently for some little time. Mrs.
Joyce was the first to speak again.

"Would it be asking too much of you, Mrs.
Peckover," said she, "to inquire how the poor
little thing really met with the accident that
caused her misfortune? I know there is an account of it in the bills of the circus, but—"

"It's the most infamous thing I ever read!"
interrupted Mr. Blyth, indignantly. "The man
who wrote it ought to be put in the pillory. I
never remember wanting to throw a rotten egg
at any of my fellow-creatures before; but I feel
certain that I should enjoy having a shy at Mr.
Jubber!"

"Gently, Valentine—gently," interposed the

rector. "I think, my love," he continued, turning to Mrs. Joyce, "that it is hardly considerate to Mrs. Peckover to expect her to comply with your request. She has already sacrificed herself once to our curiosity; and, really, to ask her now to recur a second time to recollections which I am sure must distress her—"

"It's worse than distressing, indeed, sir, even to think of that dreadful accident," said Mrs. Peckover, "and 'specially as I can't help taking some blame to myself for it. But if the lady wishes to know how it happened, I'm sure I'm agreeable to tell her. People in our way of life, ma'am—as I've often heard Peggy Burke say— are obliged to dry the tear at their eyes long before it's gone from their hearts. But pray don't think, sir, I mean that now about myself and in your company. If I *do* feel low at talking of little Mary's misfortune, I can take a look out into the garden there, and see how happy she is —and that's safe to set me right again.

"I ought to tell you first, sir," proceeded the clown's wife, after waiting thoughtfully for a moment or two before she spoke again, "that I got on much better with little Mary than ever I thought I should for the first six years of her life. She grew up so pretty that gentlefolks was always noticing her, and asking about her; and nearly in every place the circus went to they made her presents, which helped nicely in her keep and clothing. And our own people, too, petted her and were fond of her. All those six years we got on as pleasantly as could be. It

as not till she was near her seventh birthday
at I was wicked and foolish enough to consent
to her being shown in the performances.

"I was sorely tried and tempted before I did
consent.   Jubber first said he wanted her to perform with the riders; and I said 'No' at once,
though I was awful frightened of him in those
days.   But soon after, Jemmy (who wasn't the
clown then that he is now, sir; there was others
to be got for his money, to do what he did at that
time)—Jemmy comes to me, saying he's afraid
he shall lose his place, if I don't give in about
Mary.   This staggered me a good deal; for I
don't know what we should have done then, if
my husband had lost his engagement.   And, besides, there was the poor dear child herself, who
was mad to be carried up in the air on horse-
back, always begging and praying to be made a
little rider of.   And all the rest of 'em in the
circus worried and laughed at me; and, in short,
I give in at last against my conscience, but I
couldn't help it.

"I made a bargain, though, that she should
only be trusted to the steadiest, soberest man,
and the best rider of the whole lot.   They called
him 'Muley' in the bills, and stained his face to
make him look like a Turk, or something of that
sort; but his real name was Francis Yapp, and
a very good fatherly sort of man he was in his
way, having a family of his own to look after.
He used to ride splendid, at full straddle, with
three horses under him—one foot, you know, sir,
being on the outer horse's back, and one foot on

the inner.   Him and Jubber made it out togeth
that he was to act a wild man, flying for his li
across some desert, with his only child, and poor
little Mary was to be the child.   They darkened
her face to look like his; and put an outlandish
kind of white dress on her; and buckled a red
belt round her waist, with a sort of handle in it
for Yapp to hold her by.   After first making believe in all sorts of ways, that him and the child
was in danger of being taken and shot, he had to
make believe afterward that they had escaped;
and to hold her up, in a sort of triumph, at the
full stretch of his arm—galloping round and
round the ring all the while.   He was a tremendous strong man, and could do it as easy as I
could hold up a bit of that plum-cake.

"Poor little love! she soon got over the first
fright of the thing, and had a sort of mad fondness for it that I never liked to see, for it wasn't
natural to her.   Yapp, he said, she'd got the
heart of a lion, and would grow up the finest
woman-rider in the world.   I was very unhappy
about it, and lived a miserable life, always fearing some accident.   But for some time nothing
near an accident happened; and lots of money
come into the circus to see Yapp and little Mary
—but that was Jubber's luck and not ours.   One
night—when she was a little better than seven
year old—

"Oh, ma'am, how I ever lived over that dreadful night I don't know!   I was a sinful, miserable wretch not to have starved sooner than let
the child go into danger; but I was so sorely

tempted and driven to it, God knows!—No, sir! no, ma'am; and many thanks for your kindness, I'll go on now I've begun. Don't mind me crying; I'll manage to tell it somehow. The strap —no, I mean the handle; the handle in the strap gave way all of a sudden—just at the last, too! just at the worst time, when he couldn't catch her!

"Never—oh, never, never to my dying day shall I forget the horrible screech that went up from the whole audience; and the sight of the white thing lying huddled dead-still on the boards! We hadn't such a number in as usual that night; and she fell on an empty place between the benches. I got knocked down by the horses in running to her—I was clean out of my senses, and didn't know where I was going— Yapp had fallen among them, and hurt himself badly, trying to catch her; they were running wild in the ring—the horses was—frantic-like with the noise all round them. I got up somehow, and a crowd of people jostled me, and I saw my innocent darling carried among them. I felt hands on me, trying to pull me back; but I broke away, and got into the waiting-room along with the rest.

"There she was—my own, own little Mary, that I'd promised her poor mother to take care of —there she was, lying all white and still on an old box, with my cloak rolled up as a pillow for her. And people crowding round her. And a doctor feeling her head all over. And Yapp among them, held up by two men, with his face

all over blood. I wasn't able to speak or move;
I didn't feel as if I was breathing even, till the
doctor stopped and looked up; and then a great
shudder went through all of us together, as if
we'd been one body, instead of twenty or more.

"'It's not killed her,' says the doctor. 'Her
brain's escaped injury.'

"I didn't hear another word.

"I don't know how long it was before I seemed
to wake up like, with a dreadful feeling of pain
and tearing of everything inside me. I was on
the landlady's bed, and Jemmy was standing
over me with a bottle of salts. 'They've put her
to bed,' he says to me, 'and the doctor's setting
her arm.' I didn't recollect at first; but when I
did, it was almost as bad as seeing the dreadful
accident all over again.

"It was some time before any of us found out
what had really happened. The breaking of her
arm, the doctor said, had saved her head; which
was only cut and bruised a little, not half as bad
as was feared. Day after day, and night after
night, I sat by her bedside, comforting her
through her fever, and the pain of the splints on
her arm, and never once suspecting—no more, I
believe, than she did—the awful misfortune that
had really happened. She was always wonderful quiet and silent for a child, poor lamb, in
little illnesses that she'd had before; and somehow I didn't wonder—at least at first—why she
never said a word, and never answered me when
I spoke to her.

"This went on, though, after she got better in

her health; and a strange look came over her eyes. They seemed to be always wondering and frightened, in a confused way, about something or other. She took, too, to rolling her head about restlessly from one side of the pillow to the other; making a sort of muttering and humming now and then, but still never seeming to notice or to care for anything I said to her. One day I was warming her a nice cup of beef-tea over the fire, when I heard, quite sudden and quite plain, these words from where she lay on the bed: 'Why are you always so quiet here? Why doesn't somebody speak to me?'

"I knew there wasn't another soul in the room but the poor child at that time; and yet the voice as spoke those words was no more like little Mary's voice than my voice, sir, is like yours. It sounded, somehow, hoarse and low, and deep and faint, all at the same time; the strangest, shockingest voice to come from a child, who always used to speak so clearly and prettily before, that ever I heard. If I was only cleverer with my words, ma'am, and could tell you about it properly—but I can't. I only know it gave me such a turn to hear her that I upset the beef-tea and ran back in a fright to the bed. 'Why, Mary! Mary!' says I, quite loud, 'are you so well already that you're trying to imitate Mr. Jubber's gruff voice?'

"There was the same wondering look in her eyes—only wilder than I had ever seen it yet—while I was speaking. When I'd done, she says in the same strange way, 'Speak out, mother; I

can't hear you when you whisper like that.'
She was as long saying these words, and bungled
over them as much, as if she was only just learning to speak. I think I got the first suspicion,
then, of what had really happened. 'Mary!' I
bawled out as loud as I could, 'Mary! can't you
hear me?' She shook her head, and stared up at
me with the frightened, bewildered look again:
then seemed to get pettish and impatient all of a
sudden—the first time I ever saw her so—and
hid her face from me on the pillow.

"Just then the doctor came in. 'Oh, sir!'
says I, whispering to him—just as if I hadn't
found out a minute ago that she couldn't hear
me at the top of my voice—'I'm afraid there's
something gone wrong with her hearing—'
'Have you only just now suspected that?' says
he; 'I've been afraid of it for some days past,
but I thought it best to say nothing till I'd tried
her; and she's hardly well enough yet, poor
child, to be worried with experiments on her
ears.' 'She's much better,' says I; 'indeed, she's
much better to-day, sir! Oh, do try her now,
for it's so dreadful to be in doubt a moment
longer than we can help.'

"He went up to the bedside, and I followed
him. She was lying with her face hidden away
from us on the pillow, just as it was when I left
her. The doctor says to me: 'Don't disturb her,
don't let her look round, so that she can see us—
I'm going to call to her.' And he called 'Mary'
out loud, twice; and she never moved. The third
time he tried her, it was with such a shout at the

top of his voice, that the landlady come up, thinking something had happened. I was looking over his shoulder, and saw that my dear child never started in the least. 'Poor little thing,' says the doctor, quite sorrowful, 'this is worse than I expected.' He stooped down and touched her, as he said this; and she turned round directly, and put out her hand to have her pulse felt as usual. I tried to get out of her sight, for I was crying, and didn't wish her to see it; but she was too sharp for me. She looked hard in my face and the landlady's, then in the doctor's, which was downcast enough; for he had got very fond of her, just as everybody else did who saw much of little Mary.

" 'What's the matter?' she says, in the same sort of strange, unnatural voice again. We tried to pacify her, but only made her worse. 'Why do you keep on whispering?' she asks. 'Why don't you speak out loud, so that I can—' and then she stopped, seemingly in a sort of helpless fright and bewilderment. She tried to get up in bed, and her face turned red all over. 'Can she read writing?' says the doctor. 'Oh, yes, sir,' says I; 'she can read and write beautiful for a child of her age; my husband taught her.' 'Get me paper and pen and ink directly,' says he to the landlady; who went at once and got him what he wanted. 'We must quiet her at all hazards,' says the doctor, 'or she'll excite herself into another attack of fever. She feels what's the matter with her, but don't understand it; and I'm going to tell her by means of this paper. It's a risk,' he says, writing down on the paper in large letters: *You Are Deaf;* 'but I must try all I can do for her ears immediately; and this will prepare her,' says he, going to the bed, and holding the paper before her eyes.

"She shrank back on the pillow, as still as death, the instant she saw it; but didn't cry, and looked more puzzled and astonished, I should say, than distressed. But she was breathing dreadful quick—I felt that, as I stooped down and kissed her. 'She's too young,' says the doctor, 'to know what the extent of her calamity really is. You stop here and keep her quiet till I come back, for I trust the case is not hopeless yet.' 'But whatever has made her deaf, sir?' says the landlady, opening the door for him. 'The shock of that fall in the circus,' says he, going out in a very great hurry. I thought I should never have held up my head again, as I heard them words, looking at little Mary, with my arm round her neck all the time.

"Well, sir, the doctor come back; and he syringed her ears first—and that did no good. Then he tried blistering, and then he put on leeches; and still it was no use. 'I'm afraid it *is* a hopeless case,' says he; 'but there's a doctor who's had more practice than I've had with deaf people, who comes from where he lives to our Dispensary once a week. To-morrow's his day, and I'll bring him here with me.'

"And he did bring this gentleman, as he promised he would—an old gentleman, with

such a pleasant way of speaking that I understood everything he said to me directly. 'I'm
afraid you must make up your mind to the
worst,' says he. 'I have been hearing about the
poor child from my friend who's attended her;
and I'm sorry to say I don't think there's much
hope.' Then he goes to the bed and looks at
her. 'Ah,' says he, 'there's just the same expression in her face that I remember seeing in a
mason's boy—a patient of mine—who fell off a
ladder, and lost his hearing altogether by the
shock. You don't hear what I'm saying, do
you, my dear?' says he, in a hearty, cheerful
way. 'You don't hear me saying that you're
the prettiest little girl I ever saw in my life?'
She looked up at him confused, and quite silent.
He didn't speak to her again, but told me to turn
her on the bed, so that he could get at one of her
ears.

"He pulled out some instruments, while I did
what he asked, and put them into her ear, but so
tenderly that he never hurt her. Then he looked
in, through a sort of queer spy-glass thing.
Then he did it all over again with the other ear;
and then he laid down the instruments and pulled
out his watch. 'Write on a piece of paper,' says
he to the other doctor: '*Do you know that the
watch is ticking?*' When this was done, he
makes signs to little Mary to open her mouth,
and puts as much of his watch in as would go
between her teeth, while the other doctor holds
up the paper before her. When he took the
watch out again, she shook her head, and said

'No,' just in the same strange voice as ever.
The old gentleman didn't speak a word as he put
the watch back in his fob; but I saw by his face
that he thought it was all over with her hearing,
after what had just happened.

"'Oh, try and do something for her, sir!' says
I. 'Oh, for God's sake, don't give her up, sir!'
'My good soul,' says he, 'you must set her an
example of cheerfulness, and keep up her spirits
—that's all that can be done for her now.' 'Not
all, sir,' says I, 'surely not *all!*' 'Indeed, it is,'
says he; 'her hearing is completely gone; the
experiment with my watch proves it. I had an
exactly similar case with the mason's boy,' he
says, turning to the other doctor. 'The shock of
that fall has, I believe, paralyzed the auditory
nerve in her, as it did in him.' I remember
those words exactly, sir, though I didn't quite
understand them at the time. But he explained
himself to me very kindly; telling me over
again, in a plain way, what he'd just told the
doctor. He reminded me, too, that the remedies
which had been already tried had been of no
use; and told me I might feel sure that any
others would only end in the same way, and put
her to useless pain into the bargain. 'I hope,'
says he, 'the poor child is too young to suffer
much mental misery under her dreadful misfortune. Keep her amused, and keep her talking,
if you possibly can—though I doubt very much
whether, in a little time, you won't fail completely in getting her to speak at all.'

"'Don't say that, sir,' says I; 'don't say she'll

be dumb as well as deaf; it's enough to break one's heart only to think of it.' 'But I *must* say so,' says he; 'for I'm afraid it's the truth.' And then he asks me whether I hadn't noticed already that she was unwilling to speak; and that, when she did speak, her voice wasn't the same voice it used to be. I said 'Yes,' to that; and asked him whether the fall had had anything to do with it. He said, taking me up very short, it had everything to do with it, because the fall had made her what they call stone deaf, which prevented her from hearing the sound of her own voice. So it was changed, he told me, because she had no ear now to guide herself by in speaking, and couldn't know in the least whether the few words she said were spoken soft or loud, or deep or clear. 'So far as the poor child herself is concerned,' says he, 'she might as well be without a voice at all; for she has nothing but her memory left to tell her that she has one.'

"I burst out a-crying as he said this; for somehow I'd never thought of anything so dreadful before. 'I've been a little too sudden in telling you the worst, haven't I?' says the old gentleman, kindly; 'but you must be taught how to make up your mind to meet the full extent of this misfortune for the sake of the child, whose future comfort and happiness depend greatly on you.' And then he bid me keep up her reading and writing, and force her to use her voice as much as I could, by every means in my power. He told me I should find her grow more and more unwilling to speak every day, just for the shocking reason that she couldn't hear a single word she said, or a single tone of her own voice. He warned me that she was already losing the wish and the want to speak; and that it would very soon be little short of absolute pain to her to be made to say even a few words; but he begged and prayed me not to let my good-nature get the better of my prudence on that account, and not to humor her, however I might feel tempted to do so—for if I did, she would be dumb as well as deaf, most certainly. He told me my own common sense would show me the reason why; but I suppose I was too distressed or too stupid to understand things as I ought. He had to explain it to me in so many words, that if she wasn't constantly exercised in speaking, she would lose her power of speech altogether, for want of practice—just the same as if she'd been born dumb. 'So, once again,' says he, 'mind you make her use her voice. Don't give her her dinner, unless she asks for it. Treat her severely in that way, poor little soul, because it's for her own good.'

"It was all very well for *him* to say that, but it was impossible for *me* to do it. The dear child, ma'am, seemed to get used to her misfortune, except when we tried to make her speak. It was the saddest, prettiest sight in the world to see how patiently and bravely she bore with her hard lot from the first. As she grew better in her health, she kept up her reading and writing quite cleverly with my husband and me; and all her nice natural, cheerful ways came back to her just the same as ever. I've read or heard somewhere, sir, about God's goodness in tempering the wind to the shorn lamb. I don't know who said that first; but it might well have been spoken on account of my own darling little Mary in those days. Instead of us being the first to comfort her, it was she that was first to comfort us. And so she's gone on ever since—bless her heart! Only treat her kindly, and, in spite of her misfortune, she's the merriest, happiest little thing—the easiest pleased and amused, I do believe, that ever lived.

"If we were wrong in not forcing her to speak more than we did, I must say this much for me and my husband, that we hadn't the heart to make her miserable and keep on tormenting her from morning to night, when she was always happy and comfortable if we would only let her alone. We tried our best for some time to do what the gentleman told us; but it's so hard—as you've found, I dare say, ma'am—not to end by humoring them you love! I never see the tear in her eye, except when we forced her to speak to us; and then she always cried, and was fretful and out of sorts for the whole day. It seemed such a dreadful difficulty and pain to her to say only two or three words; and the shocking husky moaning voice, that sounded somehow as if it didn't belong to her, never changed. My husband first gave up worrying her to speak. He practiced her with her book and writing, but let her have her own will in everything else; and he teached her all sorts of tricks on the cards, for amusement, which was a good way of keeping her going with her reading and her pen pleasantly, by reason, of course, of him and her being obliged to put down everything they had to say to each other on a little slate that we bought for her after she got well.

"It was Mary's own notion, if you please, ma'am, to have the slate always hanging at her side. Poor dear! she thought it quite a splendid ornament, and was as proud of it as could be. Jemmy, being neat-handed at such things, did the frame over for her prettily with red morocco, and got our property-man to do it all round with a bright golden border. And then we hung it at her side, with a nice little bit of silk cord—just as you see it now.

"I held out in making her speak some time after my husband: but at last I gave in, too. I know it was wrong and selfish of me; but I got a fear that she wouldn't like me as well as she used to do, and would take more kindly to Jemmy than to me, if I went on. Oh, how happy she was the first day I wrote down on her slate that I wouldn't worry her about speaking any more! She jumped up on my knees—being always as nimble as a squirrel—and kissed me over and over again with all her heart. For the rest of the day she run about the room and all over the house like a mad thing, and when Jemmy came home at night from performing, she would get out of bed and romp with him, and ride pickaback on him, and try and imitate the funny faces she'd seen him make in the ring. I do believe, sir, that was the first regular happy night we had all had together since the dreadful time when she met with her accident.

"Long after that my conscience was uneasy though, at times, about giving in as I had. At last I got a chance of speaking to another doctor about little Mary; and he told me that if we had kept her up in her speaking ever so severely, it would still have been a pain and a difficulty to her to say her words to her dying day. He said, too, that he felt sure—though he couldn't explain it to me—that people afflicted with such stone deafness as hers didn't feel the loss of speech, because they never had the want to use their speech; and that they took to making signs, and writing, and such like, quite kindly, as a sort of second nature to them. This comforted me, and settled my mind a good deal. I hope in God what the gentleman said was true; for if I was in fault in letting her have her own way and be happy, it's past mending by this time. For more than two years, ma'am, I've never heard her say a single word, no more than if she'd been born dumb, and it's my belief that all the doctors in the world couldn't make her speak now.

"Perhaps, sir, you might wish to know how she first come to show her tricks on the cards in the circus. There was no danger in her doing that, I know—and yet I'd have given almost everything I have not to let her be shown about as she is. But I was threatened again, in the vilest, wickedest way—I hardly know how to tell it, gentlemen, in the presence of such as you—Jubber, you must know—"

Just as Mrs. Peckover, with very painful hesitation, pronounced the last words, the hall clock of the Rectory struck two. She heard it, and stopped instantly.

"Oh, if you please, sir, was that two o'clock?" she asked, starting up with a look of alarm.

"Yes, Mrs. Peckover," said the rector; "but really, after having been indebted to you for so much that has deeply interested and affected us, we can't possibly think of letting you and little Mary leave the Rectory yet."

"Indeed we must, sir; and many thanks to you for wanting to keep us longer," said Mrs. Peckover. "What I was going to say isn't much; it's quite as well you shouldn't hear it—and indeed, indeed, ma'am, we must go directly. I told this gentleman here, Mr. Blyth, when I come in, that I'd stolen to you unawares, under pretense of taking little Mary out for a walk. If we are not back to the two o'clock dinner in the circus, it's unknown what Jubber may not do. This gentleman will tell you how infamously he treated the poor child last night—we must go, sir, for her sake; or else—"

"Stop!" cried Valentine, all his suppressed excitability bursting bounds in an instant, as he took Mrs. Peckover by the arm and pressed her back into her chair. "Stop!—hear me; I must speak, or I shall go out of my senses! Don't interrupt me, Mrs. Peckover; and don't get up. All I want to say is this: you must never take that little angel of a child near Jubber again— no, never! By heavens! if I thought he was likely to touch her any more, I should go mad, and murder him!—Let me alone, doctor! I beg Mrs. Joyce's pardon for behaving like this; I'll never do it again. Be quiet, all of you! I *must* take the child home with me—oh, Mrs. Peckover, don't, don't say no! I'll make her as happy as the day is long. I've no child of my own: I'll watch over her, and love her, and teach her all my life. I've got a poor, suffer- ing, bed-ridden wife at home, who would think such a companion as little Mary the greatest blessing God could send her. My own dear, patient Lavvie! Oh, doctor, doctor! think how kind Lavvie would be to that afflicted little child; and try if you can't make Mrs. Peckover consent. I can't speak any more—I know I'm wrong to burst out in this way; and I beg all your pardons for it, I do, indeed! Speak to her, doctor—pray speak to her directly, if you don't want to make me miserable for the rest of my life!"

With these words, Valentine darted precipi- tately into the garden, and made straight for the spot where the little girls were still sitting together in their shady resting-place among the trees.

CHAPTER VI.

MADONNA GOES TO LONDON.

THE clown's wife had sat very pale and very quiet under the whole overwhelming torrent of Mr. Blyth's apostrophes, exclamations, and entreaties. She seemed quite unable to speak, after he was fairly gone; and only looked round in a bewildered manner at the rector, with fear as well as amazement expressed vividly in her hearty, healthy face.

"Pray compose yourself, Mrs. Peckover," said Doctor Joyce; "and kindly give me your best attention to what I am about to say. Let me beg you, in the first place, to excuse Mr. Blyth's odd behavior, which I see has startled and astonished you. But, however wildly he may talk, I assure you he means honorably and truthfully in all that he says. You will understand this better if you will let me temperately explain to you the proposal, which he has just made so abruptly and confusedly in his own words."

"Proposal, sir!" exclaimed Mrs. Peckover, faintly, looking more frightened than ever— "Proposal! Oh, sir! you don't mean to say that you're going to ask me to part from little Mary?"

"I will ask you to do nothing that your own good sense and kind heart may not approve," answered the rector. "In plain terms then, and

not to waste time by useless words of preface,
my friend, Mr. Blyth, feels such admiration for
your little Mary, and such a desire to help her,
as far as may be, in her great misfortune, that
he is willing and eager to make her future prospects in life his own peculiar care, by adopting
her as his daughter. This offer, though coming,
as I am aware, from a perfect stranger, can
hardly astonish you, I think, if you reflect on the
unusually strong claims which the child has to
the compassion and kindness of all her fellow-
creatures. Other strangers, as you have told us,
have shown the deepest interest in her on many
occasions. It is not, therefore, at all wonderful
that a gentleman, whose Christian integrity of
motive I have had opportunities of testing during a friendship of nearly twenty years, should
prove the sincerity of his sympathy for the poor
child, by such a proposal as I have now communicated to you."

"Don't ask me to say yes to it, sir!" pleaded
Mrs. Peckover, with tears in her eyes. "Don't
ask me to do that! Anything else to prove my
gratitude for your kindness to us; but how can I
part from my own little Mary? You can't have
the heart to ask it of me!"

"I have the heart, Mrs. Peckover, to feel deeply for your distress at the idea of parting from
the child; but, for her sake, I must again ask
you to control your feelings. And, more than
that, I must appeal to you by your love to her,
to grant a fair hearing to the petition which I
now make on Mr. Blyth's behalf."

"I would, indeed, if I could, sir—but it's just because I love her so that I can't! Besides, as you yourself said, he's a perfect stranger."

"I readily admit the force of that objection on your part, Mrs. Peckover; but let me remind you that I vouch for the uprightness of his character, and his fitness to be trusted with the child, after twenty years' experience of him. You may answer to that, that I am a stranger, too; and I can only ask you, in return, frankly to accept my character and position as the best proofs I can offer you that I am not unworthy of your confidence. If you placed little Mary for instruction (as you well might) in an asylum for the deaf and dumb, you would be obliged to put implicit trust in the authorities of that asylum, on much the same grounds as those I now advance to justify you in putting trust in me."

"Oh, sir! don't think—pray don't think I am unwilling to trust you—so kind and good as you have been to us to-day—and a clergyman, too—I should be ashamed of myself, if I could doubt—"

"Let me tell you, plainly and candidly, what advantages to the child Mr. Blyth's proposal holds out. He has no family of his own, and his wife is, as he has hinted to you, an invalid for life. If you could only see the gentleness and sweet patience with which she bears her affliction, you would acknowledge that little Mary could appeal for an affectionate welcome to no kinder heart than Mrs. Blyth's. I assure you most seriously that the only danger I fear for the child in my friend's house is, that she would be spoiled by excessive indulgence. Though by no means a rich man, Mr. Blyth is in an independent position, and can offer her all the comforts of life. In one word, the home to which he is ready to take her is a home of love and happiness and security, in the best and purest meaning of those words."

"Don't say any more, sir! Don't break my heart by making me part with her!"

"You will live, Mrs. Peckover, to thank me for trying your fortitude as I try it now. Hear me a little longer, while I tell you what terms Mr. Blyth proposes. He is not only willing but anxious—if you give the child into his charge—that you should have access to her whenever you like. He will leave his address in London with you. He desires, from motives alike honorable to you and to himself, to defray your traveling expenses whenever you wish to see the child. He will always acknowledge your prior right to her affection and her duty. He will offer her every facility in his power for constantly corresponding with you; and if the life she leads in his house be, even in the slightest respect, distasteful to her, he pledges himself to give her up to you again—if you and she desire it—at any sacrifice of his own wishes and his own feelings. These are the terms he proposes, Mrs. Peckover, and I can most solemnly assure you, on my honor as a clergyman and a gentleman, that he will hold sacred the strict performance of all and each of these conditions, exactly as I have stated them."

"I ought to let her go, sir—I know I ought to show how grateful I am for Mr. Blyth's generosity by letting her go—but how can I, after all the long time she's been like my own child to me? Oh, ma'am, say a word for me!—I seem so selfish for not giving her up—say a word for me!"

"Will you let me say a word for little Mary instead?" rejoined Mrs. Joyce. "Will you let me remind you that Mr. Blyth's proposal offers her a secure protection against that inhuman wretch who has ill-used her already, and who may often ill-use her again, in spite of everything you can do to prevent him. Pray think of that, Mrs. Peckover—pray do!"

Poor Mrs. Peckover showed that she thought of it bitterly enough, by a fresh burst of tears.

The rector poured out a glass of water, and gave it to her. "Do not think us inconsiderate or unfeeling," he said, "in pressing Mr. Blyth's offer on you so perseveringly. Only reflect on Mary's position, if she remains in the circus as she grows up! Would all your watchful kindness be sufficient to shield her against dangers to which I hardly dare allude?—against wickedness which would take advantage of her defenselessness, her innocence, and even her misfortune? Consider all that Mr. Blyth's proposal promises for her future life; for the sacred preservation of her purity of heart and mind. Look forward to the day when little Mary will have grown up to be a young woman; and I will answer, Mrs. Peckover, for your doing full justice to the importance of my friend's offer."

"I know it's all true, sir; I know I'm an ungrateful, selfish wretch—but only give me a little time to think; a little time longer to be with the poor darling that I love like my own child!"

Doctor Joyce was just drawing his chair closer to Mrs. Peckover before he answered, when the door opened, and the respectable Vance softly entered the room.

"What do you want here?" said the rector, a little irritably. "Didn't I tell you not to come in again till I rang for you?"

"I beg your pardon, sir," answered Vance, casting rather a malicious look at the clown's wife as he closed the door behind him—"but there's a person waiting in the hall, who says he comes on important business, and must see you directly."

"Who is he? What's his name?"

"He says his name is Jubber, if you please, sir."

Mrs. Peckover started from her chair with a scream. "Don't—pray, for mercy's sake, sir, don't let him into the garden where Mary is!" she gasped, clutching Doctor Joyce by the arm in the extremity of her terror. "He's found us out, and come here in one of his dreadful passions! He cares for nothing and for nobody, sir: he's bad enough to ill-treat her even before *you.* What am I to do? Oh, good gracious heavens! what am I to do?"

"Leave everything to me, and sit down again," said the rector, kindly. Then, turning to Vance, he added: "Show Mr. Jubber into the cloak-room, and say I will be with him directly."

"Now, Mrs. Peckover," continued Doctor Joyce, in the most perfectly composed manner, "before I see this man (whose business I can guess at) I have three important questions to ask of you. In the first place, were you not a witness, last night, of his cruel ill-usage of that poor child? (Mr. Blyth told me of it.) The fellow actually beat her, did he not?"

"Oh, indeed he did, sir!—beat her most cruelly with a cane."

"And you saw it all yourself?"

"I did, sir. He'd have used her worse, if I hadn't been by to prevent him."

"Very well. Now tell me if you or your husband have signed any agreement—any papers, I mean, giving this man a right to claim the child as one of his performers?"

"*Me* sign an agreement, sir! I never did such a thing in all my life. Jubber would think himself insulted, if you only talked of his signing an agreement with such as me or Jemmy."

"Better and better. Now, my third question refers to little Mary herself. I will undertake to put it out of this blackguard's power ever to lay a finger on her again—but I can only do so on one condition, which it rests entirely with you to grant."

"I'll do anything to save her, sir; I will, indeed."

"The condition is that you consent to Mr.

Blyth's proposal; for I can only insure the
child's safety on those terms."

"Then, sir, I consent to it," said Mrs. Peckover, speaking with a sudden firmness of tone
and manner which almost startled Mrs. Joyce,
who stood by listening anxiously. "I consent to
it; for I should be the vilest wretch in the world
if I could say 'no' at such a time as this. I will
trust my precious darling treasure to you, sir, and
to Mr. Blyth, from this moment. God bless *her*,
and comfort *me!* for I want comfort badly enough.
Oh, Mary! Mary! my own little Mary! to think
of you and me ever being parted like this!" The
poor woman turned toward the garden as she
pronounced those words; all her fortitude for-
sook her in an instant; and she sank back in her
chair, sobbing bitterly.

"Take her out into the shrubbery where the
children are, as soon as she recovers a little,"
whispered the rector to his wife, as he opened
the dining-room door.

Though Mr. Jubber presented, to all appearance, the most scoundrelly aspect that humanity
can assume, when he was clothed in his evening
uniform, and illuminated by his own circus
lamp-light, he nevertheless reached an infinitely
loftier climax of blackguard perfection when he
was arrayed in his private costume, and was
submitted to the tremendous ordeal of pure
daylight. The most monstrous ape that could
be picked from the cages of the Zoological Gardens would have gained by comparison with
him as he now appeared, standing in the Rec-

tory cloak-room, with his debauched bloodshot eyes staring grimly contemptuous all about him, with his yellow flabby throat exposed by a turn-down collar and a light-blue necktie, with the rouge still smeared over his gross unhealthy cheeks, with his mangy shirt-front bespattered with bad embroidery and false jewelry that had not even the politic decency to keep itself clean. He had his hat on, and was sulkily running his dirty fingers through the greasy black ringlets that flowed over his coat-collar, when Doctor Joyce entered the cloak-room.

"You wish to speak with me?" said the rector, not sitting down himself, and not asking Mr. Jubber to sit down.

"Oh! you're Doctor Joyce?" said the fellow, assuming his most insolent familiarity of manner directly.

"That is my name," said Doctor Joyce, very quietly. "Will you have the goodness to state your business with me immediately, and in the fewest possible words?"

"Halloo! You take that tone with me, do you?" said Jubber, setting his arms akimbo, and tapping his foot fiercely on the floor; "you're trying to come Tommy Grand over me already, are you? Very good! I'm the man to give you change in your own coin—so here goes! What do you mean by enticing away my Mysterious Foundling? What do you mean by this private swindle of talent that belongs to my circus?"

"You had better proceed a little," said the

rector, more quietly than before. "Thus far I understand nothing whatever, except that you wish to behave offensively to me; which, in a person of your appearance, is, I assure you, of not the slightest consequence. You had much better save time by stating what you have to say in plain words."

"You want plain words—eh?" cried Jubber, losing his temper. "Then, by God, you shall have them, and plain enough!"

"Stop a minute!" said Doctor Joyce. "If you use oaths in my presence again, I shall ring for my servant, and 'order him to show you out of the house."

"You will?"

"I will, most çertainly."

There was a moment's pause, and the black-guard and the gentleman looked one another straight in the face. It was the old, invariable struggle, between the quiet firmness of good breeding, and the savage obstinacy of bad; and it ended in the old, invariable way. The black-guard flinched first.

"If your servant lays a finger on me, I'll thrash him within an inch of his life," said Jubber, looking toward the door, and scowling as he looked. "But that's not the point just now—the point is, that I charge you with getting my deaf and dumb girl into your house, to perform before you on the sly. If you're too virtuous to come to my circus—and better than you have been there—you ought to have paid the proper price for a private performance. What do you mean by treating a public servant like me with your infernal aristocratic looks, as if I was dirt under your feet, after such shabby doings as you've been guilty of—eh?"

"May I ask how you know that the child you refer to has been at my house to-day?" asked Doctor Joyce, without taking the slightest notice of Mr. Jubber's indignation.

"One of my people saw that swindling hypocrite of a Peckover taking her in, and told me of it when I missed them at dinner. There! that's good evidence, I rather think! Deny it if you can."

"I have not the slightest intention of denying it. The child is now in my house."

"And has gone through all her performances, of course? Ah! shabby! shabby! I should be ashamed of myself, if *I'd* tried to do a man out of his rights like that."

"I am most unaffectedly rejoiced to hear that you are capable, under any circumstances, of being ashamed of yourself at all," rejoined the rector. "The child, however, has gone through no performances here, not having been sent for with any such purpose as you suppose. But, as you said just now, that's not the point. Pray, why did you speak of the little girl, a moment ago, as *your* child?"

"Because she's one of my performers, of course. But come! I've had enough of this; I can't stop talking here all day; I want the child—so just deliver her up at once, will you?—and turn out Peck as soon as you like after. I'll cure them both of ever doing this sort of thing again! I'll make them stick tight to the circus for the future! I'll show them—"

"You would be employing your time much more usefully," said Doctor Joyce, "if you occupied it in altering the bills of your performance, so as to inform the public that the deaf and dumb child will not appear before them again."

"Not appear again?—not appear to-night in my circus? Why, hang me! if I don't think you're trying to be funny all of a sudden! Alter my bills—eh? Not bad! Upon my soul, not at all bad for a parson! Give us another joke, sir; I'm all attention." And Mr. Jubber put his hand to his ear, grinning in a perfect fury of sarcasm.

"I am quite in earnest," said the rector. "A friend of mine has adopted the child, and will take her home with him to-morrow morning. Mrs. Peckover (the only person who has any right to exercise control over her) has consented to this arrangement. If your business here was to take the child back to your circus, it is right to inform you that she will not leave my house till she goes to London to-morrow with my friend."

"And you think I'm the sort of man to stand this?—and give up the child?—and alter the bills?—and lose money?—and be as mild as mother's milk all the time? Oh! yes, of course! I'm so devilish fond of you and your friend! You're such nice men, you can make me do anything! D—n all this jabber and nonsense!" roared the ruffian, passing suddenly from insolence to fury, and striking his fist on the table. "Give me the child at once, do you hear? Give her up, I say. I won't leave the house till I've got her!"

Just as Mr. Jubber swore for the second time, Dr. Joyce rang the bell. "I told you what I should do if you used oaths in my presence again," said the rector.

"And *I* told *you* I'd kill the servant, if he laid a finger on me," said Jubber, knocking his hat firmly on his head, and tucking up his cuffs.

Vance appeared at the door, much less pompous than usual, and displaying an interesting paleness of complexion. Jubber spat into the palm of each of his hands, and clinched his fists.

"Have you done dinner downstairs?" asked Doctor Joyce, reddening a little, but still very quiet.

"Yes, sir," answered Vance, in a remarkably conciliating voice.

"Tell James to go to the constable, and say I want him; and let the gardener wait with you outside there in the hall."

"Now," said the rector, shutting the door again after issuing these orders, and placing himself once more face to face with Mr. Jubber —"now I have a last word or two to say, which I recommend you to hear quietly. In the first place, you have no right over the child whatever; for I happen to know that you are without a signed agreement promising you her services. (You had better hear me out for your own sake.) You have no legal right, I say, to control the child in any manner. She is a perfectly free agent, so far as you are concerned.—Yes! yes! you deny it, of course! I have only to say that, if you attempt to back that denial by still asserting your claim to her, and making a disturbance in my house, as sure as you stand there, I'll ruin you in Rubbleford and in all the country round. (It's no use laughing—I can do it!) You beat the child in the vilest manner last night. I am a magistrate; and I have my prosecutor and my witness of the assault ready whenever I choose to call them. I can fine or imprison you, which I please. You know the public; you know what they think of people who ill-use helpless children. If you appeared in that character before me, the Rubbleford paper would report it; and, so far as the interests of your circus are concerned, you would be a ruined man in this part of the country—you would, you know it! Now I will spare you this—not from any tenderness toward *you*—on condition that you take yourself off quietly, and never let us hear from you again. I strongly advise you to go at once; for if you wait till the constable comes, I will not answer for it that my sense of duty may not force me into giving you into custody." With which words, Doctor Joyce threw open the door, and pointed to the hall.

Throughout the delivery of this speech, violent indignation, ungovernable surprise, abject terror, and impotent rage ravaged by turns the breast of Mr. Jubber. He stamped about the room, and uttered fragments of oaths, but did not otherwise interrupt Dr. Joyce while that gentleman was speaking to him. When the rector had done, the fellow had his insolent answer ready directly. To do him justice, he was consistent, if he was nothing else—he was bully and blackguard to the very last.

"Magistrate or parson," he cried, snapping his fingers, "I don't care a d—n for you in either capacity. You keep the child here at your peril! I'll go to the first lawyer in Rubbleford and bring an action against you. I'll show you a little legal law! *You* ruin me, indeed! I can prove that I only thrashed the little toad, the nasty deaf idiot, because she deserved it. I'll be even with you! I'll have the child back, wherever you take her to. I'll show you a little legal law! (Here he stepped to the hall door.) I'll be even with you, damme! I'll charge you with setting on your menial servants to assault me. (Here he looked fiercely at the gardener, a freckled Scotch giant, of six feet three, and instantly descended five steps.) Lay a finger on me, if you dare! I'm going straight from this house to the lawyer's. I'm a free Englishman, and I'll have my rights and my legal law! I'll bring my action! I'll ruin you! I'll strip your gown off your back! I'll stop your mouth in your own pulpit!" Here he strutted into the front garden; his words grew indistinct, and his gross voice became gradually less and less audible. The coachman at the outer gate saw the last of him, and reported that he made his exit striking viciously at the flowers with his cane, and swearing that he would ruin the doctor with "legal law."

After leaving certain directions with his servants, in the very improbable event of Mr. Jubber's return, Doctor Joyce repaired immediately to his dining-room. No one was there, so he went on into the garden.

Here he found the family and the visitors all assembled together; but a great change had passed over the whole party during his absence. Mr. Blyth, on being informed of the result of the rector's conversation with Mrs. Peckover, acted with his usual impetuosity and utter want of discretion; writing down delightedly on little Mary's slate, without the slightest previous preparation or coaxing, that she was to go home with him to-morrow, and be as happy as the day was long, all the rest of her life. The result of this incautious method of proceeding was that the child became excessively frightened, and ran away from everybody to take refuge with Mrs. Peckover. She was still crying, and holding tight by the good woman's gown with both hands; and Valentine was still loudly declaring to everybody that he loved her all the better for showing such faithful affection to her earliest and best friend, when the rector joined the party under the coolly-murmuring trees.

Doctor Joyce spoke but briefly of his interview with Mr. Jubber, concealing much that had passed at it, and making very light of the threats which the fellow had uttered on his departure. Mrs. Peckover, whose self-possession seemed in

imminent danger of being overthrown by little
Mary's mute demonstrations of affection, listened anxiously to every word the Doctor uttered; and, as soon as he had done, said that she
must go back to the circus directly, and tell her
husband the truth about all that had occurred,
as a necessary set-off against the slanders that
were sure to be spoken against her by Mr. Jubber.

"Oh, never mind *me*, ma'am!" she said, in
answer to the apprehensions expressed by Mrs.
Joyce about her reception when she got to the
circus. "The dear child's safe; and that's all I
care about. I'm big enough and strong enough
to take my own part; and Jemmy, he's always
by to help me when I can't. May I come back, if
you please, sir, this evening, and say—and say—"

She would have added, "and say good-by;"
but the thoughts which now gathered round that
one word made it too hard to utter. She silently
courtesied her thanks for the warm invitation
that was given to her to return; stooped down to
the child; and, kissing her, wrote on the slate:
"I shall be back, dear, in the evening, at seven
o'clock"—then disengaged the little hands that
still held fast by her gown, and hurried from the
garden, without once venturing to look behind
her as she crossed the sunny lawn.

Mrs. Joyce, and the young ladies, and the
rector, all tried their best to console little Mary;
and all failed. She resolutely, though very
gently, resisted them; walking away into corners by herself, and looking constantly at her
slate, as if she could only find comfort in read-

ing the few words which Mrs. Peckover had
written on it. At last, Mr. Blyth took her up
on his knee. She struggled to get away, for a
moment—then looked intently in his face; and,
sighing very mournfully, laid her head down on
his shoulder. There was a world of promise for
the future success of Valentine's affectionate
project in that simple action, and in the prefer-
ence which it showed.

The day wore on quietly—evening came—
seven o'clock struck—then half-past—then eight
—and Mrs. Peckover never appeared. Doctor
Joyce grew uneasy, and sent Vance to the circus
to get some news of her.

It was again Mr. Blyth—and Mr. Blyth only
—who succeeded in partially quieting little Mary
under the heavy disappointment of not seeing
Mrs. Peckover at the appointed time. The child
had been restless at first, and had wanted to go
to the circus. Finding that they tenderly, but
firmly, detained her at the Rectory, she wept
bitterly—wept so long that at last she fairly
cried herself asleep in Valentine's arms. He
sat anxiously supporting her with a patience that
nothing could tire. The sunset rays, which he
had at first carefully kept from falling on her
face, vanished from the horizon; the quiet luster
of twilight overspread the sky—and still he refused to let her be taken from him; and said he
would sit as he was all through the night rather
than let her be disturbed.

Vance came back, and brought word that Mrs.
Peckover would follow him in half an hour.

They had given her some work to do at the circus, which she was obliged to finish before she could return to the Rectory.

Having delivered this message, Vance next produced a handbill, which he said was being widely circulated all over Rubbleford; and which proved to be the composition of Mr. Jubber himself. That ingenious ruffian, having doubtless discovered that "legal law" was powerless to help him to his revenge, and that it would be his wisest proceeding to keep clear of Doctor Joyce in the rector's magisterial capacity, was now artfully attempting to turn the loss of the child to his own profit, by dint of prompt lying in his favorite large type, sprinkled with red letters. He informed the public, through the medium of his handbills, that the father of the Mysterious Foundling had been "most providentially" discovered, and that he (Mr. Jubber) had given the child up immediately, without a thought of what he might personally suffer, in pocket as well as in mind, by his generosity. After this, he appealed confidently to the sympathy of people of every degree, and of "fond parents" especially, to compensate him by flocking in crowds to the circus; adding, that if additional stimulus were wanting to urge the public into "rallying round the Ring," he was prepared to administer it forthwith, in the shape of the smallest dwarf in the world, for whose services he was then in treaty, and whose first appearance before a Rubbleford audience would certainly take place in the course of a few days.

Such was Mr. Jubber's ingenious contrivance for turning to good pecuniary account the ignominious defeat which he had suffered at the hands of Dr. Joyce.

After much patient reasoning and many earnest expostulations, Mrs. Joyce at last succeeded in persuading Mr. Blyth that he might carry little Mary upstairs to her bed, without any danger of awakening her. The moonbeams were streaming through the windows over the broad, old-fashioned landings of the rectory staircase, and bathed the child's sleeping face in their lovely light, as Valentine carefully bore her in his own arms to her bedroom. "Oh!" he whispered to himself, as he paused for an instant where the moon shone clearly on the landing; and looked down on her—"oh! if my poor Lavvie could only see little Mary now."

They laid her, still asleep, on the bed, and covered her over lightly with a shawl, then went downstairs again to wait for Mrs. Peckover.

The clown's wife came in half an hour, as she had promised. They saw sorrow and weariness in her face, as they looked at her. Besides a bundle with the child's few clothes in it, she brought the hair bracelet and the pocket-handkerchief which had been found on little Mary's mother.

"Wherever the child goes," she said, "these two things must go with her." She addressed Mr. Blyth as she spoke, and gave the hair bracelet and the handkerchief into his own hands.

It seemed rather a relief than a disappointment to Mrs. Peckover to hear that the child was asleep above stairs. All pain of parting would now be spared, on one side at least. She went up to look at her on her bed, and kissed her—but so lightly that little Mary's sleep was undisturbed by that farewell token of tenderness and love.

"Tell her to write to me, sir," said poor Mrs. Peckover, holding Valentine's hand fast, and looking wistfully in his face through her gathering tears. "I shall prize my first letter from her so much, if it's only a couple of lines. God bless you, sir; and good-by. It ought to be a comfort to me, and it is, to know that you will be kind to her—I hope I shall get up to London some day, and see her myself. But don't forget the letter, sir: I shan't fret so much after her when once I've got that!"

She went away, sadly murmuring these last words many times over, while Valentine was trying to cheer and re-assure her, as they walked together to the outer gate. Doctor Joyce accompanied them down the front-garden path, and exacted from her a promise to return often to the Rectory while the circus was at Rubbleford; saying also that he and his family desired her to look on them always as her fast and firm friends in any emergency. Valentine entreated her, over and over again, to remember the terms of their agreement, and to come and judge for herself of the child's happiness in her new home. She only answered: "Don't forget the letter, sir!" And so they parted,

Early the next morning, Mr. Blyth and little Mary left the Rectory, and started for London by the first coach.

CHAPTER VII.

MADONNA IN HER NEW HOME.*

THE result of Mr. Blyth's adventure in the traveling circus, and of the events which followed it, was that little Mary at once became a member of the painter's family, and grew up happily, in her new home, into the young lady who was called "Madonna" by Valentine, by his wife,

---

* I do not know that any attempt has yet been made in English fiction to draw the character of a "Deaf-Mute" simply and exactly after nature, or, in other words, to exhibit the peculiar effects produced by the loss of the senses of hearing and speaking on the disposition of the person so afflicted. The famous Fenella, in Scott's "Peveril of the Peak," only *assumes* deafness and dumbness, and the whole family of dumb people on the stage have the remarkable faculty—so far as my experience goes—of always being able to hear what is said to them. When the idea first occurred to me of representing the character of a "Deaf-Mute" as literally as possible according to nature, I found the difficulty of getting at tangible and reliable materials to work from much greater than I had anticipated; so much greater, indeed, that I believe my design must have been abandoned, if a lucky chance had not thrown in my way Dr. Kitto's delightful little book, "The Lost Senses." In the first division of that work, which contains the author's interesting and touching narrative of his own sensations

and by all intimate friends who were in the habit of frequenting the house.

Mr. Blyth's first proceeding, after he had brought the little girl home with him, was to take her to the most eminent aural surgeon of the day. He did this, not in the hope of any curative result following the medical examination, but as a first duty which he thought he owed to her, now that she was under his sole charge. The surgeon was deeply interested in the case; but, after giving it the most careful attention, he declared that it was hopeless. Her

---

under the total loss of the sense of hearing, and its consequent effect on the faculties of speech, will be found my authority for most of those traits in Madonna's character which are especially and immediately connected with the deprivation from which she is represented as suffering. The moral purpose to be answered by the introduction of such a personage as this, and of the kindred character of the painter's wife, lies, I would fain hope, so plainly on the surface, that it can be hardly necessary for me to indicate it even to the most careless reader. I know of nothing which more firmly supports our faith in the better parts of human nature, than to see—as we all may—with what patience and cheerfulness the heavier bodily afflictions of humanity are borne, for the most part, by those afflicted; and also to note what elements of kindness and gentleness the spectacle of these afflictions constantly develops in the persons of the little circle by which the sufferer is surrounded. Here is the ever bright side, the ever noble and consoling aspect of all human calamity; and the object of presenting this to the view of others as truly and as tenderly as in him lies, seems to me to be a fit object for any writer who desires to address himself to the best sympathies of his readers.

sense of hearing, he said, was entirely gone; but her faculty of speech, although it had been totally disused (as Mrs. Peckover had stated) for more than two years past, might, he thought, be imperfectly regained, at some future time, if a tedious, painful, and uncertain process of education were resorted to, under the direction of an experienced teacher of the deaf and dumb. The child, however, had such a horror of this resource being tried, when it was communicated to her, that Mr. Blyth instinctively followed Mrs. Peckover's example, and consulted the little creature's feelings, by allowing her in this particular—and indeed in most others—to remain perfectly happy and contented in her own way.

The first influence which reconciled her almost immediately to her new life was the influence of Mrs. Blyth. The perfect gentleness and patience with which the painter's wife bore her incurable malady, seemed to impress the child in a very remarkable manner from the first. The sight of that frail, wasted life, which they told her, by writing, had been shut up so long in the same room, and had been condemned to the same weary inaction for so many years past, struck at once to Mary's heart, and filled her with one of those new and mysterious sensations which mark epochs in the growth of a child's moral nature. Nor did these first impressions ever alter. When years had passed away, and when Mary, being "little" Mary no longer, possessed those marked characteristics of feature and expression which gained for her the name of "Madonna," she still preserved all her child's feeling for the painter's wife. However playful her manner might often be with Valentine, it invariably changed when she was in Mrs. Blyth's presence; always dis-playing at such times the same anxious tender-ness, the same artless admiration, and the same watchful and loving sympathy. There was something secret and superstitious in the girl's fondness for Mrs. Blyth. She appeared unwill-ing to let others know what this affection really was in all its depth and fullness: it seemed to be intuitively preserved by her in the most sacred privacy of her own heart, as if the feeling had been part of her religion, or rather, as if it had been a religion in itself.

Her love for her new mother, which testified itself thus strongly and sincerely, was returned by that mother with equal fervor. From the day when little Mary first appeared at her bed-side, Mrs. Blyth felt, to use her own expression, as if a new strength had been given to her to enjoy her new happiness. Brighter hopes, bet-ter health, calmer resignation, and purer peace seemed to follow the child's footsteps and be always inherent in her very presence, as she moved to and fro in the sick-room. All the lit-tle difficulties of communicating with her and teaching her, which her misfortune rendered in-evitable, and which might sometimes have been felt as tedious by others, were so many distinct sources of happiness, so many exquisite occupa-tions of once-weary time to Mrs. Blyth. All the friends of the family declared that the child had succeeded where doctors, and medicines, and luxuries, and the sufferer's own courageous resignation had hitherto failed—for she had succeeded in endowing Mrs. Blyth with a new life. And they were right. A fresh object for the affections of the heart and the thoughts of the mind, is a fresh life for every feeling and thinking human being, in sickness even as well as in health.

In this sense, indeed, the child brought fresh life with her to all who lived in her new home— to the servants, as well as to the master and mistress. The cloud had rarely found its way into that happy dwelling in former days; now the sunshine seemed fixed there forever. No more beautiful and touching proof of what the heroism of patient dispositions and loving hearts can do toward guiding human existence, unconquered and unsullied, through its hardest trials, could be found anywhere than was presented by the aspect of the painter's household. Here were two chief members of one little family circle, afflicted by such incurable bodily calamity as it falls to the lot of but few human beings to suffer —yet here were no sighs, no tears, no vain repinings with each new morning, no gloomy thoughts to set woe and terror watching by the pillow at night. In this homely sphere, life, even in its frailest aspects, was still greater than its greatest trials; strong to conquer by virtue of its own innocence and purity, its simple unworldly aspirations, its self-sacrificing devotion to the happiness and the anxieties of others.

As the course of her education proceeded, many striking peculiarities became developed in Madonna's disposition, which seemed to be all more or less produced by the necessary influence of her affliction on the formation of her character. The social isolation to which that affliction condemned her, the solitude of thought and feeling into which it forced her, tended from an early period to make her mind remarkably self-reliant for so young a girl. Her first impression of strangers seemed invariably to decide her opinion of them at once and forever. She liked or disliked people heartily; estimating them apparently from considerations entirely irrespective of age, or sex, or personal appearance. Sometimes the very person who was thought certain to attract her proved to be absolutely repulsive to her—sometimes people who, in Mr. Blyth's opinion, were sure to be unwelcome visitors to Madonna, turned out, incomprehensibly, to be people whom she took a violent liking to directly. She always betrayed her pleasure or uneasiness in the society of others with the most diverting candor—showing the extremest anxiety to conciliate and attract those whom she liked; running away and hiding herself, like a child, from those whom she disliked. There were some unhappy people in this latter class, whom no persuasion could ever induce her to see a second time.

She could never give any satisfactory account of how she proceeded in forming her opinions of others. The only visible means of arriving at them, which her deafness and dumbness permitted her to use, consisted simply in examination of a stranger's manner, expression, and play of features at a first interview. This process, however, seemed always amply sufficient for her; and in more than one instance events proved that her judgment had not been misled by it. Her affliction had tended, indeed, to sharpen her faculties of observation and her powers of analysis to such a remarkable degree, that she often guessed the general tenor of a conversation quite correctly merely by watching the minute varieties of expression and gesture in the persons speaking—fixing her attention always with especial intentness on the changeful and rapid motions of their lips.

Exiled alike from the worlds of sound and speech, the poor girl's enjoyment of all that she could still gain of happiness, by means of the seeing sense that was left her, was hardly conceivable to her speaking and hearing fellow-creatures. All beautiful sights, and particularly the exquisite combinations that Nature presents, filled her with an artless rapture, which it affected the most unimpressible people to witness. Trees were beyond all other objects the greatest luxuries that her eyes could enjoy. She would sit for hours, on fresh summer evenings, watching the mere waving of the leaves; her face flushed, her whole nervous organization trembling with the sensations of deep and perfect happiness which that simple sight imparted to her. All the riches and honors which this

world can afford would not have added to her
existence a tithe of that pleasure which Valentine
easily conferred on her, by teaching her to draw;
he might almost be said to have given her a new
sense in exchange for the senses that she had
lost. She used to dance about the room with the
reckless ecstasy of a child, in her ungovernable
delight at the prospect of a sketching expedition
with Mr. Blyth in the Hampstead fields.

. At a very early date of her sojourn with Valentine, it was discovered that her total deafness
did not entirely exclude her from every effect of
sound. She was acutely sensitive to the influence of percussion—that is to say (if so vague
and contradictory an expression may be allowed),
she could, under certain conditions, *feel* the
sounds that she could not hear. For example,
if Mr. Blyth wished to bring her to his side
when they were together in the painting-room,
and when she happened neither to be looking at
him nor to be within reach of a touch, he used
to rub his foot or the end of his maul-stick gently
against the floor. The slight concussion so produced reached her nerves instantly; provided
always that some part of her body touched the
floor on which such experiments were tried.

As a means of extending her faculties of social
communication, she was instructed in the deaf
and dumb alphabet by Valentine's directions;
he and his wife, of course, learning it also; and
many of their intimate friends, who were often
in the house, following their example for Madonna's sake. Oddly enough, however, she fre-

quently preferred to express herself, or to be addressed by others, according to the clumsier and slower system of signs and writing, to which she had been accustomed from childhood. She carefully preserved her little slate, with its ornamented frame, and kept it hanging at her side, just as she wore it on the morning of her visit to the Rectory-house at Rubbleford.

In one exceptional case, and one only, did her misfortune appear to have the power of affecting her tranquillity seriously. Whenever, by any accident, she happened to be left in the dark, she was overcome by the most violent terror. It was found, even when others were with her, that she still lost her self-possession at such times. Her own explanation of her feelings on these occasions suggested the simplest of reasons to account for this weakness in her character. "Remember," she wrote on her slate, when a new servant was curious to know why she always slept with a light in her room—"remember that I am deaf *and blind, too,* in the darkness. You, who can hear, have a sense to serve you, instead of sight, in the dark—your ears are of use to you then, as your eyes are in the light. *I* hear nothing, and see nothing—I lose all my senses together in the dark."

It was only by rare accidents, which there was no providing against, that she was ever terrified in this way, after her peculiarity had first disclosed itself. In small things as well as in great, Valentine never forgot that her happiness was his own especial care. He was more nerv-

ously watchful over her than any one else in the
house—for she cost him those secret anxieties
which make the objects of our love doubly precious to us.   In all the years that she had lived
under his roof, he had never conquered his morbid dread that Madonna might be one day traced
and discovered by her father, or by relatives,
who might have a legal claim to her.   Under
this apprehension, he had written to Doctor
Joyce and Mrs. Peckover a day or two after the
child's first entry under his roof, pledging both
the persons whom he addressed to the strictest
secrecy in all that related to Madonna and to the
circumstances which had made her his adopted
child.   As for the hair bracelet, if his conscience
had allowed him, he would have destroyed it
immediately; but feeling that this would be an
inexcusable breach of trust, he was fain to be
content with locking it up, as well as the pocket-
handkerchief, in an old bureau in his painting-
room, the key of which he always kept attached
to his own watch-chain.

Not one of his London friends ever knew how
he first met with Madonna.   He boldly baffled
all forms of inquiry by requesting that they
would consider her history before she came into
his house as a perfect blank, and by simply presenting her to them as his adopted child.   This
method of silencing troublesome curiosity succeeded certainly to admiration; but at the expense of Mr. Blyth's own moral character.   Persons who knew little or nothing of his real disposition and his early life, all shook their heads,

and laughed in secret; asserting that the mystery was plain enough to the most ordinary capacity, and that the young lady could be nothing more nor less than a natural child of his own.

Mrs. Blyth was far more indignant at this report than her husband, when in due time it reached the painter's house. Valentine rather approved of the scandal than not, because it was likely to lead inquisitive people in the wrong direction. He might have been now perfectly easy about the preservation of his secret, but for the distrust which still clung to him, in spite of himself, on the subject of Mrs. Peckover's discretion. He never wearied of warning that excellent woman to be careful in keeping the important secret, every time she came to London to see Madonna. Whether she only paid them a visit for the day, and went away again; or whether she spent her Christmas with them, Valentine's greeting always ended nervously with the same distrustful question: "Excuse me for asking, Mrs. Peckover, but are you quite sure you have kept what you know about little Mary and her mother, and dates and places and all that, properly hidden from prying people, since you were here last?" At which point Mrs. Peckover generally answered by repeating, always with the same sarcastic emphasis: "Properly hidden, did you say, sir? Of course I keep what I know properly hidden, for of course I can hold my tongue. In my time, sir, it used always to take two parties to play at a game of Hide-and-seek. Who in the world is seeking after little Mary, I should like to know?''

Perhaps Mrs. Peckover's view of the case was the right one; or, perhaps, the extraordinary discretion observed by the persons who were in the secret of Madonna's history prevented any disclosure of the girl's origin from reaching her father or friends—presuming them to be still alive and anxiously looking for her. But, at any rate this much at least is certain: Nobody appeared to assert a claim to Valentine's adopted child, from the time when he took her home with him as his daughter, to the time when the reader first made his acquaintance, many pages back, in the congenial sphere of his own painting-room.*

CHAPTER VIII.

MENTOR AND TELEMACHUS.

IT is now some time since we left Mr. Blyth and Madonna in the studio. The first was engaged, it may be remembered, in the process of brushing up Bacchanalian Nymphs in the foreground of a Classical landscape. The second was modestly occupied in making a copy of the head of the Venus de' Medici.

The clock strikes one—and a furious ring is heard at the house-bell.

"There he is!" cries Mr. Blyth to himself;

* See note, p. 165.

"there's Zack! I know his ring among a thousand; it's worse even than the postman's; it's like an alarm of fire!"

Here Valentine drums gently with his maulstick on the floor. Madonna looks toward him directly; he waves his hand round and round rapidly above his head. This is the sign which means "Zack." The girl smiles brightly, and blushes as she sees it. Zack is apparently one of her special favorites.

While the young gentleman is being admitted at the garden-gate, there is a leisure moment to explain how he became acquainted with Mr. Blyth.

Valentine's father and Mrs. Thorpe's father (the identical Mr. Goodworth who figures at the beginning of this narrative as one of the actors in the Sunday Drama at Baregrove Square) had been intimate associates of the drowsy-story-telling and copious-port-drinking old school. The friendly intercourse between these gentlemen spread, naturally enough, to the sons and daughters who formed their respective families. From the time of Mr. Thorpe's marriage to Miss Goodworth, however, the connection between the junior Goodworths and Blyths began to grow less intimate—so far, at least, as the new bride and Valentine were concerned. The rigid modern Puritan of Baregrove Square, and the eccentric votary of the Fine Arts, mutually disapproved of each other from the very first. Visits of ceremony were exchanged at long intervals; but even these were discontinued on Madonna's

arrival under Valentine's roof: Mr. Thorpe being
one of the first of the charitable friends of the
family who suspected her to be the painter's natural child.   An almost complete separation accordingly ensued for some years, until Zack grew
up to boy's estate, and was taken to see Valentine, one day in holiday time, by his grandfather.   He and the painter became friends directly.   Mr. Blyth liked boys, and boys of all degrees
liked him.   From this time, Zack frequented
Valentine's house at every opportunity, and
never neglected his artist-friend in after years.
At the date of this story, one of the many points
in his son's conduct of which Mr. Thorpe disapproved on the highest moral grounds, was the
firm determination the lad showed to keep up
his intimacy with Mr. Blyth.

We may now get back to the ring at the bell.

Zack's approach to the painting-room was her-
alded by a scuffling of feet, a loud noise of talking, and a great deal of suspicious giggling on
the part of the housemaid, who had let him in.
Suddenly these sounds ceased—the door was
dashed open — and Mr. Thorpe, junior, burst
into the room.

"Dear old Blyth! how are you?" cried Zack.
"Have you had any leap-frog since I was here
last?   Jump up, and let's celebrate my return to
the painting-room with a bit of manly exercise
in our old way.   Come on!   I'll give the first
back.   No shirking!   Put down your palette;
and one, two, three—and over!"

Pronouncing these words, Zack ran to the end

of the room opposite to Valentine; and signalized his entry into the studio by the extraordinary process of giving its owner what is termed, in the technical language of leap-frog, "a capital back."

Mr. Blyth put down his palette, brushes, and maul-stick—tucked up his cuffs and smiled—took a little trial skip into the air—and, running down the room with the slightly tremulous step of a gentleman of fifty, cleared Zack in gallant style; fell over on the other side, all in a lump on his hands and feet; gave the return "back" conscientiously, at the other end of the studio; and was leaped over in an instant, with a shout of triumph, by Zack. The athletic ceremonies thus concluded, the two stood up together and shook hands heartily.

"Too stiff, Blyth—too stiff and shaky by half," said young Thorpe. "I haven't kept you up enough in your gymnastics lately. We must have some more leap-frog in the garden; and I'll bring my boxing-gloves next time, and open your chest by teaching you to fight. Splendid exercise, and so good for your sluggish old liver."

Delivering this opinion, Zack ran off to Madonna, who had been keeping the Venus de' Medici from being shaken down, while she looked on at the leap-frog. "How is the dearest, prettiest, gentlest love in the world?" cried Zack, taking her hand, and kissing it with boisterous fondness. "Ah! she lets other old friends kiss her cheek, and only lets *me* kiss her hand! I say, Blyth, what a little witch she is—I'll lay you two to one she's guessed what I've just been saying to her."

A bright flush overspread the girl's face while Zack addressed her. Her tender blue eyes looked up at him, shyly conscious of the pleasure that their expression was betraying; and the neat folds of her pretty gray dress, which had lain so still over her bosom when she was drawing, began to rise and fall gently now, when Zack was holding her hand. If young Thorpe had not been the most thoughtless of human beings—as much a boy still, in many respects, as when he was locked up in his father's dressing-room for bad behavior at church—he might have guessed long ago why he was the only one of Madonna's old friends whom she did not permit to kiss her on the cheek!

But Zack neither guessed, nor thought of guessing, anything of this sort. His flighty thoughts flew off in a moment from the young lady to his cigar-case; and he walked away to the hearth-rug, twisting up a piece of waste paper into a lighter as he went.

When Madonna returned to her drawing, her eyes wandered timidly once or twice to the place where Zack was standing, when she thought he was not looking at her; and, assuredly, so far as personal appearance was concerned, young Thorpe was handsome enough to tempt any woman into glancing at him with approving eyes. He was over six feet in height; and, though then little more than nineteen years old, was well developed in proportion to his stature. His box-

"HOW IS THE DEAREST, PRETTIEST, GENTLEST LOVE IN THE WORLD?"
CRIED ZACK, TAKING HER HAND, AND KISSING IT WITH BOISTEROUS
FONDNESS.—HIDE-AND-SEEK, Vol. XI., page 179.

ing, rowing and other athletic exercises had done
wonders toward bringing his naturally vigorous, upright frame to the perfection of healthy
muscular condition.   Tall and strong as he was,
there was nothing stiff or ungainly in his movements.   He trod easily and lightly, with a certain youthful suppleness and hardy grace in all
his actions which set off his fine bodily formation to the best advantage.   He had keen, quick,
mischievous gray eyes—a thoroughly English
red-and-white complexion—admirably bright and
regular teeth—and curly light-brown hair, with
a very peculiar golden tinge in it, which was
only visible when his head was placed in a particular light.   In short, Zack was a manly, handsome fellow, a thorough Saxon, every inch of
him; and (physically speaking, at least) a credit
to the parents and the country that had given
him birth.

"I say, Blyth, do you and Madonna mind
smoke?" asked Zack, lighting his cigar before
there was time to answer him.

"No—no," said Valentine.   "But, Zack, you
wrote me word that your father had taken all
your cigars away from you—"

"So he has, and all my pocket-money, too.
But I've taken to helping myself, and I've got
some splendid cigars.   Try one, Blyth," said
the young gentleman, luxuriously puffing out a
stream of smoke through each nostril.

"Taken to helping yourself!" exclaimed Mr.
Blyth.   "What do you mean?"

"Oh!" said Zack, "don't be afraid.   It's not

thieving—it's only barter. Look here, my dear
fellow, this is how it is: A friend of mine, a
junior clerk in our office, has three dozen cigars,
and I have two staring flannel shirts, which are
only fit for a snob to wear. The junior clerk
gives me the three dozen cigars, and I give the
junior clerk the two staring flannel shirts.
That's barter, and barter's commerce, old boy!
It's all my father's fault: he will make a tradesman of me. Dutiful behavior, isn't it, to be doing a bit of commerce already on my own account?"

"I'll tell you what, Zack," said Mr. Blyth, "I
don't like the way you're going on in at all.
Your last letter made me very uneasy, I can
promise you."

"You can't be half as uneasy as I am," rejoined Zack. "I'm jolly enough here, to be
sure, because I can't help it somehow; but at
home I'm the most miserable devil on the face
of the earth. My father balks me in everything, and makes me turn hypocrite, and take
him in, in all sorts of ways—which I hate myself for doing; and yet can't help doing, because
he forces me to it. Why does he want to make
me live in the same slow way that he does himself? There's some difference in our ages, I
rather think! Why does he bully me about being always home by eleven o'clock? Why does
he force me into a tea-merchant's office, when I
want to be an artist, like you? I'm a perfect
slave to commerce already. What do you think?
I'm supposed to be sampling in the city at this

very moment. The junior clerk's doing the
work for me; and he's to have one of my dress-
waistcoats to compensate him for the trouble.
First my shirts; then my waistcoat; then my—
confound it, sir, I shall be stripped to the skin,
if this sort of thing goes on much longer!"

"Gently, Zack, gently. What would your
father say if he heard you?"

"Oh yes! it's all very well, you old humbug,
to shake your head at me; but you wouldn't like
being forced into an infernal tea-shop, and having all your pocket-money stopped, if it was
your case. I won't stand it—I have the patience
of Job—but I won't stand it! My mind's made
up: I want to be an artist, and I *will* be an artist. Don't lecture, Blyth—it's no use; but just
tell me how I'm to begin learning to draw."

Here Zack cunningly touched Valentine on
his weak point. Art was his grand topic; and
to ask his advice on that subject was to administer the sweetest flattery to his professional pride.
He wheeled his chair round directly, so as to face
young Thorpe. "If you're really set on being
an artist," he began, enthusiastically, "I rather
fancy, Master Zack, I'm the man to help you.
First of all, you must purify your taste by copying the glorious works of Greek sculpture—in
short, you must form yourself on the Antique.
Look there!—just what Madonna's doing now;
she's forming herself on the Antique."

Zack went immediately to look at Madonna's
drawing, the outline of which was now finished.
"Beautiful! Splendid! Ah! confound it! yes!

the glorious Greeks, and so forth, just as you
say, Blyth. A most wonderful drawing! the
finest thing of the kind I ever saw in my life!''
Here he transferred his superlatives to his fingers, communicating them to Madonna through
the medium of the deaf and dumb alphabet,
which he had superficially mastered with extraordinary rapidity under Mr. and Mrs. Blyth's
tuition. Whatever Zack's friends did, Zack always admired with the wildest enthusiasm, and
without an instant's previous consideration.
Any knowledge of what he praised, or why he
praised it, was a slight superfluity of which he
never felt the want. If Madonna had been a
great astronomer, and had shown him pages of
mathematical calculations, he would have overwhelmed her with eulogies just as glibly as—by
means of the finger alphabet—he was overwhelming her now.

But Valentine's pupil was used to be criticised
as well as praised; and her head was in no danger of being turned by Zack's admiration of her
drawing. Looking up at him with a sly expression of incredulity, she signed these words in
reply: "I am afraid it ought to be a much better
drawing than it is. Do you really like it?"
Zack rejoined impetuously by a fresh torrent of
superlatives. She watched his face, for a moment, rather anxiously and inquiringly, then
bent quickly down over her drawing. He walked
back to Valentine. Her eyes followed him—
then returned once more to the paper before her.
The color began to rise again· in her cheek; a

thoughtful expression stole calmly over her clear, happy eyes; she played nervously with the port-crayon that held her black and white chalk; looked attentively at the drawing; and, smiling very prettily at some fancy of her own, proceeded assiduously with her employment, altering and amending, as she went on, with more than usual industry and care.

What was Madonna thinking of? If she had been willing and able to utter her thoughts, she might have expressed them thus: "I wonder whether he likes my drawing? Shall I try hard if I can't make it better worth pleasing him? I will! it shall be the best thing I have ever done. And then, when it is nicely finished, I will take it secretly to Mrs. Blyth to give from me, as my present to Zack."

"Look there," said Valentine, turning from his picture toward Madonna, "look, my boy, how carefully that dear good girl there is working from the Antique! Only copy her example, and you may be able to draw from the life in less than a year's time."

"You don't say so? I should like to sit down and begin at once. But, look here, Blyth, when you say 'draw from the life,' there can't be the smallest doubt, of course, about what you mean —but, at the same time, if you would only be a little less professional in your way of expressing yourself—"

"Good heavens, Zack, in what barbarous ignorance of art your parents must have brought you up! 'Drawing from the life,' means drawing the living human figure from the living human being which sits at a shilling an hour, and calls itself a model.''

"Ah, to be sure! Some of these very models whose names are chalked up here over your fire-place?—Delightful! Glorious! Drawing from the life—just the very thing I long for most. Halloo!'' exclaimed Zack, reading the memoranda, which it was Mr. Blyth's habit to scrawl, as they occurred to him, on the wall over the chimney-piece—"halloo! here's a woman-model; 'Amelia Bibby'—Blyth! let me dash at once into drawing from the life, and let me begin with Amelia Bibby.''

"Nothing of the sort, Master Zack,'' said Valentine. "You may end with Amelia Bibby, when you are fit to study at the Royal Academy. She's a capital model, and so is her sister Sophia. The worst of it is, they quarreled mortally a little while ago; and now, if an artist has Sophia, Amelia won't come to him. And Sophia, of course, returns the compliment, and won't sit to Amelia's friends. It's awkward for people who used to employ them both, as I did.''

"What did they quarrel about?'' inquired Zack.

"About a tea-pot,'' answered Mr. Blyth. "You see, they are daughters of one of the late king's footmen, and are desperately proud of their aristocratic origin. They used to live together as happy as birds, without a hard word ever being spoken between them, till, one day, they happened to break their tea-pot, which of course set them talking about getting a new one. Sophia said it ought to be earthenware, like the last; Amelia contradicted her, and said it ought to be metal. Sophia said all the aristocracy used earthenware; Amelia said all the aristocracy used metal. Sophia said she was oldest, and knew best; Amelia said she was youngest, and knew better. Sophia said Amelia was an impudent jackanapes; Amelia said Sophia was a plebeian wretch. From that moment they parted. Sophia sits in her own lodging, and drinks tea out of earthenware; Amelia sits in *her* own lodging, and drinks tea out of metal. They swear never to make it up, and abuse each other furiously to everybody who will listen to them. Very shocking, and very curious at the same time—isn't it, Zack?''

"Oh, capital! A perfect picture of human nature to us men of the world,'' exclaimed the young gentleman, smoking with the air of a profound philosopher. "But tell me, Blyth, which is the prettiest, Amelia or Sophia? Metal or Earthenware? My mind's made up, beforehand, to study from the best-looking of the two, if you have no objection.''

"I have the strongest possible objection, Zack, to talking nonsense where a serious question is concerned. Are you, or are you not, in earnest in your dislike of commerce and your resolution to be an artist?''

"I mean to be a painter, or I mean to leave home,'' answered Zack, resolutely. "If you don't help me, I'll be off as sure as fate! I have half a mind to cut the office from this moment. Lend me a shilling, Blyth; and I'll toss up for it. Heads—liberty and the fine arts! Tails— the tea-merchant!"

"If you don't go back to the city to-day," said Valentine, "and stick to your engagements, I wash my hands of you—but if you wait patiently, and promise to show all the attention you can to your father's wishes, I'll teach you myself to draw from the Antique. If somebody can be found who has influence enough with your father to get him to enter you at the Royal Academy, you must be prepared beforehand with a drawing that's fit to show. Now, if you promise to be a good boy, you shall come here, and learn the A B C of Art, every evening if you like. We'll have a regular little academy," continued Valentine, putting down his palette and brushes, and rubbing his hands in high glee; "and if it isn't too much for Lavvie, the evening studies shall take place in her room; and she shall draw, poor dear soul, as well as the rest of us. There's an idea for you, Zack! Mr. Blyth's Drawing Academy, open every evening—with light refreshment for industrious students. What do you say to it?"

"Say? by George, sir, I'll come every night, and get through acres of chalk and miles of drawing-paper!" cried Zack, catching all Valentine's enthusiasm on the instant. "Let's go upstairs and tell Mrs. Blyth about it directly."

"Stop a minute, Zack," interposed Mr. Blyth.

"What time ought you to be back in the City? it's close on two o'clock now."

"Oh! three o'clock will do. I've got lots oj time yet—I can walk it in half an hour."

"You have got about ten minutes more to stay," said Valentine, in his firmest manner. "Occupy them, if you like, in going upstairs to Mrs. Blyth, and take Madonna with you. I'll follow as soon as I've put away my brushes."

Saying those words, Mr. Blyth walked to the place where Madonna was still at work. She was so deeply engaged over her drawing that she had never once looked up from it, for the last quarter of an hour or more; and when Valentine patted her shoulder approvingly, and made her a sign to leave off, she answered by a gesture of entreaty, which eloquently enough implored him to let her proceed a little longer with her employment. She had never at other times claimed an indulgence of this kind, when she was drawing from the Antique—but, then, she had never, at other times, been occupied in making a copy which was secretly intended as a present for Zack.

Valentine, however, easily induced her to relinquish her port-crayon. He laid his hand on his heart, which was the sign that had been adopted to indicate Mrs. Blyth. Madonna started up, and put her drawing materials aside immediately.

Zack, having thrown away the end of his cigar, gallantly advanced and offered her his arm. As she approached, rather shyly, to take it, he also laid his hand on his heart, and pointed upstairs. The gesture was quite enough for her. She understood at once that they were going together to see Mrs. Blyth.

"Whether Zack really turns out a painter or not," said Valentine to himself, as the door closed on the two young people, "I believe I have hit on the best plan that ever was devised for keeping him steady. As long as he comes to me regularly, he can't break out at night, and get into mischief. Upon my word, the more I think of that notion of mine the better I like it. I shouldn't at all wonder if my evening Academy doesn't end in working the reformation of Zack!"

When Mr. Blyth pronounced those last words, if he could only have looked a little way into the future—if he could only have suspected how strangely the home-interests dearest to his heart were connected with his success in working the reformation of Zack—the smile which was now on his face would have left it in a moment; and for the first time in his life he would have sat before one of his own pictures in the character of an unhappy man.

CHAPTER IX.

THE TRIBULATIONS OF ZACK.

A WEEK elapsed before Mrs. Blyth's wavering health permitted her husband to open the sittings of his evening drawing academy in the invalid room.

During every day of that week, the chances of taming down Zack into a reformed character grew steadily more and more hopeless. The lad's home position, at this period, claims a moment's serious attention. Zack's resistance to his father's infatuated severity was now shortly to end in results of the last importance to himself, to his family, and to his friends.

A specimen has already been presented of Mr. Thorpe's method of religiously educating his son, at six years old, by making him attend a church service of two hours in length; as, also, of the manner in which he sought to drill the child into premature discipline by dint of Sabbath restrictions and Select Bible Texts. When that child grew to a boy, and when the boy developed to a young man, Mr. Thorpe's educational system still resolutely persisted in being what it had always been from the first. His idea of Religion defined it to be a system of prohibitions; and, by a natural consequence, his idea of Education defined *that* to be a system of prohibitions also.

His method of bringing up his son once settled, no earthly consideration could move him from it an inch, one way or the other. He had two favorite phrases to answer every form of objection, every variety of reasoning, every citation of examples. No matter with what arguments the surviving members of Mrs. Thorpe's family from time to time assailed him, the same two replies were invariably shot back at them in turn from the parental quiver. Mr. Thorpe calmly—always calmly—said, first, that he "would never compound with vice" (which was what nobody asked him to do); and, secondly, that he would in no instance, great or small, "consent to act from a principle of expediency": this last assertion, in the case of Zack, being about equivalent to saying that if he set out to walk due north, and met a lively young bull galloping with his head down, due south, he would not consent to save his own bones, or yield the animal space enough to run on, by stepping aside a single inch in a lateral direction, east or west.

"My son requires the most unremitting parental discipline and control," Mr. Thorpe remarked, in explanation of his motives for forcing Zack to adopt a commercial career. "When he is not under my own eye at home, he must be under the eyes of devout friends, in whom I can place unlimited confidence. One of these devout friends is ready to receive him into his counting-house; to keep him industriously occupied from nine in the morning till six in the evening; to surround him with estimable examples; and, in short, to share with me the solemn responsibility of managing his moral and religious training. Persons who ask me to allow motives of this awfully important nature to be modified in the smallest degree by any considerations connected with the lad's natural disposition (which has been a source of grief to me from his childhood);

with his bodily gifts of the flesh (which have
nitherto only served to keep him from the cultivation of the gifts of the spirit); or with his own
desires (which I know by bitter experience to be
all of the world, worldly); persons, I say, who
ask me to do any of these things, ask me also to
act from a godless principle of expediency, and
to violate moral rectitude by impiously compounding with vice.''

Acting on such principles of parental discipline as these, Mr. Thorpe conscientiously believed that he had done his duty, when he had at
last forced his son into the merchant's office. He
had, in truth, perpetrated one of the most serious
mistakes which it is possible for a wrong-headed
father to commit. For once Zack had not exaggerated in saying that his aversion to employment in a counting-house amounted to absolute
horror. His physical peculiarities, and the habits which they had entailed on him from boyhood, made life in the open air, and the constant
use of his hardy thews and sinews, a constitu-
tional necessity. He felt—and there was no
self-delusion in the feeling—that he should mope
and pine, like a wild animal in a cage, under
confinement in an office, only varied from morning to evening by commercial walking expeditions of a miserable mile or two in close and
crowded streets. These forebodings — to say
nothing of his natural yearning toward adventure, change of scene, and exhilarating bodily
exertion—would have been sufficient of themselves to have decided him to leave his home and

battle his way through the world (he cared not
where or how, so long as he battled it freely),
but for one consideration. Reckless as he was,
that consideration stayed his feet on the brink
of a sacred threshold which he dared not pass,
perhaps to leave it behind him forever — the
threshold of his mother's door.

Strangely as it expressed itself, and irregularly as it influenced his conduct, Zack's love
for his mother was yet, in its own nature, a
beautiful and admirable element in his character; full of promise for the future, if his father
had been able to discover it, and had been wise
enough to be guided by the discovery. As to
outward expression, the lad's fondness for Mrs.
Thorpe was a wild, boisterous, inconsiderate,
unsentimental fondness, noisily in harmony with
his thoughtless, rattle-pated disposition. It
swayed him by fits and starts; influencing him
nobly to patience and forbearance at one time;
abandoning him, to all appearance, at another.
But it was genuine, ineradicable fondness, nevertheless—however often heedlessness and temptation might overpower the still small voice in
which its impulses spoke to his conscience, and
pleaded with his heart.

Among other unlucky results of Mr. Thorpe's
conscientious imprisonment of his son in a merchant's office, was the vast increase which Zack's
commercial penance produced in his natural ap-
petite for the amusements and dissipations of the
town. After nine hours of the most ungrateful
daily labor that could well have been inflicted

on him, the sight of play-bills and other wayside advertisements of places of public recreation appealed to him, on his way home, with irresistible fascination.

Mr. Thorpe drew the line of demarkation between permissible and forbidden evening amusements at the lecture-rooms of the Royal and Polytechnic Institutions, and the oratorio performances in Exeter Hall. All gates opening on the outer side of the boundary thus laid down were gates of Vice—gates that no son of his should ever be allowed to pass. The domestic laws which obliged Zack to be home every night at eleven o'clock, and forbade the possession of a door-key, were directed especially to the purpose of closing up against him the forbidden entrances to theaters and public gardens—places of resort which Mr. Thorpe characterized, in a strain of devout allegory, as "Labyrinths of National Infamy." It was perfectly useless to suggest to the father (as some of Zack's maternal relatives did suggest to him), that the son was originally descended from Eve, and was consequently possessed of an hereditary tendency to pluck at forbidden fruit; and that his disposition and age made it next to a certainty that, if he were restrained from enjoying openly the amusements most attractive to him, he would probably end in enjoying them by stealth. Mr. Thorpe met all arguments of this kind by registering his usual protest against "compounding with vice"; and then drew the reins of discipline tighter than ever, by way of warning off all in-

trusive hands from attempting to relax them for
the future.

Before long, the evil results predicted by the
opponents of the father's plan for preventing the
son from indulging in public amusements, actually occurred. At first, Zack gratified his
taste for the drama by going to the theater
whenever he felt inclined; leaving the performances early enough to get home by eleven
o'clock, and candidly acknowledging how he
had occupied the evening when the question
was asked at breakfast next morning. This
frankness of confession was always rewarded
by rebukes, threats, and reiterated prohibitions,
administered by Mr. Thorpe with a crushing
assumption of superiority to every mitigating
argument, entreaty, or excuse that his son could
urge, which often irritated Zack into answering
defiantly, and recklessly repeating his offense.
Finding that all menaces and reproofs only
ended in making the lad ill-tempered and insub-
ordinate for days together, Mr. Thorpe so far
distrusted his own powers of correction as to
call in the aid of his prime clerical adviser, the
Reverend Aaron Yollop; under whose ministry
he sat, and whose portrait, in lithograph, hung
in the best light on the dining-room wall at
Baregrove Square.

Mr. Yollop's interference was at least weighty
enough to produce a positive and immediate result: it drove Zack to the very last limits of
human endurance. The reverend gentleman's
imperturbable self-possession defied the young

rebel's utmost powers of irritating reply, no matter how vigorously he might exert them. Once
vested with the paternal commission to rebuke,
prohibit, and lecture, as the spiritual pastor and
master of Mr. Thorpe's disobedient son, Mr. Yollop flourished in his new vocation in exact proportion to the resistance offered to the exercise
of his authority. He derived a grim encouragement from the wildest explosions of Zack's fury
at being interfered with by a man who had no
claim of relationship over him, and who gloried,
professionally, in experimenting on him, as a
finely - complicated case of spiritual disease.
Thrice did Mr. Yollop, in his capacity of a moral
surgeon, operate on his patient, and triumph in
the responsive yells which his curative exertions
elicited. At the fourth visit of attendance, however, every angry symptom suddenly and marvelously disappeared before the first significant
flourish of the clerical knife. Mr. Yollop had
triumphed where Mr. Thorpe had failed! The
case which had defied lay treatment had yielded
to the parsonic process of cure; and Zack, the
rebellious, was tamed at last into spending his
evenings in decorous dullness at home!

It never occurred to Mr. Yollop to doubt, or to
Mr. Thorpe to ascertain, whether the young gentleman really went to bed, after he had retired
obediently, at the proper hour, to his sleeping-
room. They saw him come home from business
sullenly docile and speechlessly subdued, take
his dinner and his book in the evening, and go
upstairs quietly after the house door had been

bolted for the night. They saw him thus acknowledge, by every outward proof, that he was
crushed into thorough submission; and the sight
satisfied them to their heart's content. No men
are so short-sighted as persecuting men. Both
Mr. Thorpe and his coadjutor were persecutors
on principle, wherever they encountered opposition; and both were consequently incapable of
looking beyond immediate results. The sad
truth was, however, that they had done something more than discipline the lad. They had
fairly worried his native virtues of frankness
and fair · dealing out of his heart; they had
beaten him back, inch by inch, into the miry
refuge of sheer duplicity. Zack was deceiving
them both.

Eleven o'clock was the family hour for going
to bed at Baregrove Square. Zack's first proceeding on entering his room was to open his
window softly, put on an old traveling-cap, and
light a cigar. It was December weather at that
time; but his hardy constitution rendered him
as impervious to cold as a young Polar bear.
Having smoked quietly for half an hour, he listened at his door till the silence in Mr. Thorpe's
dressing-room below assured him that his father
was safe in bed, and invited him to descend on
tiptoe—with his boots under his arm—into the
hall. Here he placed his candle, with a box of
matches by it, on a chair, and proceeded to open
the house door with the noiseless dexterity of a
practiced burglar—being always careful to facil-
itate the safe performance of this dangerous

operation by keeping lock, bolt, and hinges well oiled. Having secured the key, blown out the candle, and noiselessly closed the door behind him, he left the house, and started for the Haymarket, Covent Garden, or the Strand, a little before midnight—or, in other words, set forth on a nocturnal tour of amusement, just at the time when the doors of respectable places of public recreation (which his father prevented him from attending) were all closed, and the doors of disreputable places all thrown open.

One precaution, and one only, did Zack observe while enjoying the dangerous diversions into which paternal prohibitions, assisted by filial perversity, now thrust him headlong. He took care to keep sober enough to be sure of getting home before the servants had risen, and to be certain of preserving his steadiness of hand and stealthiness of foot while bolting the door and stealing upstairs for an hour or two of bed. Knowledge of his own perilous weakness of brain, as a drinker, rendered him thus uncharacteristically temperate and self-restrained, so far as indulgence in strong liquor was concerned. His first glass of grog comforted him; his second agreeably excited him; his third (as he knew by former experience) reached his weak point on a sudden, and robbed him treacherously of his sobriety.

Three or four times a week, for nearly a month, had he now enjoyed his unhallowed nocturnal rambles with perfect impunity—keeping them secret even from his friend Mr. Blyth, whose toleration, expansive as it was, he well knew would not extend to viewing leniently such offenses as haunting night-houses at two in the morning, while his father believed him to be safe in bed. But one mitigating circumstance can be urged in connection with the course of misconduct which he was now habitually following. He had still grace enough left to feel ashamed of his own successful duplicity, when he was in his mother's presence.

But circumstances unhappily kept him too much apart from Mrs. Thorpe, and so prevented the natural growth of a good feeling, which flourished only under her influence; and which, had it been suffered to arrive at maturity, might have led to his reform. All day he was at the office, and his irksome life there only inclined him to look forward with malicious triumph to the secret frolic of the night. Then, in the evening, Mr. Thorpe often thought it advisable to harangue him seriously, by way of not letting the reformed rake relapse for want of a little encouraging admonition of the moral sort. Nor was Mr. Yollop at all behindhand in taking similar precautions to secure the new convert permanently, after having once caught him. Every word these two gentlemen spoke only served to harden the lad afresh, and to deaden the reproving and reclaiming influence of his mother's affectionate looks and confiding words. "I should get nothing by it, even if I *could* turn over a new leaf," thought Zack, shrewdly and angrily, when his father or his father's friend

favored him with a little improving advice:
"Here they are, worrying away again already at
their pattern good boy, to make him a better."

Such was the point at which the Tribulations
of Zack had arrived, at the period when Mr.
Valentine Blyth resolved to set up a domestic
Drawing Academy in his wife's room; with the
double purpose of amusing his family circle in
the evening, and reforming his wild young
friend by teaching him to draw from the "glorious Antique."

CHAPTER X.

MR. BLYTH'S DRAWING ACADEMY.

WHEN the week of delay had elapsed, and
when Mrs. Blyth felt strong enough to receive
company in her room, Valentine sent the promised invitation to Zack which summoned him to
his first drawing-lesson.

The locality in which the family drawing
academy was to be held deserves a word of preliminary notice. It formed the narrow world
which bounded, by day and night alike, the existence of the painter's wife.

By throwing down a partition-wall, Mrs.
Blyth's room had been so enlarged as to extend
along the whole breadth of one side of the house,
measuring from the front to the back garden
windows. Considerable as the space was which
had been thus obtained, every part of it from

floor to ceiling was occupied by objects of beauty
proper to the sphere in which they were placed:
some solid and serviceable, where usefulness was
demanded; others light and elegant, where ornament alone was necessary—and all won gloriously by Valentine's brush; by the long, loving, unselfish industry of many years. Mrs.
Blyth's bed, like everything else that she used
in her room, was so arranged as to offer her the
most perfect comfort and luxury obtainable in
her suffering condition. The frame-work was
broad enough to include within its dimensions a
couch for day and a bed for night. Her read-
ing-easel and work-table could be moved within
reach, in whatever position she lay. Immediately above her hung an extraordinary compli-
cation of loose cords, which ran through ornamented pulleys of the quaintest kind, fixed at
different places in the ceiling, and communicating with the bell, the door, and a pane of glass
in the window, which opened easily on hinges.
These were Valentine's own contrivances to enable his wife to summon attendance, admit visitors, and regulate the temperature of her room at
will, by merely pulling at any one of the loops
hanging within reach of her hand, and neatly
labeled with ivory tablets, inscribed "Bell,"
"Door," "Window." The cords comprising
this rigging for invalid use were at least five
times more numerous than was necessary for the
purpose they were designed to serve; but Mrs.
Blyth would never allow them to be simplified
by dexterous hands. Clumsy as their arrange-

ment might appear to others, in her eyes it was without a fault: every useless cord was sacred from the reforming knife, for Valentine's sake.

Imprisoned to one room, as she had now been for years, she had not lost her natural womanly interest in the little occupations and events of household life. From the studio to the kitchen, she managed every day, through channels of communication invented by herself, to find out the latest domestic news; to be present in spirit at least, if not in body, at family consultations which could not take place in her room; to know exactly how her husband was getting on downstairs with his pictures; to rectify in time any omission of which Mr. Blyth or Madonna might be guilty in making the dinner arrangements, or in sending orders to tradespeople; to keep the servants attentive to their work, and to indulge or control them, as the occasion might require. Neither by look nor manner did she betray any of the sullen listlessness or fretful impatience sometimes attendant on long, incurable illness. Her voice, low as its tones were, was always cheerful, and varied musically and pleasantly with her varying thoughts. On her days of weakness, when she suffered much under her malady, she was accustomed to be quite still and quiet, and to keep her room darkened—these being the only signs by which any increase in her disorder could be detected by those about her. She never complained when the bad symptoms came on; and never voluntarily admitted, even on being questioned, that the spine was more painful to her than usual.

She was dressed very prettily for the opening night of the Drawing Academy, wearing a delicate lace cap, and a new silk gown of Valentine's choosing, made full enough to hide the emaciation of her figure. Her husband's love, faithful through all affliction and change to the girlish image of its first worship, still affectionately exacted from her as much attention to the graces and luxuries of dress as she might have bestowed on them of her own accord, in the best and gayest days of youth and health. She had never looked happier and better in any new gown than in that which Mr. Blyth had insisted on giving her to commemorate the establishment of the domestic drawing-school in her own room.

Seven o'clock had been fixed as the hour at which the business of the academy was to begin. Always punctual, wherever his professional engagements were concerned, Valentine put the finishing touch to his preparations as the clock struck; and perching himself gayly on a corner of Mrs. Blyth's couch, surveyed his drawing-boards, his lamps, and the plaster cast set up for his pupils to draw from, with bland artistic triumph.

"Now, Lavvie," he said, "before Zack comes and confuses me, I'll just check off all the drawing things one after another, to make sure that nothing's left downstairs in the studio which ought to be up here."

As her husband said these words, Mrs. Blyth

touched Madonna gently on the shoulder. For some little time the girl had been sitting thoughtfully, with her head bent down, her cheek resting on her hand, and a bright smile just parting her lips very prettily. The affliction which separated her from the worlds of hearing and speech —which set her apart among her fellow-creatures, a solitary living being in a sphere of death-silence, that others might approach but might never enter—gave a touching significance to the deep, meditative stillness that often passed over her suddenly, even in the society of her adopted parents, and of friends who were all talking around her. Sometimes the thoughts by which she was thus absorbed—thoughts only indicated to others by the shadow of their mysterious presence, moving in the expression that passed over her face—held her long under their influence: sometimes they seemed to die away in her mind almost as suddenly as they had arisen to life in it. It was one of Valentine's many eccentric fancies that she was not meditating only, at such times as these, but that, deaf and dumb as she was with the creatures of this world, she could talk with the angels, and could hear what the heavenly voices said to her in return.

The moment she was touched on the shoulder she looked up, and nestled close to her adopted mother; who, passing one arm round her neck, explained to her, by means of the manual signs of the deaf and dumb alphabet, what Valentine was saying at that moment.

Nothing was more characteristic of Mrs. Blyth's warm sympathies and affectionate consideration for Madonna than this little action. The kindest people rarely think it necessary, however well practiced in communicating by the fingers with the deaf, to keep them informed of any ordinary conversation which may be proceeding in their presence. Wise disquisitions, witty sayings, curious stories, are conveyed to their minds by sympathizing friends and relatives, as a matter of course; but the little chatty nothings of every-day talk, which most pleasantly and constantly employ our speaking and address our hearing faculties, are thought too slight and fugitive in their nature to be worthy of transmission by interpreting fingers or pens, and are consequently seldom or never communicated to the deaf. No deprivation attending their affliction is more severely felt by them than the special deprivation which thus ensues; and which exiles their sympathies, in a great measure, from all share in the familiar social interests of life around them.

Mrs. Blyth's kind heart, quick intelligence, and devoted affection for her adopted child, had long since impressed it on her, as the first of duties and pleasures, to prevent Madonna from feeling the excluding influences of her calamity, while in the society of others, by keeping her well informed of every one of the many conversations, whether jesting or earnest, that were held in her presence, in the invalid-room. For years and years past, Mrs. Blyth's nimble fingers had been accustomed to interpret all that was said by her bedside before the deaf and dumb girl, as they were interpreting for her now.

"Just stop me, Lavvie, if I miss anything out, in making sure that I've got all that's wanted for everybody's drawing lesson," said Valentine, preparing to reckon up the list of his materials correctly, by placing his right forefinger on his left thumb. "First, there's the statue that all my students are to draw from—the 'Dying Gladiator.' Secondly, the drawing-boards and paper. Thirdly, the black and white chalk. Fourthly— where are the port-crayons to hold the chalk? Down in the painting-room, of course. No! no! don't trouble Madonna to fetch them. Tell her to poke the fire instead : I'll be back directly." And Mr. Blyth skipped out of the room as nimbly as if he had been fifteen instead of fifty.

No sooner was Valentine's back turned than Mrs. Blyth's hand was passed under the pretty swan's-down coverlet that lay over her couch, as if in search of something hidden beneath it. In a moment the hand re-appeared, holding a chalk drawing very neatly framed. It was Madonna's copy from the head of the Venus de' Medici—the same copy which Zack had honored with his most superlative exaggeration of praise at his last visit to the studio. She had not since forgotten, or altered her purpose of making him a present of the drawing which he had admired so much. It had been finished with the utmost care and completeness which she could bestow upon it; had been put into a very pretty frame which she had paid for out of her own little savings of pocket-money; and was now hidden under Mrs. Blyth's coverlet, to be drawn forth as a grand surprise for Zack, and for Valentine, too, on that very evening.

After looking once or twice backward and forward between the copyist and the copy, her pale, kind face beaming with the quiet merriment that overspread it, Mrs. Blyth laid down the drawing, and began talking with her fingers to Madonna.

"So you will not even let me tell Valentine who this is a present for?" were the first words which she signed.

The girl was sitting with her back half turned on the drawing; glancing at it quickly from time to time with a strange shyness and indecision, as if the work of her own hands had undergone some transformation which made her doubt whether she was any longer privileged to look at it. She shook her head in reply to the question just put to her, then moved round suddenly on her chair; her fingers playing nervously with the fringes of the coverlet at her side.

"We all like Zack," proceeded Mrs. Blyth, enjoying the amusement which her womanly instincts extracted from Madonna's confusion; "but you must like him very much, love, to take more pains with this particular drawing than with any drawing you ever did before."

This time Madonna neither looked up nor moved an inch in her chair, her fingers working more and more nervously amid the fringe; her treacherous cheeks, neck, and bosom answered for her.

Mrs. Blyth touched her shoulder gayly, and, after placing the drawing again under the coverlet, made her look up, while signing these words:

"I shall give the drawing to Zack very soon after he comes in. It is sure to make him happy for the rest of the evening, and fonder of you than ever."

Madonna's eyes followed Mrs. Blyth's fingers eagerly to the last letter they formed; then rose softly to her face with the same wistful, questioning look which they had assumed before Valentine years and years ago, when he first interfered to protect her in the traveling circus. There was such an irresistible tenderness in the faint smile that wavered about her lips; such a sadness of innocent beauty in her face, now growing a shade paler than it was wont to be, that Mrs. Blyth's expression became serious the instant their eyes met. She drew the girl forward and kissed her. The kiss was returned many times, with a passionate warmth and eagerness remarkably at variance with the usual gentleness of all Madonna's actions. What had changed her thus? Before it was possible to inquire or to think, she had broken away from the kind arms that were round her, and was kneeling with her face hidden in the pillows that lay over the head of the couch.

"I must quiet her directly. I ought to make her feel that this is wrong," said Mrs. Blyth to herself, looking startled and grieved as she withdrew her hand, wet with tears, after trying vainly to raise the girl's face from the pillows.

"She has been thinking too much lately—too much about that drawing; too much, I am afraid, about Zack."

Just at that moment Mr. Blyth opened the door. Feeling the slight shock, as he let it bang to after entering, Madonna instantly started up and ran to the fireplace. Valentine did not notice her when he came in.

He bustled about the neighborhood of the "Dying Gladiator," talking incessantly, arranging his port-crayons by the drawing-boards, and trimming the lamps that lit the model. Mrs. Blyth cast many an anxious look toward the fireplace. After the lapse of a few minutes Madonna turned round and came back to the couch. The traces of tears had almost entirely disappeared from her face. She made a little appealing gesture that asked Mrs. Blyth to be silent about what had happened while they were alone; kissed, as a sign that she wished to be forgiven, the hand that was held out to her; and then sat down quietly again in her accustomed place.

At the same moment a voice was heard talking and laughing boisterously in the hall. Then followed a long whispering, succeeded by a burst of giggling from the housemaid, who presently ascended to Mrs. Blyth's room alone, and entered —after an explosion of suppressed laughter behind the door—holding out at arms-length a pair of boxing-gloves.

"If you please, sir," said the girl, addressing Valentine, and tittering hysterically at every third word, "Master Zack's downstairs on the landing, and he says you're to be so kind as put on these things (he's putting another pair on hisself), and give him the pleasure of your company for a few minutes in the painting-room."

"Come on, Blyth," cried the voice from the stairs. "I told you I should bring the gloves, and make a fighting-man of you, last time I was here, you know. Come on! I only want to open your chest by knocking you about a little in the painting-room before we begin to draw."

The servant still held the gloves away from her at the full stretch of her arm, as if she feared they were yet alive with the pugilistic energies that had been imparted to them by their last wearer. Mrs. Blyth burst out laughing, Valentine followed her example. The housemaid began to look bewildered, and begged to know if her master would be so kind as to take "the things" away from her.

"Did you say, come upstairs?" continued the voice outside. "All right; I have no objection, if Mrs. Blyth hasn't." Here Zack came in with his boxing-gloves fitted on. "How are you, Blyth? These are the pills for that sluggish old liver of yours that you're always complaining of. Put 'em on. Stand with your left leg forward— keep your right leg easily bent—and fix your eye on me!"

"Hold your tongue!" cried Mr. Blyth, at last recovering breath enough to assert his dignity as master of the new drawing-school. "Take off those things directly! What do you mean, sir, by coming into my academy, which is devoted to the peaceful arts, in the attitude of a prize-fighter?"

"Don't lose your temper, my dear fellow," re-joined Zack; "you will never learn to use your fists prettily if you do. Here, Patty, the box-ing-lesson's put off till to-morrow. Take the gloves upstairs into your master's dressing-room and put them in the drawer where his clean shirts are, because they must be kept nice and dry. Shake hands, Mrs. Blyth: it does one good to see you laugh like that, you look so much the better for it. And how is Madonna? I'm afraid she's been sitting before the fire and trying to spoil her pretty complexion. Why, what's the matter with her? Poor little darling, her hands are quite cold!"

"Come to your lesson, sir, directly," said Val-entine, assuming his most despotic voice, and leading the disorderly student by the collar to his appointed place.

"Halloo!" cried Zack, looking at the "Dying Gladiator." "The gentleman in plaster's mak-ing a face—I'm afraid he isn't quite well. I say, Blyth, is that the statue of an ancient Greek patient, suffering under the prescription of an ancient Greek physician?"

"*Will* you hold your tongue, and take up your drawing-board?" cried Mr. Blyth. "You young barbarian, you deserve to be expelled my acad-emy for talking in that way of the 'Dying Glad-iator.' Now then; where's Madonna? No! stop where you are, Zack. I'll show her her place, and give her the drawing-board. Wait a

minute, Lavvie! Let me prop you up comfortably with the pillows before you begin. There!
I never saw a more beautiful effect of light and
shade, my dear, than there is on your view of
the model. Has everybody got a port-crayon
and two bits of chalk? Yes, everybody has.
Order! order! order!" shouted Valentine, suddenly forgetting his assumed dignity in the exultation of the moment. "Mr. Blyth's drawing
academy for the promotion of family Art is
now open, and ready for general inspection.
Hooray!"

"Hooray!" echoed Zack, "hooray for family
Art! I say, Blyth, which chalk do I begin with
—the white or the black? The black—eh? Do
I start with the what's his name's wry face?
and if so, where am I to begin? With his eyes,
or his nose, or his mouth, or the top of his head,
or the bottom of his chin—or what?"

"First sketch in the general form with a light
and flowing stroke, and without attention to details," said Mr. Blyth, illustrating these directions by waving his hand gracefully about his
own person. "Then measure with the eye, assisted occasionally by the port-crayon, the proportion of the parts. Then put dots on the
paper; a dot where his head comes; another dot
where his elbows and knees come, and so forth.
Then strike it all in boldly—it's impossible to
give you better advice than that—strike it in,
Zack; strike it in boldly!"

"Here goes at his head and shoulders to begin
with," said Zack, taking one comprehensive and

confident look at the "Dying Gladiator," and drawing a huge half circle, with a preliminary flourish of his hand on the paper. "Oh, confound it, I've broken the chalk!"

"Of course you have," retorted Valentine. "Take another bit; the Academy grants supplementary chalk to ignorant students, who dig their lines on the paper instead of drawing them. Now, break off a bit of that bread-crumb and rub out what you have done. 'Buy a penny loaf, and rub it all out,' as Mr. Fuseli once said to me in the Schools of the Royal Academy, when I showed him my first drawing, and was excessively conceited about it."

"I remember," said Mrs. Blyth, "when my father was working at his great engraving, from Mr. Scumble's picture of the 'Fair Gleaner Surprised,' that he used often to say how much harder his art was than drawing, because you couldn't rub out a false line on copper, like you could on paper. We all thought he never would get that print done, he used to groan over it so in the front drawing-room, where he was then at work. And the publishers paid him infamously, all in bills, which he had to get discounted; and the people who gave him the money cheated him. My mother said it served him right for being always so imprudent; which I thought very hard on him, and I took his part—so harassed too as he was by the tradespeople at that time."

"I can feel for him, my love," said Valentine, pointing a piece of chalk for Zack. "The tradespeople have harassed *me*—not because I could not pay them, certainly, but because I could not add up their bills. Never owe any man enough, Zack, to give him the chance of punishing you for being in his debt, with a sum to do in simple addition. At the time when I had bills (go on with your drawing; you can listen, and draw, too), I used, of course, to think it necessary to check the tradespeople, and see that their total was right. You will hardly believe me, but I don't remember ever making the sum what the shop made it, on more than about three occasions. And, what was worse, if I tried a second time, I could not even get it to agree with what I had made it myself the first time. Thank Heaven, I've no difficulties of that sort to grapple with now! Everything's paid for the moment it comes in. If the butcher hands a leg of mutton to the cook over the area railings, the cook hands him back six-and-nine—or whatever it is—and takes his bill and receipt. I eat my dinners now with the blessed conviction that they won't all disagree with me, in an arithmetical point of view, at the end of the year. What are you stopping and scratching your head for in that way?"

"It's no use," replied Zack; "I've tried it a dozen times, and I find I can't draw a Gladiator's nose."

"Can't!" cried Mr. Blyth; "what do you mean by applying the word 'can't' to any process of art in *my* presence? There, that's the line of the 'Gladiator's' nose. Go over it yourself

with this fresh piece of chalk. No; wait a minute. Come here first, and see how Madonna is
striking in the figure—the front view of it, remember, which is the most difficult. She hasn't
worked as fast as usual, though. Do you find
your view of the model a little too much for you,
my love?" continued Valentine, transferring the
last words to his fingers, to communicate them
to Madonna.

She shook her head in answer. It was not the
difficulty of drawing from the cast before her,
but the difficulty of drawing at all, which was
retarding her progress. Her thoughts would
wander to the copy of the Venus de' Medici that
was hidden under Mrs. Blyth's coverlet; would
vibrate between trembling eagerness to see it
presented without longer delay, and groundless
apprehension that Zack might, after all, not remember it, or not care to have it when it was
given to him. And as her thoughts wandered,
so her eyes followed them. Now she stole an
anxious, inquiring look at Mrs. Blyth, to see if
her hand was straying toward the hidden drawing. Now she glanced shyly at Zack—only by
moments at a time, and only when he was hardest at work with his port-crayon—to assure herself that he was always in the same good-humor,
and likely to receive her little present kindly,
and with some appearance of being pleased to
see what pains she had taken with it. In this
way her attention wandered incessantly from
her employment; and thus it was that she made
so much less progress than usual, and caused

Mr. Blyth to suspect that the task he had set her was almost beyond her abilities.

"Splendid beginning, isn't it?" said Zack, looking over her drawing. "I defy the whole Royal Academy to equal it," continued the young gentleman, scrawling this uncompromising expression of opinion on the blank space at the bottom of Madonna's drawing, and signing his name with a magnificent flourish at the end.

His arm touched her shoulder while he wrote. She colored a little, and glanced at him, playfully affecting to look very proud of his sentence of approval—then hurriedly resumed her drawing as their eyes met. He was sent back to his place by Valentine before he could write anything more. She took some of the bread-crumbs near her to rub out what he had written—hesitated as her hand approached the lines—colored more deeply than before, and went on with her drawing, leaving the letters beneath it to remain just as young Thorpe had traced them.

"I shall never be able to draw as well as she does," said Zack, looking at the little he had done with a groan of despair. "The fact is, I don't think drawing's my forte. It's color, depend upon it. Only wait till I come to that, and see how I'll lay on the paint! Didn't you find drawing infernally difficult, Blyth, when you first began?"

"I find it difficult still, Master Zack," replied Mr. Blyth. "Art wouldn't be the glorious thing it is, if it wasn't all difficulty from beginning to end; if it didn't force out all the fine points in a man's character as soon as he takes to it. Just eight o'clock," continued Valentine, looking at his watch. "Put down your drawing-boards for the present. I pronounce the sitting of this Academy to be suspended till after tea."

"Valentine, dear," said Mrs. Blyth, smiling mysteriously, as she slipped her hand under the coverlet of the couch, "I can't get Madonna to look at me, and I want her here. Will you oblige me by bringing her to my bedside?"

"Certainly, my love," returned Mr. Blyth, obeying the request. "You have a double claim on my services to-night, for you have shown yourself the most promising of my pupils. Come here, Zack, and see what Mrs. Blyth has done. The best drawing of the evening—just what I thought it would be—the best drawing of the evening!"

Zack, who had been yawning disconsolately over his own copy, with his fists stuck into his cheeks, and his elbows on his knees, bustled up to the couch directly. As he approached, Madonna tried to get back to her former position at the fireplace, but was prevented by Mrs. Blyth, who kept tight hold of her hand. Just then, Zack fixed his eyes on her and increased her confusion.

"She looks prettier than ever to-night, don't she, Mrs. Blyth?" he said, sitting down and yawning again. "I always like her best when her eyes brighten up and look twenty different ways in a minute, just as they're doing now. She may not be so like Raphael's pictures at such times, I dare say (here he yawned once more); but for my part—What's she wanting to get away for? And what are you laughing about, Mrs. Blyth? I say, Valentine, there's some joke going on here between the ladies!"

"Do you remember this, Zack?" asked Mrs. Blyth, tightening her hold of Madonna with one hand, and producing the framed drawing of the Venus de' Medici with the other.

"Madonna's copy from my bust of the Venus!" cried Valentine, interposing with his usual readiness, and skipping forward with his accustomed alacrity.

"Madonna's copy from Blyth's bust of the Venus," echoed Zack, coolly; his slippery memory not having preserved the slightest recollection of the drawing at first sight of it.

"Dear me! how nicely it's framed, and how beautifully she has finished it!" pursued Valentine, gently patting Madonna's shoulder, in token of his high approval and admiration.

"Very nicely framed, and beautifully finished, as you say, Blyth," glibly repeated Zack, rising from his chair, and looking rather perplexed, as he noticed the expression with which Mrs. Blyth was regarding him.

"But who got it framed?" asked Valentine. "She would never have any of her drawings framed before. I don't understand what it all means."

"No more do I," said Zack, dropping back into his chair in lazy astonishment. "Is it some riddle, Mrs. Blyth? Something about why is Madonna like the Venus de' Medici, eh? If it is, I object to the riddle, because she's a deal prettier than any plaster face that ever was made. Your face beats Venus's hollow," continued Zack, communicating this bluntly sincere compliment to Madonna by the signs of the deaf and dumb alphabet.

She smiled as she watched the motion of his fingers—perhaps at his mistakes, for he made two in expressing one short sentence of five words—perhaps at the compliment, homely as it was.

"Oh, you men, how dreadfully stupid you are sometimes!" exclaimed Mrs. Blyth. "Why, Valentine, dear, it's the easiest thing in the world to guess what she has had the drawing framed for. To make it a present to somebody, of course! And who does she mean to give it to?"

"Ah! who indeed?" interrupted Zack, sliding down cozily in his chair, resting his head on the back rail, and spreading his legs out before him at full stretch.

"I have a great mind to throw the drawing at your head, instead of giving it to you!" cried Mrs. Blyth, losing all patience.

"You don't mean to say the drawing's a present to *me!*" exclaimed Zack, starting from his chair with one prodigious jump of astonishment.

"You deserve to have your ears well boxed for not having guessed that it was long ago!" retorted Mrs. Blyth. "Have you forgotten how you praised that very drawing when you saw it begun in the studio? Didn't you tell Madonna—"

"Oh! the dear, good, generous, jolly little soul!" cried Zack, snatching up the drawing from the couch, as the truth burst upon him at last in a flash of conviction. "Tell her on *your* fingers, Mrs. Blyth, how proud I am of my present. I can't do it with mine, because I can't let go of the drawing. Here, look here!—make her look here, and see how I like it!" And Zack hugged the copy of the Venus de' Medici to his waistcoat, by way of showing how highly he prized it.

At this outburst of sentimental pantomime, Madonna raised her head and glanced at young Thorpe. Her face, downcast, anxious, and averted even from Mrs. Blyth's eyes during the last few minutes (as if she had guessed every word that could pain her, out of all that had been said in her presence), now brightened again with pleasure as she looked up—with innocent, childish pleasure, that affected no reserve, dreaded no misconstruction, foreboded no disappointment. Her eyes, turning quickly from Zack, and appealing gayly to Valentine, beamed with triumph when he pointed to the drawing, and smilingly raised his hands in astonishment, as a sign that he had been pleasantly surprised by the presentation of her drawing to his new pupil. Mrs. Blyth felt the hand which she still held in hers, and which had hitherto trembled a little from time to time, grow steady and warm in her grasp, and dropped it. There was no fear that Madonna would now leave the side of the couch and steal away by herself to the fireplace.

"Go on, Mrs. Blyth—you never make mistakes in talking on your fingers, and I always do—go on, please, and tell her how much I thank her," continued Zack, holding out the drawing at arms-length, and looking at it with his head on one side, by way of imitating Valentine's manner of studying his own pictures. "Tell her I'll take such care of it as I never took of anything before in my life. Tell her I'll hang it up in my bedroom, where I can see it every morning as soon as I wake. Have you told her that?—or shall I write it on her slate? Halloo! here comes the tea. And, by heavens, a whole bagful of muffins! What!!! the kitchen fire's too black to toast them. *I'll* undertake the whole lot in the drawing academy. Here, Patty, give us the toasting-fork: I'm going to begin. I never saw such a splendid fire for toasting muffins before in my life! Rum-dum-diddy-iddy-dum-dee, dum-diddy-iddy-dum!" And Zack fell on his knees at the fireplace, humming "Rule Britannia," and toasting his first muffin in triumph; utterly forgetting that he had left Madonna's drawing lying neglected, with its face downward, on the end of Mrs. Blyth's couch.

Valentine, who in the innocence of his heart suspected nothing, burst out laughing at this new specimen of Zack's inveterate flightiness. His kind instincts, however, guided his hand at the same moment to the drawing. He took it up carefully, and placed it on a low book-case at the opposite side of the room. If any increase had been possible in his wife's affection for him, she would have loved him better than ever at the moment when he performed that one little action.

As her husband removed the drawing, Mrs. Blyth looked at Madonna. The poor girl stood shrinking close to the couch, with her hands clasped tightly together in front of her, and with no trace of their natural lovely color left on her cheeks. Her eyes followed Valentine listlessly to the book-case, then turned toward Zack, not reproachfully nor angrily—not even tearfully—but again with that same look of patient sadness, of gentle resignation to sorrow, which used to mark their expression so tenderly in the days of her bondage among the mountebanks of the traveling circus. So she stood, looking toward the fireplace and the figure kneeling at it, bearing her new disappointment just as she had borne many a former mortification that had tried her sorely while she was yet a little child. How carefully she had labored at that neglected drawing in the secrecy of her own room! How happy she had been in anticipating the moment when it would be given to young Thorpe; in imagining what he would say on receiving it, and how he would communicate his thanks to her; in wondering what he would do with it when he got it: where he would hang it, and whether he would often look at his present after he had got used to seeing it on the wall! Thoughts such as these had made the moment of presenting that drawing the moment of a great event in her life—and there it was now, placed on one side by other hands than the hands into which it had been given; laid down carelessly at the mere entrance of a servant with a tea-tray; neglected for the childish pleasure of kneeling on the hearth-rug and toasting a muffin at a clear coal-fire!

Mrs. Blyth's generous, impulsive nature, and sensitively-tempered affection for her adopted child, impelled her to take instant and not very merciful notice of Zack's unpardonable thoughtlessness. Her face flushed, her dark eyes sparkled, as she turned quickly on her couch toward the fireplace. But, before she could utter a word, Madonna's hand was on her lips, and Madonna's eyes were fixed with a terrified, imploring expression on her face. The next instant the girl's trembling fingers rapidly signed these words:

"Pray—pray don't say anything! I would not have you speak to him just now for the world!"

Mrs. Blyth hesitated, and looked toward her husband; but he was away at the other end of the room, amusing himself professionally by casting the drapery of the window-curtains hither and thither into all sorts of picturesque folds. She looked next at Zack. Just at that moment he was turning his muffin and singing louder than ever. The temptation to startle him out of his provoking gayety by a good sharp reproof was almost too strong to be resisted; but

Mrs. Blyth forced herself to resist it, nevertheless, for Madonna's sake. She did not, however, communicate with the girl, either by signs or writing, until she had settled herself again in her former position; then her fingers expressed these sentences of reply:

"If you promise not to let his thoughtlessness distress you, my love, I promise not to speak to him about it. Do you agree to that bargain? If you do, give me a kiss."

Madonna only paused to repress a sigh that was just stealing from her, before she gave the required pledge. Her cheeks did not recover their color, nor her lips the smile that had been playing on them earlier in the evening; but she arranged Mrs. Blyth's pillow even more carefully than usual, before she left the couch, and went away to perform, as neatly and prettily as ever, her own little household duty of making the tea.

Zack, entirely unconscious of having given pain to one lady and cause of anger to another, had got on to his second muffin, and had changed his accompanying song from "Rule Britannia" to the "Lass o' Gowrie," when the hollow, ringing sound of rapidly-running wheels penetrated into the room from the frosty road outside; advancing nearer and nearer, and then suddenly ceasing opposite Mr. Blyth's own door.

"Dear me!—surely that's at our gate," exclaimed Valentine; "who can be coming to see us so late, on such a cold night as this? And in a carriage, too!"

"It's a cab, by the rattling of the wheels, and

it brings us the 'Lass o' Gowrie,'" sang Zack, combining the original text of his song, and the suggestion of a possible visitor, in his concluding words.

"Do leave off singing nonsense out of tune, and let us listen when the door opens," said Mrs. Blyth, glad to seize the slightest opportunity of administering the smallest reproof to Zack.

"Suppose it should be Mr. Gimble, come to deal at last for that picture of mine that he has talked of buying so long," exclaimed Valentine.

"Suppose it should be my father!" exclaimed Zack, suddenly turning round on his knees, with a very blank face. "Or that infernal old Yollop, with his gooseberry eyes and his hands full of tracts. They're both of them quite equal to coming after me and spoiling my pleasure here, just as they spoil it everywhere else."

"Hush!" said Mrs. Blyth. "The visitor has come in, whoever it is. It can't be Mr. Gimble, Valentine; he always runs up two stairs at a time."

"And this is one of the heavy-weights. Not an ounce less than sixteen stone, I should say, by the step," remarked Zack, letting his muffin burn while he listened.

"It can't be that tiresome old Lady Brambledown come to worry you again about altering her picture," said Mrs. Blyth.

"Stop! surely it isn't—" began Valentine. But before he could say another word, the door opened, and, to the utter amazement of every-

body but the poor girl whose ear no voice could
reach, the servant announced:

"MRS. PECKOVER."

CHAPTER XI.

THE BREWING OF THE STORM.

TIME had lavishly added to Mrs. Peckover's
size, but had generously taken little or nothing
from her in exchange. Her hair had certainly
turned gray since the period when Valentine first
met her at the circus; but the good-humored face
beneath was just as hearty to look at now as ever
it had been in former days. Her cheeks had
ruddily expanded; her chin had passed from the
double to the triple stage of jovial development
—any faint traces of a waist which she might
formerly have possessed, were utterly obliterated
—but it was pleasantly evident, to judge only
from the manner of her bustling entry into Mrs.
Blyth's room, that her active disposition had lost
nothing of its early energy, and could still gayly
defy all corporeal obstructions to the very last.

Nodding and smiling at Mr. and Mrs. Blyth,
and Zack, till her vast country bonnet trembled
aguishly on her head, the good woman advanced,
shaking every movable object in the room,
straight to the tea-table, and enfolded Madonna
in her capacious arms. The girl's light figure
seemed to disappear in a smothering circum-
ambient mass of bonnet ribbons and unintelligi-

ble drapery, as Mrs. Peckover saluted her with a rattling fire of kisses, the report of which was audible above the voluble talking of Mr. Blyth and the boisterous laughter of Zack.

"I'll tell you all about how I came here directly, sir; only I couldn't help saying how-d'ye-do in the old way to little Mary to begin with," said Mrs. Peckover, apologetically. It had been found impossible to prevail on her to change the familiar name of "little Mary," which she had pronounced so often and so fondly in past years, for the name which had superceded it in Valentine's house. The truth was, that this worthy creature knew nothing whatever about Raphael; and, considering "Madonna" to be an outlandish foreign word intimately connected with Guy Fawkes and the Gunpowder Plot, firmly believed that no respectable Englishwoman ought to compromise her character by attempting to pronounce it.

"I'll tell you, sir—I'll tell you directly why I've come to London," repeated Mrs. Peckover, backing majestically from the tea-table, and rolling round easily on her own axis in the direction of the couch, to ask for the fullest particulars of the state of Mrs. Blyth's health.

"Much better, my good friend—much better," was the cheerful answer; "but do tell us (we are so glad to see you!) how you came to surprise us all in this way."

"Well, ma'am," began Mrs. Peckover, "it's almost as great a surprise to me to be in London, as it is— Be quiet, young Good-for-nothing; I won't even shake hands with you, if you don't behave yourself!" these last words she addressed to Zack, whose favorite joke it had always been, from the day of their first acquaintance at Valentine's house, to pretend to be violently in love with her. He was now standing with his arms wide open, the toasting-fork in one hand and the muffin he had burned in the other, trying to look languishing, and entreating Mrs. Peckover to give him a kiss.

"When you know how to toast a muffin properly, p'raps I may give you one," said she, chuckling as triumphantly over her own small retort as if she had been a professed wit. "Do, Mr. Blyth, sir, please to keep him quiet, or I shan't be able to get on with a single word of what I've got to say. Well, you see, ma'am, Doctor Joyce—"

"How is he?" interrupted Valentine, handing Mrs. Peckover a cup of tea.

"He's the best gentleman in the world, sir, but he *will* have his glass of port after dinner; and the end of it is, he's laid up again with the gout."

"And Mrs. Joyce?"

"Laid up too, sir—it's a dreadful sick house at the Rectory—laid up with the inferlenzer."

"Have any of the children caught the influenza, too?" asked Mrs. Blyth. "I hope not."

"No, ma'am, they're all nicely, except the youngest; and it's on account of her—don't you remember her, sir, growing so fast, when you was last at the Rectory?—that I'm up in London."

"Is the child ill?" asked Valentine, anxiously. "She's such a picturesque little creature, Lavvie! I long to paint her."

"I'm afraid, sir, she's not fit to be put into a picter now," said Mrs. Peckover. "Mrs. Joyce is in sad trouble about her, because of one of her shoulders which has growed out somehow. The doctor at Rubbleford don't doubt but what it may be got right again; but he said she ought to be shown to some great London doctor as soon as possible. So, neither her papa nor her mamma being able to take her up to her aunt's house, they trusted her to me. As you know, sir, ever since Doctor Joyce got my husband that situation at Rubbleford, I've been about the Rectory, helping with the children and the housekeeping, and all that: and Miss Lucy being used to me, we come along together in the railroad quite pleasant and comfortable. I was glad enough, you may be sure, of the chance of getting here, after not having seen little Mary for so long. So I just left Miss Lucy at her aunt's, where they were very kind, and wanted me to stop all night. But I told them that, thanks to your goodness, I always had a bed here when I was in London; and I took the cab on, after seeing the little girl safe and comfortable upstairs. That's the whole story of how I come to surprise you in this way, ma'am—and now I'll finish my tea."

Having got to the bottom of her cup, and to the end of a muffin amorously presented to her by the incorrigible Zack, Mrs. Peckover had leisure to turn again to Madonna; who, having relieved her of her bonnet and shawl, was now sitting close at her side.

"I didn't think she was looking quite so well as usual, when I first come in," said Mrs. Peckover, patting the girl's cheek with her chubby fingers; "but she seems to have brightened up again now." (This was true: the sad stillness had left Madonna's face, at sight of the friend and mother of her early days.) "Perhaps she's been sticking a little too close to her drawing lately—"

"By-the-by, talking of drawings, what's become of *my* drawing?" cried Zack, suddenly recalled for the first time to the remembrance of Madonna's gift.

"Dear me!" pursued Mrs. Peckover, looking toward the three drawing-boards, which had been placed together round the pedestal of the cast; "are all those little Mary's doings? She's cleverer at it, I suppose, by this time, than ever. Ah, Lord! what an old woman I feel, when I think of the many years ago—"

"Come and look at what she has done to-night," interrupted Valentine, taking Mrs. Peckover by the arm, and pressing it very significantly as he glanced at the part of the table where young Thorpe was sitting.

"My drawing — where's my drawing?" repeated Zack. "Who put it away when tea came in? Oh, there it is, all safe on the bookcase."

"I congratulate you, sir, on having succeeded at last in remembering that there *is* such a thing in the world as Madonna's present," said Mrs. Blyth, sarcastically.

Zack looked up bewildered from his tea, and asked directly what those words meant.

"Oh, never mind," said Mrs. Blyth, in the same tone, "they're not worth explaining. Did you ever hear of a young gentleman who thought more of a plate of muffins than of a lady's gift? I dare say not! *I* never did. It's too ridiculously improbable to be true, isn't it? There! don't speak to me; I've got a book here that I want to finish. No, it's no use; I shan't say another word."

"What have I done that's wrong?" asked Zack, looking piteously perplexed as he began to suspect that he had committed some unpardonable mistake earlier in the evening. "I know I burned a muffin; but what has that got to do with Madonna's present to me?" (Mrs. Blyth shook her head, and, opening her book, became quite absorbed over it in a moment.) "Didn't I thank her properly for it? I'm sure I meant to." (Here he stopped; but Mrs. Blyth took no notice of him.) "I suppose I've got myself into some scrape? Make as much fun as you like about it; but tell me what it is. You won't? Then I'll find out all about it from Madonna. She knows, of course; and she'll tell me. Look here, Mrs. Blyth; I'm not going to get up till she's told me everything." And Zack, with a comic gesture of entreaty, dropped on his knees by Madonna's chair, preventing her from leaving it, which she tried to do, by taking immediate possession of the slate that hung at her side.

While young Thorpe was scribbling questions, protestations and extravagances of every kind, in rapid succession, on the slate; and while Madonna, her face half smiling, half tearful, as she felt that he was looking up at it, was reading what he wrote, trying hard, at first, not to believe in him too easily when he scribbled an explanation, and not to look down on him too leniently when he followed it up by an entreaty; and ending at last, in defiance of Mrs. Blyth's private signs to the contrary, in forgiving his carelessness, and letting him take her hand again as usual, in token that she was sincere—while this little scene of the home drama was proceeding at one end of the room, a scene of another kind—a dialogue in mysterious whispers—was in full progress between Mr. Blyth and his visitor from the country, at the other.

Time had in no respect lessened Valentine's morbid anxiety about the strict concealment of every circumstance attending Mrs. Peckover's first connection with Madonna and Madonna's mother. The years that had now passed and left him in undisputed possession of his adopted child had not diminished that excess of caution in keeping secret all the little that was known of her early history, which had even impelled him to pledge Doctor and Mrs. Joyce never to mention in public any particulars of the narrative related at the Rectory. Still, he had not got over his first dread that she might one day be traced, claimed, and taken away from him, if that narrative, meager as it was, should ever be trusted to other ears than those which had originally listened to it. Still, he kept the hair bracelet and the handkerchief that had belonged to her mother carefully locked up out of sight in his bureau; and still, he doubted Mrs. Peckover's discretion in the government of her tongue, as he had doubted it in the by-gone days when the little girl was first established in his own home.

After making a pretense of showing her the drawings begun that evening, Mr. Blyth artfully contrived to lead Mrs. Peckover past them into a recess at the extreme end of the room.

"Well," he said, speaking in an unnecessarily soft whisper, considering the distance which now separated him from Zack—"well, I suppose you're quite sure of not having let out anything by chance, since I last saw you, about how you first met with our darling girl? or about her poor mother? or—?"

"What, you're at it again, sir," interrupted Mrs. Peckover, loftily, but dropping her voice in imitation of Mr. Blyth—"a clever man, too, like you! Dear, dear me! how often must I keep on telling you that I'm old enough to be able to hold my tongue? How much longer are you to worrit yourself about hiding what nobody's seeking after?"

"I'm afraid I shall always worry myself about it," replied Valentine, seriously. "Whenever I see you, my good friend, I fancy I hear all that melancholy story over again about our darling child, and that poor lost forsaken mother of hers, whose name even we don't know. I feel, too, when you come and see us, almost more than at other times, how inexpressibly precious the daughter whom you have given to us is to Lavvie and me; and I think with more dread than I well know how to describe, of the horrible chance, if anything was incautiously said, and carried from mouth to mouth—about where you met with her mother, for instance, or what time of the year it was, and so forth—that it might lead, nobody knows how, to some claim being laid to her, by somebody who might be able to prove the right to make it."

"Lord, sir! after all these years, what earthly need have you to be anxious about such things as that?"

"I'm never anxious long, Mrs. Peckover. My good spirits always get the better of every anxiety, great and small. But while I don't know that relations of hers—perhaps her vile father himself—may not be still alive, and seeking for her—"

"Bless your heart, Mr. Blyth, none of her relations are alive; or if they are, none of them care about her, poor lamb; I'll answer for it."

"I hope in God you are right," said Valentine, earnestly. "But let us think no more about it now," he added, resuming his usual manner. "I have asked my regular question, that I can't help asking whenever I see you; and you have forgiven me, as usual, for putting it; and now I

am quite satisfied. Take my arm, Mrs. Peckover: I mean to give the students of my new
drawing academy a holiday for the rest of the
night, in honor of your arrival. What do you
say to devoting the evening in the old way to a
game at cards?"

"Just what I was thinking I should like myself, as long as it's only sixpence a game, sir,"
said Mrs. Peckover, gayly. "I say, young gentleman," she continued, addressing Zack, after
Mr. Blyth had left her to look for the cards,
"what nonsense are you writing on our darling's
slate that puts her all in a flutter, and makes her
blush up to the eyes, when she's only looking at
her poor old Peck? Bless her heart! she's just
as easily amused now as when she was a child.
Give us another kiss, my own little love. You
understand what I mean, don't you, though you
can't hear me? Ah, dear, dear! when she stands
and looks at me with her eyes like that, she's the
living image of—"

"Cribbage," cried Mr. Blyth, knocking a tri-
angular board for three players on the table, and
regarding Mrs. Peckover with the most reproach-
ful expression that his features could assume.

She felt that the look had been deserved, and
approached the card-table rather confusedly,
without uttering another word. But for Valentine's second interruption she would have declared, before young Thorpe, that "little Mary"
was the living image of her mother.

"Madonna's going to play, as usual. Will
you make the third, Lavvie?" inquired Valen-

tine, shuffling the cards. "It's no use asking
Zack; he can't even count yet."

"No, thank you, dear. I shall have quite
enough to do in going on with my book, and
trying to keep Master Madcap in order while
you play," replied Mrs. Blyth.

The game began. It was a regular custom,
whenever Mrs. Peckover came to Mr. Blyth's
house, that cribbage should be played, and that
Madonna should take a share in it. This was
done, on her part, principally in affectionate remembrance of the old times when she lived under
the care of the clown's wife, and when she had
learned cribbage from Mr. Peckover to amuse
her, while the frightful accident which had befallen her in the circus was still a recent event.
It was characteristic of the happy peculiarity of
her disposition that the days of suffering and
affliction, and the after-period of hard tasks in
public, with which cards were connected in her
case, never seemed to recur to her remembrance
painfully when she saw them in later life. The
pleasanter associations which belonged to them,
and which reminded her of homely kindness that
had soothed her in pain, and self-denying affection that had consoled her in sorrow, were the
associations instinctively dwelt on by her heart
to the exclusion of all others.

To Mrs. Blyth's great astonishment, Zack, for
full ten minutes, required no keeping in order
whatever while the rest were playing at cards.
It was the most marvelous of human phenomena,
but there he certainly was, standing quietly by

the fireplace with the drawing in his hand, actually thinking! Mrs. Blyth's amazement at this unexampled change in his manner so completely overcame her, that she fairly laid down her book to look at him. He noticed the action, and approached the couch directly.

"That's right," he said; "don't read any more. I want to have a serious consultation with you."

First, a visit from Mrs. Peckover, then a serious consultation with Zack. This is a night of wonders! thought Mrs. Blyth.

"I've made it all right with Madonna," Zack continued. "She don't think a bit the worse of me because I went on like a fool about the muffins at tea-time. But that's not what I want to talk about now: it's a sort of secret. In the first place—"

"Do you usually mention your secrets in a voice that everybody can hear?" asked Mrs. Blyth, laughing.

"Oh, never mind about that," he replied, not lowering his tone in the least; "it's only a secret from Madonna, and we can talk before *her*, poor little soul, just as if she wasn't in the room. Now this is the thing: she's made me a present, and I think I ought to show my gratitude by making her another in return." (He resumed his ordinary manner as he warmed with the subject, and began to walk up and down the room in his usual flighty way.) "Well, I have been thinking what the present ought to be—something pretty, of course. I can't do her a drawing worth a farthing; and even if I could—"

"Suppose you come here and sit down, Zack," interposed Mrs. Blyth. "While you are wandering backward and forward in that way before the card-table, you take Madonna's attention off the game."

No doubt he did. How could she see him walking about close by her, and carrying her drawing with him wherever he went—as if he prized it too much to be willing to put it down—without feeling gratified in more than one of the innocent little vanities of her sex, without looking after him much too often to be properly alive to the interests of her game?

Zack took Mrs. Blyth's advice, and sat down by her, with his back toward the cribbage players.

"Well, the question is, What present am I to give her?" he went on. "I've been twisting and turning it over in my mind, and the long and the short of it is—"

("Fifteen two, fifteen four, and a pair's six," said Valentine, reckoning up the tricks he had in his hand at that moment.)

"Did you ever notice that she has a particularly pretty hand and arm?" proceeded Zack, somewhat evasively. "I'm rather a judge of these things myself; and of all the other girls I ever saw—"

"Never mind about other girls," said Mrs. Blyth. "Tell me what you mean to give Madonna."

("Two for his heels," cried Mrs. Peckover, turning up a knave with great glee.)

"I mean to give her a bracelet," said Zack.

Valentine looked up quickly from the card-table.

("Play, please, sir," said Mrs. Peckover; "little Mary's waiting for you.")

"Well, Zack," rejoined Mrs. Blyth, "your idea of returning a present only errs on the side of generosity. I should recommend something less costly. Don't you know that it's one of Madonna's oddities not to care about jewelry? She might have bought herself a bracelet long ago, out of her own savings, if trinkets had been things to tempt her."

"Wait a bit, Mrs. Blyth," said Zack, "you haven't heard the best of my notion yet: all the pith and marrow of it has got to come. The bracelet I mean to give her is one that she will prize to the day of her death, or she's not the affectionate, warm-hearted girl I take her for. What do you think of a bracelet that reminds her of you and Valentine, and jolly old Peck there—and a little of me, too, which I hope won't make her think the worse of it. I've got a design against all your heads," he continued, imitating the cutting action of a pair of scissors with two of his fingers, and raising his voice in high triumph. "It's a splendid idea: I mean to give Madonna a hair bracelet!"

Mrs. Peckover and Mr. Blyth started back in their chairs, and stared at each other as amazedly as if Zack's last words had sprung from a charged battery, and had struck them both at the same moment with a smart electrical shock.

"Of all the things in the world, how came he ever to think of giving her that!" ejaculated Mrs. Peckover under her breath; her memory reverting, while she spoke, to the mournful day when strangers had searched the body of Madonna's mother, and had found the hair bracelet hidden away in a corner of the dead woman's pocket.

"Hush! let's go on with the game," said Valentine. He, too, was thinking of the hair bracelet—thinking of it as it now lay locked up in his bureau downstairs, remembering how he would fain have destroyed it years ago, but that his conscience and sense of honor forbade him; pondering on the fatal discoveries to which, by bare possibility, it might yet lead, if ever it should fall into strangers' hands.

"A hair bracelet," continued Zack, quite unconscious of the effect he was producing on two of the card-players behind him; "and *such* hair, too, as I mean it to be made of! Why, Madonna will think it more precious than all the diamonds in the world. I defy anybody to have hit on a better idea of the sort of present she's sure to like; it's elegant and appropriate, and all that sort of thing—isn't it?"

"Oh, yes! very nice and pretty indeed," replied Mrs. Blyth, rather absently and confusedly. She knew as much of Madonna's history as her husband did; and was wondering what he would think of the present which young Thorpe proposed giving to their adopted child.

"The thing I want most to know," said Zack,

"is what you think would be the best pattern for the bracelet. There will be two kinds of hair in it, which can be made into any shape, of course —your hair and Mrs. Peckover's."

("Not a morsel of my hair shall go toward the bracelet!" muttered Mrs. Peckover, who was listening to what was said, while she went on playing.)

"The difficult hair to bring in will be mine and Valentine's," pursued Zack. "Mine's long enough, to be sure; I ought to have got it cut a month ago; but it's so stiff and curly; and Blyth keeps his cropped so short—I don't see what they can do with it (do you?), unless they make rings, or stars, or knobs, or something stumpy, in the way of a cross-pattern of it."

"The people at the shop will know best," said Mrs. Blyth, resolving to proceed cautiously.

"One thing I'm determined on, though, beforehand," cried Zack; "the clasp shall be a serpent, with turquoise eyes and a carbuncle tail, and all our initials scored up somehow on his scales. Won't that be splendid? I should like to surprise Madonna with it this very evening."

("You shall never give it to her, if _I_ can help it," grumbled Mrs. Peckover, still soliloquizing under her breath. "If anything in this world can bring her ill luck, it will be a hair bracelet!")

These last words were spoken with perfect seriousness; for they were the result of the strongest superstitious conviction.

From the time when the hair bracelet was found

on Madonna's mother, Mrs. Peckover had persuaded herself—not unnaturally, in the absence
of any information to the contrary—that it had
been in some way connected with the ruin and
shame which had driven its unhappy possessor
forth as an outcast, to die among strangers.   To
believe, in consequence, that a hair bracelet had
brought "ill luck" to the mother, and to derive
from that belief the conviction that a hair bracelet would, therefore, also bring "ill luck" to the
child, was a perfectly direct and inevitable de-
ductive process to Mrs. Peckover's superstitious
mind.   The motives which had formerly influenced her to forbid her "little Mary" ever to begin anything important on a Friday, or ever to
imperil her prosperity by walking under a ladder, were precisely the motives by which she was
now actuated in determining to prevent the
presentation of young Thorpe's ill-omened gift.

Although Valentine had only caught a word
here and there, to guide him to the subject of
Mrs. Peckover's mutterings to herself while the
game was going on, he guessed easily enough
the general tenor of her thoughts, and suspected
that she would, ere long, begin to talk louder
than was at all desirable, if Zack proceeded
much further with his present topic of conversation.   Accordingly, he took advantage of a
pause in the game, and of a relapse into another
restless fit of walking about the room on young
Thorpe's part, to approach his wife's couch, as if
he wanted to find something lying near it, and
to whisper to her, "Stop his talking any more

about that present to Madonna; I'll tell you why another time."

Mrs. Blyth very readily and easily complied with this injunction by telling Zack (with perfect truth) that she had been already a little too much excited by the events of the evening; and that she must put off all further listening or talking, on her part, till the next night, when she promised to advise him about the bracelet to the best of her power. He was, however, still too full of his subject to relinquish it easily under no stronger influence than the influence of a polite hint. Having lost one listener in Mrs. Blyth, he boldly tried the experiment of inviting two others to replace her, by addressing himself to the players at the card-table.

"I dare say you have heard what I have been talking about to Mrs. Blyth?" he began.

"Lord, Master Zack!" said Mrs. Peckover, "do you think we haven't had something else to do here besides listening to you? There, now, don't talk to us, please, till we are done, or you'll throw us out altogether. Don't, sir, on any account, because we are playing for money —sixpence a game."

Repelled on both sides, Zack was obliged to give way. He walked off to try and amuse himself at the bookcase. Mrs. Peckover, with a very triumphant air, nodded and winked several times at Valentine across the table; desiring, by these signs, to show him that she could not only be silent herself when the conversation was in danger of approaching a forbidden subject, but

could make other people hold their tongues
too.

The room was now perfectly quiet, and the
game at cribbage proceeded smoothly enough,
but not so pleasantly as usual on other occasions. Valentine did not regain his customary
good spirits; and Mrs. Peckover relapsed into
whispering discontentedly to herself—now and
then looking toward the bookcase, where young
Thorpe was sitting sleepily, with a volume of
engravings on his knee. It was, more or less, a
relief to everybody when the supper tray came
up, and the cards were put away for the night.

Zack, becoming quite lively again at the prospect of a little eating and drinking, tried to return to the dangerous subject of the hair bracelet; addressing himself, on this occasion, directly
to Valentine. He was interrupted, however,
before he had spoken three words. Mr. Blyth
suddenly remembered that he had an important
communication of his own to make to young
Thorpe.

"Excuse me, Zack," he said, "I have some
news to tell you, which Mrs. Peckover's arrival
drove out of my head; and which I must mention at once, while I have the opportunity. Both
my pictures are done—what do you think of
that?—done, and in their frames. I settled the
titles yesterday. The classical landscape is to be
called 'The Golden Age,' which is a pretty poetical sort of name; and the figure-subject is to be
'Columbus in Sight of the New World'; which
is, I think, simple, affecting, and grand. Wait

a minute! the best of it has yet to come. I am going to exhibit both the pictures in the studio to my friends, and my friends' friends, as early as Saturday next.''

"You don't mean it!" exclaimed Zack. "Why it's only January now; and you always used to have your private view of your own pictures in April, just before they were sent into the Academy Exhibition.''

"Quite right," interposed Valentine, "but I am going to make a change this year. The fact is, I have got a job to do in the provinces, which will prevent me from having my picture-show at the usual time. So I mean to have it now. The cards of invitation are coming home from the printer's to-morrow morning. I shall reserve a pack, of course, for you and your friends, when we see you to-morrow night.''

Just as Mr. Blyth spoke those words, the clock on the mantel-piece struck the half hour after ten. Having his own private reasons for continuing to preserve the appearance of perfect obedience to his father's domestic regulations, Zack rose at once to say good-night, in order to insure being home before the house door was bolted at eleven o'clock. This time he did not forget Madonna's drawing; but, on the contrary, showed such unusual carefulness in tying his pocket-handkerchief over the frame to preserve it from injury as he carried it through the streets, that she could not help—in the fearless innocence of her heart—unreservedly betraying to him, both by look and manner, how warmly she ap-

preciated his anxiety for the safe preservation
of her gift.   Never had the bright, kind young
face been lovelier in its artless happiness than it
appeared at the moment when she was shaking
hands with Zack.

Just as Valentine was about to follow his
guest out of the room, Mrs. Blyth called him
back, reminding him that he had a cold, and
begging him not to expose himself to the wintry
night air by going down to the door.

"But the servants must be going to bed by
this time; and somebody ought to fasten the
bolts," remonstrated Mr. Blyth.

"I'll go, sir," said Mrs. Peckover, rising with
extraordinary alacrity.   "I'll see Master Zack
out, and do up the door.   Bless your heart! it's
no trouble to me.   I'm always moving about at
home from morning to night, to prevent myself
getting fatter.   Don't say no, Mr. Blyth, unless
you are afraid of trusting an old gossip like me
alone with your visitors."

The last words were intended as a sarcasm,
and were whispered into Valentine's ear.   He
understood the allusion to their private conversation together easily enough; and felt that unless
he let her have her own way without further
contest, he must risk offending an old friend by
implying a mistrust of her, which would be simply ridiculous, under the circumstances in which
they were placed.   So, when his wife nodded to
him to take advantage of the offer just made, he
accepted it forthwith.

"Now, I'll stop his giving Mary a hair brace-

let!'' thought Mrs. Peckover, as she bustled out
after young Thorpe, and closed the room door
behind her.

"Wait a bit, young gentleman," she said, ar-
resting his further progress on the first landing.
"Just leave off talking a minute, and let me
speak. I've got something to say to you. Do
you really mean to give Mary that hair bracelet?"

"Oho! then you did hear something at the
card-table about it, after all?" said Zack.
"Mean? Of course I mean!"

"And you want to put some of my hair in it?"

"To be sure I do! Madonna wouldn't like it
without."

"Then you had better make up your mind at
once to give her some other present; for not one
morsel of my hair shall you have. There now!
what do you think of that?"

"I don't believe it, my old darling."

"It's true enough, I can tell you. Not a hair
of my head shall you have."

"Why not?"

"Never mind why. I've got my own reasons."

"Very well: if you come to that, I've got *my*
reasons for giving the bracelet; and I mean to
give it. If you won't let any of your hair be
plaited up along with the rest, it's Madonna you
will disappoint—not me."

Mrs. Peckover saw that she must change her
tactics, or be defeated.

"Don't you be so dreadful obstinate, Master
Zack, and I'll tell you the reason," she said, in
an altered tone, leading the way lower down into

the passage.   "I don't want you to give her a hair bracelet, because I believe it will bring ill luck to her—there!"

Zack burst out laughing.   "Do you call that a reason?   Who ever heard of a hair bracelet being an unlucky gift?"

At this moment the door of Mrs. Blyth's room opened.

"Anything wrong with the lock?" asked Valentine from above.   He was rather surprised at the time that elapsed without his hearing the house door shut.

"All quite right, sir," said Mrs. Peckover; adding in a whisper to Zack—"Hush! don't say a word!"

"Don't let him keep you in the cold with his nonsense," said Valentine.

"My nonsense—!" began Zack, indignantly.

"He's going, sir," interrupted Mrs. Peckover. "I shall be upstairs in a moment."

"Come in, dear, pray!   You're letting all the cold air into the room," exclaimed the voice of Mrs. Blyth.

The door of the room closed again.

"What *are* you driving at?" asked Zack, in extreme bewilderment.

"I only want you to give her some other present," said Mrs. Peckover, in her most persuasive tones.   "You may think it all a whim of mine, if you like—I dare say I'm an old fool; but I don't want you to give her a hair bracelet."

"A whim of yours!!!" repeated Zack, with a look which made Mrs. Peckover's cheeks redden

with rising indignation. "What! a woman at
your time of life subject to whims! My darling
Peckover, it won't do.! My mind's made up to
give her the hair bracelet. Nothing in the world
can stop me—except, of course, Madonna's having a hair bracelet already, which I know she
hasn't."

"Oh! you know that, do you, you mischievous
imp? Then, for once in a way, you just know
wrong!" exclaimed Mrs. Peckover, losing her
temper altogether.

"You don't mean to say so? How very remarkable, to think of her having a hair bracelet
already, and of my not knowing it!—Mrs. Peckover," continued Zack, mimicking the tone and
manner of his old clerical enemy, the Reverend
Aaron Yollop, "what I am now about to say
grieves me deeply; but I have a solemn duty to
discharge, and in the conscientious performance
of that duty, I now unhesitatingly express my
conviction that the remark you have just made
is—a flam."

"It isn't—Monkey!" returned Mrs. Peckover,
her anger fairly boiling over, as she nodded her
head vehemently in Zack's face.

Just then, Valentine's step became audible in
the room above; first moving toward the door,
then suddenly retreating from it, as if he had
been called back.

"I haven't let out what I oughtn't, have I?"
thought Mrs. Peckover, calming down directly
when she heard the movement upstairs.

"Oh, you stick to it, do you?" continued

Zack. "It's rather odd, old lady, that Mrs. Blyth should have said nothing about this newly-discovered hair bracelet of yours while I was talking to her. But she doesn't know, of course: and Valentine doesn't know either, I suppose? By Jove! he's not gone to bed yet: I'll run back, and ask him if Madonna really *has* got a hair bracelet!"

"For God's sake don't!—don't say a word about it, or you'll get me into dreadful trouble!" exclaimed Mrs. Peckover, turning pale as she thought of possible consequences, and catching young Thorpe by the arm when he tried to pass her in the passage.

The step upstairs crossed the room again.

"Well, upon my life," cried Zack, "of all the extraordinary old women—!"

"Hush! he's going to open the door this time; he is, indeed!"

"Never mind if he does; I won't say anything," whispered young Thorpe, his natural good-nature prompting him to relieve Mrs. Peckover's distress, the moment he became convinced that it was genuine.

"That's a good chap! that's a dear good chap!" exclaimed Mrs. Peckover, squeezing Zack's hand in a fervor of unbounded gratitude.

The door of Mrs. Blyth's room opened for the second time.

"He's gone, sir; he's gone at last!" cried Mrs. Peckover, shutting the house door on the parting guest with inhospitable rapidity, and locking it with elaborate care and extraordinary noise.

"I must manage to make it all safe with Master Zack to-morrow night; though I don't believe I have said a single world I oughtn't to say," thought she, slowly ascending the stairs. "But Mr. Blyth makes such fusses, and works himself into such fidgets about the poor thing being traced and taken away from him (which is all stuff and nonsense), that he would go half distracted if he knew what I said just now to Master Zack. Not that it's so much what I said to *him*, as what he made out somehow and said to *me*. But they're so sharp, these young London chaps—they are so awful sharp!"

Here she stopped on the landing to recover her breath; then whispered to herself, as she went on and approached Mr. Blyth's door:

"But one thing I'm determined on; little Mary shan't have that hair bracelet!"

* * * * * * *

Even as Mrs. Peckover walked thinking all the way upstairs, so did Zack walk wondering all the way home.

What the deuce could these extraordinary remonstrances about his present to Madonna possibly mean? Was it not at least clear from Mrs. Peckover's terror, when he talked of asking Blyth whether Madonna really had a hair bracelet, that she had told the truth after all? And was it not even plainer still that she had let out a secret in telling that truth, which Blyth must have ordered her to keep? Why keep it? Was this mysterious hair bracelet mixed up somehow with the grand secret about Madonna's past history,

which Valentine had always kept from him and
from everybody? Very likely it was—but why
cudgel his brains about what didn't concern him?
Was it not—considering the fact, previously forgotten, that he had but fifteen shillings-and-
threepence of disposable money in the world—
rather lucky than otherwise that Mrs. Peckover
had taken it into her head to stop him from buying what he hadn't the means of paying for?
What other present could he buy for Madonna
that was pretty, and cheap enough to suit the
present state of his pocket? Would she like a
thimble, or an almanac, or a pair of cuffs, or a
pot of bear's grease?

Here Zack suddenly paused in his mental in-
terrogatories; for he had arrived within sight of
his home in Baregrove Square.

A change passed over his handsome face: he
frowned, and his color deepened as he looked up
at the light in his father's window.

"I'll slip out again to-night, and see life,"
he muttered doggedly to himself, approaching
the door. "The more I'm bullied at home, the
oftener I'll go out on the sly."

This rebellious speech was occasioned by the
recollection of a domestic scene, which had con-
tributed, early that evening, to swell the list of
the Tribulations of Zack. Mr. Thorpe had moral
objections to Mr. Blyth's profession, and moral
doubts on the subject of Mr. Blyth himself—
these last being strengthened by that gentleman's own refusal to explain away the mystery
which enveloped the birth and parentage of his

adopted child. As a necessary consequence, Mr. Thorpe considered the painter to be no fit companion for a devout young man; and expressed, severely enough, his unmeasured surprise at finding that his son had accepted an invitation from a person of doubtful character. Zack's rejoinder to his father's reproof was decisive, if it was nothing else. He denied everything alleged or suggested against his friend's reputation— lost his temper on being sharply rebuked for the "indecent vehemence" of his language—and left the paternal tea-table in defiance, to go and cultivate the Fine Arts in the doubtful company of Mr. Valentine Blyth.

"Just in time, sir," said the page, grinning at his young master as he opened the door. "It's on the stroke of eleven."

Zack muttered something savage in reply, which it is not, perhaps, advisable to report. The servant secured the lock and bolts, while he put his hat on the hall table and lit his bedroom candle.

*　　*　　*　　*　　*　　*　　*

Rather more than an hour after this time—or, in other words, a little past midnight—the door opened again softly, and Zack appeared on the step, equipped for his nocturnal expedition.

He hesitated, as he put the key into the lock from outside, before he closed the door behind him. He had never done this on former occasions; he could not tell why he did it now. We are mysteries even to ourselves; and there are times when the Voices of the future that are in us, yet not ours, speak, and make the earthly part of us conscious of their presence. Oftenest our mortal sense feels that they are breaking their dread silence at those supreme moments of existence, when on the choice between two apparently trifling alternatives hangs suspended the whole future of a life. And thus it was now with the young man who stood on the threshold of his home, doubtful whether he should pursue or abandon the purpose which was then uppermost in his mind. On his choice between the two alternatives of going on or going back—which the closing of a door would decide—depended the future of his life, and of other lives that were mingled with it.

He waited a minute undecided, for the warning Voices within him were stronger than his own will: he waited, looking up thoughtfully at the starry loveliness of the winter's night—then closed the door behind him as softly as usual—hesitated again at the last step that led on to the pavement—and then fairly set forth from home, walking at a rapid pace through the streets.

He was not in his usual good spirits. He felt no inclination to sing as was his wont, while passing through the fresh, ·frosty air: and he wondered why it was so.

The Voices were still speaking faintly and more faintly within him. But we must die before we can become immortal as they are; and their language to us in this life is often as an unknown tongue.

BOOK II.—THE SEEKING.

CHAPTER I.

THE MAN WITH THE BLACK SKULL—CAP.

THE Roman poet who, writing of vice, ascribed its influence entirely to the allurement of the fair disguises that it wore, and asserted that it only needed to be seen with the mask off to excite the hatred of all mankind, uttered a very plausible moral sentiment, which wants nothing to recommend it to the admiration of posterity, but a seasoning of practical truth. Even in the most luxurious days of old Rome, it may safely be questioned whether vice could ever afford to disguise itself to win recruits, except from the wealthier classes of the population. But in these modern times it may be decidedly asserted as a fact that vice, in accomplishing the vast majority of its seductions, uses no disguise at all; appears impudently in its naked deformity; and, instead of horrifying all beholders, in accordance with the prediction of the classical satirist, absolutely attracts a much more numerous congregation of worshipers than has ever yet been brought together by the divinest beauties that virtue can display for the allurement of mankind.

That famous place of public amusement known, a few years since, to the late-roaming youth of

London by the name of the Snuggery, affords, among hosts of other instances which might be cited, a notable example to refute the assertion of the ancient poet. The place was principally devoted to the exhibition of musical talent, and opened at a period of the night when the performances at the theaters were over. The orchestral arrangements were comprised in one bad piano, to which were occasionally added, by way of increasing the attractions, performances on the banjo and guitar. All the singers were called "ladies and gentlemen"; and the one long room in which the performances took place was simply furnished with a double row of benches, bearing troughs at their backs for the reception of glasses of liquor.

Innocence itself must have seen at a glance that the Snuggery was an utterly vicious place. Vice never so much as thought of wearing any disguise here. No glimmer of wit played over the foul substance of the songs that were sung, and hid it in dazzle from too close observation. No relic of youth and freshness, no artfully-assumed innocence and vivacity, concealed the squalid deterioration of the worn-out human counterfeits which stood up to sing, and were coarsely painted and padded to look like fine women. Their fellow-performers among the men were such sodden-faced blackguards as no shop-boy who applauded them at night would dare to walk out with in the morning. The place itself had as little of the allurement of elegance and beauty about it as the people. Here was no bright gilding on the ceiling—no charm of ornament, no comfort of construction even, in the furniture. Here were no viciously-attractive pictures on the walls—no enervating sweet odors in the atmosphere—no contrivances of ventilation to cleanse away the stench of bad tobacco-smoke and brandy-flavored human breath with which the room reeked all night long. Here, in short, was vice wholly undisguised; recklessly showing itself to every eye, without the varnish of beauty, without the tinsel of wit, without even so much as the flavor of cleanliness to recommend it. Were all beholders instinctively overcome by horror at the sight? Far from it. The Snuggery was crammed to its last benches every night; and the proprietor filled his pockets from the purses of applauding audiences. For, let classical moralists say what they may, vice gathers followers as easily, in modern times, with the mask off, as ever it gathered them in ancient times with the mask on.

It was two o'clock in the morning, and the entertainments in the Snuggery were fast rising to the climax of joviality. A favorite comic song had just been sung by a bloated old man with a bald head and a hairy chin. There was a brief lull of repose, before the amusements resumed their noisy progress. Orders for drink were flying abroad in all directions. Friends were talking at the tops of their voices, and strangers were staring at each other—except at the lower end of the room, where the whole attention of the company was concentrated strangely upon one man.

The person who thus attracted to himself the wandering curiosity of all his neighbors had come in late, had taken the first vacant place he could find near the door, and had sat there listening and looking about him very quietly. He drank and smoked like the rest of the company; but never applauded, never laughed, never exhibited the slightest symptom of astonishment, or pleasure, or impatience, or disgust—though it was evident, from his manner of entering and giving his orders to the waiters, that he visited the Snuggery that night for the first time.

He was not in mourning, for there was no band round his hat; but he was dressed, nevertheless, in a black frock-coat, waistcoat, and trousers, and wore black kid gloves. He seemed to be very little at his ease in this costume, moving his limbs, whenever he changed his position, as cautiously and constrainedly as if he had been clothed in gossamer instead of stout black broadcloth, shining with its first new gloss on it. His face was tanned to a perfectly Moorish brown, was scarred in two places by the marks of old wounds, and was overgrown by coarse, iron-gray whiskers, which met under his chin. His eyes were light, and rather large, and seemed to be always quietly, but vigilantly on the watch. Indeed the whole expression of his face, coarse and heavy as it was in form, was remarkable for its acuteness, for its cool, collected penetration, for its habitually observant, passively-watchful

look.   Any one guessing at his calling from his
manner and appearance would have set him
down immediately as the captain of a merchant-
man, and would have been willing to lay any
wager that he had been several times round the
world.

But it was not his face, nor his dress, nor his
manner, that drew on him the attention of all
his neighbors; it was his head.   Under his hat
(which was brand-new, like everything else he
wore) there appeared, fitting tight round his
temples and behind his ears, a black velvet skull-
cap.   Not a vestige of hair peeped from under
it.   All round his head, as far as could be seen
beneath his hat, which he wore far back over his
coat-collar, there was nothing but bare flesh, encircled by a rim of black velvet.

From a great proposal for reform, to a small
eccentricity in costume, the English are the most
intolerant people in the world in their reception
of anything which presents itself to them under
the form of a perfect novelty.   Let any man display a new project before the Parliament of England, or a new pair of light-green trousers before the inhabitants of London, let the project
proclaim itself as useful to all listening ears,
and the trousers eloquently assert themselves as
beautiful to all beholding eyes—the nation will
shrink suspiciously, nevertheless, both from the
one and the other; will order the first to "lie on
the table," and will hoot, laugh, and stare at the
second; will, in short, resent either novelty as
an unwarrantable intrusion, for no other dis-

cernible reason than that people in general are not used to it.

Quietly as the strange man in black had taken his seat in the Snuggery, he and his skull-cap attracted general attention; and our national weakness displayed itself immediately.

Nobody paused to reflect that he probably wore his black velvet head-dress from necessity; nobody gave him credit for having objections to a wig, which might be perfectly sensible and well-founded; and nobody, even in this free country, was liberal enough to consider that he had really as much right to put on a skull-cap under his hat, if he chose, as any other man present had to put on a shirt under his waistcoat. The audience saw nothing but the novelty in the way of a head-dress which the stranger wore, and they resented it unanimously, because it was a novelty. First, they expressed this resentment by staring indignantly at him, then by laughing at him, then by making sarcastic remarks on him. He bore their ridicule with the most perfect and provoking coolness. He did not expostulate, or retort, or look angry, or grow red in the face, or fidget in his seat, or get up to go away. He just sat smoking and drinking as quietly as ever, not taking the slightest notice of any of the dozens of people who were all taking notice of him.

His unassailable composure only served to encourage his neighbors to take further liberties with him. One rickety little man, with a spirituous nose and watery eyes, urged on by some women near him, advanced to the stranger's

ONE RICKETY LITTLE MAN, WITH A SPIRITUOUS NOSE AND WATERY
EYES, URGED ON BY SOME WOMEN NEAR HIM, ADVANCED TO THE
STRANGER'S BENCH.—HIDE-AND-SEEK, Vol. XI., page 262.

bench, and, expressing his admiration of a skull-cap as a becoming ornamental addition to a hat, announced, with a bow of mock politeness, his anxiety to feel the quality of the velvet. He stretched out his hand as he spoke, not a word of warning or expostulation being uttered by the victim of the intended insult; but the moment his fingers touched the skull-cap, the strange man, still without speaking, without even removing his cigar from his mouth, very deliberately threw all that remained of the glass of hot brandy-and-water before him in the rickety gentleman's face.

With a scream of pain as the hot liquor flew into his eyes, the miserable little man struck out helplessly with both his fists, and fell down between the benches. A friend who was with him advanced to avenge his injuries, and was thrown sprawling on the floor. Yells of "Turn him out!" and "Police!" followed; people at the other end of the room jumped up excitably on their seats; the women screamed, the men shouted and swore, glasses were broken, sticks were waved, benches were cracked, and, in one instant, the stranger was assailed by every one of his neighbors who could get near him, on pretense of turning him out.

Just as it seemed a matter of certainty that he must yield to numbers, in spite of his gallant resistance, and be hurled out of the door down the flight of stairs that led to it, a tall young gentleman, with a quantity of light curly hair on his hatless head, leaped up on one of the benches at the opposite side of the gangway running down the middle of the room, and apostrophized the company around him with vehement fistic gesticulation. Alas for the tranquillity of parents with pleasure-loving sons!—alas for Mr. Valentine Blyth's idea of teaching his pupil to be steady, by teaching him to draw!—this furious young gentleman was no other than Mr. Zachary Thorpe, Junior, of Baregrove Square.

"D—n you all, you cowardly counter-jumping scoundrels!" roared Zack, his eyes aflame with valor, generosity, and gin-and-water. "What do you mean by setting on one man in that way? Hit out, sir—hit out right and left! I saw you insulted, and I'm coming to help you!"

With these words Zack tucked up his cuffs, and jumped into the crowd about him. His height, strength, and science as a boxer carried him triumphantly to the opposite bench. Two or three blows on the ribs, and one on the nose which drew blood plentifully, only served to stimulate his ardor and increase the pugilistic ferocity of his expression. In a minute he was by the side of the man with the skull-cap; and the two were fighting back to back, amid roars of applause from the audience at the upper end of the room, who were only spectators of the disturbance.

In the meantime the police had been summoned. But the waiters downstairs, in their anxiety to see a struggle between two men on one side, and somewhere about two dozen on the other, had neglected to close the street door.

The consequence was, that all the cabmen on the stand outside, and all the vagabond night-idlers in the vagabond neighborhood of the Snuggery, poured into the narrow passage, and got up an impromptu riot of their own with the waiters, who tried, too late, to turn them out. Just as the police were forcing their way through the throng below, Zack and the stranger had fought their way out of the throng above, and had got clear of the room.

On the right of the landing, as they approached it, was a door, through which the man with the skull-cap now darted, dragging Zack after him. His temper was just as cool, his quick eye just as vigilant as ever. The key of the door was inside. He locked it, amid a roar of applauding laughter from the people on the staircase, mixed with cries of "Police!" and "Stop 'em in the Court!" from the waiters. The two then descended a steep flight of stairs at headlong speed, and found themselves in a kitchen, confronting an astonished man-cook and two female servants. Zack knocked the man down before he could use the rolling-pin which he had snatched up on their appearance; while the stranger coolly took a hat that stood on the dresser, and jammed it tight, with one smack of his large hand, on young Thorpe's bare head. The next moment they were out in a court into which the kitchen opened, and were running at the top of their speed.

The police, on their side, lost no time; but they had to get out of the crowd in the passage and go round the front of the house, before they could arrive at the turning which led into the court from the street. This gave the fugitives a start; and the neighborhood of alleys, lanes, and by-streets in which their flight immediately involved them, was the neighborhood of all others to favor their escape. While the springing of rattles and the cries of "Stop thief!" were rending the frosty night air in one direction, Zack and the stranger were walking away quietly, arm in arm, in the other.

The man with the skull-cap had taken the lead hitherto, and he took it still; though, from the manner in which he stared about him at corners of streets, and involved himself and his companion every now and then in blind alleys, it was clear enough that he was quite unfamiliar with the part of the town through which they were now walking. Zack, having treated himself that night to his fatal third glass of grog, and having finished half of it before the fight began, was by this time in no condition to care about following any particular path in the great labyrinth of London. He walked on, talking thickly and incessantly to the stranger, who never once answered him. It was of no use to applaud his bravery; to criticise his style of fighting, which was anything but scientific; to express astonishment at his skill in knocking his hat on again, all through the struggle, every time it was knocked off; and to declare admiration of his quickness in taking the cook's hat to cover his companion's bare head, which might have exposed him to suspicion and capture as he passed through the streets. It was of no use to speak on these subjects, or on any others. The imperturbable hero, who had not uttered a word all through the fight, was as imperturbable as ever, and would not utter a word after it.

They strayed at last into Fleet Street, and walked to the foot of Ludgate Hill. Here the stranger stopped, glanced toward the open space on the right, where the river ran, gave a rough gasp of relief and satisfaction, and made directly for Blackfriars Bridge. He led Zack, who was still thick in his utterance, and unsteady on his legs, to the parapet wall; let go of his arm there, and, looking steadily in his face by the light of the gas-lamp, addressed him, for the first time, in a remarkably grave, deliberate voice, and in these words:

"Now, then, young 'un, suppose you pull a breath, and wipe that bloody nose of yours."

Zack, instead of resenting this unceremonious manner of speaking to him—which he might have done had he been sober—burst into a frantic fit of laughter. The remarkable gravity and composure of the stranger's tone and manner, contrasted with the oddity of the proposition by which he opened the conversation, would have been irresistibly ludicrous even to a man whose faculties were not in an intoxicated condition.

While Zack was laughing till the tears rolled down his cheeks, his odd companion was leaning over the parapet of the bridge, and pulling off his black kid gloves, which had suffered considerably during the progress of the fight. Having rolled them up into a ball, he jerked them contemptuously into the river.

"There goes the first pair of gloves as ever I had on, and the last as ever I mean to wear," he said, spreading out his brawny hands to the sharp night breeze.

Young Thorpe heaved a few last expiring gasps of laughter, then became quiet and serious from sheer exhaustion.

"Go it again," said the man of the skull-cap, staring at him as gravely as ever, "I like to hear you."

"I can't go it again," answered Zack, faintly; "I'm out of breath. I say, old boy, you're quite a character! Who are you?"

"I ain't nobody in particular; and I don't know as I've got a single friend to care about who I am in all England," replied the other. "Give us your hand, young 'un! In the foreign parts where I come from, when one man stands by another as you've stood by me to-night, them two are brothers together afterward. You needn't be a brother to me, if you don't like. I mean to be a brother to you, whether you like it or not. My name's Mat. What's yours?"

"Zack," returned young Thorpe, clapping his new acquaintance on the back with brotherly familiarity already. "You're a glorious fellow, and I like your way of talking. Where do you come from, Mat? And what do you wear that queer cap under your hat for?"

"I come from America last," replied Mat, as grave and deliberate as ever. "And I wear this cap because I haven't got no scalp on my head."

"What do you mean?" cried Zack, startled into temporary sobriety, and taking his hand off his new friend's shoulder as quickly as if he had put it on red-hot iron.

"I always mean what I say," continued Mat; "I've got that much good about me, if I haven't got no more. Me and my scalp parted company years ago. I'm here, on a bridge in London, talking to a young chap of the name of Zack. My scalp's on the top of a high pole in some Indian village, anywhere you like about the Amazon country. If there's any puffs of wind going there like there is here, it's rattling just now like a bit of dry parchment; and all my hair's a flip-flapping about like a horse's tail, when the flies is in season. I don't know nothing more about my scalp or my hair than that. If you don't believe me, just lay hold of my hat, and I'll show you—"

"No, thank you!" exclaimed Zack, recoiling from the offered hat. "I don't want to see it. But how the deuce do you manage without a scalp?—I never heard of such a thing before in my life—how is it you're not dead? eh?"

"It takes a deal more to kill a tough man than you London chaps think," said Mat. "I was found before my head got cool, and plastered over with leaves and ointment. They'd left a bit of scalp at the back, being in rather too great a hurry to do their work as handily as usual; and a new skin growed over, after a little—a babyish sort of skin, that wasn't half thick enough, and wouldn't bear no new crop of hair. So I had to eke out and keep my head comfortable with an old yellow handkercher; which I always wore till I got to San Francisco, on my way back here. I met with a priest at San Francisco, who told me that I should look a little less like a savage if I wore a skull-cap like his, instead of a handkercher, when I got back into what he called the civilized world. So I took his advice and bought this cap. I suppose it looks better than my old yellow handkercher; but it ain't half as comfortable.''

"But how did you lose your scalp?'' asked Zack; "tell us all about it. Upon my life, you're the most interesting fellow I ever met with! And, I say, lets walk about while we talk. I feel steadier on my legs now; and it's so infernally cold standing here.''

"Which way can we soonest get out of this muck of houses and streets?'' asked Mat, surveying the London view around him with an expression of grim disgust. "There ain't no room, even on this bridge, for the wind to blow fairly over a man. I'd just as soon be smothered up in a bed, as smothered up in smoke and stink here.''

"What a delightful fellow you are! so entirely out of the common way! Steady, my dear friend. The grog's not quite out of my head yet; and I find I've got the hiccoughs. Here's

my way home, and your way into the fresh air,
if you really want it.   Come along; and tell me
how you lost your scalp."

"There ain't nothing particular to tell.   What's
your name again?"

"Zack."

"Well, Zack, I was out on a tramp, dodging
about after any game that turned up, on the
banks of the Amazon—"

"Amazon? what's that? a woman—or a
place?"

"Did you ever hear of South America?"

"I can't positively swear to it; but, to the best
of my belief, I think I have."

"Well; the Amazon's a longish bit of river in
those parts.   I was out, as I told you, on the
tramp."

"So I should think! you look like the sort of
man who has tramped everywhere, and done
everything."

"You're about right there, for a wonder!   I've
druv cattle in Mexico; I've been out with a gang
that went to find an overland road to the North
Pole; I've worked through a season or two in
catching wild horses on the Pampas; and another season or two in digging gold in California.   I went away from England, a tidy lad
aboard ship; and here I am back again now, an
old vagabond as hasn't a friend to own him.   If
you want to know exactly who I am, and what
I've been up to all my life, that's about as much
as I can tell you."

"You don't say so!   Wait a minute, though;

there's one thing—you're not troubled with the hiccoughs, are you, after eating supper? (I've been a martyr to hiccoughs ever since I was a child.) But, I say, there's one thing you haven't told me yet; you haven't told me what your other name is besides Mat. Mine's Thorpe."

"I haven't heard the sound of the other name you're asking after for a matter of better than twenty year: and I don't care if I never hear it again." His voice sank huskily, and he turned his head a little away from Zack as he said those words. "They nicknamed me 'Marksman,' when I used to go out with the exploring gangs, because I was the best shot of all of them. *You* call me Marksman, too, if you don't like Mat. Mister Matthew Marksman, if you please: everybody seems to be a 'mister' here. You're one, of course. I don't mean to call you 'Mister,' for all that. I shall stick to Zack; it's short, and there's no bother about it."

"All right, old fellow! and I'll stick to Mat, which is shorter still by a whole letter. But, I say, you haven't told the story yet about how you lost your scalp."

"There's no story in it. Do you know what it is to have a man dodging after you through these odds and ends of streets here? I dare say you do. Well, I had three skulking thieves of Indians dodging after me, over better than four hundred miles of lonesome country, where I might have bawled for help for a whole week on end, and never made anybody hear me. They wanted my scalp, and they wanted my rifle, and they goth both at last, at the end of their man-hunt, because I couldn't get any sleep.''

"Not get any sleep. Why not?"

"Because they was three, and I was only one, to be sure! One of them kep' watch while the other two slept. I hadn't nobody to keep watch for me; and my life depended on my eyes being open night and day. I took a dog's snooze once, and was woke out of it by an arrow in my face. I kep' on a long time after that before I give out; but at last I got the horrors, and thought the prairie was all afire, and run from it. I don't know how long I run on in that mad state; I only know that the horrors turned out to be the saving of my life. I missed my own trail, and struck into another, which was a trail of friend-ly Indians—people I'd traded with, you know. And I came up with 'em somehow, near enough for the stragglers of their hunting-party to hear me skreek when my scalp was took. Now, you know as much about it as I do; I can't tell you no more, except that I woke up like, in an In-dian wigwam, with a crop of cool leaves on my head, instead of a crop of hair.''

"A crop of leaves! What a jolly old Jack-in-the-Green you must have looked like! Which of those scars on your face is the arrow-wound, eh? Oh, that's it—is it? I say, old boy, you've got a black eye! Did any of those fellows in the Snuggery hit hard enough to hurt you?''

"Hurt me? Chaps like them *hurt Me!!*'' Tickled by the exrtavagance of the idea which Zack's question suggested to him, Mat shook his sturdy shoulders, and indulged himself in a gruff chuckle, which seemed to claim some sort of barbarous relationship with a laugh.

"Ah! of course they haven't hurt you: I didn't think they had," said Zack, whose pugilistic sympathies were deeply touched by the contempt with which his new friend treated the bumps and bruises received in the fight. "Go on, Mat, I like adventures of your sort. What did you do after your head healed up?"

"Well, I got tired of dodging about the Amazon, and went South, and learned to throw a lasso, and took a turn at the wild horses. Galloping did my head good."

"It's just what would do my head good too. Yours is the sort of life, Mat, for me! How did you first come to lead it? Did you run away from home?"

"No; I served aboard ship, where I was put out, being too idle a vagabond to be kep' at home. I always wanted to run wild somewheres for a change; but I didn't really go to do it, till I picked up a letter which was waiting for me, in port, at the Brazils. There was news in that letter which sickened me of going home again; so I deserted, and went off on the tramp. And I've been mostly on the tramp ever since, till I got here last Sunday."

"What! have you only been in England since Sunday?"

"That's all. I made a good time of it in California, where I've been last, digging gold. My mate, as was with me, got a-talking about the

Old Country, and wrought on me so that I went back with him to see it again. So, instead of gambling away all my money over there" (Mat carelessly jerked his hand in a westerly direction), "I've come to spend it over here; and I'm going down into the country to-morrow, to see if anybody lives to own me at the old place."

"And suppose nobody does? What then?"

"Then I shall go back again. After twenty years among the savages, or little better, I'm not fit for the sort of thing as goes on among you here. I can't sleep in a bed; I can't stop in a room; I can't be comfortable in decent clothes; I can't stray into a singing-shop, as I did to-night, without a dust being kicked up all round me, because I haven't got a proper head of hair like everybody else. I can't shake up along with the rest of you, nohow; I'm used to hard lines and a wild country; and I shall go back and die over there among the lonesome places, where there's plenty of room for me." And· again Mat jerked his hand carelessly in the direction of the American continent.

"Oh, don't talk about going back!" cried Zack; "you're sure to find somebody left at home—don't you think so yourself, old fellow?"

Mat made no answer. He suddenly slackened, then as suddenly increased his pace, dragging young Thorpe with him at a headlong rate

"You're sure to find somebody," continued Zack, in his off-hand, familiar way. "I don't know—gently! we're not walking for a wager— I don't know whether you're married or not?"

(Mat still made no answer, and walked faster than ever.) "But if you haven't got wife or child, every fellow's got a father and mother, you know; and most fellows have got brothers or sisters—"

"Good-night," said Mat, stopping short, and abruptly holding out his hand.

"Why! what's the matter now?" asked Zack, in astonishment. "What do you want to part company for already? We are not near the end of the streets yet. Have I said anything that's offended you?"

"No, you haven't. You can come and talk to me if you like, the day after to-morrow. I shall be back then, whatever happens. I said I'd be like a brother to you; and that means, in my lingo, doing anything you ask. Come and smoke a pipe along with me, as soon as I'm back again. Do you know Kirk Street? It's nigh on the Market. Do you know a 'bacco-shop in Kirk Street? It's got a green door, and Fourteen written on it in yaller paint. When I *am* shut up in a room of my own, which isn't often, I'm shut up there. I can't give you the key of the house, because I want it myself."

"Kirk Street? That's my way. Why can't we go on together? What do you want to say good-night here for?"

"Because I want to be left by myself. It's not your fault; but you've set me thinking of something that don't make me easy in my mind. I've led a lonesome life of it, young 'un; stray-ing away months and months out in the wilderness, without a human being to speak to.   I dare say that wasn't a right sort of life for a man to take up with; but I *did* take up with it; and I can't get over liking it sometimes still.   When I'm not easy in my mind, I want to be left lonesome as I used to be.   I want it now.   Goodnight."

Before Zack could enter his new friend's address in his pocket-book, Mat had crossed the road and had disappeared in the dark distance dotted with gaslights.   In another moment the last thump of his steady footstep died away on the pavement, in the morning stillness of the street.

"That's rather an odd fellow"—thought Zack, as he pursued his own road—"and we have got acquainted with each other in rather an odd way.   I shall certainly go and see him though, on Thursday; something may come of it one of these days."

Zack was a careless guesser; but in this case he guessed right.   Something *did* come of it.

CHAPTER II.

THE PRODIGAL'S RETURN.

WHEN Zack reached Baregrove Square, it was four in the morning.   The neighboring church clock struck the hour as he approached his own door.

Immediately after parting with Mat, malicious

Fate so ordained it that he passed one of those late—or, to speak more correctly, early—public-houses, which are open to customers during the "small hours" of the morning. He was parched with thirst; and the hiccoughing fit which had seized him in the company of his new friend had not yet subsided. "Suppose I try what a drop of brandy will do for me," thought Zack, stopping at the fatal entrance of the public-house.

He went in easily enough—but he came out with no little difficulty. However, he had achieved his purpose of curing the hiccoughs. The remedy employed acted, to be sure, on his legs as well as his stomach—but that was a trifling physiological eccentricity quite unworthy of notice.

He was far too exclusively occupied in chuckling over the remembrance of the agreeably riotous train of circumstances which had brought his new acquaintance and himself together, to take any notice of his own personal condition, or to observe that his course over the pavement was of a somewhat sinuous nature as he walked home. It was only when he pulled the door-key out of his pocket, and tried to put it into the keyhole, that his attention was fairly directed to himself; and then he discovered that his hands were helpless, and that he was also by no means rigidly steady on his legs.

There are some men whose minds get drunk, and some men whose bodies get drunk, under the influence of intoxicating liquor. Zack belonged to the second class. He was perfectly capable of understanding what was said to him, and of knowing what he said himself, long after his utterance had grown thick and his gait had become uncertain. He was now quite conscious that his visit to the public-house had by no means tended to sober him; and quite awake to the importance of noiselessly stealing up to bed —but he was, at the same time, totally unable to put the key into the door at the first attempt, or to look comfortably for the keyhole, without previously leaning against the area railings at his side.

"Steady," muttered Zack, "I'm done for if I make any noise." Here he felt for the keyhole and guided the key elaborately, with his left hand, into its proper place. He next opened the door, so quietly that he was astonished at himself—entered the passage with marvelous stealthiness—then closed the door again, and cried "Hush!" when he found that he had let the lock go a little too noisily.

He listened before he attempted to light his candle. The air of the house felt strangely close and hot, after the air out-of-doors. The dark stillness above and around him was instinct with an awful and virtuous repose; and was deepened ominously by the solemn *tick-tick* of the kitchen clock—never audible from the passage in the day-time: terribly and incomprehensibly distinct at this moment.

"I won't bolt the door," he whispered to himself, "till I have struck a—" Here the unreliability of brandy as a curative agent in cases of

fermentation in the stomach was palpably dem-
onstrated by a sudden return of thĕ hiccoughing
fit. "Hush!" cried Zack for the second time,
terrified at the violence and suddenness of the
relapse, and clapping his hand to his mouth
when it was too late.

After groping on his knees with extraᴼrdinary
perseverance all round the rim of his bedroom
candlestick, which stood on one of the hall
chairs, he succeeded—not in finding the box of
matches—but in knocking it off the chair, and
sending it rolling over the stone floor, until it
was stopped by the opposite wall. With some
difficulty he captured it, and struck a light.
Never, in all Zack's experience, had any former
matches caught flame with such a shrill report
as was produced from the one disastrous match
which he happened to select to light his candle
with.

The next thing to be done was to bolt the door.
He succeeded very well with the bolt at the top,
but failed signally with the bolt at the bottom,
which appeared particularly difficult to deal with
that night. It first of all creaked fiercely on
being moved, then stuck spitefully just at the
entrance of the staple, then slipped all of a sudden, under moderate pressure, and ran like light-
ning into its appointed place, with a bang of
malicious triumph. "If that doesn't bring my
father down," thought Zack, listening with all
his ears, and stifling the hiccoughs with all his
might, "he's a harder sleeper than I take him
for."

But no door opened, no voice called, no sound of any kind broke the mysterious stillness of the bedroom regions. Zack sat down on the stairs and took his boots off, got up again with some little difficulty, listened, took his candlestick, listened once more, whispered to himself, "Now for it!" and began the perilous ascent to his own room.

He held tight by the banisters, only falling against them, and making them crack from top to bottom once, before he reached the drawing-room landing. He ascended the second flight of stairs without casualties of any kind, until he got to the top step, close by his father's bedroom door. Here, by a dire fatality, the stifled hic-coughs burst beyond all control; and distinctly asserted themselves by one convulsive yelp, which betrayed Zack into a start of horror. The start shook his candlestick: the extin-guisher, which lay loose in it, dropped out, hopped playfully down the stone stairs, and rolled over the landing with a loud and lively ring—a devilish and brazen flourish of exulta-tion in honor of its own activity.

"Oh, Lord!" faintly ejaculated Zack, as he heard somebody's voice speaking, and some-body's body moving, in the bedroom; and re-membered that he had to mount another flight of stairs—wooden stairs this time—before he got to his own quarters on the garret floor.

He went up, however, directly, with the reck-lessness of despair; every separate stair creaking and cracking under him, as if a young elephant had been retiring to bed instead of a young man. He blew out his light, tore off his clothes, and, slipping between the sheets, began to breathe elaborately, as if he was fast asleep—in the desperate hope of being still able to deceive his father, if Mr. Thorpe came upstairs to look after him.

No sooner had he assumed a recumbent position, than a lusty and ceaseless singing began in his ears, which bewildered and half-deafened him. His bed, the room, the house, the whole world tore round and round, and heaved up and down frantically with him. He ceased to be a human being: he became a giddy atom, spinning drunkenly in illimitable space. He started up in bed, and was recalled to a sense of his humanity by a cold perspiration and a deathly qualm. Hiccoughs burst from him no longer; but they were succeeded by another and a louder series of sounds—sounds familiar to everybody who has ever been at sea—sounds nautically and lamentably associated with white basins, whirling waves, and misery of mortal stomachs wailing in emetic despair.

In the momentary pauses between the rapidly successive attacks of the malady which now overwhelmed him, and which he attributed in after-life entirely to the dyspeptic influences of toasted cheese, Zack was faintly conscious of the sound of slippered feet ascending the stairs. His back was to the door. He had no strength to move, no courage to look round, no voice to raise in supplication. He knew that his door was

opened—that a light came into the room—that
a voice cried "Degraded beast!"—that the door
was suddenly shut again with a bang—and that
he was left once more in total darkness.   He did
not care for the light, or the voice, or the banging of the door: he did not think of them afterward; he did not mourn over the past, or speculate on the future.   He just sank back on his
pillow with a gasp, drew the clothes over him
with a groan, and fell asleep, blissfully reckless
of the retribution that was to come with the
coming daylight.

When he woke, late the next morning, conscious of nothing at first except that it was thawing fast out-of-doors, and that he had a violent
headache, but gradually recalled to a remembrance of the memorable fight in the Snuggery
by a sense of soreness in the ribs, and a growing
conviction that his nose had become too large
for his face, Zack's memory began, correctly
though confusedly, to retrace the circumstances
attending his return home, and his disastrous
journey upstairs to bed.   With these recollections were mingled others of the light which
had penetrated into his room, after his own candle was out; of the voice which had denounced
him as a "Degraded beast"; and of the banging
of the door which had followed.   There could be
no doubt that it was his father who had entered
the room and apostrophized him in the briefly
emphatic terms which he was now calling to
mind.   Never had Mr. Thorpe, on any former
occasion, been known to call names or bang

doors. It was quite clear that he had discovered everything, and was exasperated with his son as he had never been exasperated with any other human being before in his life.

Just as Zack arrived at this conclusion, he heard the rustling of his mother's dress on the stairs, and Mrs. Thorpe, with her handkerchief to her eyes, presented herself wofully at his bedside. Profoundly and penitently wretched, he tried to gain his mother's forgiveness before he encountered his father's wrath. To do him justice, he was so thoroughly ashamed to meet her eye, that he turned his face to the wall, and in that position appealed to his mother's compassion in the most moving terms, and with the most vehement protestations which he had ever addressed to her.

The only effect he produced on Mrs. Thorpe was to make her walk up and down the room in violent agitation, sobbing bitterly. Now and then a few words burst lamentably and incoherently from her lips. They were just articulate enough for him to gather from them that his father had discovered everything, had suffered in consequence from an attack of palpitation of the heart, and had felt himself, on rising that morning, so unequal, both in mind and body, to deal unaided with the enormity of his son's offense, that he had just gone out to request the co-operation of the Reverend Aaron Yollop. On discovering this, Zack's penitence changed instantly into a curious mixture of indignation and alarm. He turned round quickly toward

his mother. But before he could open his lips
she informed him, speaking with an unexampled
severity of tone, that he was on no account to
think of going to the office as usual, but was to
wait at home until his father's return, and then
hurried from the room.   The fact was, that Mrs.
Thorpe distrusted her own inflexibility, if she
stayed too long in the presence of her penitent
son; but Zack could not, unhappily, know this.
He could only see that she left him abruptly
after delivering an ominous message, and could
only place the gloomiest interpretation on her
conduct.

"When mother turns against me, I've lost my
last chance." He stopped before he ended the
sentence, and sat up in bed, deliberating with
himself for a minute or two. "I could make up
my mind to bear anything from my father, because he has a right to be angry with me, after
what I've done. But if I stand old Yollop
again, I'll be—" Here, whatever Zack said
was smothered in the sound of a blow, expressive of fury and despair, which he administered
to the mattress on which he was sitting.   Having relieved himself thus, he jumped out of bed,
pronouncing at last in real earnest those few
words of fatal slang which had often burst from
his lips in other days as an empty threat:

"It's all over with me; I must bolt from
home."

He refreshed both mind and body by a good
wash; but still his resolution did not falter.   He
hurried on his clothes, looked out of window,

listened at his door; and all this time his purpose never changed. Remembering but too well
the persecution he had already suffered at the
hands of Mr. Yollop, the conviction that it would
now be repeated, with fourfold severity, was
enough of itself to keep him firm to his desperate intention. When he had done dressing, his
thoughts were suddenly recalled by the sight of
his pocket-book to his companion of the past
night. As he reflected on the appointment for
Thursday morning, his eyes brightened, and he
said to himself aloud, while he turned resolutely
to the door, "That queer fellow talked of going
back to America. If I can't do anything else,
I'll go back with him!"

Just as his hand was on the lock, he was
startled by a knock at the door. He opened it,
and found the housemaid on the landing with
a letter for him. Returning to the window,
he hastily undid the envelope. Several gayly-
printed invitation-cards with gilt edges dropped
out. There was a letter among them which
proved to be in Mr. Blyth's handwriting, and
ran thus:

"Wednesday.

"MY DEAR ZACK—The inclosed are the tickets for my picture-show, which I told you about
yesterday evening. I send them now, instead of
waiting to give them to you to-night, at Lavvie's
suggestion. She thinks only three days' notice,
from now to Saturday, rather short, and consid-
ers it advisable to save even a few hours, so as
to enable you to give your friends the most time

possible to make their arrangements for coming to my studio. Post all the invitation tickets, therefore, that you send about among your connection, at once, as I am posting mine; and you will save a day by that means, which is a good deal. Patty is obliged to pass your house this morning on an errand, so I send my letter by her. How conveniently things sometimes turn out, don't they?

"Introduce anybody you like; but I should prefer *intellectual* people; my figure-subject of 'Columbus in sight of the New World' being treated mystically, and, therefore, adapted to tax the popular mind to the utmost. Please warn your friends beforehand that it is a work of high art, and that nobody can hope to understand it in a hurry.

"Affectionately yours,
"V. BLYTH."

The perusal of this letter reminded Zack of certain recent aspirations in the direction of the fine arts, which had escaped his slippery memory altogether, while he was thinking of his future prospects. "I'll stick to my first idea," he thought, "and be an artist, if Blyth will let me, after what's happened. If he won't, I've got Mat to fall back upon; and I'll run as wild in America as ever he did."

Reflecting thus, Zack descended cautiously to the back parlor, which was called a "library." The open door showed him that no one was in the room. He went in, and in great haste scrawled the following answer to Mr. Blyth's letter:

"My dear Blyth—Thank you for the tickets. I have got into a dreadful scrape, having been found out coming home tipsy at four in the morning, which I did by stealing the family door-key. My prospects after this are so extremely unpleasant that I am going to make a bolt of it. I write these lines in a tearing hurry, for fear my father should come home before I have done—he having gone to Yollop's to set the parson at me again worse than ever.

"I can't come to you to-night, because your house would be the first place they would send to after me. But I mean to be an artist, if you won't desert me. Don't, my dear fellow! I know I'm a scamp; but I'll try and be a reformed character, if you will only stick by me. When you take your walk to-morrow, I shall be at the turnpike in the Laburnum Road, waiting for you, at three o'clock. If you won't come there, or won't speak to me when you do come, I shall leave England and take to something desperate.

"I have got a new friend—the best and most interesting fellow in the world. He has been half his life in the wilds of America; so, if you don't give me the go-by, I shall bring him to see your picture of Columbus.

"I feel so miserable, and have got such a headache, that I can't write any more.

"Ever yours,   Z. Thorpe, Jun."

After directing this letter, and placing it in his pocket to be put into the post by his own hand, Zack looked toward the door and hesitated —advanced a step or two to go out—and ended by returning to the writing-table, and taking a fresh sheet of paper out of the portfolio before him.

"I can't leave the old lady (though she won't forgive me) without writing a line to keep up her spirits and say good-by," he thought, as he dipped the pen in the ink, and began in his usual dashing, scrawling way. But he could not get beyond "My dear Mother." The writing of those three words seemed to have suddenly paralyzed him. The strong hand that had struck out so sturdily all through the fight, trembled now at merely touching a sheet of paper. Still, he tried desperately to write something, even if it were only the one word, "Good-by"—tried till the tears came into his eyes, and made all further effort hopeless.

He crumpled up the paper and rose hastily, brushing away the tears with his hand, and feeling a strange dread and distrust of himself as he did so. It was rarely, very rarely, that his eyes were moistened as they were moistened now. Few human beings have lived to be twenty years of age without shedding more tears than had ever been shed by Zack.

"I can't write to her while I'm at home, and I know she's in the next room to me. I will send her a letter when I'm out of the house, saying it's only for a little time, and that I'm coming back when the angry part of this infernal business is all blown over.'' Such was his resolution, as he tore up the crumpled paper, and went out quickly into the passage.

He took his hat from the table. *His* hat? No: he remembered that it was the hat which had been taken from the man at the tavern. At the most momentous instant of his life—when his heart was bowing down before the thought of his mother—when he was leaving home in secret, perhaps forever — the current of his thoughts could be incomprehensibly altered in its course by the influence of such a trifle as this!

It was thus with him; it is thus with all of us. Our faculties are never more completely at the mercy of the smallest interests of our being, than when they appear to be most fully absorbed by the mightiest. And it is well for us that there exists this seeming imperfection in our nature. The first cure of many a grief, after the hour of parting, or in the house of death, has begun, insensibly to ourselves, with the first moment when we were betrayed into thinking of so little a thing even as a daily meal.

The rain which had accompanied the thaw was falling faster and faster; inside the house was dead silence, and outside it damp desolation, as Zack opened the street door, and, without hesitating a moment, dashed out desperately through mud and wet, to cast himself loose on the thronged world of London as a fugitive from his own home.

He paused before he took the turning out of the square; the recollections of weeks, months, years past, all whirling through his memory in a few moments of time. He paused, looking through the damp, foggy atmosphere at the door which he had just left—never, it might be, to approach it again; then moved away, buttoned his coat over his chest with trembling, impatient fingers, and saying to himself, "I've done it, and nothing can undo it now," turned his back resolutely on Baregrove Square.

CHAPTER III.

THE SEARCH BEGUN.

THE street which Mat had chosen for his place of residence in London was situated in a densely populous, and by no means respectable neighborhood. In Kirk Street the men of the fustian jacket and seal-skin cap clustered tumultuous round the lintels of the gin-shop doors. Here ballad-bellowing, and organ-grinding, and voices of costermongers, singing of poor men's luxuries, never ceased all through the hum of day, and penetrated far into the frowzy repose of latest night. Here, on Saturday evenings especially, the butcher smacked, with appreciating hand, the fat carcasses that hung around him; and, flourishing his steel, roared aloud to every woman who passed the shop door with a basket, to come in and buy—buy—buy! Here, with foul frequency, the language of the natives was interspersed with such words as reporters indicate in the newspapers by an expressive black line; and on this "beat," more than on most others, the night police were chosen from men of mighty strength to protect the sober part of the street community, and of notable cunning to persuade the drunken part to retire harmlessly brawling into the seclusion of their own homes.

Such was the place in which Mat had set up his residence, after twenty years of wandering amid the wilds of the great American Continent.

Never was tenant of any order or degree known to make such conditions with a landlord as were made by this eccentric stranger. Every household convenience with which the people at the lodgings could offer to accommodate him, Mat considered to be a domestic nuisance which it was particularly desirable to get rid of. He stipulated that nobody should be allowed to clean his room but himself; that the servant-of-all-work should never attempt to make his bed, or offer to put sheets on it, or venture to cook him a morsel of dinner when he stopped at home; and that he should be free to stay away unexpectedly for days and nights together, if he chose, without either landlord or landlady presuming to be anxious or to make inquiries about him, as long as they had his rent in their pockets. This rent he willingly covenanted to pay beforehand, week by week, as long as his stay lasted; and he was also ready to fee the servant occasionally, provided she would engage sol-

emnly "not to upset his temper by doing anything for him."

The proprietor of the house (and tobacco-shop)
was at first extremely inclined to be distrustful;
but as he was likewise extremely familiar with
poverty, he was not proof against the auriferous
halo which the production of a handful of bright
sovereigns shed gloriously over the oddities of
the new lodger. The bargain was struck; and
Mat went away directly to fetch his personal
baggage.

After an absence of some little time, he returned with a large corn-sack on his back, and a
long rifle in his hand. This was his luggage.

First putting the rifle on his bed in the back
room, he cleared away all the little second-hand
furniture with which the front room was decorated; packing the three rickety chairs together
in one corner, and turning up the cracked round
table in another. Then, untying a piece of cord
which secured the mouth of the corn-sack, he
emptied it over his shoulder into the middle of
the room—just (as the landlady afterward said)
as if it was coals coming in instead of luggage.
Among the things which fell out on the floor in
a heap, were—some bear-skins and a splendid
buffalo-hide, neatly packed; a pipe, two red flannel shirts, a tobacco-pouch, and an Indian blanket; a leather bag, a gunpowder flask, two
squares of yellow soap, a bullet-mold, and a
night-cap; a tomahawk, a paper of nails, a
scrubbing-brush, a hammer, and an old grid-
iron. Having emptied the sack, Mat took up

the buffalo-hide, and spread it out on his bed, with a very expressive sneer at the patch-work counterpane and meager curtains. He next threw down the bear-skins, with the empty sack under them, in an unoccupied corner; propped up the leather bag between two angles of the wall; took his pipe from the floor; left everything else lying in the middle of the room; and, sitting down on the bear-skins with his back against the bag, told the astonished landlord that he was quite settled and comfortable, and would thank him to go downstairs and send up a pound of the strongest tobacco he had in the shop.

Mat's subsequent proceedings during the rest of the day—especially such as were connected with his method of laying in a stock of provisions and cooking his own dinner—exhibited the same extraordinary disregard of all civilized precedent which had marked his first entry into the lodgings. After he had dined, he took a nap on his bear-skins; woke up grumbling at the close air and the confined room; smoked a long series of pipes, looking out of window all the time with quietly observant, constantly attentive eyes; and, finally, rising to the climax of all his previous oddities, came down when the tobacco-shop was being shut up after the closing of the neighboring theater, and coolly asked which was his nearest way into the country, as he wanted to clear his head, and stretch his legs, by making a walking night of it in the fresh air.

He began the next morning by cleaning both

his rooms thoroughly with his own hands; and seemed to enjoy the occupation mightily in his own grim, grave way. His dining, napping, smoking, and observant study of the street view from his window, followed as on the previous day. But at night, instead of setting forth into the country as before, he wandered into the streets; and, in the course of his walk, happened to pass the door of the Snuggery. What happened to him there is already known; but what became of him afterward remains to be seen.

On leaving Zack, he walked straight on; not slackening his pace, not noticing whither he went, not turning to go back till day-break. It was past nine o'clock before he presented himself at the tobacco-shop, bringing in with him a goodly share of mud and wet from the thawing ground and rainy sky outside. His long walk did not seem to have relieved the uneasiness of mind which had induced him to separate so suddenly from Zack. He talked almost perpetually to himself in a muttering, incoherent way; his heavy brow was contracted, and the scars of the old wounds on his face looked angry and red. The first thing he did was to make some inquiries of his landlord relating to railway traveling, and to the part of London in which a certain terminus that he had been told of was situated. Finding it not easy to make him understand any directions connected with this latter point, the shop-keeper suggested sending for a cab to take him to the railway. He briefly assented to that arrangement; occupying the time before the vehicle arrived in walking sullenly backward and forward over the pavement in front of the shop door.

When the cab came to take him up, he insisted, with characteristic regardlessness of appearances, on riding upon the roof, because he could get more air to blow over him, and more space for stretching his legs in, there than inside. Arriving in this irregular and vagabond fashion at the terminus, he took his ticket for DIBBLE- DEAN, a quiet little market-town in one of the midland counties.

When he was set down at the station, he looked about him rather perplexedly at first; but soon appeared to recognize a road, visible at some little distance, which led to the town, and toward which he immediately directed his steps, scorning all offers of accommodation from the local omnibus.

It did not happen to be market-day; and the thaw looked even more dreary at Dibbledean than it looked in London. Down the whole perspective of the High Street there appeared only three human figures—a woman in pattens; a child under a large umbrella; and a man with a hamper on his back, walking toward the yard of the principal inn.

Mat had slackened his pace more and more as he approached the town, until he slackened it altogether at last, by coming to a dead standstill under the walls of the old church, which stood at one extremity of the High Street, in what seemed to be the suburban district of Dibbledean. He waited for some time, looking over the low parapet wall which divided the church-yard from the road—then slowly approached a gate leading to a path among the gravestones—stopped at it—apparently changed his purpose—and, turning off abruptly, walked up the High Street.

He did not pause again till he arrived opposite a long, low, gabled house, evidently one of the oldest buildings in the place, though brightly painted and whitewashed, to look as new and unpicturesque as possible. The basement story was divided into two shops; which, however, proclaimed themselves as belonging now, and having belonged also in former days, to one and the same family. Over the larger of the two was painted in letters of goodly size:

BRADFORD AND SON
(*late* JOSHUA GRICE),
Linen-drapers, Hosiers, etc., etc.

The board on which these words were traced was continued over the smaller shop, where it was additionally superscribed thus:

MRS. BRADFORD
(*late* JOANNA GRICE)
Milliner and Dressmaker.

Regardless of rain, and droppings from eaves that trickled heavily down his hat and coat, Mat stood motionless, reading and re-reading these inscriptions from the opposite side of the way. Though the whole man, from top to toe, was the very impersonation of firmness, he nevertheless hesitated most unnaturally now. At one moment he seemed to be on the point of entering the shop before him—at another, he turned half round toward the churchyard which he had left behind him. At last he decided to go back to the churchyard, and retraced his steps accordingly.

He entered quickly by the gate at which he had delayed before, and pursued the path among the graves a little way. Then striking off over the grass, after a moment's consideration and looking about him, he wound his course hither and thither among the turf mounds, and stopped suddenly at a plain flat tombstone, raised horizontally above the earth by a foot or so of brickwork. Bending down over it, he read the characters engraven on the slab.

There were four inscriptions, all of the simplest and shortest kind, comprising nothing but a record of the names, ages, and birth and death dates of the dead who lay beneath. The first two inscriptions notified the deaths of children: "Joshua Grice, son of Joshua and Susan Grice, of this parish, aged four years;" and "Susan Grice, daughter of the above, aged thirteen years." The next death recorded was the mother's: and the last was the father's at the age of sixty-two. Below this followed a quotation from the New Testament: *Come unto Me all ye that are weary and heavy laden, and I will give you rest.* It was on these lines, and on the record above them of the death of Joshua Grice the elder, that the eyes of the lonely reader rested longest; his lips murmuring several times, as he looked down on the letters: "He lived to be an old man—he lived to be an old man after all!"

There was sufficient vacant space left toward the bottom of the tombstone for two or three more inscriptions; and it appeared as if Mat expected to have seen more. He looked intently at the vacant space, and measured it roughly with his fingers, comparing it with the space above, which was occupied by letters. "Not there, at any rate!" he said to himself as he left the churchyard, and walked back to the town.

This time he entered the double shop—the hosiery division of it—without hesitation. No one was there, but the young man who served behind the counter. And right glad the young man looked, having been long left without a soul to speak to on that rainy morning, to see some one—even a stranger with an amazing skull-cap under his hat—enter the shop at last.

What could he serve the gentleman with? The gentleman had not come to buy. He only desired to know whether Joanna Grice, who used to keep the dressmaker's shop, was still living?

Still living, certainly! the young man replied, with brisk civility. Miss Grice, whose brother once had the business now carried on by Bradford and Son, still resided in the town; and was a very curious old person, who never went out, and let nobody inside her doors. Most of her old friends were dead; and those who were still alive she had broken with. She was full of fierce, wild ways; was suspected of being crazy; and was execrated by the boys of Dibbledean as an "old tiger-cat." In all probability her intellects were a little shaken, years ago, by a dreadful scandal in the family, which quite crushed them down, being very respectable, religious people—

At this point the young man was interrupted, in a very uncivil manner, by the stranger, who desired to hear nothing about the scandal, but who had another question to ask. This question seemed rather a difficult one to put; for he began it two or three times, in two or three different forms of words, and failed to get on with it. At last he ended by asking, generally, whether any other members of old Mr. Grice's family were still alive.

For a moment or so the shopman was stupid and puzzled, and asked what other members the gentleman meant. Old Mrs. Grice had died some time ago; and there had been two children who died young, and whose names were in the churchyard. Did the gentleman mean the second daughter, who lived and grew up beautiful, and was, as the story went, the cause of all the scandal? If so, the young person ran away, and died miserably somehow—nobody knew how; and was supposed to have been buried like a pauper somewhere—nobody knew where, unless it was Miss Grice—"

The young man stopped and looked perplexed. A sudden change had passed over the strange gentleman's face. His swarthy cheeks had turned to a cold clay color, through which his two scars seemed to burn fiercer than ever, like streaks of fire. His heavy hand and arm trembled a little as he leaned against the counter. Was he going to be taken ill? No: he walked at once from the counter to the door—turned round there, and asked where Joanna Grice lived. The young man answered, the second turning to the right, down a street which ended in a lane of cottages. Miss Grice's was the last cottage on the left hand; but he could assure the gentleman that it would be quite useless to go there, for she let nobody in. The gentleman thanked him, and went, nevertheless.

"I didn't think it would have took me so," Mat said, walking quickly up the street; "and it wouldn't if I'd heard it anywhere else. But I'm not the man I was, now I'm in the old place again. Over twenty year of hardening don't seem to have hardened me yet!"

He followed the directions given him, correctly enough, arrived at the last cottage on his left hand, and tried the garden gate. It was locked; and there was no bell to ring. But the paling was low, and Mat was not scrupulous. He got over it, and advanced to the cottage door. It opened, like other doors in the country, merely by turning the handle of the lock. He went in without any hesitation, and entered the first room into which the passage led him. It was a small parlor; and at the back window, which looked out on a garden, sat Joanna Grice, a thin, dwarfish old woman, poring over a big book which looked like a Bible. She started from her chair, as she heard the sound of footsteps, and tottered up fiercely, with wild wandering gray eyes and horny threatening hands, to meet the intruder. He let her come close to him; then mentioned a name—pronouncing it twice, very distinctly.

She paused instantly, livid pale, with gaping lips, and arms hanging rigid at her side; as if that name, or the voice in which it had been uttered, had frozen up in a moment all the little life left in her. Then she moved back slowly, groping with her hands like one in the dark— back, till she touched the wall of the room. Against this she leaned, trembling violently; not speaking a word; her wild eyes staring panic-stricken on the man who was confronting her.

He sat down unbidden, and asked if she did not remember him. No answer was given; no movement made that might serve instead of an answer. He asked again; a little impatiently this time. She nodded her head and stared at him—still speechless, still trembling.

He told her what he had heard at the shop; and using the shopman's phrases, asked whether it was true that the daughter of old Mr. Grice, who was the cause of all the scandal in the family, had died long since, away from her home, and in a miserable way?

There was something in his look, as he spoke,

which seemed to oblige her to answer against her
will. She said Yes; and trembled more violently than ever.

He clasped his hands together; his head
drooped a little; dark shadows seemed to move
over his bent face; and the scars of the old
wounds deepened to a livid violet hue.

His silence and hesitation seemed to inspire
Joanna Grice with sudden confidence and courage. She moved a little away from the wall,
and a gleam of triumph lightened over her face,
as she reiterated her last answer of her own accord. "Yes! the wretch who ruined the good
name of the family *was* dead—dead, and buried
far off, in some grave by herself—not there, in
the churchyard with her father and mother—
no, thank God, not there!"

He looked up at her instantly when she said
those words. There was some warning influence
in his eye, as it rested on her, which sent her
cowering back again to her former place against
the wall. Mentioning the name for the first
time, he asked sternly where Mary was buried.
The reply — doled out doggedly and slowly,
forced from her word by word—was, that Mary
was buried among strangers, as she deserved to
be—at a place called Bangbury—far away in the
next county, where she died, and where money
was sent to bury her.

His manner became less roughly imperative;
his eyes softened; his voice saddened in tone,
when he spoke again. And yet, the next question that he put to Joanna Grice seemed to pierce

her to the quick, to try her to the heart, as no
questioning had tried her before. The muscles
were writhing on her haggard face, her breath
burst from her in quick, fierce pantings, as he
asked plainly whether it was only suspicion, or
really the truth, that Mary was with child when
she left her home.

No answer was given to him. He repeated
the question, and insisted on having one. Was
it suspicion, or truth? The reply hissed out at
him in one whispered word—Truth.

Was the child born alive?

The answer came again in the same harsh
whisper—Yes: born alive.

What became of it?

She never saw it—never asked about it—never
knew. While she replied thus, her whispering
accents changed, and rose sullenly to hoarse, distinct tones. But it was not till the questioner
spoke to her once more that the smothered fury
flashed out into flaming rage. Then, even as he
raised his head and opened his lips, she staggered, with outstretched arms, up to the table at
which she had been reading when he came in;
and struck her bony hands on the open Bible;
and swore by the Word of Truth in that Book,
that she would answer him no more.

He rose up calmly; and with something of
contempt in his look, approached the table and
spoke. But his voice was drowned by hers,
bursting from her in screams of fury. No! no!
no! Not a word more! How dare he come
there, with his shameless face and his threaten-

ing eyes, and make her speak of what should never have passed her lips again—never till she went up to render her account at the Judgment-seat! Relations! let him not speak to her of relations. The only kindred she ever cared to own, lay heart-broken under the great stone in the churchyard. Relations! if they all came to life this very minute, what could she have to do with them, whose only relation was Death? Yes; Death, that was father, mother, brother, sister to her now! Death, that was waiting to take her in God's good time. What! would he stay on in spite of her? stay after she had sworn not to answer him another word?

Yes; he was resolved to stay—and resolved to know more. Had Mary left nothing behind her on the day when she fled from her home?

Some suddenly-conceived resolution seemed to calm the first fury of Joanna Grice's passion while he said those words. She stretched out her hand quickly, and griped him by the arm, and looked up in his face with a wicked exultation in her wild eyes.

He was bent on knowing what that ruined wretch left behind her? Well! he should see for himself!

Between the leaves of Joanna Grice's Bible there was a key, which seemed to be used as a marker. She took it out, and led the way, with toilsome step, and hands outstretched for support to the wall on one side and the banisters on the other, up the one flight of stairs which communicated with the bedroom story of the cottage.

He followed close behind her: and was standing by her side, when she opened a door, and pointed into a room, telling him to take what he found there, and then go—she cared not whither, so long as he went from her.

She descended the stairs again, as he entered the room. There was a close, faint, airless smell in it. Cobwebs, pendulous and brown with dirt, hung from the ceiling. The grimy window-panes saddened all the light that poured through them faintly. He looked round him, and saw no furniture anywhere; no sign that the room had ever been lived in, ever entered even, for years and years past. He looked again, more carefully: and detected, in one dim corner, something covered with dust and dirt, which looked like a small box.

He pulled it out toward the window. Dust flew from it in clouds. Loathsome, crawling creatures crept from under it and from off it. He stirred it with his foot still nearer to the faint light, and saw that it was a common deal-box, corded. He looked closer, and through cobwebs, and dead insects, and foul stains of all kinds, spelled out a name that was painted on it: MARY GRICE.

At the sight of that name, and of the pollution which covered it, he paused, silent and thoughtful; and, at the same moment, heard the parlor door below locked. He stooped hastily, took up the box by the cord round it, and left the room. His hand touched a substance, as he grasped the cord, which did not feel like wood. Examining the box by the clearer light falling on the landing from a window in the roof, he discovered a letter nailed to the cover. There was something written on it; but the paper was dusty, the ink was faded by time, and the characters were hard to decipher. By dint of perseverance, however, he made out from them this inscription: "Justification of my conduct toward my niece; to be read after my death. Joanna Grice."

As he passed the parlor door, he heard her voice, reading. He stopped and listened. The words that reached his ears seemed familiar to them; and yet he knew not, at first, what book they came from. He listened a little longer; his recollections of his boyhood and of home helped him; and he knew that the book from which Joanna Grice was reading aloud to herself was the Bible.

His face darkened, and he went out quickly into the garden; but stopped before he reached the paling, and, turning back to the front window of the parlor, looked in. He saw her sitting with her back to him, with elbows on the table, and hands working feverishly in her tangled gray hair. Her voice was still audible; but the words it pronounced could no longer be distinguished. He waited at the window for a few moments; then left it suddenly, saying to himself, "I wonder the book don't strike her dead!" Those were his only words of farewell. With that thought in his heart, he turned his back on the cottage, and on Joanna Grice.

He went on through the rain, taking the box

with him, and looking about for some sheltered place in which he could open it. After walking nearly a mile, he saw an old cattle-shed, a little way off the road—a rotten, deserted place; but it afforded some little shelter, even yet; so he entered it.

There was one dry corner left; dry enough, at least, to suit his purpose. In that he knelt down, and cut the cord round the box—hesitated before he opened it—and began by tearing away the letter outside, from the nail that fastened it to the cover.

It was a long letter, written in a close crabbed hand. He ran his eye over it impatiently, till his attention was accidentally caught and arrested by two or three lines, more clearly penned than the rest, near the middle of a page. For many years he had been unused to reading any written characters; but he spelled out resolutely the words in the few lines which first struck his eye, and found that they ran thus:

"I have now only to add, before proceeding to the miserable confession of our family dishonor, that I never afterward saw, and only once heard of, the man who tempted my niece to commit the deadly sin, which was her ruin in this world, and will be her ruin in the next."

Beyond those words, he made no effort to read further. Thrusting the letter hastily into his pocket, he turned once more to the box.

It was sealed up with strips of tape, but not

locked. He forced the lid open, and saw inside a few simple articles of woman's wearing apparel; a little work-box; a lace collar, with the needle and thread still sticking in it; several letters, here tied up in a packet, there scattered carelessly; a gayly-bound album; a quantity of dried ferns and flower leaves that had apparently fallen from between the pages; a piece of canvas with a slipper-pattern worked on it; and a black dress-waistcoat with some unfinished embroidery on the collar. It was plain to him, at a first glance, that these things had been thrown into the box anyhow, and had been left just as they were thrown. For a moment or two, he kept his eyes fixed on the sad significance of the confusion displayed before him; then turned away his head, whispering to himself, mournfully and many times, that name of "Mary," which he had already pronounced while in the presence of Joanna Grice. After a little, he mechanically picked out the letters that lay scattered about the box; mechanically eyed the broken seals and the addresses on each; mechanically put them back again unopened, until he came to one which felt as if it had something inside it. This circumstance stimulated him into unfolding the inclosure, and examining what the letter might contain.

Nothing but a piece of paper neatly folded. He undid the folds, and found part of a lock of hair inside, which he wrapped up again the moment he saw it, as if anxious to conceal it from view as soon as possible. The letter he examined more deliberately. It was in a woman's handwriting; was directed to "Miss Mary Grice, Dibbledean"; and was only dated "Bond Street, London. Wednesday." The post-mark, however, showed that it had been written many years ago. It was not very long; so he set himself to the task of making it all out from beginning to end.

This was what he read:

"MY DEAREST MARY—I have just sent you your pretty hair bracelet by the coach, nicely sealed and packed up by the jeweler. I have directed it to you by your own name, as I direct this, remembering what you told me about your father making it a point of honor never to open your letters and parcels; and forbidding that ugly Aunt Joanna of yours ever to do so either. I hope you will receive this and the little packet about the same time.

"I will answer for your thinking the pattern of your bracelet much improved since the new hair has been worked in with the old. How slyly you will run away to your own room, and *blush unseen*, like the flower in the poem, when you look at it. You may be rather surprised, perhaps, to see some little gold fastenings introduced as additions; but this, the jeweler told me, was a matter of necessity. Your poor dear sister's hair being the only material of the bracelet, when you sent it up to me to be altered, was very different from the hair of that faultless true-love of yours which you also sent to be worked in with it. It was, in fact, hardly half long enough to plait up properly with poor Susan's, from end to end; so the jeweler had to join it with little gold clasps, as you will see. It is very prettily run in along with the old hair, though. No country jeweler could have done it half as nicely, so you did well to send it to London after all. I consider myself rather a judge of these things; and I say positively that it is now the prettiest hair bracelet I ever saw.

"Do you see him as often as ever? He ought to be true and faithful to you, when you show how dearly you love him, by mixing his hair with poor Susan's, whom you were always so fondly attached to. I say he *ought;* but *you* are sure to say he *will*—and I am quite ready, love, to believe that you are the wiser of the two.

"I would write more, but have no time. It is just the regular London season now, and we are worked out of our lives. I envy you dressmakers in the country; and almost wish I was back again at Dibbledean, to be tyrannized over from morning to night by Miss Joanna. I know she is your aunt, my dear; but I can't help saying that I hate her very name! Ever your affectionate friend,   JANE HOLDSWORTH.

"P.S.—The jeweler sent back the hair he did not want; and I, as in duty bound, return it inclosed to you, its lawful owner."

Those scars on Mat's face, which indicated the stir of strong feelings within him more palpably than either his expression or his manner, began

to burn redly again while he spelled his way
through this letter. He crumpled it up hastily
round the inclosure, instead of folding it as it
had been folded before; and was about to cast it
back sharply into the box, when the sight of the
wearing apparel and half-finished work lying
inside seemed to stay his hand, and teach it on a
sudden to move tenderly. He smoothed out the
paper with care, and placed it very gently
among the rest of the letters—then looked at the
box thoughtfully for a moment or two; took
from his pocket the letter that he had first examined, and dropped it in among the others—then
suddenly and sharply closed the lid of the box
again.

"I can't touch any more of her things," he
said to himself; "I can't so much as look at
'em, somehow, without its making me—" he
stopped to tie up the box; straining at the cords
as if the mere physical exertion of pulling hard
at something were a relief to him at that moment. "I'll open it again and look it over in a
day or two, when I'm away from the old place
here," he resumed, jerking sharply at the last
knot—"when I'm away from the old place, and
have got to be my own man again."

He left the shed, regained the road, and
stopped, looking up and down, and all round
him, indecisively. Where should he go next?
To the grave, where he had been told that Mary
lay buried? No: not until he had first read all
the letters and carefully examined all the objects
in the box. Back to London, and to his prom-

ised meeting next morning with Zack? Yes: nothing better was left to be done—back to London.

Before nightfall he was journeying again to the great city, and to his meeting with Zack; journeying (though he little thought it) to the place where the clew lay hid—the clew to the Mystery of Mary Grice.

CHAPTER IV.

FATE WORKS, WITH ZACK FOR AN INSTRUMENT.

A QUARTER of an hour's rapid walking from his father's door took Zack well out of the neighborhood of Baregrove Square, and launched him in vagabond independence loose on the world. He had a silk handkerchief and sevenpence half-penny in his pockets—his available assets consisted of a handsome gold watch and chain—his only article of baggage was a blackthorn stick—and his anchor of hope was the pawnbroker.

His first action, now that he had become his own master, was to go direct to the nearest stationer's shop that he could find, and there to write the penitent letter to his mother over which his heart had failed him in the library at Baregrove Square. It was about as awkward, scrambling, and incoherent an epistolary production as ever was composed. But Zack felt easier when he had completed it—easier still when he had actually dropped it into the post-office along with his other letter to Mr. Valentine Blyth.

The next duty that claimed him was the first great duty of civilized humanity—the filling of an empty purse. Most young gentlemen in his station of life would have found the process of pawning a watch in the streets of London, and in broad daylight, rather an embarrassing one. But Zack was born impervious to a sense of respectability. He marched into the first pawnbroker's he came to with as solemn an air of business, and marched out again with as serene an expression of satisfaction, as if he had just been drawing a handsome salary, or just been delivering a heavy deposit into the hands of his banker.

Once provided with pecuniary resources, Zack felt himself at liberty to indulge forthwith in a holiday of his own granting. He opened the festival by a good long ride in a cab, with a bottle of pale ale and a packet of cigars inside, to keep the miserable state of the weather from affecting his spirits. He closed the festival with a visit to the theater, a supper in mixed company, total self-oblivion, a bed at a tavern, and a blinding headache the next morning. Thus much, in brief, for the narrative of his holiday. The proceedings, on his part, which followed that festival, claim attention next; and are of sufficient importance, in the results to which they led, to be mentioned in detail.

The new morning was the beginning of an important day in Zack's life. Much depended on

the interviews he was about to seek with his
new friend, Mat, in Kirk Street, and with Mr.
Blyth, at the turnpike in the Laburnum Road.
As he paid his bill at the tavern, his conscience
was not altogether easy, when he recalled a certain passage in his letter to his mother, which
had assured her that he was on the highroad to
reformation already. "I'll make a clean breast
of it to Blyth, and do exactly what he tells me,
when I meet him at the turnpike." Fortifying
himself with this good resolution, Zack arrived
at Kirk Street, and knocked at the private door
of the tobacconist's shop.

Mat, having seen him from the window, called
to him to come up, as soon as the door was
opened. The moment they shook hands, young
Thorpe noticed that his new friend looked altered. His face seemed to have grown downcast
and weary, his eyes heavy and vacant, since
they had last met.

"What's happened to you?" asked Zack.
"You have been somewhere in the country,
haven't you? What news do you bring back,
my dear fellow? Good, I hope?"

"Bad as can be," returned Mat, gruffly.
"Don't you say another word to me about it.
If you do, we part company again. Talk of
something else. Anything you like; and the
sooner the better."

Forbidden to discourse any more concerning
his friend's affairs, Zack veered about directly,
and began to discourse concerning his own.
Candor was one of his few virtues: and he now

confided to Mat the entire history of his tribulations, without a single reserved point at any part
of the narrative, from beginning to end.

Without putting a question or giving an answer, without displaying the smallest astonishment or the slightest sympathy, Mat stood gravely listening until Zack had quite done.   He then
went to the corner of the room where the round
table was; pulled the upturned lid back upon the
pedestal; drew from the breast-pocket of his coat
a roll of beaver-skin; slowly undid it; displayed
upon the table a goodly collection of bank-notes;
and pointing to them, said to young Thorpe,
"Take what you want."

It was not easy to surprise Zack; but this proceeding so completely astonished him that he
stared at the bank-notes in speechless amazement.   Mat took his pipe from a nail in the
wall, filled the bowl with tobacco, and pointing
with the stem toward the table, gruffly repeated,
"Take what you want."

This time Zack found words in which to express himself, and used them pretty freely to
praise his new friend's unexampled generosity,
and to decline taking a single farthing.   Mat
deliberately lit his pipe, in the first place, and
then bluntly answered in these terms:

"Take my advice, young 'un, and keep all
that talking for somebody else: it's gibberish to
me.   Don't bother; and help yourself to what
you want.   Money's what you want—though
you won't own it.   That's money.   When it's
gone, I can go back to California and get more.

While it lasts, make it spin. What is there to stare at? I told you I'd be brothers with you, because of what you done for me the other night. Well: I'm being brothers with you now. Get your watch out of pawn, and shake a loose leg at the world. *Will* you take what you want? And when you have, just tie up the rest, and chuck 'em over here." With those words the man of the black skull-cap sat down on his bear-skins, and sulkily surrounded himself with clouds of tobacco-smoke.

Finding it impossible to make Mat understand those delicacies and refinements of civilized life which induce one gentleman (always excepting a clergyman at Easter-time) to decline accepting money from another gentleman as a gift—perceiving that he was resolved to receive all remonstrances as so many declarations of personal enmity and distrust—and well knowing, moreover, that a little money to go on with would be really a very acceptable accommodation under existing circumstances, Zack consented to take two ten-pound notes as a loan. At this reservation Mat chuckled contemptuously; but young Thorpe enforced it, by tearing a leaf out of his pocket-book, and writing an acknowledgment for the sum he had borrowed. Mat roughly and resolutely refused to receive the document; but Zack tied it up along with the bank-notes, and threw the beaver-skin roll back to its owner, as requested.

"Do you want a bed to sleep in?" asked Mat next. "Say yes or no at once! I won't have no more gibberish. I'm not a gentleman, and I can't shake up along with them as are. It's no use trying it on me, young 'un. I'm not much better than a cross between a savage and a Christian. I'm a battered, lonesome, scalped old vagabond—that's what I am! But I'm brothers with you for all that. What's mine is yours; and if you tell me it isn't again, me and you are likely to quarrel! Do you want a bed to sleep in? Yes? or No?"

Yes; Zack certainly wanted a bed; but—

"There's one for you," remarked Mat, pointing through the folding-doors into the back room. "*I* don't want it. I haven't slep' in a bed these twenty years and more, and I can't do it now. I take dog's snoozes in this corner; and I shall take more dog's snoozes out-of-doors in the day-time, when the sun begins to shine. I haven't been used to much sleep, and I don't want much. Go in and try if the bed's long enough for you."

Zack tried to expostulate again, but Mat interrupted him more gruffly than ever.

"I suppose you don't care to sleep next door to such as me," he said. "You wouldn't turn your back on a bit of my blanket, though, if we were out in the lonesome places together. Never mind! You won't cotton to me all at once, I dare say. Well: I cotton to *you* in spite of that. D—n the bed! Take it or leave it, which you like."

Zack the reckless, who was always ready at five minutes' notice to make friends with any living being under the canopy of heaven—Zack the gregarious, who in his days of roaming the country, before he was fettered to an office-stool, had "cottoned" to every species of rustic vagabond, from a traveling tinker to a resident poacher—at once declared that he would sleep in the offered bed that very night, by way of showing himself worthy of his host's assistance and regard, if worthy of nothing else. Greatly relieved by this plain declaration, Mat crossed his legs luxuriously on the floor, shook his great shoulders with a heartier chuckle than usual, and made his young friend free of the premises in these hospitable words:

"There! now the bother's over at last, I suppose," cried Mat. "Pull in the buffalo-hide, and bring your legs to an anchor anywhere you like. I'm smoking. Suppose you smoke too.— Hoi! Bring up a clean pipe," cried this rough diamond, in conclusion, turning up a loose corner of the carpet, and roaring through a crack in the floor into the shop below.

The pipe was brought. Zack sat down on the buffalo-hide, and began to ask his queer friend about the life he had been leading in the wilds of North and South America. From short replies at first, Mat was gradually beguiled into really relating some of his adventures. Wild, barbarous fragments of narrative they were; mingling together in one darkly-fantastic record, fierce triumphs and deadly dangers; miseries of cold, and hunger, and thirst; glories of hunters' feasts in mighty forests; gold-findings among desolate rocks; gallopings for life from the flames of the blazing prairie; combats with wild beasts and with men wilder still; weeks of awful solitude in primeval wastes; days and nights of perilous orgies among drunken savages; visions of meteors in heaven, of hurricanes on earth, and of icebergs blinding bright, when the sunshine was beautiful over the Polar seas.

Young Thorpe listened in a fever of excitement. Here was the desperate, dangerous, roving life of which he had dreamed! He longed already to engage in it: he could have listened to descriptions of it all day long. But Mat was the last man in the world to err, at any time, on the side of diffuseness in relating the results of his own experience. And he now provokingly stopped, on a sudden, in the middle of an adventure among the wild horses on the Pampas; declaring that he was tired of feeling his own tongue wag, and had got so sick of talking of himself, that he was determined not to open his mouth again—except to put a rump-steak and a pipe in it—for the rest of the day.

Finding it impossible to make him alter this resolution, Zack thought of his engagement with Mr. Blyth, and asked what time it was. Mat, having no watch, conveyed this inquiry into the shop by the same process of roaring through the crack in the ceiling which he had already employed to produce a clean pipe. The answer showed Zack that he had barely time enough left to be punctual to his appointment in the Laburnum Road.

K—11

"I must be off to my friend at the turnpike," he said, rising and putting on his hat; "but I shall be back again in an hour or two. I say, have you thought seriously yet about going back to America?" His eyes sparkled eagerly as he put this question.

"There ain't no need to think about it," answered Mat. "I mean to go back; but I haven't settled what day yet. I've got something to do first." His face darkened, and he glanced aside at the box which he had brought from Dibbledean, and which was now covered with one of his bear-skins. "Never mind what it is; I've got it to do, and that's enough. Don't you go asking again whether I've brought news from the country, or whether I haven't. Don't you ever do that, and we shall sail along together easy enough. I like you, Zack, when you don't bother me. If you want to go, what are you stopping for? Why don't you clear out at once?"

Young Thorpe departed, laughing. It was a fine clear day and the bright sky showed signs of a return of the frost. He was in high spirits as he walked along thinking of Mat's wild adventures. What was the happiest painter's life, after all, compared to such a life as he had just heard described? Zack was hardly in the Laburnum Road before he began to doubt whether he had really made up his mind to be guided entirely by Mr. Blyth's advice, and to devote all his energies for the future to the cultivation of the fine arts.

Near the turnpike stood a tall gentleman making a sketch in a note-book of some felled timber lying by the road-side. This could be no other than Valentine—and Valentine it really was.

Mr. Blyth looked unusually serious, as he shook hands with young Thorpe. "Don't begin to justify yourself, Zack," he said; "I'm not going to blame you now. Let's walk on a little. I have some news to tell you from Baregrove Square."

It appeared from the narrative on which Valentine now entered, that, immediately on the receipt of Zack's letter, he had called on Mr. Thorpe, with the kindly purpose of endeavoring to make peace between father and son. His mission had entirely failed. Mr. Thorpe had grown more and more irritable as the interview proceeded; and had accused his visitor of unwarrantable interference, when Valentine suggested the propriety of holding out some prospect of forgiveness to the runaway son.

This outbreak Mr. Blyth had abstained from noticing, out of consideration for the agitated state of the speaker's feelings. But when the Reverend Mr. Yollop (who had been talking with Mrs. Thorpe upstairs) came into the room soon afterward, and joined in the conversation, words had been spoken which had obliged Valentine to leave the house. The reiteration of some arguments on the side of mercy which he had already advanced, had caused Mr. Yollop to hint, with extreme politeness and humility, that Mr. Blyth's profession was not of a nature to render him capable of estimating properly the nature and consequences of moral guilt; while Mr. Thorpe had referred almost openly to the scandalous reports which had been spread abroad in certain quarters, years ago, on the subject of Madonna's parentage. These insinuations had roused Valentine instantly. He had denounced them as false in the strongest terms he could employ; and had left the house, resolved never to hold any communication again either with Mr. Yollop or Mr. Thorpe.

About an hour after his return home, a letter marked "Private" had been brought to him from Mrs. Thorpe. The writer referred, with many expressions of sorrow, to what had occurred at the interview of the morning; and earnestly begged Mr. Blyth to take into consideration the state of Mr. Thorpe's health, which was such, that the family doctor (who had just called) had absolutely forbidden him to excite himself in the smallest degree by receiving any visitors, or by taking any active steps toward the recovery of his absent son. If these rules were not strictly complied with for many days to come, the doctor declared that the attack of palpitation of the heart, from which Mr. Thorpe had suffered on the night of Zack's return, might occur again, and might be strengthened into a confirmed malady. As it was, if proper care was taken, nothing of an alarming nature need be apprehended.

Having referred to her husband in these terms, Mrs. Thorpe next reverted to herself. She men-

tioned the receipt of a letter from Zack; but said
it had done little toward calming her anxiety
and alarm. Feeling certain that Mr. Blyth
would be the first friend her son would go to,
she now begged him to use his influence to keep
Zack from abandoning himself to any desperate
courses, or from leaving the country, which she
greatly feared he might be tempted to do. She
asked this of Mr. Blyth as a favor to herself, and
hinted that if he would only enable her, by
granting it, to tell her husband, without entering into details, that their son was under safe
guidance for the present, half the anxiety from
which she was now suffering would be allevi-
ated. Here the letter ended abruptly, a request
for a speedy answer being added in the post-
script.

"Now, Zack," said Valentine, after he had
related the result of his visit to Baregrove Square,
and had faithfully reported the contents of Mrs.
Thorpe's letter, "I shall only add that whatever
has happened between your father and me,
makes no difference in the respect I have always
felt for your mother, and in my earnest desire to
do her every service in my power. I tell you
fairly—as between friends—that I think you
have been very much to blame; but I have sufficient confidence and faith in you to leave everything to be decided by your own sense of honor,
and by the affection which I am sure you feel
for your mother."

This appeal, and the narrative which had preceded it, had their due effect on Zack. His

ardor for a wandering life of excitement and peril began to cool in the quiet temperature of the good influences that were now at work within him. "It shan't be my fault, Blyth, if I don't deserve your good opinion," he said, warmly. "I know I've behaved badly; and I know, too, that I have had some severe provocations. Only tell me what you advise, and I'll do it—I will, upon my honor, for my mother's sake."

"That's right! that's talking like a man!" cried Valentine, clapping him on the shoulder. "In the first place, it would be no use your going back home at once—even if you were willing, which I am afraid you are not. In your father's present state, your return to Baregrove Square would do *him* a great deal of harm, and do *you* no good. Employed, however, you must be somehow while you're away from home; and what you're fit for—unless it's Art—I'm sure I don't know. You have been talking a great deal about wanting to be a painter; and now is the time to test your resolution. If I get you an order to draw in the British Museum, to fill up your mornings; and if I enter you at some private Academy, to fill up your evenings (mine at home is not half strict enough for you)—will you stick to it?"

"With all my heart," replied Zack, resolutely dismissing his dreams of life in the wilds to the limbo of oblivion. "I ask nothing better, Blyth, than to stick to you and your plan for the future."

"Bravo!" cried Valentine, in his old gay, hearty manner. "The heaviest load of anxiety that has been on my shoulders for some time past is off now. I will write and comfort your mother this very afternoon—"

"Give her my love," interposed Zack.

"Giving her your love; in the belief, of course, that you are going to prove yourself worthy to send such a message," continued Mr. Blyth. "Let us turn, and walk back at once. The sooner I write, the easier and happier I shall be. By-the-by, there's another important question starts up now, which your mother seems to have forgotten, in the hurry and agitation of writing her letter. What are you going to do about money matters? Have you thought about a place to live in for the present? Can I help you in any way?"

These questions admitted of but one candid form of answer, which the natural frankness of Zack's character led him to adopt without hesitation. He immediately related the whole history of his first meeting with Mat (formally describing him, on this occasion, as Mr. Matthew Marksman), and of the visit to Kirk Street which had followed it that very morning.

Though in no way remarkable for excess of caution, or for the possession of any extraordinary fund of worldly wisdom, Mr. Blyth frowned and shook his head suspiciously, while he listened to the curious narrative now addressed to him. As soon as it was concluded, he expressed the most decided disapprobation of the careless

readiness with which Zack had allowed a perfect
stranger to become intimate with him—reminding him that he had met his new acquaintance
(of whom, by his own confession, he knew next
to nothing) in a very disreputable place—and
concluded by earnestly recommending him to
break off all connection with so dangerous an
associate, at the earliest possible opportunity.

Zack, on his side, was not slow in mustering
arguments to defend his conduct. He declared
that Mr. Marksman had gone into the Snuggery
innocently, and had been grossly insulted before
he became the originator of the riot there. As
to his family affairs and his real name, he might
have good and proper reasons for concealing
them; which was the more probable, as his account of himself in other respects was straightforward and unreserved enough. He might be
a litttle eccentric, and might have led an ad-
venturous life; but it was surely not fair to condemn him, on that account only, as a bad character. In conclusion, Zack cited the loan he had
received, as a proof that the stranger could not
be a swindler, at any rate; and referred to the
evident familiarity with localities and customs
in California which he had shown in conversation that afternoon, as affording satisfactory
proof in support of his own statement that he
had gained his money by gold-digging.

Mr. Blyth, however, still held firmly to his
original opinion; and, first offering to advance
the money from his own purse, suggested that
young Thorpe should relieve himself of the obli-

gation which he had imprudently contracted, by
paying back what he had borrowed that very
afternoon.

"Get out of his debt," said Valentine, earnestly; "get out of his debt, at any rate."

"You don't know him as well as I do," replied Zack. "He wouldn't think twice about
knocking me down, if I showed I distrusted him
in that way—and let me tell you, Blyth, he's one
of the few men alive who could really do it."

"This is no laughing matter, Zack," said
Valentine, shaking his head doubtfully.

"I never was more serious in my life," rejoined Zack. "I won't say I should be afraid,
but I will say I should be ashamed to pay him
his money back on the day when I borrowed it.
Why, he even refused to accept my written acknowledgment of the loan! I only succeeded
in forcing it on him unawares, by slipping it in
among his bank-notes; and, if he finds it there,
I'll lay you any wager you like, he tears it up,
or throws it into the fire."

Mr. Blyth began to look a little puzzled. The
stranger's behavior about the money was rather
staggering, to say the least of it.

"Let me bring him to your picture-show,"
pursued Zack. "Judge of him yourself, before
you condemn him. Surely I can't say fairer
than that? May I bring him to see the pictures?
Or will you come back at once with me to Kirk
Street, where he lives?"

"I must write to your mother, before I do
anything else; and I have work in hand besides

for to-day and to-morrow," said Valentine. "All things considered, you had better bring your friend, as you proposed just now. But remember the distinction I always make between my public studio and my private house. I consider the glorious mission of Art to apply to everybody; so I am proud to open my painting-room to any honest man who wants to look at my pictures. But the freedom of my other rooms is only for my own friends. I can't have strangers brought upstairs: remember that."

"Of course! I shouldn't think of it, my dear fellow. Only you look at old Rough and Tough, and hear him talk; and I'll answer for the rest."

"Ah, Zack! Zack! I wish you were not so dreadfully careless about whom you get acquainted with. I have often warned you that you will bring yourself or your friends into trouble some day, when you least expect it. Where are you going to now?"

"Back to Kirk Street. This is my nearest way; and I promised Mat—"

"Remember what you promised *me*, and what I am going to promise your mother—"

"I'll remember everything, Blyth. Good-by, and thank you. Only wait till we meet on Saturday, and you see my new friend, and you will find it all right."

"I hope I shan't find it all wrong," said Mr. Blyth, forebodingly, as he followed the road to his own house.

CHAPTER V.

FATE WORKS, WITH MR. BLYTH FOR AN INSTRUMENT.

THE great day of the year in Valentine's house was always the day on which his pictures for the Royal Academy Exhibition were shown in their completed state to friends and admiring spectators, congregated in his own painting-room. His visitors represented almost every variety of rank in the social scale; and grew numerous in proportion as they descended from the higher to the lower degrees. Thus, the aristocracy of race was usually impersonated, in his studio, by his one noble patron, the Dowager Countess of Brambledown; the aristocracy of art by two or three Royal Academicians; and the aristocracy of money by eight or ten highly respectable families, who came quite as much to look at the Dowager Countess as to look at the pictures. With these last, the select portion of the company might be said to terminate; and, after them, flowed in promiscuously the obscure majority of the visitors—a heterogeneous congregation of worshipers at the shrine of art, who were some of them of small importance, some of doubtful importance, some of no importance at all; and who included within their numbers not only a sprinkling of Mr. Blyth's old-established tradesmen, but also his gardener, his wife's old nurse, the brother of his housemaid, and the fa-

ther of his cook.   Some of his respectable friends
deplored, on principle, the "leveling tendencies"
which induced him thus to admit a mixture of
all classes into his painting-room, on the days
when he exhibited his pictures.   But Valentine
was warmly encouraged in taking this course by
no less a person than Lady Brambledown herself, whose perverse pleasure it was to exhibit
herself to society as an uncompromising Radical,
a reviler of the Peerage, a teller of scandalous
Royal anecdotes, and a worshiper of the memory
of Oliver Cromwell.

On the eventful Saturday which was to display his works to an applauding public of private friends, Mr. Blyth's studio, thanks to Madonna's industry and attention, looked really in
perfect order—as neat and clean as a room could
be.   A semicircle of all the available chairs in
the house—drawing-room and bedroom chairs
intermingled—ranged itself symmetrically in
front of the pictures.   That imaginative classical landscape, "The Golden Age," reposed
grandly on its own easel; while "Columbus in
Sight of the New World"—the largest canvas
Mr. Blyth had ever worked on, encased in the
most gorgeous frame he had ever ordered for one
of his own pictures—was hung on the wall at an
easy distance from the ground, having proved
too bulky to be safely accommodated by any
easel in Valentine's possession.

Except Mr. Blyth's bureau, all the ordinary
furniture and general litter of the room had
been cleared out of it, or hidden away behind

convenient draperies in corners. Backward and
forward over the open space thus obtained, Mr.
Blyth walked expectant, with the elastic skip
peculiar to him; looking ecstatically at his pictures, as he passed and repassed them—now singing, now whistling; sometimes referring mysteriously to a small manuscript which he carried
in his hand, jauntily tied round with blue ribbon; sometimes following the lines of the composition in "Columbus," by flourishing his right
hand before it in the air, with dreamy artistic
grace; always, turn where he would, instinct
from top to toe with an excitable activity which
defied the very idea of rest—and always hospitably ready to rush to the door and receive the
first enthusiastic visitor with open arms at a
moment's notice.

Above stairs, in the invalid room, the scene
was of a different kind. Here, also, the arrival
of the expected visitors was an event of importance; but it was awaited in perfect tranquillity
and silence. Mrs. Blyth lay in her usual position on the couch-side of the bed, turning over a
small portfolio of engravings; and Madonna
stood at the front window, where she could command a full view of the garden gate, and of the
approach from it to the house. This was always
her place on the days when the pictures were
shown; for, while occupying this position, she
was able, by signs, to indicate the arrival of the
different guests to her adopted mother, who lay
too far from the window to see them. On all
other days of the year, it was Mrs. Blyth who

devoted herself to Madonna's service, by interpreting for her advantage the pleasant conversations that she could not hear. On this day, it
was Madonna who devoted herself to Mrs. Blyth's
service, by identifying for her amusement the
visitors whose approach up the garden walk she
could not safely leave her bed to see.

No privilege that the girl enjoyed under Valentine's roof was more valued by her than this;
for by the exercise of it she was enabled to make
some slight return in kind for the affectionate
attention of which she was the constant object.
Mrs. Blyth always encouraged her to indicate
who the different guests were, as they followed
each other, by signs of her own choosing, these
signs being almost invariably suggested by some
characteristic peculiarity of the person represented, which her quick observation had detected at a first interview, and which she copied
with the quaintest exactness of imitation. The
correctness with which her memory preserved
these signs, and retained, after long intervals,
the recollection of the persons to whom they
alluded, was very extraordinary. The name of
any mere acquaintance, who came seldom to the
house, she constantly forgot, having only perhaps had it interpreted to her once or twice, and
not hearing it, as others did, whenever it accidentally occurred in conversation. But if the
sign by which she herself had once designated
that acquaintance—no matter how long ago—
happened to be repeated by those about her,
it was then always found that the forgotten

person was recalled to her recollection immediately.

From eleven till three had been notified in the invitation-cards as the time during which the pictures would be on view. It was now long past ten. Madonna still stood patiently by the window, going on with a new purse which she was knitting for Valentine, and looking out attentively now and then toward the road. Mrs. Blyth, humming a tune to herself, slowly turned over the engravings in her portfolio, and became so thoroughly absorbed in looking at them, that she forgot altogether how time was passing, and was quite astonished to hear Madonna suddenly clap her hands at the window, as a signal that the first punctual visitor had passed the garden gate.

Mrs. Blyth raised her eyes from the prints directly, and smiled as she saw the girl puckering up her fresh, rosy face into a childish imitation of old age, bending her light figure gravely in a succession of formal bows, and kissing her hand several times with extreme suavity and deliberation. These signs were meant to indicate Mrs. Blyth's father, the poor engraver, whose old-fashioned habit it was to pay homage to all his friends among the ladies, by saluting them from afar off with tremulous bows and gallant kissings of the hand.

"Ah!" thought Mrs. Blyth, nodding, to show that she understood the signs—"Ah! there's father. I felt sure he would be the first; and I know exactly what he will do when he gets in.

He will admire the pictures more than anybody, and have a better opinion to give of them than anybody else has; but before he can mention a word of it to Valentine, there will be dozens of people in the painting-room, and then he will get taken suddenly nervous, and come up here to me."

While Mrs. Blyth was thinking about her father, Madonna signalized the advent of two more visitors. First, she raised her hand sharply, and began pulling at an imaginary whisker on her own smooth cheek—then stood bolt upright, and folded her arms majestically over her bosom. Mrs. Blyth immediately recognized the originals of these two pantomime portrait-sketches. The one represented Mr. Hemlock, the small critic of a small newspaper, who was principally remarkable for never letting his whiskers alone for five minutes together. The other portrayed Mr. Bullivant, the aspiring fair-haired sculptor, who wrote poetry and studied dignity in his attitudes so unremittingly, that he could not even stop to look in at a shop-window, without standing before it as if he was his own statue.

In a minute or two more, Mrs. Blyth heard a prodigious grating of wheels, and trampling of horses, and banging of carriage-steps violently let down. Madonna immediately took a seat on the nearest chair, rolled the skirt of her dress up into her lap, tucked both her hands inside it, then drew one out, and imitated the action of snuff-taking—looking up merrily at Mrs. Blyth, as much as to say, "You can't mistake that, I think?"—Impossible! old Lady Brambledown, with her muff and snuff-box, to the very life.

Close on the Dowager Countess followed a visitor of low degree. Madonna—looking as if she was a little afraid of the boldness of her own imitation—began chewing an imaginary quid of tobacco; then pretended to pull it suddenly out of her mouth, and throw it away behind her. It was all over in a moment; but it represented to perfection Mangles, the gardener; who, though an inveterate chewer of tobacco, always threw away his quid whenever he confronted his betters, as a duty that he owed to his own respectability.

Another carriage. Madonna put on a supposititious pair of spectacles, pretended to pull them off, rub them bright, and put them on again; then, retiring a little from the window, spread out her dress into the widest dimensions that it could be made to assume. The new arrivals thus portrayed were the doctor, whose spectacles were never clean enough to please him; and the doctor's wife, an emaciated fine lady, who deceitfully suggested the presence of vanished charms by wearing a balloon under her gown—which benevolent rumor pronounced to be only a crinoline petticoat.

Here there was a brief pause in the procession of visitors. Mrs. Blyth beckoned to Madonna, and began talking on her fingers.

"No signs of Zack yet—are there, love?"

The girl looked anxiously toward the window, and shook her head.

"If he ventures up here, when he does come, we must not be so kind to him as usual. He has been behaving very badly, and we must see if we can't make him ashamed of himself."

Madonna's color rose directly. She looked amazed, sorry, perplexed, and incredulous, by turns. Zack behaving badly?—she would never believe it!

"*I* mean to make him ashamed of himself, if he ventures near *me!*" pursued Mrs. Blyth.

"And *I* shall try if I can't console him afterward," thought Madonna, turning away her head for fear her face should betray her.

Another ring at the bell! "There he is, perhaps," continued Mrs. Blyth, nodding in the direction of the window, as she signed those words.

Madonna ran to look: then turned round, and with a comic air of disappointment, hooked her thumbs in the armholes of an imaginary waistcoat. Only Mr. Gimble, the picture dealer, who always criticised works of art with his hands in that position.

Just then, a soft knock sounded at Mrs. Blyth's door; and her father entered, sniffing with a certain perpetual cold of his which nothing could cure—bowing, kissing his hand, and frightened upstairs by the company, just as his daughter had predicted.

"Oh, Lavvie! the Dowager Countess is downstairs, and her ladyship likes the pictures," exclaimed the old man, snuffling and smiling infirmly in a flutter of nervous glee.

"Come and sit down by me, father, and see Madonna doing the visitors. It's funnier than any play that ever was acted."

"And her ladyship likes the pictures," repeated the engraver, his poor old watery eyes sparkling with pleasure as he told his little morsel of good news over again, and sat down by the bedside of his favorite child.

The rings at the bell began to multiply at compound interest. Madonna was hardly still at the window for a moment, so many were the visitors whose approach up the garden walk it was now necessary for her to signalize. Down-stairs, all the vacant seats left in the painting-room were filling rapidly; and the ranks of standers in the back places were getting two-deep already.

There was Lady Brambledown (whose calls at the studio always lasted the whole morning), sitting in the center, or place of honor, taking snuff fiercely, talking liberal sentiments in a cracked voice, and apparently feeling extreme pleasure in making the respectable middle classes stare at her in reverent amazement. Also, two Royal Academicians—a saturnine Academician, swaddled in a voluminous cloak; and a benevolent Academician, with a slovenly umbrella and a perpetual smile. Also, the doctor and his wife, who admired the massive frame of "Columbus," but said not a word about the picture itself. Also, Mr. Bullivant, the sculptor, and Mr. Hemlock, the journalist, exchanging solemnly that critical small talk, in which such words as "sensuous," "æsthetic," "object-ive," and "subjective," occupy prominent places, and out of which no man ever has succeeded, or ever will succeed, in extricating an idea. Also, Mr. Gimble, fluently laudatory, with the whole alphabet of Art Jargon at his fingers' ends, and without the slightest comprehension of the sub-ject to embarrass him in his flow of language. Also, certain respectable families who tried vainly to understand the pictures, opposed by other respectable families who never tried at all, but confined themselves exclusively to the Dowager Countess. Also, the obscure general visitors, who more than made up in enthusiasm what they wanted in distinction. And, finally, the absolute democracy, or downright low-life party among the spectators—represented for the time being by Mr. Blyth's gardener, and Mr. Blyth's cook's father—who, standing together modestly outside the door, agreed, in awestruck whispers, that the "Golden Age" was a tasty thing, and "Columbus in Sight of the New World" a beautiful piece.

All Valentine's restlessness before the visitors arrived was as nothing compared with his raptur-ous activity, now that they were fairly assem-bled. Not once had he stood still, or ceased talk-ing, since the first spectator entered the room. And not once, probably, would he have permitted either his legs or his tongue to take the slightest repose until the last guest had departed from the Studio, but for Lady Brambledown, who accidentally hit on the only available means of fixing his attention to one thing and keeping him comparatively quiet in one place.

"I say, Blyth," cried her ladyship (she never prefixed the word "Mister" to the names of any of her male friends)—"I say, Blyth, I can't for the life of me understand your picture of Columbus. You talked some time ago about explaining it in detail. When are you going to begin?"

"Directly, my dear madam, directly: I was only waiting till the room got well filled," answered Valentine, taking up the long wand which he used to steady his hand while he was painting, and producing the manuscript tied round with blue ribbon. "The fact is—I don't know whether you mind it?—I have just thrown together a few thoughts on art, as a sort of introduction to—to Columbus, in short. They are written down on this paper—the thoughts are. Would anybody be kind enough to read them, while I point out what they mean on the picture? I only ask, because it seems egotistical to be reading my opinions about my own works.—*Will* anybody be kind enough?" repeated Mr. Blyth, walking all along the semicircle of chairs, and politely offering his manuscript to anybody who would take it.

Not a hand was held out. Bashfulness is frequently infectious; and it proved to be so on this particular occasion.

"Nonsense, Blyth!" exclaimed Lady Brambledown. "Read it yourself. Egotistical? Stuff! Everybody's egotistical. I hate modest men;

they are all rascals. Read it, and assert your own importance. You have a better right to do so than most of your neighbors, for you belong to the aristocracy of talent—the only aristocracy, in my opinion, that is worth a straw.'' Here her ladyship took a pinch of snuff, and looked at the middle-class families, as much as to say, ''There! what do you think of that from a Member of your darling Peerage?''

Thus encouraged, Valentine took his station (wand in hand) beneath ''Columbus,'' and unrolled the manuscript.

''What a very peculiar man Mr. Blyth is!'' whispered one of the lady visitors to an acquaintance behind her.

''And what a very unusual mixture of people he seems to have asked!'' rejoined the other, looking toward the doorway, where the democracy loomed diffident in Sunday clothes.

''The pictures which I have the honor to exhibit,'' began Valentine from the manuscript, '' have been painted on a principle—''

''I beg your pardon, Blyth,'' interrupted Lady Brambledown, whose sharp ears had caught the remark made on Valentine and his ''mixture of people,'' and whose liberal principles were thereby instantly stimulated into publicly asserting themselves. ''I beg your pardon; but where's my old ally, the gardener, who was here last time?—Out at the door, is he? What does he mean by not coming in? Here, gardener! come behind my chair.''

The gardener approached, internally writhing

under the honor of public notice, and covered with confusion in consequence of the noise his boots made on the floor.

"How do you do? and how are your family? What did you stop out at the door for? You're one of Mr. Blyth's guests, and have as much right inside as any of the rest of us. Stand there, and listen, and look about you, and inform your mind. This is an age of progress, gardener; your class is coming uppermost, and time it did, too. Go on, Blyth." And again the Dowager Countess took a pinch of snuff, looking contemptuously at the lady who had spoken of the "mixture of people."

"I take the liberty," continued Valentine, resuming the manuscript, "of dividing all art into two great classes, the landscape subjects, and the figure subjects; and I venture to describe these classes, in their highest development, under the respective titles of Art Pastoral and Art Mystic. The 'Golden Age' is an attempt to exemplify Art Pastoral. 'Columbus in Sight of the New World' is an effort to express myself in Art Mystic. In the 'Golden Age' "—(everybody looked at Columbus immediately)—"in the 'Golden Age,' " continued Mr. Blyth, waving his wand persuasively toward the right picture, "you have, in the foreground bushes, the middle distance trees, the horizon mountains, and the superincumbent sky, what I would fain hope is a tolerably faithful transcript of mere Nature. But in the group of buildings to the right" (here the wand touched the architectural city, with

its acres of steps and forests of pillars), "in the
dancing nymphs, and the musing philosopher"
(Mr. Blyth rapped the philosopher familiarly on
the head with the padded end of his wand), "you
have the Ideal—the elevating poetical view of
ordinary objects, like cities, happy female peas-
ants, and thoughtful spectators. Thus Nature
is exalted; and thus Art Pastoral—no!—thus
Art Pastoral exalts—no! I beg your pardon—
thus Art Pastoral and Nature exalt each other,
and—I beg your pardon again!—in short, exalt
each other—"

Here Valentine broke down at the end of a
paragraph; and the gardener made an abortive
effort to get back to the doorway.

"Capital, Blyth!" cried Lady Brambledown.
"Liberal, comprehensive, progressive, profound.
Gardener, don't fidget!"

"The true philosophy of art—the true philosophy of art, my lady," added Mr. Gimble, the
picture-dealer.

"Crude?" said Mr. Hemlock, the critic, appealing confidentially to Mr. Bullivant, the
sculptor.

"What?" inquired that gentleman.

"Blyth's principles of criticism," answered
Mr. Hemlock.

"Oh yes! extremely so," said Mr. Bullivant.

"Having glanced at Art Pastoral, as attempted
in the 'Golden Age,'" pursued Valentine, turning over a leaf, "I will now, with your permission, proceed to Art Mystic and 'Columbus.' Art

"CAPITAL, BLYTH!" CRIED LADY BRAMBLEDOWN. "LIBERAL, COM-
PREHENSIVE, PROGRESSIVE, PROFOUND! GARDENER, DON'T FIDGET!"
—HIDE-AND-SEEK, Vol. XI., page 344.

Mystic I would briefly endeavor to define as aiming at the illustration of fact on the highest imaginative principles. It takes a scene, for instance, from history, and represents that scene as exactly and naturally as possible. And here the ordinary thinker might be apt to say, Art Mystic has done enough." ("So it has," muttered Mr. Hemlock.) "On the contrary, Art Mystic has only begun. Besides the representation of the scene itself, the spirit of the age"—("Ah! quite right," said Lady Brambledown; "yes, yes, the spirit of the age")—"the spirit of the age which produced that scene must also be indicated, mystically, by the introduction of those angelic or infernal winged forms—those cherubs and airy female geniuses—those demons and dragons of darkness—which so many illustrious painters have long since taught us to recognize as impersonating to the eye the good and evil influences, Virtue and Vice, Glory and Shame, Success and Failure, Past and Future, Heaven and Earth—all on the same canvas." Here Mr. Blyth stopped again: this passage had cost him some trouble, and he was proud of having got smoothly to the end of it.

"Glorious!" cried enthusiastic Mr. Gimble.

"Turgid," muttered critical Mr. Hemlock.

"Very," assented compliant Mr. Bullivant.

"Go on — get to the picture — don't stop so often," said Lady Brambledown. "Bless my soul, how the man *does* fidget!" This was not directed at Valentine (who, however, richly deserved it), but at the unhappy gardener, who

had made a second attempt to escape to the shel-
tering obscurity of the doorway, and had been
betrayed by his boots.

"To exemplify what has just been remarked,
by the picture at my side," proceeded Mr. Blyth.
"The moment sought to be represented is sun-
rise on the 12th of October, 1492, when the great
Columbus first saw land clearly at the end of his
voyage. Observe, now, in the upper portions of
the composition, how the spirit of the age is mystically developed before the spectator. Of the
two winged female figures hovering in the morning clouds, immediately over Columbus and his
ship, the first is the Spirit of Discovery, holding
the orb of the world in her left hand, and pointing with a laurel crown (typical of Columbus's
fame) toward the newly-discovered Continent.
The other figure symbolizes the Spirit of Royal
Patronage, impersonated by Queen Isabella, Columbus's warm friend and patron, who offered
her jewels to pay his expenses, and who, throughout his perilous voyage, was with him in spirit,
as here represented. The tawny figure with feath-
ered head, floating hair, and wildly-extended
pinions, soaring upward from the western horizon, represents the Genius of America advancing
to meet her great discoverer; while the shadowy
countenances, looming dimly through the morning mist behind her, are portrait-types of Washington and Franklin, who would never have
flourished in America if that continent had not
been discovered, and who are here, therefore,

associated prophetically with the first voyages from the Old World to the New."

Pausing once more, Mr. Blyth used his explanatory wand freely on the Spirit of Discovery, the Spirit of Royal Patronage, and the Genius of America—not forgetting an indicative knock apiece for the embryo physiognomies of Washington and Franklin. Everybody's eyes followed the progress of the wand vacantly; but nobody spoke, except Mr. Hemlock, who frowned, and whispered "Bosh!" to Mr. Bullivant; who smiled, and whispered "Quite so," to Mr. Hemlock.

"Let me now ask your attention," resumed Valentine, "to the same mystic style of treatment, as carried from the sky into the sea. Writhing defeated behind Columbus's ship, in the depths of the transparent Atlantic, you have shadowy types of the difficulties and enemies that the dauntless navigator had to contend with. Crushed headlong into the water, sinks first the Spirit of Superstition, delineated by monastic robes—the council of monks having set itself against Columbus from the very first. Behind the Spirit of Superstition, and impersonated by a fillet of purple grapes around her head, descends the Genius of Portugal — the Portuguese having repulsed Columbus, and having treacherously sent out frigates to stop his discovery, by taking him prisoner. The scaly forms entwined around these two represent Envy, Hatred, Malice, Ignorance, and Crime generally; and thus the mystic element is, so

to speak, led through the sea out of the picture.''

(Another pause. Nobody said a word, but
everybody was relieved by the final departure
of the mystic element.

"All that now remains to be noticed,'' continued Mr. Blyth, "is the central portion of the
composition, which is occupied by Columbus and
his ships, and which represents the scene as it
may actually be supposed to have occurred.
Here we get to Reality, and to that sort of cor-
rectly-imitative art which is simple enough to
explain itself. As a proof of this, let me point
attention to the rig of the ships, the actions of the
sailors, and, more than all, to Columbus himself. Weeks of the most laborious consultation
of authorities of which the artist is capable have
been expended over the impersonation of that
one figure—expended, I would say, in obtaining
that faithful representation of individual character, which it is my earnest desire to combine
with the higher or mystic element. One instance of this fidelity to Nature I may perhaps
be permitted to point out in the person of Columbus, in conclusion. Pray observe him, standing
rapturously on the high stern of his vessel—and
oblige me, at the same time, by minutely in-
specting his outstretched arms. First, however,
let me remind you that this great man went to
sea at the age of fourteen, and cast himself freely
into all the hardships of nautical life; next, let
me beg you to enter into my train of thought,
and consider these hardships as naturally com-

prising, among other things, industrious haul-
ings at ropes and manful tuggings at long oars;
and, finally, let me now direct your direction to
the manner in which the muscular system of the
famous navigator is developed about the arms in
anatomical harmony with this idea. Follow the
wand closely, and observe, bursting, as it were,
through his sleeves, the characteristic vigor of
Columbus's *Biceps Flexor Cubiti*—"

"Mercy on us! what's that?" cried Lady
Brambledown. "Anything improper?"

"The *Biceps Flexor Cubiti*, your ladyship,"
began the Doctor, delighted to pour professional
information into the mind of a Dowager Countess, "may be literally interpreted as the Two-
headed Bender of the Elbow, and is a muscle
situated on what we term the Os—"

"Follow the wand, my dear madam, pray follow the wand! This is the *Biceps*," interrupted
Valentine, tapping till the canvas quivered again
on the upper part of Columbus's arms, which
obtruded their muscular condition through a pair
of tight-fitting chamois leather sleeves. "The
Biceps, Lady Brambledown, is a tremendously
strong muscle—"

"Which arises in the human body, your ladyship," interposed the Doctor, "by two heads—"

"Which is used," continued Valentine, cutting him short—"I beg your pardon, Doctor, but
this is important—which is used—"

"I beg yours," rejoined the Doctor, testily.
"The origin of the muscle, or place where it
arises, is the first thing to be described. The

use comes afterward.   It is an axiom of anatomical science—"

"But, my dear sir!" cried Valentine.

"No," said the Doctor, peremptorily, "you
must really excuse me. This is a professional
point. If I allow erroneous explanations of the
muscular system to pass unchecked in my
presence—"

"I don't want to make any!" cried Mr. Blyth,
gesticulating violently in the direction of Columbus. "I only want to—"

"To describe the use of a muscle before you
describe the place of its origin in the human
body," persisted the Doctor. "No, my dear sir!
I can't sanction it. No, indeed! I really *can*
NOT sanction it!"

"Will you let me say two words?" asked Valentine.

"Two hundred thousand, my good sir, on any
other subject," assented the Doctor, with a sarcastic smile; "but on *this* subject—"

"On art?" shouted Mr. Blyth, with a tap on
Columbus, which struck a sound from the canvas like a thump on a muffled drum. "On art,
Doctor? I only want to say that, as Columbus's
early life must have exercised him considerably
in hauling ropes and pulling oars, I have shown
the large development of his *Biceps* muscle
(which is principally used in those actions)
through his sleeves, as a good characteristic
point to insist on in his physical formation.—
That's all! As to the origin—"

"The origin of the *Biceps Flexor Cubiti*,

your Ladyship," resumed the pertinacious Doctor, "is by two heads. The first begins, if I may so express myself, *tendinous*, from the glenoid cavity of the scapula—"

"That man is a pedantic jackass," whispered Mr. Hemlock to his friend.

"And yet he hasn't a bad head for a bust!" rejoined Mr. Bullivant.

"Pray, Mr. Blyth," pleaded the polite and ever-admiring Mr. Gimble; "pray let me beg you, in the name of the company, to proceed with your most interesting and suggestive explanations and views on art!"

"Indeed, Mr. Gimble," said Valentine, a little crestfallen under the anatomical castigation inflicted on him by the Doctor, "I am very much delighted and gratified by your approval; but I have nothing more to read. I thought that point about Columbus a good point to leave off with, and considered that I might safely allow the rest of the picture to explain itself to the intelligent spectator."

Hearing this, some of the spectators, evidently distrusting their own intelligence, rose to take leave—new visitors making their appearance, however, to fill the vacant chairs and receive Mr. Blyth's hearty welcome. Meanwhile, through all the bustle of departing and arriving friends, and through all the fast-strengthening hum of general talk, the voice of the unyielding doctor still murmured solemnly of "capsular ligaments," "adjacent tendons," and "corracoid processes," to Lady Brambledown, who listened to him with satirical curiosity, as a species of polite medical buffoon whom it rather amused her to become acquainted with.

Among the next applicants for admission at the painting-room door were two whom Valentine had expected to see at a much earlier period of the day—Mr. Matthew Marksman and Zack.

"How late you are!" he said, as he shook hands with young Thorpe.

"I wish I could have come earlier, my dear fellow," answered Zack, rather importantly; "but I had some business to do" (he had been recovering his watch from the pawnbroker); "and my friend here had some business to do also" (Mr. Marksman had been toasting red herrings for an early dinner); "and so somehow we couldn't get here before. Mat, let me introduce you. This is my old friend, Mr. Blyth, whom I told you of."

Valentine had barely time to take the hand of the new guest before his attention was claimed by fresh visitors. Young Thorpe did the honors of the painting-room in the artist's absence. "Lots of people, as I told you. My friend's a great genius," whispered Zack, wondering, as he spoke, whether the scene of civilized life now displayed before Mr. Marksman would at all tend to upset his barbarian self-possession.

No: not in the least. There stood Mat, just as grave, cool, and quietly observant of things about him as ever. Neither the pictures, nor the company, nor the staring of many eyes that wondered at his black skull-cap and scarred swarthy face, were capable of disturbing the Olympian serenity of this Jupiter of the backwoods.

"There!" cried Zack, pointing triumphantly across the room to "Columbus." "Cudgel your brains, old boy, and guess what that is a picture of, without coming to me to help you."

Mat attentively surveyed the figure of Columbus, the rig of his ship, and the wings of the typical female spirits, hovering overhead in the morning clouds—thought a little—then gravely and deliberately answered:

"Peter Wilkins taking a voyage along with his flying wives."

Zack pulled out his handkerchief, and stifled his laughter as well as he could, out of consideration for Mat, who, however, took not the smallest notice of him, but added, still staring intently at the picture:

" 'Peter Wilkins' was the only book I had when I was a lad aboard ship. I used to read it over and over again, at odds and ends of spare time, till I pretty nigh got it by heart. That was many a year ago; and a good lot of what I knowed then I don't know now. But, mind ye, it's my belief that Peter Wilkins was something of a sailor."

"Well!" whispered Zack, humoring him, "suppose he was, what of that?"

"Do you think a man as was anything of a sailor would ever be fool enough to put to sea in such a craft as that?" asked Mr. Marksman, pointing scornfully to Columbus's ship.

"Hush! old Rough and Tough: the picture hasn't anything to do with Peter Wilkins," said Zack. "Keep quiet, and wait here a minute for me. There are some friends of mine at the other end of the room that I must go and speak to. And I say, if Blyth comes up to you and asks you about the picture, say it's Columbus, and remarkably like him."

Left by himself, Mat looked about for better standing-room than he then happened to occupy; and seeing a vacant space left between the door-post and Mr. Blyth's bureau, retreated to it. Putting his hands in his pockets, he leaned comfortably against the wall, and began to examine the room and everything in it at his leisure. It was not long, however, before he was disturbed. One of his neighbors, seeing that his back was against a large paper sketch nailed on the wall behind him, told him bluntly that he was doing mischief there, and made him change his position. He moved accordingly to the door-post; but even here he was not left in repose. A fresh relay of visitors arrived, and obliged him to make way for them to pass into the room—which he did by politely rolling himself round the door-post into the passage.

As he disappeared in this way, Mr. Blyth bustled up to the place where Mat had been standing, and received his guests there, with great cordiality, but also with some appearance of flurry and perplexity of mind. The fact was, that Lady Brambledown had just remembered that she had not examined Valentine's works yet through one of those artistic tubes which effectively concentrate the rays of light on a picture, when applied to the eye. Knowing, by former experience, that the studio was furnished with one of these little instruments, her ladyship now intimated her ardent desire to use it instantly on "Columbus." Valentine promised to get it, with his usual ready politeness; but he had not the slightest idea where it actually was, for all that. Among the litter of small things that had been cleared out of the way when the painting-room was put in order, there were several which he vaguely remembered having huddled together for safety in the bottom of his bureau. The tube might possibly have been among them; so in this place he determined to look for it—being quite ignorant, if the search turned out unsuccessful, where he ought to look next.

After begging the new visitors to walk in, he opened the bureau, which was large and old-fashioned, with a little bright key hanging by a chain that he unhooked from his watch-guard, and began searching inside, amid infinite confusion—all his attention concentrated in the effort to discover the lost tube. It was not to be found in the bottom of the bureau. He next looked, after a little preliminary hesitation, into a long narrow drawer opening beneath some pigeon-hole recesses at the back.

The tube was not there either; and he shut the drawer to again, carefully and gently—for inside it was the hair bracelet that had belonged to Madonna's mother, lying on the white handkerchief, which had also been taken from the dead woman's pocket. Just as he closed the drawer he heard footsteps at his right hand, and turned in that direction rather suspiciously, locking down the lid of the bureau as he looked round. It was only the civil Mr. Gimble, wanting to know what Mr. Blyth was searching for, and whether he could help him. Valentine mentioned the loss of the tube; and Mr. Gimble immediately volunteered to make one of pasteboard. "Ten thousand thanks," said Mr. Blyth, hooking the key to his watch-guard again, as he returned to Lady Brambledown with his friend. "Ten thousand thanks; but the worst of it is, I don't know where to find the pasteboard."

If, instead of turning to the right hand to speak to Mr. Gimble, Valentine had turned to the left, he would have seen that, just as he opened the bureau and began to search in it, Mr. Marksman, finding the way into the painting-room clear once more, had rolled himself quietly round the door-post again; and had then, just as quietly, bent forward a little, so as to look sidewise into the bureau with those observant eyes of his which nothing could escape, and which had been trained by his old Indian experience to be always unscrupulously at work watching something. Little did Mr. Blyth think, as he walked away, talking with Mr. Gimble, and carefully hooking his key on to its swivel again, that Zack's strange friend had seen as much of the inside of the bureau as he had seen of it himself.

"He shut up his big box uncommon sharp, when that smilin' little chap come near him," thought Mat. "And yet there didn't seem nothing in it that strangers mightn't see. There wasn't no money there—at least none that *I* set eyes on. Well! it's not my business. Let's have another look at the picter."

In the affairs of art, as in other matters, important discoveries are sometimes made, and great events occasionally accomplished, by very ignoble agencies. Mat's deplorable ignorance of Painting in general, and grossly illiterate misunderstanding of the subject represented by Columbus in particular, seemed to mark him out as the last man in the world who could possibly be associated with Art Mystic in the character of guardian genius. Yet such was the proud position which he was now selected by Fate to occupy. In plain words, Mr. Blyth's greatest historical work had been for some little time in imminent danger of destruction by falling; and Mat's "look at the picter" was the all-important look which enabled him to be the first person in the room who perceived that it was in peril.

The eye with which Mr. Marksman now regarded the picture was certainly the eye of a barbarian; but the eye with which he afterward examined the supports by which it was suspended was the eye of a sailor, and of a good practical carpenter to boot. He saw directly that one of the two iron clamps to which the frame-lines of "Columbus" were attached had been carelessly driven into a part of the wall that was not strong enough to hold it against the downward stress of the heavy frame. Little warning driblets of loosened plaster had been trickling down rapidly behind the canvas; but nobody heard them fall, in the general buzz of talking; and nobody noticed the thin, fine crack above the iron clamp, which was now lengthening stealthily minute by minute.

"Just let me by, will you?" said Mat, quietly, to some of his neighbors. "I want to stop those flying women and the man in the crank ship from coming down by the long run."

Dozens of alarmed ladies and gentlemen started up from their chairs. Mat pushed through them unceremoniously, and was indebted to his want of politeness for being in time to save the picture. With a grating crack, and an accompanying descent of a perfect slab of plaster, the loose clamp came clean out of the wall, just as Mat seized the unsupported end and side of the frame in his sturdy hands, and so prevented the picture from taking the fatal swing downward, which would have infallibly torn it from the remaining fastening, and precipitated it on the chairs beneath.

A prodigious confusion and clamoring of tongues ensued; Mr. Blyth being louder, wilder, and more utterly useless in the present emergency than any of his neighbors. Mat, cool as ever, kept his hold of the picture; and, taking no notice of the confused advice and cumbersome help offered to him, called to Zack to fetch a ladder, or, failing that, to "get a hoist" on some chairs, and cut the rope from the clamp that remained firm. Wooden steps, as young

Thorpe knew, were usually kept in the paint-ing-room. Where had they been removed to now? Mr. Blyth's memory was lost altogether in his excitement. Zack made a speculative dash at the flowing draperies which concealed the lum-ber in one corner, and dragged out the steps in triumph.

"All right; take your time, young 'un: there's a knife in my left-hand breeches-pocket," said Mat. "Now then, cut away at that bit of rope's-end, and hold on tight at top, while I lower away at bottom. Steady! Take it easy, and—there you are!" With which words, the guardian genius left Art Mystic resting safely on the floor, and began to shake his coat-tails free of the plaster that had dropped on them.

"My dear sir! you have saved the finest picture I ever painted," cried Valentine, warmly seizing him by both hands. "I can't find words to express my gratitude and admiration—"

"Don't worry yourself about that," answered Mat; "I don't suppose I should understand you if you *could* find 'em. If you want the picter put up again, I'll do it. And if you want the carpenter's muddle-head punched who put it up before, I shouldn't much mind doing that either," added Mat, looking at the hole from which the clamp had been torn with an expres-sion of the profoundest workman-like disgust.

A new commotion in the room—near the door this time—prevented Mr. Blyth from giving an immediate answer to the two friendly proposi-tions just submitted to him.

At the first alarm of danger, all the ladies—headed by the Dowager Countess, in whom the instinct of self-preservation was largely developed—had got as far away as they could from the falling picture before they ventured to look round at the process by which it was at last safely landed on the floor. Just as this had been accomplished, Lady Brambledown—who stood nearest to the doorway—caught sight of Madonna in the passage that led to it. Mrs. Blyth had heard the noise and confusion downstairs; and finding that her bell was not answered by the servants, and that it was next to impossible to overcome her father's nervous horror of confronting the company alone, had sent Madonna downstairs with him, to assist in finding out what had happened in the studio.

While descending the stairs with her companion, the girl had anticipated that they might easily discover whether anything was amiss without going further than the passage, by merely peeping through the studio door. But all chance of escaping the ordeal of the painting-room was lost the moment Lady Brambledown set eyes on her. The Dowager Countess was one of Madonna's warmest admirers; and now expressed that admiration by pouncing on her with immense affection and enthusiasm from the painting-room doorway. Other people, to whom the deaf and dumb girl was a much more interesting sight than "Columbus" or the "Golden Age," crowded round her; all trying together, with great amiability and small intelligence, to explain what had happened by signs which no human being could possibly understand. Fortunately for Madonna, Zack (who ever since he had cut the picture down had been assailed by an incessant fire of questions about his strange friend from dozens of inquisitive gentlemen) happened to look toward her over the ladies' heads, and came directly to explain the danger from which "Columbus" had escaped. She tried hard to get away, and bear the intelligence to Mrs. Blyth; but Lady Brambledown, feeling amiably unwilling to resign her too soon, pitched on the poor engraver standing tremulous in the passage, as being quite clever enough to carry a message upstairs, and sent him off to take the latest news from the studio to his daughter immediately.

Thus it was that, when Mr. Blyth left Zack's friend to see what was going on near the door, he found Madonna in the painting-room, surrounded by sympathizing and admiring ladies. The first words of explanation by which Lady Brambledown answered his mute look of inquiry reminded him of the anxiety and alarm that his wife must have suffered; and he ran upstairs directly, promising to be back again in a minute or two.

Mat carelessly followed Valentine to the group at the doorway, carelessly looked over some ladies' bonnets, and saw Madonna offering her slate to the Dowager Countess at that moment.

The sweet feminine gentleness and youthful softness of the girl's face looked inexpressibly

lovely, as she now stood shy and confused under
the eager eyes that were all gazing on her.   Her
dress, too, had never more powerfully aided the
natural attractions of her face and figure by its
own lovable charms of simplicity and modesty
than now, when the plain gray merino gown,
and neat little black silk apron which she always wore, were contrasted with the fashionable
frippery of fine colors shining all around her.
Was the rough Mr. Marksman himself lured at
first sight into acknowledging her influence?   If
he was, his face and manner showed it very
strangely.

Almost at the instant when his eyes fell on
her, that clay-cold change which had altered
the color of his swarthy cheeks in the hosier's
shop at Dibbledean passed over them again.   The
first amazed look that he cast on her slowly darkened, while his eyes rested on her face, into a
fixed, heavy, vacant stare of superstitious awe.
He never moved—he hardly seemed to breathe
—until the head of a person before him accidentally intercepted his view.   Then he stepped
back a few paces, looked about him bewildered,
as if he had forgotten where he was, and turned
quickly toward the door, as if resolved to leave
the room immediately.

But there was some inexplicable influence at
work in his heart that drew him back, in spite
of his own will.   He retraced his steps to the
group round Madonna, looked at her once more,
and from that moment never lost sight of her
till she went upstairs again.   Whichever way

her face turned, he followed the direction, outside the circle, so as to be always in front of it.
When Valentine re-appeared in the studio, and
Madonna besought him by a look to set her free
from general admiration, and send her back to
Mrs. Blyth, Mat was watching her over the
painter's shoulder. And when young Thorpe,
who had devoted himself to helping her in communicating with the visitors, nodded to her as
she left the room, his friend from the backwoods
was close behind him.

CHAPTER VI.

THE FINDING OF THE CLEW.

Mr. Blyth's visitors, now that their common
center of attraction had disappeared, either dis-
persed again in the painting-room, or approached
the door to take their departure. Zack, turning
round sharply after Madonna had left the studio,
encountered his queer companion, who had not
stirred an inch, while other people were all moving about him.

"In the name of wonder, what has come to
you now? Are you ill? Have you hurt yourself with that picture?" asked Zack, startled by
the incomprehensible change which he beheld in
his friend's face and manner.

"Come out," said Mat. Young Thorpe looked
at him in amazement; even the sound of his voice
had altered!

"What's wrong?" asked Zack. No answer. They went quickly along the passage and down to the garden gate in silence. As soon as they had got into one of the lonely by-roads of the new suburb, Mat stopped short, and, turning full on his companion, said: "Who is she?" The sudden eagerness with which he spoke, so strangely at variance with his usual deliberation of tone and manner, made those three common words almost startling to hear.

"*She?* Who do you mean?" inquired young Thorpe.

"I mean that young woman they were all staring at."

For a moment Zack contemplated the anxiety visible in his friend's face with an expression of blank astonishment; then burst into one of his loudest, heartiest, and longest fits of laughter. "Oh, by Jove, I wouldn't have missed this for fifty pounds. Here's old Rough and Tough smitten with the tender passion, like all the rest of us! Blush, you brazen old beggar, blush! You've fallen in love with Madonna at first sight!"

"D—n your laughing! Tell me who she is."

"Tell you who she is? That's exactly what I can't do."

"Why not? What do you mean? Does she belong to that painter-man?"

"Oh, fie, Mat. You mustn't talk of a young lady *belonging* to anybody as if she was a piece of furniture, or money in the Three per Cents, or something of that sort. Confound it, man, don't shake me in that way! You'll pull my arm off. Let me have my laugh, and I'll tell you everything."

"Tell it, then, and be quick about it."

"Well, first of all, she is not Blyth's daughter —though some scandal-mongering people have said she is—"

"Nor yet his wife?"

"Nor yet his wife. What a question! He adopted her, as they call it, years ago, when she was a child. But who she is, or where he picked her up, or what is her name, Blyth never *has* told anybody, and never *will*. She's the dearest, kindest, prettiest little soul that ever lived; and that's all I know about her. It's a short story, old boy; but surprisingly romantic—isn't it?"

Mat did not immediately answer. He paid the most breathless attention to the few words of information which Zack had given him—repeated them over again to himself—reflected for a moment—then said,

"Why won't the painter-man tell anybody who she is?"

"How should I know? It's a whim of his. And, I'll tell you what, here's a piece of serious advice for you: If you want to go there again and make her acquaintance, don't you ask Blyth who she is, or let him fancy you want to know. He's touchy on that point—I can't say why; but he is. Every man has a raw place about him somewhere: that's Blyth's raw place; and if you hit him on it, you won't get inside of his house again in a hurry, I can tell you."

Still Mat's attention fastened greedily on every word—still his eyes fixed eagerly on his informant's face—still he repeated to himself what Zack was telling him.

"By-the-by, I suppose you saw the poor dear little soul is deaf and dumb," young Thorpe continued. "She's been so from a child. Some accident; a fall, I believe. But it don't affect her spirits a bit. She's as happy as the day is long —that's one comfort."

"Deaf and dumb! So like her, it was a'most as awful as seeing the dead come to life again. She had Mary's turn with her head; Mary's— poor creature! poor creature!" He whispered those words to himself under his breath, his face turned aside, his eyes wandering over the ground at his feet with a faint, troubled, vacantly anxious expression.

"Come! come! don't be getting into the dolefuls already," cried Zack, administering an exhilarating thump on the back to his friend. "Cheer up! We're all in love with her; you're rowing in the same boat with Bullivant, and Gimble, and me, and lots more; and you'll get used to it in time, like the rest of us. I'll act the generous rival with you, brother Mat! You shall have all the benefit of my advice gratis; and shall lay siege to our little beauty in regular form. I don't think your own experience among the wild Indians will help you much over here. How do you mean to make love to her? Did you ever make love to a squaw?"

"She isn't his wife, and she isn't his daugh-

ter; he won't say where he picked her up, or
who she is." Repeating these words to himself
in a quick, quiet whisper, Mat did not appear to
be listening to a single word that young Thorpe
said. His mind was running now on one of the
answers that he had wrested from Joanna Grice
at Dibbledean—the answer which had informed
him that Mary's child had been born alive!

"Wake up, Mat! You shall have your fair
chance with the lady, along with the rest of us;
and I'll undertake to qualify you on the spot for
civilized courtship," continued Zack, pitilessly
carrying on his joke. "In the first place, always
remember that you mustn't go beyond admiration at a respectful distance, to begin with. At
the second interview, you may make ámorous
faces at close quarters—what you call looking
unutterable things, you know. At the third,
you may get bold, and try her with a little present. Lots of people have done that before you.
Gimble tried it, and Bullivant wanted to; but
Blyth wouldn't let him; and I mean to give
her— Oh, by-the-by, I have another important
caution for you." Here he indulged himself in
a fresh burst of laughter, excited by the remembrance of his interview with Mrs. Peckover, in
Mr. Blyth's hall. "Remember that the whole
round of presents is open for you to choose from,
except one; and that one is a hair bracelet."

Zack's laughter came to an abrupt termination. Mat had raised his head suddenly, and
was now staring him full in the face again with
a bright, searching look—an expression in which

suspicious amazement and doubting curiosity were very strangely mingled together.

"You're not angry with me for cracking a few respectable old jokes?" said Zack. "Have I said anything? Stop! yes, I have, though I didn't mean it. You looked up at me in that savage manner, when I warned you not to give her a hair bracelet. Surely you don't think me brute enough to make fun of your not having any hair on your own head to give anybody? Surely you have a better opinion of me than that? I give you my word of honor, I never thought of you, or your head, or that infernal scalping business, when I said what I did. It was true—it happened to *me*."

"How did it happen?" said Mat, with eager, angry curiosity.

"Only in this way. I wanted to give her a hair bracelet myself—my hair and Blyth's, and so on. And an addle-headed old woman, who seems to know Madonna (that's a name we give her) as well as Blyth himself, and keeps what she knows just as close, got me into a corner, and talked nonsense about the whole thing, as old women will."

"What did she say?" asked Mat, more eager, more angry, and more curious than ever.

"She talked nonsense, I tell you. She said a hair bracelet would be unlucky to Madonna; and then told me Madonna had one already; and then wouldn't let me ask Blyth whether it was true, because I should get her into dreadful trouble if I said anything to him about it;

besides a good deal more which you wouldn't care to be bothered with. But I have told you enough—haven't I?—to show I was not thinking of *you*, when I said that just now by way of a joke. Come, shake hands, old fellow. You're not offended with me, now I have explained everything?"

Mat gave his hand, but he put it out like a man groping in the dark. His mind was full of that memorable letter about a hair bracelet, which he had found in the box given to him by Joanna Grice.

"A hair bracelet?" he said, vacantly.

"Don't be sulky!" cried Zack, clapping him on the shoulder.

"A hair bracelet is unlucky to the young woman—and she's got one already" (he was weighing attentively the lightest word that Zack had spoken to him). "What's it like?" he asked aloud, turning suddenly to young Thorpe.

"What's what like?"

"A hair bracelet."

"Still harping on that, after all my explanations! Like? Why it's hair plaited up, and made to fasten round the wrist, with gold at each end to clasp it by. What are you stopping for again? I'll tell you what, Mat, I can make every allowance for a man in your love-struck situation; but if I didn't know how you had been spending the morning, I should say you were drunk."

They had been walking along quickly, while Mat asked what a hair bracelet was like. But

no sooner had Zack told him than he came to a
dead pause—started and changed color—opened
his lips to speak—then checked himself, and remained silent. The information which he had
just received had recalled to him a certain object
that he had seen in the drawer of Mr. Blyth's
bureau; and the resemblance between the two
had at once flashed upon him. The importance
which this discovery assumed in his eyes, in
connection with what he had already heard,
may be easily estimated, when it is remembered
that his barbarian life had kept him totally ignorant that a hair bracelet is in England one of the
commonest ornaments of woman's wear.

"Are we going to stop here all day?" asked
Zack. "If you're turning from sulky to sentimental again, I shall go back to Blyth's and
pave the way for you with Madonna, old boy!"
He turned gayly in the direction of Valentine's
house as he said those words.

Mat did not offer to detain him; did not say a
word at parting. He passed his hand wearily
over his eyes as Zack left him. "I'm sober,"
he said, vacantly, to himself; "I'm not dreaming; I'm not light-headed, though I feel a'most
like it. I saw that young woman as plain as I
see them houses in front of me now; and by
God, if she had been Mary's ghost, she couldn't
have been more like her!"

He stopped. His hand fell to his side; then
fastened mechanically on the railings of a house
near him. His rough, misshapen fingers trembled round the iron. Recollections that had

slumbered for years and years past were awakening again awfully to life within him. Through the obscurity and oblivion of long absence, through the changeless darkness of the tomb, there was shining out now, vivid and solemn on his memory, the image—as she had been in her youth-time—of the dead woman whose name was "Mary." And it was only the sight of that young girl, of that poor, shy, gentle, deaf and dumb creature, that had wrought the miracle!

He tried to shake himself clear of the influences which were now at work on him. He moved forward a step or two and looked up. Zack?—where was Zack?

Away, at the other end of the solitary suburban street, just visible, sauntering along and swinging his stick in his hand.

Without knowing why he did so, Mat turned instantly and walked after him, calling to him to come back. The third summons reached him: he stopped, hesitated, made comic gesticulations with his stick in the air—then began to retrace his steps.

The effort of walking and calling after him had turned Mat's thoughts in another direction. They now occupied themselves again with the hints that Zack had dropped of some incomprehensible connection between a hair bracelet, and the young girl who was called by the strange name of "Madonna." With the remembrance of this, there came back also the recollection of the letter about a bracelet, and its inclosure of

hair, which he had examined in the lonely cattle-shed at Dibbledean, and which still lay in
the little box bearing on it the name of "Mary
Grice."

"Well!" cried Zack, speaking as he came on.
"Well, Cupid! what do you want with me
now?"

Mat did not immediately answer. His
thoughts were still traveling back cautiously
over the ground which they had already ex-
plored. Once more he was pondering on that
little circle of plaited hair, having gold at each
end, and looking just big enough to go round a
woman's wrist, which he had seen in the drawer
of Mr. Blyth's bureau. And once again, the
identity between this object and the ornament
which young Thorpe had described as being the
thing called a hair bracelet, began surely and
more surely to establish itself in his mind.

"Now, then, don't keep me waiting," continued Zack, laughing again as he came nearer;
"clap your hand on your heart, and give me
your tender message for the future Mrs. Marksman."

It was on the tip of Mat's tongue to emulate
the communicativeness of young Thorpe, and to
speak unreservedly of what he had seen in the
drawer of the bureau—but he suddenly restrained
the words just as they were dropping from his
lips. At the same moment his eyes began to
lose their vacant, perturbed look, and to brighten
again with something of craft and cunning,
added to their customary watchful expression.

"What's the young woman's real name?" he asked, carelessly, just as Zack was beginning to banter him for the third time.

"Is that all you called me back for? Her real name's Mary."

Mat had made his inquiry with the air of a man whose thoughts were far away from his words, and who only spoke because he felt obliged to say something. Zack's reply to his question startled him into instant and anxious attention.

"Mary!" he repeated, in a tone of surprise. "What else besides Mary?"

"How should I know? Didn't I try and beat it into your muddled old head, half an hour ago, that Blyth won't tell his friends anything about her?"

There was another pause. The secrecy in which Mr. Blyth chose to conceal Madonna's history, and the sequestered place in the innermost drawer of his bureau where he kept the hair bracelet, began vaguely to connect themselves together in Mat's mind. A curious smile hovered about his lips, and the cunning look brightened in his eyes. "The painter-man won't tell anything about her, won't he? Perhaps that thing in his drawer will." He muttered the words to himself, putting his hands in his pockets, and mechanically kicking away a stone which happened to lie at his feet on the pavement.

"What are you grumbling about now?" asked Zack. "Do you think I'm going to stop here all

day for the pleasure of hearing you talk to yourself?" As he spoke, he vivaciously rapped his
friend on the shoulder with his stick. "Trust
me to pave the way for you with Madonna!" he
called out mischievously, as he turned back in
the direction of Mr. Blyth's house.

"Trust *me* to have another look at your friend's
hair bracelet," said Mat, quietly, to himself.
"I'll handle it this' time, before I'm many days
older."

He nodded over his shoulder at Zack, and
walked away quickly in the direction of Kirk
Street.

CHAPTER VII.

THE BOX OF LETTERS.

THE first thing Mat did when he got to his
lodgings, was to fill and light his pipe. He then
sat down on his bear-skins, and dragged the box
close to him which he had brought from Dibbledean.

Although the machinery of Mat's mind was
constructed of very clumsy and barbaric materials; although book-learning had never oiled it,
and wise men's talk had never quickened it;
nevertheless, it always contrived to work on—
much as it was working now—until it reached,
sooner or later, a practical result. Solitude and
Peril are stern schoolmasters, but they do their
duty for good or evil, thoroughly with some
men; and they had done it thoroughly, amid

the rocks and wildernesses of the great American
continent, with Mat.

Many a pipe did he empty and fill again, many
a dark change passed over his heavy features, as
he now pondered long and laboriously over every
word of the dialogue that had just been held between himself and Zack. But not so much as
five minutes out of all the time he thus consumed
was, in any true sense of the word, time wasted.
He had sat down to his first pipe, resolved that,
if any human means could compass it, he would
find out how the young girl whom he had seen
in Mr. Blyth's studio had first come there, and
who she really was. When he rose up at last,
and put the pipe away to cool, he had thought
the matter fairly out from beginning to end, had
arrived at his conclusions and had definitely settled his future plans.

Reflection had strengthened him in the resolution to follow his first impulse when he parted
from Zack in the street, and begin the attempt
to penetrate the suspicious secret that hid from
him and from every one the origin of Valentine's adopted child, by getting possession of the
hair bracelet which he had seen laid away in
the inner drawer of the bureau. As for any as-
signable reason for justifying him in associating
this hair bracelet with Madonna, he found it, to
his own satisfaction, in young Thorpe's account
of the strange words spoken by Mrs. Peckover
in Mr. Blyth's hall—the suspicions resulting
from these hints being also immensely strengthened, by his recollections of the letter signed

"Jane Holdsworth," and containing an inclosure of hair, which he had examined in the cattle-shed at Dibbledean.

According to that letter, a hair bracelet (easily recognizable, if still in existence, by comparing it with the hair inclosed in Jane Holdsworth's note) had once been the property of Mary Grice. According to what Zack had said, there was apparently some incomprehensible confusion and mystery in connection with a hair bracelet and the young woman whose extraordinary likeness to what Mary Grice had been in her girlhood had first suggested to him the purpose he was now pursuing. Lastly, according to what he himself now knew, there was actually a hair bracelet lying in the innermost drawer of Mr. Blyth's bureau—this latter fragment of evidence assuming in his mind, as has been already re-marked, an undue significance in relation to the fragments preceding it, from his not knowing that hair bracelets are found in most houses where there are women in a position to wear any jewelry ornament at all.

Vague as they might be, these coincidences were sufficient to startle him at first—then to fill him with an eager, devouring curiosity—and then to suggest to him the uncertain and desperate course which he was now firmly resolved to follow. How he was to gain possession of the hair bracelet without Mr. Blyth's knowledge, and without exciting the slightest suspicion in the painter's family, he had not yet determined. But he was resolved to have it, he was perfectly

unscrupulous as to means, and he felt certain
beforehand of attaining his object.   Whither, or
to what excesses, that object might lead him, he
never stopped and never cared to consider.   The
awful face of the dead woman (now fixed forever in his memory by the living copy of it that
his own eyes had beheld) seemed to be driving
him on swiftly into unknown darkness, to bring
him out into unexpected light at the end.   The
influence which was thus sternly at work in him
was not to be questioned—it was to be obeyed.

His resolution in reference to the hair bracelet
was not more firmly settled than his resolution
to keep his real sensations on seeing Madonna,
and the purpose which had grown out of them,
a profound secret from young Thorpe, who was
too warmly Mr. Blyth's friend to be trusted.
Every word that Zack had let slip had been of
vital importance hitherto; every word that might
yet escape him might be of the most precious
use for future guidance.   "If it's his fun and
fancy," mused Mat, "to go on thinking I'm
sweet on the girl, let him think it.   The more
he thinks, the more he'll talk.   All I've got to
do is to *hold in*, and then he's sure to *let out*."

While schooling himself thus as to his future
conduct toward Zack, he did not forget another
person who was less close at hand certainly, but
who might also be turned to good account.   Before he fairly decided on his plan of action, he
debated with himself the propriety of returning
to Dibbledean, and forcing from the old woman,
Joanna Grice, more information than she had

been willing to give him at their first interview.
But, on reflection, he considered that it was better to leave this as a resource to be tried, in case
of the failure of his first experiment with the
hair bracelet.   One look at that—one close comparison of the hair it was made of with the
surplus hair which had not been used by the
jeweler, in Mary Grice's bracelet, and which
had been returned to her in her friend's letter
—was all he wanted in the first place; for this
would be enough to clear up every present uncertainty and suspicion connected with the ornament in the drawer of Mr. Blyth's bureau.

These were mainly the resolutions to which
his long meditation had now crookedly and
clumsily conducted him.   His next immediate
business was to examine those letters in the box
which he had hitherto not opened; and also to
possess himself of the inclosure of hair in the
letter to "Mary Grice," so that he might have
it always about him ready for any emergency.
Before he opened the box, however, he took a
quick, impatient turn or two up and down his
miserable little room.   Not once, since he had
set forth to return to his own country, and to the
civilization from which, for more than twenty
years, he had been an outcast, had he felt (to
use his favorite expression) that he was "his
own man again," until now.   A thrill of the
old, breathless, fierce suspense of his days of
deadly peril ran through him, as he thought on
the forbidden secret into which he was about to

pry, and for the discovery of which he was ready
to dare any hazard and use any means. "It goes
through and through me, a'most like dodging for
life again among the bloody Indians," muttered
Mat to himself, as he trod restlessly to and fro
in his cage of a room, rubbing all the while at
the scars on his face, as his way was when any
new excitement got the better of him.

At the very moment when this thought was
rising ominously in his mind, Valentine was ex-
pounding anew the whole scope and object of
"Columbus" to a fresh circle of admiring spectators—while his wife was interpreting to Madonna
above stairs Zack's wildest jokes about his friend's
love-stricken condition; and all three were laughing gayly at a caricature, which he was malicious-
ly drawing for them, of "poor old Mat" in the
character of a scalped Cupid. Even the little
minor globe of each man's social sphere has its
antipode-points; and when it is all bright sunshine in one part of the miniature world, it is
all pitch darkness, at the very same moment, in
another.

Mat's face had grown suddenly swarthier than
ever, while he walked across his room, and said
those words to himself which have just been recorded. It altered again, though, in a minute
or two, and turned once more to the cold clay-
color which had overspread it in the hosier's
shop at Dibbledean, as he returned to his bear-
skins and opened the box that had belonged to
"Mary Grice."

He took out first the letter with the inclosure

of hair, and placed it carefully in the breast-
pocket of his coat. He next searched a moment
or two for the letter superscribed and signed by
Joanna Grice; and, having found it, placed it
on one side of him, on the floor. After this he
paused a moment, looking into the box with a
curious, scowling sadness on his face; while his
hand vacantly stirred hither and thither the different objects that lay about among the papers—the
gayly-bound album, the lace collar, the dried
flower-leaves, and the other little womanly pos-
sessions which had once belonged to Mary Grice.

Then he began to collect together all the letters in the box. Having got them into his
hands—some tied up in a packet, some loose—
he spread them out before him on his lap, first
drawing up an end of one of the bear-skins over
his legs for them to lie on conveniently. He began by examining the addresses. They were all
directed to "Mary Grice," in the same clear,
careful, sharply-shaped handwriting. Though
they were letters in form, they proved to be only
notes in substance, when he opened them: the
writing, in some, not extending to more than four
or five lines. At least fifteen or twenty were expressed, with unimportant variations, in this form:

"MY DEAREST MARY—Pray try all you can
to meet me to-morrow evening at the usual place.
I have been waiting and longing for you in vain
to-day. Only think of *me*, love, as I am now,
and always, thinking of *you;* and I know you
will come. Ever and only yours,   A. C."

All these notes were signed in the same way, merely with initial letters. They contained nothing in the shape of a date, except the day of the week on which they had been written, and they had evidently been delivered by some private means, for there did not appear to be a post-mark on any of them. One after another Mat opened and glanced at them—then tossed them aside into a heap. He pursued this employment quietly and methodically; but as he went on with it, a strange look flashed into his eyes from time to time, giving to them a certain sinister bright-ness which altered very remarkably the whole natural expression of his face.

Other letters, somewhat longer than the note already quoted, fared no better at his hands. Dry leaves dropped out of some, as he threw them aside; and little water-color drawings of rare flowers fluttered out of others. Hard botan-ical names which he could not spell through, and descriptions of plants which he could not un-derstand, occurred here and there in postscripts and detached passages of the longer letters. But still, whether long or short, they bore no signa-ture but the initials "A. C."; still the dates afforded no information of the year, month, or place in which they had been written; and still Mat quietly and quickly tossed them aside one after the other, without so much as a word or a sigh escaping him, but with that sinister bright-ness flashing into his eyes from time to time. Out of the whole number of the letters there were only two that he read more than once

through, and then pondered over anxiously,
before he threw them from him like the rest.
The first of the two was expressed thus:

"I shall bring the dried ferns and the passion-
flower for your album with me this evening.
You cannot imagine, dearest, how happy and
how vain I feel at having made you as enthusiastic a botanist as I am myself. Since you
have taken an interest in my favorite pursuit, it
has been more exquisitely delightful to me than
any words can express. I believe that I never
really knew how to touch tender leaves tenderly
until now, when I gather them with the knowledge that they are all to be shown to *you*, and
all to be placed in your dear hand.

"Do you know, my own love, I thought I detected an alteration in you yesterday evening?
I never saw you so serious. And then your
attention often wandered; and, besides, you
looked at me once or twice quite strangely,
Mary — I mean strangely because your color
seemed to be coming and going constantly without any imaginable reason. I really fancied,
as I walked home—and I fancy still—that you
had something to say, and were afraid to say it.
Surely, love, you can have no secrets from me!
—But we shall meet to-night, and then you will
tell me everything (will you not?) without reserve. Farewell, dearest, till seven o'clock."

Mat slowly read the second paragraph of this
letter twice over, abstractedly twisting about

his great bristly whiskers between his finger and thumb. There was evidently something in the few lines which he was thus poring over, that half saddened, half perplexed him. Whatever the difficulty was, he gave it up, and went on doggedly to the next letter, which was an exception to the rest of the collection, for it had a postmark on it. He had failed to notice this, on looking at the outside; but he detected directly, on glancing at the inside, that it was dated differently from those which had gone before it. Under the day of the week was written the word ''London''—noting which, he began to read the letter with some appearance of anxiety. It ran thus:

"I write, my dearest love, in the greatest possible agitation and despair. All the hopes I felt and expressed to you, that my absence would not last more than a few days, and that I should not be obliged to journey further from Dibbledean than London, have been entirely frustrated. I am absolutely compelled to go to Germany, and may be away as long as three or four months. You see, I tell you the worst at once, Mary, because I know your courage and high spirit, and feel sure that you will bear up bravely against this unforeseen parting, for both our sakes. How glad I am that I gave you my hair for your bracelet, when I did; and that I got yours in return! It will be such a consolation to both of us to have our keepsakes to look at now.

"If it only rested with *me* to go or not, no earthly consideration should induce me to take this journey. But the rights and interests of others are concerned in my setting forth; and I must, therefore, depart at the expense of my own wishes, and my own happiness. I go this very day, and can only steal a few minutes to write to you. My pen hurries over the paper without stopping an instant—I am so agitated that I hardly know what I am saying to you.

"If anything, dearest Mary, could add to my sense of the misfortune of being obliged to leave you, it would be the apprehension which I now feel, that I may have ignorantly offended you, or that something has happened which you don't like to tell me. Ever since I noticed, ten days ago, that little alteration in your manner, I have been afraid you had something on your mind that you were unwilling to confide to me. The very last time we saw each other I thought you had been crying; and I am sure you looked away uneasily whenever our eyes met. What is it? Do relieve my anxiety by telling me what it is in your first letter! The moment I get to the other side of the Channel, I will send you word where to direct to. I will write constantly— mind you write constantly, too. Love me, and remember me always, till I return, never, I hope, to leave you again. A. C."

Over this letter Mat meditated long before he quietly cast it away among the rest. When he had at last thrown it from him, there remained

M—11

only three more to examine. They proved to be notes of no consequence, and had been evidently written at an earlier period than the letters he had just read. After hastily looking them over, he searched carefully all through the box, but no papers of any sort remained in it. That hurried letter, with its abrupt announcement of the writer's departure from England, was the latest in date—the last of the series!

After he had made this discovery, he sat for a little while vacantly gazing out of the window. His sense of the useless result to which the search he had been prosecuting had led him thus far, seemed to have robbed him of half his energy already. He looked once or twice at the letter superscribed by Joanna Grice, mechanically reading along the line on the cover: "Justification of my conduct toward my niece"—but not attempting to examine what was written inside. It was only after a long interval of hesitation and delay that he at last roused himself. "I must sweep these things out of the way, and read all what I've got to read before Zack comes in," he said to himself, gathering up the letters heaped at his feet, and thrusting them all back again together, with an oath, into the box.

He listened carefully once or twice after he had shut down the lid, and while he was tying the cords over it, to ascertain whether his wild young friend was opening the street door yet, or not. How short a time he had passed in Zack's company, yet how thoroughly well he knew him, not as to his failings only, but as to his merits

besides!   How wisely he foreboded that his boisterous fellow-lodger would infallibly turn against
him as an enemy, and expose him without an
instant's hesitation, if young Thorpe got any
hint of his first experimental scheme for discovering poor Mr. Blyth's anxiously-treasured secret
by underhand and treacherous means! Mat's
cunning had proved an invaluable resource to
him on many a critical occasion already; but he
had never been more admirably served by it than
now, when it taught him to be cautious of betraying himself to Zack.

For the present there seemed. to be no danger
of interruption. He corded up the box at his
leisure, concealed it in its accustomed place, took
his brandy-bottle from the cupboard, opened
Joanna Grice's letter—and still there was no
sound of any one entering in the passage downstairs. Before he began to read, he drank some
of the spirit from the neck of the bottle. Was
there some inexplicable dread stealing over him
at the mere prospect of examining the contents
of this one solitary letter?

It seemed as if there was. His finger trembled so, when he tried to guide himself by it
along each successive line of the cramped writing which he was now attempting to decipher,
that he had to take a second dram to steady it.
And when he at length fairly began the letter,
he did not pursue his occupation either as quietly
or as quickly as he had followed it before.
Sometimes he read a line or two aloud, sometimes he overlooked several sentences, and went

on to another part of the long narrative—now growling out angry comments on what he was reading; and now dashing down the paper impatiently on his knees, with fierce outbursts of oaths, which he had picked up in the terrible swearing-school of the Californian gold mines.

He began, however, with perfect regularity at the proper part of the letter; sitting as near to the window as he could, and slanting the closely written page before him, so as to give himself the full benefit of all the afternoon light which still flowed into the room.

CHAPTER VIII.

JOANNA GRICE'S NARRATIVE.

"I INTEND this letter to be read after my death, and I purpose calling it plainly a Justification of my conduct toward my Niece. Not because I think my conduct wants any excuse—but because others, ignorant of my true motives, may think that my actions want justifying, and may wickedly condemn me, unless I make some such statement in my own defense as the present. There may still be living one member of my late brother's family, whose voice would, I feel sure, be raised against me for what I have done. The relation to whom I refer has been—"

(Here Mat, who had read carefully thus far, grew impatient, and growling out some angry words, guided himself hastily down the letter with his finger till he arrived at the second paragraph.)

"—It was in the April month of 1827 that the villain who was the ruin of my niece, and the dishonor of the once respectable family to which she belonged, first came to Dibbledean. He took the little four-room cottage called Jay's Cottage, which was then to be let furnished, and which stands out of the town about a quarter of a mile down Church Lane. He called himself Mr. Carr, and the few letters that came to him were directed to 'Arthur Carr, Esq.'

"He was quite a young man—I should say not more than four or five and twenty—very quiet-mannered and delicate—or rather effeminate-looking, as I thought—for he wore his hair quite long over his shoulders, in the foreign way, and had a clear, soft complexion, almost like a woman's. Though he appeared to be a gentleman, he always kept out of the way of making acquaintances among the respectable families about Dibbledean. He had no friends of his own to come and see him that I heard of, except an old gentleman who might have been his father, and who came once or twice. His own account of himself was, that he came to Jay's Cottage for quiet, and retirement, and study; but he was very reserved, and would let nobody make up to him until the miserable day when he and my brother Joshua, and then my niece Mary, all got acquainted together.

"Before I go on to anything else, I must say first, that Mr. Carr was what they call a botanist. Whenever it was fine, he was always out-of-doors, gathering bits of leaves, which it seems he carried home in a tin case, and dried, and kept by him. He hired a gardener for the bit of ground round about Jay's Cottage; and the man told me once, that his master knew more about flowers and how to grow them than anybody he ever met with. Mr. Carr used to make little pictures, too, of flowers and leaves set together in patterns. These things were thought very odd amusements for a young man to take up with; but he was as fond of them as others of his age might be of hunting or shooting. He brought down many books with him, and read a great deal; but from all that I heard, he spent more time over his flowers and his botany than anything else.

"We had, at that time, the two best shops in Dibbledean. Joshua sold hosiery, and I carried on a good dressmaking and general millinery business. Both our shops were under the same roof, with a partition-wall between. One day Mr. Carr came in Joshua's shop, and wanted something which my brother had not got as ready to hand as the common things that the towns-people generally bought. Joshua begged him to sit down for a few minutes; but Mr. Carr (the parlor door at the bottom of the shop being left open) happened to look into the garden, which he could see very well through the window, and said that he would like to wait there, and look at the flowers. Joshua was only too glad to have his garden taken such notice of by a gentleman who was a botanist; so he showed his customer in there, and then went up into the warehouse to look for what was wanted.

"My niece, Mary, worked in my part of the house, along with the other young women. The room they used to be in looked into the garden; and from the window my niece must have seen Mr. Carr, and must have slipped downstairs (I not being in the way just then) to peep at the strange gentleman—or, more likely, to make believe she was accidentally walking in the garden, and so get noticed by him. All I know is, that when I came up into the work-room and found she was not there, and looked out of the window, I saw her and Joshua, and Mr. Carr all standing together on the grass-plot, the strange gentleman talking to her quite intimate, with a flower in his hand.

"I called out to her to come back to her work directly. She looked up at me, smiling in her bold impudent way, and said, 'Father has told me I may stop and learn what this gentleman is so kind as to teach me about my geraniums.' After that, I could say nothing more before the stranger: and when he was gone, and she came back triumphing, and laughing, and singing about the room, more like a mad play-actress than a decent young woman, I kept quiet and bore with her provocation. But I went down to my brother Joshua the same day, and talked to him seriously, and warned him that she ought to be kept stricter, and never let to have her own way, and offered to keep a strict hand over her myself, if he would only support me properly. But he put me off with careless, jesting words, which he learned to repent of bitterly afterward.

"Joshua was as pious and respectable a man as ever lived: but it was his misfortune to be too easy-tempered, and too proud of his daughter. Having lost his wife, and his eldest boy and girl, he seemed so fond of Mary, that he could deny her nothing. There was, to be sure, another one left of his family of children, who—"

(Here, again, Mat lost patience. He had been muttering to himself angrliy for the last minute or two, while he read—and now once more he passed over several lines of the letter, and went on at once to a new paragraph.)

"I have said she was vain of her good looks, and bold, and flighty; and I must now add, that she was also hasty, and passionate, and reckless. But she had wheedling ways with her, which nobody was sharp enough to see through but me. When I made complaints against her to her father, and proved that I was right in making them, she always managed to get him to forgive her. She behaved, from the outset (though I stood in the place of a mother to her) as perversely toward me as usual, in respect to Mr. Carr. It had flattered her pride to be noticed and bowed to just as if she was a born lady, by a gentleman, and a customer at the shop. And the very same evening, at tea-time, she undid before my face the whole effect of the good advice I had been giving her father. What with jumping on his knee, kissing him, tying and untying his cravat, sticking flowers in his button-hole, and going on altogether more like a child than a grown-up young woman, she wheedled him into promising that he would take her next Sunday to see Mr. Carr's garden; for it seems the gentleman had invited them to look at his flowers. I had tried my best, when I heard it, to persuade my brother not to accept the invitation and let her scrape acquaintance with a stranger under her father's own nose; but all that I could say was useless now. She had got the better of me, and when I put in my word, she had her bold laugh and her light answer ready to insult me with directly. Her father said he wondered I was not amused at her high spirits. I shook my head, but said nothing in return. Poor man! he lived to see where her 'high spirits' led her to.

"On the Sunday, after church, they went to Mr. Carr's. Though my advice was set at defiance in this way, I determined to persevere in keeping a stricter watch over my niece than ever. I felt that the maintaining the credit and reputation of the family rested with me, and I determined that I would try my best to uphold our good name. It is some little comfort to me, after all that has happened, to remember that I did my utmost to carry out this resolution. The blame of our dishonor lies not at my door. I disliked and distrusted Mr. Carr from the very first; and I tried hard to make others as suspicious of him as I was. But all I could say, and all I could do, availed nothing against the wicked cunning of my niece. Watch and restrain her as I might, she was sure—"

(Once more Mat broke off abruptly in the middle of a sentence. This time, however, it was to strike a light. The brief day of winter was fast fading out—the coming darkness was deepening over the pages of Joanna Grice's narrative. When he had lit his candle, and had sat down to read again, he lost his place, and, not having patience to look for it carefully, went on at once with the first lines that happened to strike his eye.)

"Things were now come, then, to this pass, that I felt certain she was in the habit of meeting him in secret; and yet I could not prove it to my brother's satisfaction. I had no help that I could call in to assist me against the diabolical cunning that was used to deceive me. To set other people to watch them when I could not, would only have been spreading through Dibbledean the very scandal that I was most anxious to avoid. As for Joshua, his infatuation made him deaf to all that I could urge. He would see nothing suspicious in the fondness Mary had suddenly taken for botany and drawing flowers. He let Mr. Carr lend her paintings to copy from, just as if they had known each other all their lives. Next to his blind trust in his daughter, because he was so fond of her, was his blind trust in this stranger, because the gen-

tleman's manners were so quiet and kind, and
because he sent us presents of expensive flowers
to plant in our garden. He would not authorize
me to open Mary's letters, or to forbid her even
to walk out alone; and he even told me once that
I did not know how to make proper allowances
for young people.

 "Allowances! I knew my niece better, and
my duty as one of an honest family better, than
to make allowances for such conduct as hers. I
kept the tightest hand over her that l could. I
advised her, argued with her, ordered her, por-
tioned out her time for her, watched her, warned
her, told her in the plainest terms, that she
should not deceive *me*—she or her gentleman!
I was honest and open, and said I disapproved
so strongly of the terms she kept up with Mr.
Carr, that if ever it lay in my power to cut short
their acquaintance together, I would most assuredly do it. I even told her plainly that if
she once got into mischief, it would then be too
late to reclaim her; and she answered, in her
reckless, sluttish way, that if she ever did get
into mischief it would be nothing but my aggra-
vation that would drive her to it; and that she
believed her father's kindness would never find
it too late to reclaim her again. This is only
one specimen of the usual insolence and wickedness of all her replies to me."

(As he finished this paragraph, Mat dashed
the letter down angrily on his knee, and cursed
the writer of it with some of those gold-digger's

imprecations which it had been his misfortune
to hear but too often in the past days of his Californian wanderings. It was evidently only by
placing considerable constraint upon himself,
that he now refrained from crumpling up the
letter and throwing it from him in disgust.
However, he spread it out flat before him once
more—looked first at one paragraph, then at another, but did not read them; hesitated—and
then irritably turned over the leaf of paper before him, and began at a new page.)

"When I told Joshua generally what I had
observed, and particularly what I myself had
seen and heard on the evening in question, he
seemed at last a little staggered, and sent for my
niece, to insist on an explanation. On his repeating to her what I had mentioned to him, she
flung her arms round his neck, looked first at me
and then at him, burst out sobbing and crying,
and so got from bad to worse, till she had a sort
of fit. I was not at all sure that this might not
be one of her tricks; but it frightened her father
so that he forgot himself, and threw all the
blame on me, and said my prudery and conspir-
ing had tormented and frightened the poor girl
out of her wits. After being insulted in this
way, of course the only thing I could do was to
leave the room, and let her have it all her own
way with him.

"It was now the autumn, the middle of September; and I was at my wit's end to know what
I ought to think and do next—when Mr. Carr

left Dibbledean. He had been away once or twice before, in the summer, but only for a day or two at a time. On this occasion my niece received a letter from him. He had never written to her when he was away in the summer; so I thought this looked like a longer absence than usual, and I determined to take advantage of it to try if I could not break off the intimacy between them, in case it went the length of any more letter-writing.

"I most solemnly declare, and could affirm on oath if necessary, that in spite of all I had seen and all I suspected for these many months, I had not the most distant idea of the wickedness that had really been committed. I thank God I was not well enough versed in the ways of sin to be as sharp in coming to the right conclusion as other women might have been in my situation. I only believed that the course she was taking *might* be fatal to her at some future day; and, acting on that belief, I thought myself justified in using any means in my power to stop her in time. I therefore resolved with myself that if Mr. Carr wrote again she should get none of his letters; and I knew her passionate and proud disposition well enough to know that if she could once be brought to think herself neglected by him, she would break off all intercourse with him, if ever he came back, immediately.

"I thought myself perfectly justified, standing toward her as I did in the place of a mother, and having only her good at heart, in taking these measures. On that head my conscience is still quite easy. I cannot mention what the plan was that I now adopted, without seriously compromising a living person. All I can say is, that every letter from Mr. Carr to our house passed into my hands only, and was by me committed to the flames unread. These letters were at first all for my niece; but toward the end of the year two came, at different intervals, directed to my brother. I distrusted the cunning of the writer and the weakness of Joshua; and I put both those letters into the fire, unread like the rest. After that, no more came; and Mr. Carr never returned to Jay's Cottage. In reference to this part of my narrative, therefore, I have only now to add, before proceeding to the miserable confession of our family dishonor, that I never afterward saw, and only once heard of the man who tempted my niece to commit the deadly sin which was her ruin in this world, and will be her ruin in the next.

"I must return first, however, to what happened from my burning of the letters. When my niece found that week after week passed, and she never heard from Mr. Carr, she fretted about it much more than I had fancied she would. And Joshua unthinkingly made her worse by wondering, in her presence, at the long absence of the gentleman of Jay's Cottage. My brother was a man who could not abide his habits being broken in on. He had been in the habit of going on certain evenings to Mr. Carr's (and, I grieve to say, often taken his daughter with him) to fetch the London paper, to take back drawings of flowers, and to let my niece bring away new ones to copy. And now he fidgeted, and was restless, and discontented (as much as so easy-tempered a man could be) at not taking his usual walks to Jay's Cottage. This, as I have said, made his daughter worse. She fretted and fretted, and cried in secret, as I could tell by her eyes, till she grew to be quite altered. Now and then the angry fit that I had expected to see came upon her; but it always went away again in a manner not at all natural to one of her passionate disposition. All this time, she led me as miserable a life as she could; provoking and thwarting and insulting me at every opportunity. I believe she suspected me in the matter of the letters. But I had taken my measures so as to make discovery impossible; and I determined to wait, and be patient and persevering, and get the better of her and her wicked fancy for Mr. Carr, just as I had made up my mind to do.

"At last, as the winter drew on, she altered so much, and got such a strange look in her face, which never seemed to leave it, that Joshua became alarmed, and said he must send for the doctor. She seemed to be frightened out of her wits at the mere thought of it; and declared, quite passionately, all of a sudden, that she had no want of a doctor, and would see none and answer the questions of none—no! not even if her father himself insisted on it.

"This astonished me as well as Joshua; and when he asked me privately what I thought was the matter with her, I was obliged of course to tell him the truth, and say I believed that she was almost out of her mind with love for Mr. Carr. For the first time in his life, my brother flew into a violent rage with me. I suspect he was furious with his own conscience for reminding him, as it must have done then, how foolishly overindulgent he had been toward her, and how carelessly he had allowed her, as well as himself, to get acquainted with a person out of her own station, whom it was not proper for either of them to know. I said nothing of this to him at the time; he was not fit to listen to it —and still less fit, even had I been willing to confide it to him, to hear what the plan was which I had adopted for working her cure.

"As the weeks went on, and she still fretted in secret, and still looked unlike herself, I began to doubt whether this very plan, from which I had hoped so much, would after all succeed. I was sorely distressed in my mind, at times, as to what I ought to do next; and began indeed to feel the difficulty getting too much for me, just when it was drawing on fast to its shocking and shameful end. We were then close upon Christmas-time. Joshua had got his shop-bills well forward for sending out, and was gone to London on business, as was customary with him at this season of the year. I expected him back, as usual, a day or two before Christmas-day.

"For a little while past, I had noticed some change in my niece. Ever since my brother had talked about sending for the doctor, she had altered a little, in the way of going on more regularly with her work, and pretending (though she made but a bad pretense of it) that there was nothing ailed her; her object being, of course, to make her father easier about her in his mind. The change, however, to which I now refer was of another sort, and only affected her manner toward me, and her manner of dressing herself. When we were alone together now, I found her conduct quite altered. She spoke soft to me, and looked humble, and did what work I set her without idleness or murmuring; and once, even made as if she wanted to kiss me. But I was on my guard—suspecting that she wanted to entrap me, with her wheedling ways, into letting out something about Mr. Carr's having written, and my having burned his letters. It was at this time also, and a little before it, that I noticed the alteration in her dress. She fell into wearing her things in a slovenly way, and sitting at home in her shawl, on account of feeling cold, she said, when I reprimanded her for such untidiness.

"I don't know how long things might have lasted like this, or what the end might have been, if events had gone on in their own way. But the dreadful truth made itself known at last suddenly, by a sort of accident. She had a quarrel with one of the other young women in the dress-making-room, named Ellen Gough, about a certain disreputable friend of hers, one Jane Holdsworth, whom I had once employed, and had dismissed for impertinence and slatternly conduct. Ellen Gough having, it seems, been provoked past all bearing by something my niece said to her, came away to me in a passion, and in so many words told me the awful truth, that my brother's only daughter had disgraced herself and her family forever. The horror and misery of that moment is present to me now, at this distance of time. The shock I then received struck me down at once; I never have recovered from it, and I never shall.

"In the first distraction of the moment, I must have done or said something downstairs, where I was, which must have warned the wretch in the room above that I had discovered her infamy. I remember going to her bed-chamber, and finding the door locked, and hearing her refuse to open it. After that, I must have fainted, for I found myself, I did not know how, in the workroom, and Ellen Gough giving me a bottle to smell to. With her help, I got into my own room; and there I fainted away dead again.

"When I came to, I went once more to my niece's bed-chamber. The door was now open; and there was a bit of paper on the looking-glass directed to my brother Joshua. She was gone from the honest house that her sin had defiled— gone from it forever. She had written only a few scrawled wild lines to her father, but in them there was full acknowledgment of her crime, and a confession that it was the villain Carr who had caused her to commit it. She said she was gone to take her shame from our doors. She entreated that no attempt might be made to trace her, for she would die rather than return to disgrace her family, and her father in his old age. After this came some lines, which seemed to have been added, on second thoughts, to what went before. I do not remember the exact words; but the sense referred, shamelessly enough as I thought, to the child that was afterward born, and to her resolution, if it came into the world alive, to suffer all things for its sake.

"It was at first some relief to know that she was gone. The dreadful exposure and degradation that threatened us seemed to be delayed at least by her absence. On questioning Ellen Gough, I found that the other two young women who worked under me, and who were most providentially absent on a Christmas visit to their friends, were not acquainted with my niece's infamous secret. Ellen had accidentally discovered it; and she had, therefore, been obliged to confess to Ellen, and put trust in her. Everybody else in the house had been as successfully deceived as I had been myself. When I heard this, I began to have some hope that our family disgrace might remain unknown in the town.

"I wrote to my brother, not telling him what had happened, but only begging him to come back instantly. It was the bitterest part of all the bitter misery I then suffered, to think of what I had now to tell Joshua, and of what dreadful extremities his daughter's ruin might drive him to. I strove hard to prepare myself for the time of coming trial; but what really took place was worse than my worst forebodings.

"When my brother heard the shocking news I had to tell, and saw the scrawled paper she had left for him, he spoke and acted as if he was out of his mind. It was only charitable, only fair to his previous character, to believe, as I then believed, that distress had actually driven him, for the time, out of his senses. He declared that he would go away instantly and search for her, and set others seeking for her too. He said, he even swore, that he would bring her back home the moment he found her; that he would succor her in her misery, and accept her penitence, and shelter her under his roof the same as ever, without so much as giving a thought to the scandal and disgrace that her infamous situation would inflict on her family. He even wrested Scripture from its true meaning to support him in what he said, and in what he was determined to. do. And, worst of all, the moment he heard how it was that I had discovered his daughter's crime, he insisted that Ellen Gough should be turned out of the house: he declared, in such awful language as I had never believed it possible he could utter, that she should not sleep under his roof that night. It was hopeless to attempt to appease him. He put her out at the door with his own hand that very day. She was an excellent and a regular work-woman, but sullen and revengeful when her temper was once roused. By the next morning our disgrace was known all over Dibbledean.

"There was only one more degradation now to be dreaded, and that it sickened me to think of. I knew Joshua well enough to know that if he found the lost wretch he was going in search of, he would absolutely and certainly bring her home again. I had been born in our house at Dibbledean; my mother before me had been born there; our family had lived in the old place, honestly and reputably, without so much as a breath of ill report ever breathing over them, for generations and generations back. When I thought of this, and then thought of the bare possibility that an abandoned woman might soon be admitted, and a bastard child born, in the house where so many of my relations had lived virtuously and died righteously, I resolved that the day when *she* set her foot on our threshold should be the day when *I* left my home and my birthplace forever.

"While I was in this mind, Joshua came to me—as determined in his way as I secretly was in mine—to ask if I had any suspicions about what direction she had taken. All the first inquiries after her that he had made in Dibbledean had, it seems, given him no information whatever. I said I had no positive knowledge (which was strictly true), but told him I suspected she was gone to London. He asked why; I answered, because I believed she was gone to look after Mr. Carr; and said that I remembered his letter to her (the first and only one she received) had a London postmark upon it. We could not find this letter at the time: the hiding-place she had for it, and for all the others she left behind her, was not discovered till years after, when the house was repaired for the people who bought our business. Joshua, however, having nothing better to guide himself by, and being resolved to begin seeking her at once, said my suspicion was a likely one; and went away to London by that night's coach, to see what he could do, and to get advice from his lawyers about how to trace her.

"This, which I have been just relating, is the only part of my conduct, in the time of our calamity, which I now think of with an uneasy conscience. When I told Joshua I suspected she was gone to London I was not telling him the truth. I knew nothing certainly about where she was gone; but I did assuredly suspect that she had turned her steps exactly in the contrary direction to London—that is to say, far out Bangbury way. She had been constantly asking all sorts of questions of Ellen Gough, who told me of it, about roads, and towns, and people in that distant part of the country: and this was my only reason for thinking she had taken herself away in that direction. Though it was but a matter of bare suspicion at the best, still I deceived my brother as to my real opinion when he asked it of me: and this was a sin which I now humbly and truly repent of. But the thought of helping him, by so little even as a likely guess, to bring our infamy home to our own doors, by actually bringing his degraded daughter back with him into my presence, in the face of the whole town—this thought, I say, was too much for me. I believed that the day when she crossed our threshold again would be the day of my death, as well as the day of my farewell to home; and under that conviction I concealed from Joshua what my real opinion was.

"I deserved to suffer for this; and I did suffer for it.

"Two or three days after the lonely Christmas-day that I passed in utter solitude at our house in Dibbledean, I received a letter from Joshua's lawyer in London, telling me to come up and see my brother immediately, for he was taken dangerously ill. In the course of his inquiries (which he would pursue himself, although the lawyers, who knew better what ought to be done, were doing their utmost to help him), he had been misled by some false information, and had been robbed and ill-used in some place near the river, and then turned out at night in a storm of snow and sleet. It is useless now to write about what I suffered from this fresh blow, or to speak of the awful time I passed by his bedside in London. Let it be enough to say, that he escaped out of the very jaws of death; and that it was the end of February before he was well enough to be taken home to Dibbledean.

"He soon got better in his own air—better as to his body, but his mind was in a sad way. Every morning he used to ask if any news of Mary had come? and when he heard there was none, he used to sigh, and then hardly say another word, or so much as hold up his head for the rest of the day. At one time, he showed a little anxiety now and then about a letter reaching its destination, and being duly received;

peevishly refusing to mention to me even so much as the address on it. But I guessed who it had been sent to easily enough, when his lawyers told me that he had written it in London, and had mentioned to them that it was going to some place beyond the seas. He soon seemed to forget this though, and to forget everything, except his regular question about Mary, which he sometimes repeated in his dazed condition, even after I had broken it to him that she was dead.

"The news of her death came in the March month of the new year, 1828.

"All inquiries in London had failed up to that time in discovering the remotest trace of her. In Dibbledean we knew she could not be; and elsewhere Joshua was now in no state to search for her himself, or to have any clear notions of instructing others in what direction to make inquiries for him. But in this month of March, I saw in the Bangbury paper (which circulates in our county besides its own) an advertisement calling on the friends of a young woman who had just died and left behind her an infant, to come forward and identify the body, and take some steps in respect to the child. The description was very full and particular, and did not admit of a doubt, to any one that knew her as well as I did, that the young woman referred to was my guilty and miserable niece. My brother was in no condition to be spoken to in this difficulty; so I determined to act for myself. I sent, by a person I could depend upon, money enough to bury her decently in Bangbury churchyard, putting no name or date to my letter. There was no law to oblige me to do more, and more I was determined not to do. As to the child, that was the offspring of her sin; it was the infamous father's business to support and own it, and not mine.

"When people in the town, who knew of our calamity, and had seen the advertisement, talked to me of it, I admitted nothing, and denied nothing—I simply refused to speak with them, on the subject of what had happened in our family.

"Having endeavored to provide in this way for the protection of my brother and myself against the meddling and impertinence of idle people, I believed that I had now suffered the last of the many bitter trials which had assailed me as the consequences of my niece's guilt: I was mistaken; the cup of my affliction was not yet full. One day, hardly a fortnight after I had sent the burial-money anonymously to Bangbury, our servant came to me and said there was a stranger at the door who wished to see my brother, and was so bent on it that he would take no denial. I went down, and found waiting on the door-steps a very respectable-looking, middle-aged man, whom I had certainly never set eyes on before in my life.

"I told him that I was Joshua's sister, and that I managed my brother's affairs for him in the present state of his health. The stranger only answered that he was very anxious to see Joshua himself. I did not choose to expose the helpless condition into which my brother's intel-

lects had fallen, to a person of whom I knew
nothing; so I merely said, the interview he
wanted was out of the question, but that if he
had any business with Mr. Grice, he might, for
the reasons I had already given, mention it to
me. He hesitated, and smiled, and said he was
very much obliged to me; and then, making as
if he was going to step in, added that I should
probably be able to appreciate the friendly nature
of the business on which he came, when he informed me that he was confidentially employed
by Mr. Arthur Carr.

"The instant he spoke it, I felt the name go to
my heart like a knife—then my indignation got
the better of me. I told him to tell Mr. Carr
that the miserable creature whom his villainy
had destroyed, had fled away from her home,
had died away from her home, and was buried
away from her home; and with that I shut the
door in his face. My agitation, and a sort of
terror that I could not account for, so overpowered me that I was obliged to lean against the
wall of the passage, and was unable, for some
minutes, to stir a step toward going upstairs.
As soon as I got a little better, and began to
think about what had taken place, a doubt came
across me as to whether I might not have acted
wrong. I remembered that Joshua's lawyers in
London had made it a great point that this Mr.
Carr should be traced; and though, since then,
our situation had been altered by my niece's
death, still I felt uncertain and uneasy—I could
hardly tell why—at what I had done. It was as

if I had taken some responsibility on myself
which ought not to have been mine.   In short, I
ran back to the door and opened it, and looked
up and down the street.   It was too late: the
strange man was out of sight, and I never set
eyes on him again.

"This was in March, 1828, the same month in
which the advertisement appeared.   I am particular in repeating the date, because it marks
the time of the last information I have to give,
in connection with the disgraceful circumstances
which I have here forced myself to relate.   Of
the child mentioned in the advertisement, I
never heard anything, from that time to this.
I do not even know when it was born.   I only
know that its guilty mother left her home in the
December of 1827.   Whether it lived after the
date of the advertisement, or whether it died, I
never discovered, and never wished to discover.
I have kept myself retired since the days of my
humiliation, hiding my sorrow in my own heart,
and neither asking questions nor answering
them."

At this place Mat once more suspended the
perusal of the letter.   He had now read on for
an unusually long time with unflagging attention, and with the same stern sadness always in
his face, except when the name of Arthur Carr
occurred in the course of the narrative.   Almost
on every occasion, when the finger by which he
guided himself along the close lines of the letter,
came to those words, it trembled a little, and the

dangerous look grew ever brighter and brighter in his eyes. It was in them now, as he dropped the letter on his knee, and, turning round, took from the wall behind him, against which it leaned, a certain leather bag, already alluded to as part of the personal property that he brought with him on installing himself in Kirk Street. He opened it, took out a feather fan, and an Indian tobacco-pouch of scarlet cloth; and then began to search in the bottom of the bag, from which, at length, he drew forth a letter. It was torn in several places, the ink of the writing in it was faded, and the paper was disfigured by stains of grease, tobacco, and dirt generally. The direction was in such a condition, that the word "Brazils," at the end, was alone legible. Inside, it was not in a much better state. The date at the top, however, still remained tolerably easy to distinguish: it was "December 26, 1827."

Mat looked first at this, and then at the paragraph he had just been reading, in Joanna Grice's narrative. After that, he began to count on his fingers, clumsily enough—beginning with the year 1828 as Number One, and ending with the current year, 1851, as Number Twenty-three. "Twenty - three," he repeated aloud to himself, "twenty-three years: I shall remember that."

He looked down a little vacantly, the next moment, at the old torn letter again. Some of the lines, here and there, had escaped stains and dirt sufficiently to be still easily legible; and it was over these that his eyes now wandered.

The first words that caught his attention ran thus: "I am now, therefore, in this bitter affliction, more than ever desirous that all past differences between us should be forgotten, and"—here the beginning of another line was hidden by a stain, beyond which, on the cleaner part of the letter, the writing proceeded: "In this spirit, then, I counsel you, if you can get continued employment anywhere abroad, to accept it, instead of coming back"—(a rent in the paper made the next words too fragmentary to be easily legible). ". . . any good news, be sure of hearing from me again. In the meantime, I say it once more, keep away, if you can. Your presence could do no good; and it is better for you, at your age, to be spared the sight of such sorrow as that we are now suffering." (After this, dirt and the fading of the ink made several sentences near the end of the page almost totally illegible—the last three or four lines at the bottom of the letter alone remaining clear enough to be read with any ease.) ". . . the poor, lost, unhappy creature! But I shall find her, I know I shall find her; and then, let Joanna say or do what she may, I will forgive my own Mary, for I know she will deserve her pardon. As for *him*, I feel confident that he may be traced yet; and that I can shame him into making the atonement of marrying her. If he should refuse, then the black-hearted villain shall—"

At this point, Mat abruptly stopped in his reading; and, hastily folding up the letter, put it back in the bag again, along with the feather fan and the Indian pouch. "I can't go on with that part of the story now, but the time *may* come—" He pursued the thought which thus expressed itself in him no further, but sat still for a few minutes, with his head on his hand and his heavy eyebrows contracted by an angry frown, staring sullenly at the flame of the candle. Joanna Grice's letter still remained to be finished. He took it up, and looked back to the paragraph that he had last read.

"As for the child mentioned in the advertisement"—those were the words to which he was now referring. "*The child?*"—There was no mention of its sex. "I should like to know if it was a boy or a girl," thought Mat.

Though he was now close to the end of the letter, he roused himself with difficulty to attend to the last few sentences which remained to be read. They began thus:

"Before I say anything in conclusion, of the sale of our business, of my brother's death, and of the life which I have been leading since that time, I should wish to refer, once for all, and very briefly, to the few things which my niece left behind her when she abandoned her home. Circumstances may, one day, render this necessary. I desire then to state, that everything belonging to her is preserved in one of her boxes (now in my possession), just as she left it. When the letters signed 'A. C.' were discovered, as I have mentioned, on the occasion of repairs being made in the house, I threw them into the box with my own hand. They will all be found, more or less, to prove the justice of those first suspicions of mine, which my late brother so unhappily disregarded. In reference to money or valuables, I have only to mention that my niece took all her savings with her in her flight. I knew in what box she kept them, and I saw that box open and empty on her table, when I first discovered that she was gone. As for the only three articles of jewelry that she had, her brooch I myself saw her give to Ellen Gough—her earrings she always wore—and I can only presume (never having found it anywhere) that she took with her, in her flight, her hair bracelet."

"There it is again!" cried Mat, dropping the letter in astonishment, the instant those two significant words, "hair bracelet," caught his eye.

He had hardly uttered the exclamation, before he heard the door of the house flung open, then shut to again with a bang. Zack had just let himself in with his latch-key.

"I'm glad he's come," muttered Mat, snatching up the letter from the floor and crumpling it into his pocket. "There's another thing or two I want to find out before I go any further, and Zack's the lad to help me."

CHAPTER IX.

MORE DISCOVERIES.

WHEN Zack entered the room, and saw his strange friend, with legs crossed and hands in pockets, sitting gravely in the usual corner, on the floor, between a brandy bottle on one side, and a guttering, unsnuffed candle on the other, he roared with laughter, and stamped about in his usual boisterous way, till the flimsy little house seemed to be trembling under him to its very foundations. Mat bore all this noise and ridicule, and all the jesting that followed it about the futility of drowning his passion for Madonna in the brandy-bottle, with the most unruffled and exemplary patience. The self-control which he thus exhibited did not pass without its reward. Zack got tired of making jokes which were received with the serenest in-attention; and, passing at once from the fanciful to the practical, astonished his fellow-lodger by suddenly communicating a very unexpected and very important piece of news.

"By-the-by, Mat," he said, "we must sweep the place up, and look as respectable as we can, before to-morrow night. My friend Blyth is coming to spend a quiet evening with us. I stayed behind till all the visitors had gone, on purpose to ask him."

"Do you mean he's coming to have a drop of grog and smoke a pipe along with us two?" asked Mat, rather amazedly.

"I mean he's coming here, certainly; but as for grog and pipes, he never touches either. He's the best and dearest fellow in the world; but I'm ashamed to say he's spooney enough to like lemonade and tea. Smoking would make him sick directly; and, as for grog, I don't believe a drop ever passes his lips from one year's end to another. A weak head—a wretchedly weak head for drinking," concluded Zack, tapping his forehead with an air of bland Bacchanalian superiority.

Mat seemed to have fallen into one of his thoughtful fits again. He made no answer, but holding the brandy-bottle standing by his side up before the candle, looked in to see how much liquor was left in it.

"Don't begin to bother your head about the brandy: you needn't get any more of it for Blyth," continued Zack, noticing his friend's action. "I say, do you know that the best thing you ever did in your life was saving Valentine's picture in that way? You have regularly won his heart by it. He was suspicious of my making friends with you before; but now he doesn't seem to think there's a word in the English language that's good enough for you. He said he should be only too glad to thank you again, when I asked him to come and judge of what you were really like in your own lodging. Tell him some of those splendid stories of yours. I've been terrifying him already with one or two of them at second-hand. Oh, Lord! how hospitably we'll treat him—won't we? You shall make his hair stand on end, Mat; and I'll drown him in his favorite tea."

"What does he do with them pictures of his?" asked Mat. "Sell 'em?"

"Of course!" answered the other, confidently; "and gets enormous sums of money for them."

N—11

Whenever Zack found an opportunity of magnifying a friend's importance, he always rose grandly superior to mere matter-of-fact restraints, and seized the golden moment without an instant of hesitation or a syllable of compromise.

"Get lots of money, does he?" proceeded Mat. "And keeps on hoarding of it up, I dare say, like all the rest of you over here?"

"*He* hoard money!" retorted Zack. "You never made a worse guess in your life. I don't believe he ever hoarded sixpence since he was a baby. If Mrs. Blyth didn't look after him, I don't suppose there would be five pounds in the house from one year's end to another."

There was a moment's silence. (It wasn't because he had money in it, then, thought Mat, that he shut down the lid of that big chest of his so sharp. I wonder whether—)

"He's the most generous fellow in the world," continued Zack, lighting a cigar; "and the best pay: ask any of his trades-people."

This remark suspended the conjecture that was just forming in Mat's mind. He gave up pursuing it quite readily, and went on at once with his questions to Zack. Some part of the additional information that he desired to obtain from young Thorpe he had got already. He knew now that, when Mr. Blyth, on the day of the picture-show, shut down the bureau so sharply on Mr. Gimble's approaching him, it was not, at any rate, because there was money in it.

"Is he going to bring anybody else in here along with him to-morrow night?" asked Mat.

"Anybody else? Who should he bring? Why, you old barbarian, you don't expect him to bring Madonna into our jolly bachelor den to preside over the grog and pipes—do you?"

"How old is the young woman?" inquired Mat, contemplatively snuffing the candle with his fingers, as he put the question.

"Still harping on my daughter!" shouted Zack, with a burst of laughter. "She's older than she looks, I can tell you that. You wouldn't guess her at more than eighteen or nineteen.   But the fact is, she's actually twenty-three;—steady there! you'll be through the window if you don't sit quieter in your queer corner than that."

(Twenty-three! The very number he had stopped at, when he reckoned off the difference on his fingers between 1828 and 1851, just before young Thorpe came in.)

"I suppose the next cool thing you will say, is that she's too old for you," Zack went on; "or, perhaps, you may prefer asking another question or two first.   I'll tell you what, old Rough and Tough, the inquisitive part of your character is beginning to be—"

"Bother all this talking!" interrupted Mat, jumping up suddenly as he spoke, and taking a greasy pack of cards from the chimney-piece. "I don't ask no questions, and don't want no answers.   Let's have a drop of grog and a turn-to at Beggar my Neighbor.   Sixpence a time. Come on!"

They sat down at once to their cards and their

420 WORKS OF WILKIE COLLINS.

brandy-and-water; playing uninterruptedly for
an hour or more. Zack won; and—being additionally enlivened by the inspiring influences of
grog—rose to a higher and higher pitch of exhilaration with every additional sixpence which
his good luck extracted from his adversary's
pocket. His gayety seemed at last to communicate itself even to the imperturbable Mat, who,
in an interval of shuffling the cards, was heard
to deliver himself suddenly of one of those gruff
chuckles, which have been already described as
the nearest approach he was capable of making
toward a civilized laugh.

He was so seldom in the habit of exhibiting
any outward symptoms of hilarity, that Zack,
who was dealing for the new game, stopped in
astonishment, and inquired with great curiosity
what it was his friend was "grunting about."
At first, Mat declined altogether to say; then,
on being pressed, admitted that his mind was
just then running on the "old woman" Zack
had spoken of, as having "suddenly fallen foul
of him in Mr. Blyth's house, because he wanted
to give the young woman a present:" which circumstance, Mat added, "so tickled his fancy,
that he would have paid a crown piece out of his
pocket only to have seen and heard the whole
squabble all through from beginning to end."

Zack, whose fancy was now exactly in the
right condition to be "tickled" by anything that
"tickled" his friend, seized in high glee the humorous side of the topic suggested to him; and
immediately began describing poor Mrs. Peck-

over's personal peculiarities in a strain of the most ridiculous exaggeration. Mat listened, as he went on, with such admiring attention, and seemed to be so astonishingly amused by everything he said, that, in the excitement of success, he ran into the next room, snatched the two pillows off the bed, fastened one in front and the other behind him, tied the patch-work counterpane over all for a petticoat, and waddled back into his friend's presence, in the character of fat Mrs. Peckover, as she appeared on the memorble evening when she stopped him mysteriously in the passage of Mr. Blyth's house.

Zack was really a good mimic; and he now hit off all the peculiarities of Mrs. Peckover's voice, manner, and gait to the life—Mat chuckling all the while, rolling his huge head from side to side, and striking his heavy fist applaudingly on the table. Encouraged by the extraordinary effect his performances produced, Zack went through the whole of his scene with Mrs. Peckover in the passage, from beginning to end; following that excellent woman through all the various mazes of "rhodomontade" in which she then bewildered herself, and imitating her terror when he threatened to run upstairs and ask Mr. Blyth if Madonna really had a hair bracelet, with such amazing accuracy and humor, as made Mat declare that what he had just beheld for nothing, would cure him of ever paying money again to see any regular play-acting as long as he lived.

By the time young Thorpe had reached the

climax of his improvised dramatic entertainment, he had so thoroughly exhausted himself that he was glad to throw aside the pillows and the counterpane, and perfectly ready to spend the rest of the evening quietly over the newspaper. His friend did not interrupt him by a word, except at the moment when he sat down; and then Mat said, simply and carelessly enough, that he thought he should detect the original Mrs. Peckover directly by Zack's imitation, if ever he met with her in the streets. To which young Thorpe merely replied that he was not very likely to do anything of the sort; because Mrs. Peckover lived at Rubbleford, where her husband had some situation, and where she herself kept a little dairy and muffin-shop. "She don't come to town above once a year," concluded Zack, as he lit a cigar; "and then the old beauty stops indoors all the time at Blyth's!"

Mat listened to this answer attentively, but offered no further remark. He went into the back room, where the water was, and busied himself in washing up all the spare crockery of the bachelor household in honor of Mr. Blyth's expected visit.

In process of time, Zack—on whom literature of any kind, high or low, always acted more or less as a narcotic—grew drowsy over his newspaper, let his grog get cold, dropped his cigar out of his mouth, and fell fast asleep in his chair. When he woke up, shivering, his watch had stopped, the candle was burning down in the socket, the fire was out, and his fellow-lodger was not to be seen either in the front or the back room. Young Thorpe knew his friend's strange fancy for "going out over night" (as Mat phrased it) "to catch the morning the first thing in the fields" too well to be at all astonished at now finding himself alone. He moved away sleepily to bed, yawning out these words to himself: "I shall see the old boy back again as usual to-morrow morning as soon as I wake."

When the morning came, this anticipation proved to be fallacious. The first objects that greeted Zack's eyes when he lazily awoke about eleven o'clock, were an arm and a letter, introduced cautiously through his partially opened bedroom door. Though by no means contemptible in regard to muscular development, this was not the hairy and herculean arm of Mat. It was only the arm of the servant of all-work, who held the barbarian lodger in such salutary awe that she had never been known to venture her whole body into the forbidden region of his apartments since he had first inhabited them. Zack jumped out of bed and took the letter. It proved to be from Valentine, and summoned him to repair immediately to the painter's house to see Mrs. Thorpe, who earnestly desired to speak with him. His color changed as he read the few lines Mr. Blyth had written, and thought of the prospect of meeting his mother face to face for the first time since he had left his home. He hurried on his clothes, however, without a moment's delay, and went out directly—now walking at the top of his speed, now running, in his

anxiety not to appear dilatory or careless in paying obedience to the summons that had just
reached him.

On arriving at the painter's house, he was
shown into one of the parlors on the ground-
floor; and there sat Mrs. Thorpe, with Mr. Blyth
to keep her company.   The meeting between
mother and son was characteristic on both sides.
Without giving Valentine time enough to get
from his chair to the door—without waiting an
instant to ascertain what sentiments toward him
were expressed in Mrs. Thorpe's face—without
paying the smallest attention to the damage he
did to her cap and bonnet—Zack saluted his
mother with the old shower of hearty kisses,
and the old boisterously affectionate hug of his
nursery and schoolboy days.   And she, poor
woman, on her side, feebly faltered over her
first words of reproof—then lost her voice altogether, pressed into his hand a little paper packet
of money that she had brought for him, and
wept on his breast without speaking another
word.   Thus it had been with them long ago,
when she was yet a young woman and he but
a boy—thus, even as it was now in the latter
and the sadder time!

Mrs. Thorpe was long in regaining the self-
possession which she had lost on seeing her son
for the first time since his flight from home.
Zack expressed his contrition over and over again,
and many times reiterated his promise to follow
the plan Mr. Blyth had proposed to him when
they met at the turnpike, before his mother be-

came calm enough to speak three words together without bursting into tears. When she at last recovered herself sufficiently to be able to address him with some composure, she did not speak, as he had expected, of his past delinquencies or of his future prospects, but of the lodging which he then inhabited, and of the stranger whom he had suffered to become his friend. Although Mat's gallant rescue of "Columbus" had warmly predisposed Valentine in his favor, the painter was too conscientious to soften facts on that account when he told Zack's mother where her son was now living, and what sort of companion he had chosen to lodge with. Mrs. Thorpe was timid, and distrustful as all timid people are; and she now entreated him with nervous eagerness to begin his promised reform by leaving Kirk Street, and at once dropping his dangerous intimacy with the vagabond stranger who lived there.

Zack defended his friend to his mother exactly as he had already defended him to Valentine—but without shaking her opinion, until he bethought himself of promising that in this matter, as in all others, he would be finally guided by the opinion of Mr. Blyth. The assurance so given, accompanied as it was by the announcement that Valentine was about to form his own judgment of Mr. Marksman by visiting the house in Kirk Street that very night, seemed to quiet and satisfy Mrs. Thorpe. Her last hopes for her son's future, now that she was forced to admit the sad necessity of conniving at his continued

absence from home, rested one and all on Mr.
Blyth alone.

This first difficulty smoothed over, Zack asked,
with no little apprehension and anxiety, whether
his father's anger showed any symptoms of subsiding as yet. The question was an unfortunate
one. Mrs. Thorpe's eyes began to fill with tears
again, the moment she heard it. The news she
had now to tell her son, in answering his inquiries,
was of a very melancholy and a very hopeless kind.

The attack of palpitations in the heart which
had seized Mr. Thorpe on the day of his son's
flight from Baregrove Square had been immediately and successfully relieved by the medical
remedies employed; but it had been followed,
within the last day or two, by a terrible depression of spirits, under which the patient seemed
to have given way entirely, and for which the
doctor was unable to suggest any speedy process
of cure. Few in number at all times, Mr.
Thorpe's words had now become fewer than
ever. His usual energy appeared to be gone
altogether. He still went through all the daily
business of the religious societies to which he
belonged, in direct opposition to the doctor's advice; but he performed his duties mechanically,
and without any apparent interest in the persons
or events with which he was brought in contact.
He had only referred to his son once in the last
two days; and then it was not to talk of reclaiming him, not to ask where he had gone, but only
to desire briefly and despairingly that his name
might not be mentioned again.

So far as Zack's interests or apprehensions were now concerned, there was consequently no fear of any new collision occurring between his father and himself. When Mrs. Thorpe had told her husband (after receiving Valentine's answer to her letter) that their runaway son was "in safe hands," Mr. Thorpe never asked, as she had feared he would, "What hands?" And again, when she hinted that it might be perhaps advisable to assist the lad to some small extent, as long as he kept in the right way, and suffered himself to be guided by the "safe hands" already mentioned, still Mr. Thorpe made no objections and no inquiries, but bowed his head, and told her to do as she pleased: at the same time whispering a few words to himself, which were not uttered loud enough for her to hear. She could only, therefore, repeat the sad truth that, since his energies had given way, all his former plans, and all his customary opinions in reference to his son seemed to have undergone some disastrous and sudden alteration. It was only in consequence of this alteration, which appeared to render him as unfit to direct her how to act as to act himself, that she had ventured to undertake the responsibility of arranging the present interview with Zack, and of bringing him the small pecuniary assistance which Mr. Blyth had considered to be necessary in the present melancholy emergency.

The enumeration of all these particulars—interrupted, as it constantly was, by unavailing lamentations on one side, and by useless self-

reproaches on the other—occupied much more
time than either mother or son imagined. It
was not till the clock in Mr. Blyth's hall struck,
that Mrs. Thorpe discovered how much longer
her absence from home had lasted than she had
intended it should, on leaving Baregrove Square.
She rose directly, in great trepidation—took a
hurried leave of Valentine, who was loitering
about his front garden—sent the kindest mes-
sages she could think of to the ladies above
stairs—and departed at once for home. Zack
escorted her to the entrance of the square; and,
on taking leave, showed the sincerity of his contrition in a very unexpected and desperate manner, by actually offering to return home then
and there with his mother, if she wished it!
Mrs. Thorpe's heart yearned to take him at his
word, but she remembered the doctor's orders
and the critical condition of her husband's health;
and forced herself to confess to Zack that the favorable time for his return had not yet arrived.
After this—with mutual promises to communicate
again soon through Valentine—they parted very
sadly just at the entrance of Baregrove Square:
Mrs. Thorpe hurrying nervously to her own door,
Zack returning gloomily to Mr. Blyth's house. .

Meanwhile, how had Mat been occupying himself since he had left his young friend alone in
the lodging in Kirk Street?

He had really gone out, as Zack had supposed,
for one of those long night-walks of his, which
usually took him well into the country before

the first gray of daylight had spread far over the sky. On ordinary occasions, he only indulged in these oddly-timed pedestrian excursions because the restless habits engendered by his vagabond life made him incapable of conforming to civilized hours by spending the earliest part of the morning, like other people, inactively in bed. On this particular occasion, however, he had gone out with something like a special purpose; for he had left Kirk Street not so much for the sake of taking a walk, as for the sake of thinking clearly and at his ease. Mat's brain was never so fertile in expedients as when he was moving his limbs freely in the open air.

Hardly a chance word had dropped from Zack that night which had not either confirmed him in his resolution to possess himself of Valentine's hair bracelet, or helped to suggest to him the manner in which his determination to obtain it might be carried out. The first great necessity imposed on him by his present design was to devise the means of secretly opening the painter's bureau; the second was to hit on some safe method—should no chance opportunity occur—of approaching it unobserved. Mat had remarked that Mr. Blyth wore the key of the bureau attached to his watch-chain; and Mat had just heard from young Thorpe that Mr. Blyth was about to pay them a visit in Kirk Street. On the evening of that visit, therefore, the first of the two objects—the discovery of a means of secretly opening the bureau—might, in some way, be attained. How?

This was the problem which Mat set off to solve to his own perfect satisfaction, in the silence and loneliness of a long night's walk.

In what precise number of preliminary mental entanglements he involved himself, before arriving at the desired solution, it would not be very easy to say. As usual, his thoughts wandered every now and then from his subject in the most irregular manner; actually straying away, on one occasion, as far as the New World itself, and unintelligibly occupying themselves with stories he had heard, and conversations he had held in various portions of that widely-extended sphere, with vagabond chance-comrades from all parts of civilized Europe. How his mind ever got back from these past times and foreign places to present difficulties and future considerations connected with the guest who was expected in Kirk Street, Mat himself would have been puzzled to tell. But it did eventually get back, nevertheless; and, what was still more to the purpose, it definitely and thoroughly worked out the intricate problem that had been set it to solve.

Not a whispered word of the plan he had now hit on dropped from Mat's lips, as, turning it this way and that in his thoughts, he walked briskly back to town in the first fresh tranquillity of the winter morning. Discreet as he was, however, either some slight practical hints of his present project must have oozed out through his actions when he got back to London; or his notion of the sort of hospitable preparation which

ought to be made for the reception of Mr. Blyth
was more barbarously and extravagantly eccentric than all the rest of his notions put together.

Instead of going home at once, when he arrived at Kirk Street, he stopped at certain shops
in the neighborhood to make some purchases
which evidently had reference to the guest of the
evening; for the first things he bought were two
or three lemons and a pound of loaf-sugar. So
far his proceedings were no doubt intelligible
enough; but they gradually became more and
more incomprehensible when he began to walk
up and down two or three streets, looking about
him attentively, stopping at every locksmith's
and iron-monger's shop that he passed, waiting
to observe all the people who might happen to be
inside them, and then deliberately walking on
again. In this way he approached, in course
of time, a very filthy little row of houses, with
some very ill-looking male and female inhabitants visible in detached positions, staring out of
windows or lingering about public-house doors.

Occupying the lower story of one of these
houses was a small grimy shop, which, judging
by the visible stock in trade, dealt on a much
larger scale in iron and steel ware that was old
and rusty, than in iron and steel ware that was
new and bright. Before the counter no customer
appeared; behind it there stood alone a squalid,
bushy-browed, hump-backed man, as dirty as the
dirtiest bit of iron about him, sorting old nails.
Mat, who had unintelligibly passed the doors of
respectable iron-mongers, now, as unintelligibly,

entered this doubtful and dirty shop; and addressed himself to the unattractive stranger behind the counter. The conference in which the two immediately engaged was conducted in low tones, and evidently ended to the satisfaction of both; for the squalid shopman began to whistle a tune as he resumed his sorting of the nails, and Mat muttered to himself, "That's all right," as he came out on the pavement again.

His next proceeding—always supposing that it had reference to the reception of Mr. Blyth—was still more mysterious. He went into one of those grocer's shops which are dignified by the title of "Italian Warehouses," and bought a small lump of the very best refined wax! After making this extraordinary purchase, which he put into the pocket of his trousers, he next entered the public-house opposite his lodgings; and, in defiance of what Zack had told him about Valentine's temperate habits, bought and brought away with him, not only a fresh bottle of brandy, but a bottle of old Jamaica rum besides.

Young Thorpe had not returned from Mr. Blyth's when Mat entered the lodgings with these purchases. He put the bottles, the sugar, and the lemons in the cupboard—cast a satisfied look at the three clean tumblers and spoons already standing on the shelf—relaxed so far from his usual composure of aspect as to smile—lit the fire, and heaped plenty of coal on, to keep it alight—then sat down on his bear-skins—wriggled himself comfortably into the corner, and threw his handkerchief over his face; chuckling gruffly for the first time since the past night, as he put his hand in his pockets, and so accidentally touched the lump of wax that lay in one of them.

"Now, I'm all ready for the painter-man," growled Mat behind the handkerchief, as he quietly settled himself to go to sleep.

CHAPTER X.

THE SQUAW'S MIXTURE.

LIKE the vast majority of those persons who are favored by Nature with what is commonly termed "a high flow of animal spirits," Zack was liable, at certain times and seasons, to fall from the heights of exhilaration to the depths of despair, without stopping for a moment, by the way, at any intermediate stages of moderate cheerfulness, pensive depression, or tearful gloom. After he had parted from his mother, he presented himself again at Mr. Blyth's house, in such a prostrate condition of mind, and talked of his delinquencies and their effect on his father's spirits with such vehement bitterness of self-reproach, as quite amazed Valentine, and even alarmed him a little on the lad's account. The good-natured painter was no friend to contrite desperation of any kind, and no believer in repentance which could not look hopefully forward to the future as well as sorrowfully back at the past. So he laid down his brush, just as he was about to begin varnishing the "Golden Age"; and set himself to console Zack, by reminding him of all the credit and honor he might yet win, if he was regular in attending to his new studies—if he never flinched from work at the British Museum, and the private drawing-school to which he was immediately to be introduced—and if he ended as he well might end, in excusing to his father his determination to be an artist, by showing Mr. Thorpe a prize medal, won by the industry of his son's hand in the Schools of the Royal Academy.

A necessary characteristic of people whose spirits are always running into extremes is that they are generally able to pass from one change of mood to another with unusual facility. By the time Zack had exhausted Mr. Blyth's copious stores of consolation, had partaken of an excellent and plentiful hot lunch, and had passed an hour upstairs with the ladies, he predicted his own reformation just as confidently as he had predicted his own ruin about two hours before; and went away to Kirk Street, to see that his friend Mat was at home to receive Valentine that evening, stepping along as nimbly and swinging his stick as cheerfully as if he had already vindicated himself to his father by winning every prize medal that the Royal Academy could bestow.

Seven o'clock had been fixed as the hour at which Mr. Blyth was to present himself at the lodgings in Kirk Street. He arrived punctual to the appointed time, dressed jauntily for the occasion in a short blue frock-coat, famous among all his acquaintances for its smartness of cut and its fabulous old age. From what Zack had told him of Mat's lighter peculiarities of character, he anticipated a somewhat uncivilized reception from the elder of his two hosts; and when he got to Kirk Street, he certainly found that his expectations were, upon the whole, handsomely realized.

On mounting the dark and narrow wooden staircase of the tobacconist's shop, his nose was greeted by a composite smell of fried liver and bacon, brandy - and - water, and cigar-smoke, pouring hospitably down to meet him through the crevices of the drawing-room door. When he got into the room, the first object that struck his eyes at one end of it was Zack, with his hat on, vigorously engaged in freshening up the dusty carpet with a damp mop; and Mat, at the other, presiding over the frying-pan, with his coat off, his shirt-sleeves rolled up to his shoulders, a glass of steaming hot grog on the chimney-piece above him, and a long pewter toasting-fork in his hand.

"Here's the honored guest of the evening arrived before I've swabbed down the decks," cried Zack, jogging his friend in the ribs with the long handle of the mop.

"How are you, to-night?" said Mat, with familiar ease, not moving from the frying-pan, but getting his right hand free to offer to Mr. Blyth by taking the pewter toasting-fork between his teeth. "Sit down anywhere you like;

and just holler through the crack in the floor, under the bear-skins there, if you want anything out of the bocker-shop, below." ("He means tobacco when he says bocker," interposed Zack, parenthetically.) "Can you set your teeth in a baked tater or two?" continued Mat, tapping a small Dutch oven before the fire with his toasting-fork. "We've got you a lot of fizzin' hot liver and bacon to ease down the taters with what you call a relish. Nice and streaky, ain't it?" Here the host of the evening stuck his fork into a slice of bacon, and politely passed it over his shoulder for Mr. Blyth to inspect, as he stood bewildered in the middle of the room.

"Oh, delicious, delicious!" cried Valentine, smelling as daintily at the outstretched bacon as if it had been a nosegay. "Really, my dear sir—" He said no more; for at that moment he tripped himself up upon one of some ten or a dozen bottle-corks which lay about on the carpet where he was standing. There is very little doubt, if Zack had not been by to catch him, that Mr. Blyth would just then have concluded his polite remarks on the bacon by measuring his full length on the floor.

"Why don't you put him into a chair?" growled Mat, looking round reproachfully from the frying-pan, as Valentine recovered his erect position again with young Thorpe's assistance.

"I was just going to swab up that part of the carpet when you came in," said Zack, apologetically, as he led Mr. Blyth to a chair.

"Oh, don't mention it," answered Valentine, laughing. "It was all my awkwardness."

He stopped abruptly again. Zack had placed him with his back to the fire, against a table covered with a large and dirty cloth which flowed to the floor, and under which, while he was speaking, he had been gently endeavoring to insinuate his legs. Amazement bereft him of the power of speech when, on succeeding in this effort, he found that his feet came in contact with a perfect hillock of empty bottles, oyster-shells, and broken crockery, heaped under the table. "Good gracious me! I hope I'm doing no mischief!" exclaimed Valentine, as a miniature avalanche of oyster-shells clattered down on his intruding foot, and a plump bottle with a broken neck rolled lazily out from under the tablecloth, and courted observation on the open floor.

"Kick about, dear old fellow, kick about as much as you please," cried Zack, seating himself opposite Mr. Blyth, and bringing down a second avalanche of oyster-shells to encourage him. "The fact is, we are rather put to it for space here, so we keep the cloth always laid for dinner, and make a temporary lumber-room of the place under the table. Rather a new idea that, I think—not tidy perhaps, but original and ingenious, which is much better."

"Amazingly ingenious!" said Valentine, who was now beginning to be amused as well as surprised by his reception in Kirk Street. "Rather untidy, perhaps, as you say, Zack; but new, and not disagreeable, I suppose, when you're used to it. What I like about all this,'' continued Mr. Blyth, rubbing his hands cheerfully and kicking into view another empty bottle, as he settled himself in his chair—"what I like about this is, that it's so thoroughly without ceremony. Do you know I really feel at home already, though I never was here before in my life?—Curious, Zack, isn't it?''

"Look out for the taters!" roared Mat, suddenly, from the fireplace. Valentine started, first at the unexpected shout just behind him, next at the sight of a big truculently-knobbed potato which came flying over his head, and was dexterously caught and instantly deposited on the dirty tablecloth by Zack. "Two, three, four, five, six," continued Mat, keeping the frying-pan going with one hand and tossing the baked potatoes with the other over Mr. Blyth's head in quick succession, for young Thorpe to catch. "What do you think of our way of dishing up potatoes in Kirk Street?" asked Zack, in great triumph. "It's a little sudden when you're not used to it," stammered Valentine, ducking his head as each edible missile flew over him—"but it's free and easy—it's delightfully free and easy." "Ready there with your plates. The liver's a-coming," cried Mat, in a voice of martial command, suddenly showing his great red-hot perspiring face at the table, as he wheeled round from the fire, with the hissing frying-pan in one hand and the long toasting-fork in the other. "My dear sir, I'm shocked to see you

"KICK ABOUT, DEAR OLD FELLOW, KICK ABOUT AS MUCH AS YOU PLEASE," CRIED ZACK, SEATING HIMSELF OPPOSITE MR. BLYTH.

—HIDE-AND-SEEK, Vol. XI., page 437

taking all this trouble," exclaimed Mr. Blyth; "do pray let me help you!" "No, I'm d—d if I do," returned Mat, with the most polite suavity and the most perfect good-humor. "Let him have all the trouble, Blyth," said Zack; "let him help you, and don't pity him. He'll make up for his hard work, I can tell you, when he sets in seriously to his liver and bacon. Watch him when he begins—he bolts his dinner like the lion in the Zoological Gardens."

Mat appeared to receive this speech of Zack's as a well-merited compliment, for he chuckled at young Thorpe and winked grimly at Valentine, as he sat down bare-armed to his own mess of liver and bacon. It was certainly a rare and even a startling sight to see this singular man eat. Lump by lump, without one intervening morsel of bread, he tossed the meat into his mouth rather than put it there—turned it apparently once round between his teeth—and then voraciously and instantly swallowed it whole. By the time a quarter of Mr. Blyth's plateful of liver and bacon and half of Zack's had disappeared, Mat had finished his frugal meal; had wiped his mouth on the back of his hand, and the back of his hand on the leg of his trousers; had mixed two glasses of strong hot rum-and-water for himself and Zack; and had set to work on the composition of a third tumbler, into which sugar, brandy, lemon-juice, rum, and hot water all seemed to drop together in such incessant and confusing little driblets that it was impossible to tell which ingredient was uppermost in the whole mixture. When the tumbler was full, he set it down on the table, with an indicative bang, close to Valentine's plate.

"Just try a toothful of that to begin with," said Mat. "If you like it, say Yes; if you don't, say No; and I'll make it better next time."

"You are very kind, very kind indeed," answered Mr. Blyth, eying the tumbler by his side with some little confusion and hesitation; "but really, though I should be shocked to appear ungrateful, I'm afraid I must own—Zack, you ought to have told your friend—"

"So I did," said Zack, sipping his rum-and-water with infinite relish.

"The fact is, my dear sir," continued Valentine, "I have the most wretched head in the world for strong liquor of any kind—"

"Don't call it strong liquor," interposed Mat, emphatically tapping the rim of his guest's tumbler with his forefinger.

"Perhaps," pursued Mr. Blyth, with a polite smile, "I ought to have said grog."

"Don't call it grog," retorted Mat, with two disputatious taps on the rim of the glass.

"Dear me!" asked Valentine, amazedly, "what is it, then?"

"It's Squaw's Mixture," answered Mat, with three distinct taps of asseveration.

Mr. Blyth and Zack laughed, under the impression that their queer companion was joking with them. Mat looked steadily and sternly from one to the other; then repeated, with the gruffest gravity, "I tell you, it's Squaw's Mixture."

"What a very curious name! How is it made?" asked Valentine.

"Enough brandy to spile the water. Enough rum to spile the brandy-and-water. Enough lemon to spile the rum *and* brandy-*and*-water. Enough sugar to spile everything. That's 'Squaw's Mixture,'" replied Mat, with perfect calmness and deliberation.

Zack began to laugh uproariously. Mat became more inflexibly grave than ever. Mr. Blyth felt that he was growing interested on the subject of the Squaw's Mixture. He stirred it diffidently with his spoon, and asked with great curiosity how his host first learned to make it.

"When I was out, over there, in the Nor'-west," began Mat, nodding toward the particular point of the compass that he mentioned.

"When he says Nor'west, and wags his addled old head like that at the chimney-pots over the way, he means North America," Zack explained.

"When I was out Nor'west," repeated Mat, heedless of the interruption, "working along with the exploring gang, our stock of liquor fell short, and we had to make the best of it in the cold with a spurt of spirits and a pinch of sugar, drowned in more hot water than had ever got down the throat of e'er a man of the lot of us before. We christened the brew 'Squaw's Mixture,' because it was such weak stuff that even a woman couldn't have got drunk on it if she tried. Squaw means woman in those parts, you know; and mixture means—what you've got afore you now. I knowed you couldn't stand regular grog, and that's why I cooked it up for you. Don't keep on stirring of it with a spoon like that, or you'll stir it away altogether. Try it."

"Let *me* try it—let's see how weak it is," cried Zack, reaching over to Valentine.

"Don't you go a-shoving of your oar into another man's rollocks," said Mat, dexterously knocking Zack's spoon out of his hand just as it touched Mr. Blyth's tumbler. "You stick to *your* grog; I'll stick to *my* grog; and *he'll* stick to Squaw's Mixture." With those words, Mat leaned his bare elbows on the table, and watched Valentine's first experimental sip with great curiosity.

The result was not successful. When Mr. Blyth put down the tumbler, all the watery part of the Squaw's Mixture seemed to have got up into his eyes, and all the spirituous part to have stopped short at his lungs. He shook his head, coughed, and faintly exclaimed: "Too strong."

"Too hot, you mean?" said Mat.

"No, indeed," pleaded poor Mr. Blyth, "I really meant too strong."

"Try again," suggested Zack, who was far advanced toward the bottom of his own tumbler already. "Try again. Your liquor all went the wrong way last time."

"More sugar," said Mat, neatly tossing two lumps into the glass from where he sat. "More lemon" (squeezing one or two drops of juice and three or four pips into the mixture). "More water" (pouring in about a teaspoonful, with a clumsy flourish of the kettle). "Try again."

"Thank you, thank you a thousand times. Really, do you know, it tastes much nicer now," said Mr. Blyth, beginning cautiously with a spoonful of the Squaw's Mixture at a time.

Mat's spirits seemed to rise immensely at this announcement. He lit his pipe and took up his glass of grog; nodded to Valentine and young Thorpe, just as he had nodded to the northwest point of the compass a minute or two before; muttered gruffly, "Here's all our good healths;" and finished half his liquor at a draught.

"All our good healths!" repeated Mr. Blyth, gallantly attacking the Squaw's Mixture this time without any intermediate assistance from the spoon.

"All our good healths!" chimed in Zack, draining his glass to the bottom. "Really, Mat, it's quite bewildering to see how your dormant social qualities are waking up, now you're plunged into the vortex of society. What do you say to giving a ball here next? You're just the man to get on with the ladies, if you could only be prevailed on to wear your coat and give up airing your tawny old arms in public."

"Don't, my dear sir! I particularly beg you won't," cried Valentine, as Mat, apparently awakened to a sense of polite propriety by Zack's hint, began to unroll one of his tightly-tucked-up shirt-sleeves. "Pray consult your own comfort, and keep your sleeves as they were—pray do! As an artist, I have been admiring your arms from the professional point of view ever since we first sat down to table. I never remember, in all my long experience of the living model, having met with such a splendid muscular development as yours.''

Saying those words, Mr. Blyth waved his hand several times before his host's arms, regarding them with his eyes partially closed, and his head very much on one side, just as he was accustomed to look at his pictures. Mat stared, smoked vehemently, folded the objects of Valentine's admiration over his breast, and, modestly scratching his elbows, looked at young Thorpe with an expression of utter bewilderment. "Yes! decidedly the most magnificent muscular development I ever remember studying," reiterated Mr. Blyth, drumming with his fingers on the table, and concentrating the whole of his critical acumen in one eye by totally closing the other.

"Hang it, Blyth!" remonstrated Zack, "don't keep on looking at his arms as if they were a couple of bits of prize beef! You may talk about his muscular development as much as you please, but you can't have the smallest notion of what it's really equal to till you try it. I say, old Rough and Tough! jump up, and show him how strong you are. Just lift him on your toe, like you did me." (Here Zack pulled Mat unceremoniously out of his chair.) "Come along, Blyth! Get opposite to him—give him hold of your hand—stand on the toe part of his right foot—don't wriggle about—stiffen your hand and arm, and—there!—what do you say to his muscular development now?" concluded Zack, with an air of supreme triumph, as Mat slowly lifted from the ground the foot on which Mr. Blyth was standing, and, steadying himself on his left leg, raised the astonished painter with his right nearly two feet high in the air.

Any spectator observing the performance of this feat of strength and looking only at Mat, might well have thought it impossible that any human being could present a more comical aspect than he now exhibited, with his black skull-cap pushed a little on one side, and showing an inch or so of his bald head, with his grimly-grinning face empurpled by the violent physical exertion of the moment, and with his thick, heavy figure ridiculously perched on one leg. Mr. Blyth, however, was beyond all comparison the more laughable object of the two, as he soared nervously into the air on Mat's foot, tottering infirmly in the strong grasp that supported him, till he seemed to be trembling all over, from the tips of his crisp black hair to the flying tails of his frock-coat. As for the expression of his round rosy face, with the bright eyes fixed in a startled stare, and the plump cheeks crumpled up by an uneasy smile, it was so exquisitely absurd, as young Thorpe saw it over his fellow-lodger's black skull-cap, that he roared again with laughter. "Oh! look up at him!" cried Zack, falling back in his chair. "Look at his face, for Heaven's sake, before you put him down!"

But Mat was not to be moved by this appeal.

All the attention his eyes could spare during those few moments was devoted, not to Mr. Blyth's face, but to Mr. Blyth's watch-chain. There hung the bright little key of the painter's bureau, dangling jauntily to and fro over his waistcoat-pocket. As the right foot of the Samson of Kirk Street hoisted him up slowly, the key swung temptingly backward and forward between them. "Come take me! come take me!" it seemed to say, as Mat's eyes fixed greedily on it every time it dangled toward him.

"Wonderful! wonderful!" cried Mr. Blyth, looking excessively relieved when he found himself safely set down on the floor again.

"That's nothing to some of the things he can do," said Zack. "Look here! Put yourself stomach downward on the carpet; and if you think the waistband of your trousers will stand it, he'll take you up in his teeth."

"Thank you, Zack, I'm perfectly satisfied without risking the waistband of my trousers," rejoined Valentine, returning in a great hurry to the table.

"The grog's getting cold," grumbled Mat. "Do you find it slip down easy now?" he continued, handing the Squaw's Mixture in the friendliest manner to Mr. Blyth.

"Astonishingly easy!" answered Valentine, drinking this time almost with the boldness of Zack himself. "Now it's cooler, one tastes the sugar. Whenever I've tried to drink regular grog, I have never been able to get people to give it me sweet enough. The delicious part of this is that there's plenty of sugar in it. And, besides, it has the merit (which real grog has not) of being harmless. It tastes strong to *me*, to be sure; but then I'm not used to spirits. After what you say, however, of course it must be harmless — perfectly harmless, I have no doubt." Here he sipped again, pretty freely this time, by way of convincing himself of the innocent weakness of the Squaw's Mixture.

While Mr. Blyth had been speaking, Mat's hands had been gradually stealing down deeper and deeper into the pockets of his trousers, until his finger and thumb and a certain plastic substance hidden away in the left-hand pocket came gently into contact, just as Valentine left off speaking. "Let's have another toast," cried Mat, quite briskly, the instant the last word was out of his guest's mouth. "Come on, one of you, and give us another toast," he reiterated, with a roar of barbarous joviality, taking up his glass in his right hand and keeping his left still in his pocket.

"Give you another toast, you noisy old savage!" repeated Zack. "I'll give you *five*, all at once! Mr. Blyth, Mrs. Blyth, Madonna, 'Columbus,' and 'The Golden Age'—three excellent people and two glorious pictures; let's lump them all together in a friendly way, and drink long life and success to them in beakers of fragrant grog!" shouted the young gentleman, making perilously rapid progress through his second glass, as he spoke.

"Do you know, I'm afraid I must change to

some other place, if you have no objection," said Mr. Blyth, after he had duly honored the composite toast just proposed. "The fire here, behind me, is getting rather too hot."

"Change along with me," said Mat. "I don't mind heat, nor cold neither, for the matter of that."

Valentine accepted this offer with great gratitude. "By-the-by, Zack," he said, placing himself comfortably in his host's chair, between the table and the wall—"I was going to ask a favor of our excellent friend here, when you suggested that wonderful and matchless trial of strength which we have just had. You have been of such inestimable assistance to me already, my dear sir," he continued, turning toward Mat, with all his natural cordiality of disposition now fully developed, under the fostering influence of the Squaw's Mixture "You have laid me under such an inexpressible obligation in saving my picture from destruction—" .

"I wish you could make up your mind to say what you want in plain words," interrupted Mat. "I'm one of your rough-handed, thick-headed sort, *I* am. I'm not gentleman enough to understand parlarver. It don't do me no good: it only worrits me into a perspiration." And Mat, shaking down his shirt-sleeve, drew it several times across his forehead, as a proof of the truth of his last assertion.

"Quite right! quite right!" cried Mr. Blyth, patting him on the shoulder in the most friendly manner imaginable. "In plain words, then, when I mentioned, just now, how much I admired your arms in an artistic point of view, I was only paving the way for asking you to let me make a drawing of them, in black and white, for a large picture that I mean to paint later in the year. My classical figure composition, you know, Zack—you have seen the sketch—Hercules bringing to Eurystheus the Erymanthian boar—a glorious subject; and our friend's arms, and, indeed, his chest, too, if he would kindly consent to sit for it, would make the very studies I most want for Hercules."

"What on earth *is* he driving at?" asked Mat, addressing himself to young Thorpe, after staring at Valentine for a moment or two in a state of speechless amazement.

"He wants to draw your arms-of course you will be only too happy to let him-you can't understand anything about it now-but you will when you begin to sit-pass the cigars-thank Blyth for meaning to make a Hercules of you-and tell him you'll come to the painting-room whenever he likes," answered Zack, joining his sentences together in his most off-hand manner, all in a breath.

"What painting-room? Where is it?" asked Mat, still in a densely stupefied condition.

"My painting - room," replied Valentine. "Where you saw the pictures, and saved Columbus, yesterday."

Mat considered for a moment—then suddenly brightened up, and began to look quite intelligent again. "I'll come," he said, "as soon as

you like—the sooner the better," clapping his
fist emphatically on the table, and drinking to
Valentine with his heartiest nod.

"That's a worthy, good-natured fellow!"
cried Mr. Blyth, drinking to Mat in return,
with grateful enthusiasm. "The sooner the better, as you say. Come to-morrow evening."

"All right. To-morrow evening," assented
Mat. His left hand, as he spoke, began to work
stealthily round and round in his pocket, mold-
ing into all sorts of strange shapes that plastic
substance, which had lain hidden there ever
since his shopping expedition in the morning.

"I should have asked you to come in the day-
time," continued Valentine; "but, as you know,
Zack, I have the 'Golden Age' to varnish, and
one or two little things to alter in the lower part
of 'Columbus'; and then, by the latter end of the
week, I must leave home to do those portraits in
the country which I told you of, and which are
wanted before I thought they would be. You
will come with our friend, of course, Zack? I
dare say I shall have the order for you to study
at the British Museum, by to-morrow. As for
the Private Drawing Academy—"

"No offense; but I can't stand seeing you
stirring up them grounds in the bottom of your
glass any longer," Mat broke in here; taking
away Mr. Blyth's tumbler as he spoke, throwing
the sediment of sugar, the lemon-pips, and the
little liquor left to cover them, into the grate behind; and then hospitably devoting himself to
the concoction of a second supply of that pala-

table and innocuous beverage, the Squaw's Mixture.

"Half a glass," cried Mr. Blyth. "Weak— remember my wretched head for drinking, and pray make it weak."

As he spoke, the clock of the neighboring parish church struck.

"Only nine," exclaimed Zack, referring ostentatiously to the watch which he had taken out of pawn the day before. "Pass the rum, Mat, as soon as you've done with it—put the kettle on to boil—and now, my lads, we'll begin spending the evening in earnest!"

*   *   *   *   *   *   *

If any fourth gentleman had been present to assist in "spending the evening," as Zack chose to phrase it, at the small social *soirée* in Kirk Street; and if that gentleman had deserted the festive board as the clock struck nine—had walked about the streets to enjoy himself in the fresh air—and had then, as the clock struck ten, returned to the society of his convivial companions, he would most assuredly have been taken by surprise, on beholding the singular change which the lapse of one hour had been sufficient to produce in the manners and conversation of Mr. Valentine Blyth.

It might have been that the worthy and simple-hearted gentleman had been unduly stimulated by the reek of hot grog, which, in harmonious association with a heavy mist of tobacco-smoke, now filled the room; or it might have been that the second brew of the Squaw's Mixture had exceeded half a glassful in quantity, had not been diluted to the requisite weakness, and had consequently got into his head; but, whatever the exciting cause might be, the alteration that had taken place since nine o'clock, in his voice, looks, and manners, was remarkable enough to be of the nature of a moral phenomenon. He now talked incessantly about nothing but the fine arts; he differed with both his companions, and loftily insisted on his own superior sagacity, whenever either of them ventured to speak a word; he was by turns as noisy as Zack and as gruff as Mat; his hair was crumpled down over his forehead, his eyes were dimmed, his shirt-collar was turned rakishly over his cravat: in short, he was not the genuine Valentine Blyth at all—he was only a tipsy counterfeit of him.

As for young Thorpe, any slight steadiness of brain which he might naturally possess, he had long since parted with, as a matter of course, for the rest of the evening. Mat alone remained unchanged. There he sat, reckless of the blazing fire behind him, still with that left hand of his dropping stealthily every now and then into his pocket; smoking, drinking, and staring at his two companions, just as gruffly self-possessed as ever.

"There's ten," muttered Mat, as the clock struck. "I said we should be getting jolly by ten. So we are."

Zack nodded his head solemnly, and stared hard at one of the empty bottles on the floor, which had rolled out from the temporary store-room under the table.

"Hold your tongues, both of you!" cried Mr. Blyth. "I insist on clearing up that disputed point about whether artists are not just as hardy and strong as other men. I'm an artist myself, and I say they are. I'll agree with you in everything else; for you're the two best fellows in the world; but if you say a word against artists, I'm your enemy for life. You may talk to me by the hour together about admirals, generals, and prime ministers—I mention the glorious names of Michael Angelo and Raphael, and down goes your argument directly. When Michael Angelo's nose was broken, do you think he minded it? Look in his Life, and see if he did—that's all! Ha! ha! My painting-room is forty feet long (now this is an important proof). While I was painting 'Columbus' and the 'Golden Age,' one was at one end—north; and the other at the other—south. Very good. I walked backward and forward between those two pictures incessantly; and never sat down all day long. This is a fact—and the proof is, that I worked on both of them at once. A touch on 'Columbus'—a walk into the middle of the room, to look at the effect—turn round—walk up to 'The Golden Age' opposite—a touch on 'The Golden Age'—another walk into the middle of the room to look at the effect—another turn round—and back again to 'Columbus.' Fifteen miles a day of indoor exercise, according to the calculation of a mathematical friend of mine;

and *not* including the number of times I had to go up and down my portable wooden steps to get at the top parts of 'Columbus.' Isn't a man hardy and strong who can stand that? Ha! ha! Just feel my legs, Zack. Are they hard and muscular, or are they not?"

Here Mr. Blyth, rapping young Thorpe smartly on the head with his spoon, tried to skip out of his chair as nimbly as usual; but only succeeded in floundering awkwardly into an upright position, after he had knocked down his plate with all the greasy remains of the liver and bacon on it. Zack roused himself from muddled meditation with a start; and, under pretense of obeying his friend's injunction, pinched Valentine's leg with such vigorous malice that the painter fairly screamed again under the infliction. All this time Mat sat immovably serene in his place next to the fire. He just kicked Mr. Blyth's broken plate, with the scraps of liver and bacon, and the knife and fork that had fallen with them, into the temporary store-room under the table, and then pushed toward him another glass of the Squaw's Mixture, quietly concocted while he had been talking.

The effect on Valentine of this hospitable action proved to be singularly soothing and beneficial. He had been getting gradually more and more disputatious for the last ten minutes; but the moment the steaming glass touched his hand, it seemed to change his mood with the most magical celerity. As he looked down at it, and felt the fragrant rum steaming softly into his nos-

trils, his face expanded; and while his left hand
unsteadily conveyed the tumbler to his lips, his
right reached across the table and fraternally
extended itself to Mat. "My dear friend," said
Mr. Blyth, affectionately, "how kind you are!
Pray how do you make the Squaw's Mixture?"

"I say, Mat, leave off smoking, and tell us
something," interposed Zack. "Bowl away at
once with one of your tremendous stories, or
Blyth will be bragging again about his rickety
old legs. Talk, man! Tell us your famous
story of how you lost your scalp."

Mat laid down his pipe, and for a moment
looked very attentively at Mr. Blyth — then,
with the most uncharacteristic readiness and
docility, began his story at once, without requir-
ing another word of persuasion. In general, the
very reverse of tedious when he related any ex-
periences of his own, he seemed, on this occasion, perversely bent on letting his narrative ooze
out to the most interminable length. Instead of
adhering to the abridged account of his terrible
adventure, which he had given Zack when they
first talked together on Blackfriars Bridge, he
now dwelt drowsily on the minutest particulars
of the murderous chase that had so nearly cost
him his life, enumerating them one after the
other in the same heavy droning voice which
never changed its tone in the slightest degree as
he went on. After about ten minutes' endurance of the narrative-infliction which he had
himself provoked, young Thorpe was just beginning to feel a sensation of utter oblivion stealing

over him, when a sound of lusty snoring close
at his back startled him into instant wakeful-
ness. He looked round. There was Mr. Blyth
placidly and profoundly asleep, with his mouth
wide open and his head resting against the wall.

"Stop!" whispered Mat, as Zack seized on a
half-squeezed lemon and took aim at Valentine's
mouth. "Don't wake him yet. What do you
say to some oysters?"

"Give us a dish, and I'll show you," returned
young Thorpe. "Sally's in bed by this time—
I'll fetch the oysters myself from over the way.
But, I say, I must have a friendly shot with
something or other at dear old Blyth's gaping
mouth."

"Try him with an oyster, when you come
back," said Mat, producing from the cupboard
behind him a large yellow pie-dish. "Go on!
I'll see you downstairs, and leave the candle on
the landing, and the door on the jar, so as you
can get in quietly. Steady, young 'un! and
mind the dish when you cross the road." With
these words Mat dismissed Zack from the street
door to the oyster-shop, and then returned immediately to his guest upstairs.

Valentine was still fast asleep, and snoring vehemently. Mat's hand descended again
into his pocket, reappearing, however, quickly
enough on this occasion, with the piece of wax
which he had purchased that morning. Steadying his arms coolly on the table, he detached the
little chain which held the key of Mr. Blyth's
bureau from the watch-guard to which it was

fastened, took off on his wax a perfect impression of the whole key from the pipe to the handle, attached it again to the sleeper's watch-guard, pared away the rough ends of the piece of wax till it fitted into an old tin tobacco-box which he took from the chimney-piece, pocketed this box, and then quietly resumed his original place at the table.

"Now," said Mat, looking at the unconscious Mr. Blyth, after he had lighted his pipe again, "now, painter-man! wake up as soon as you like."

It was not long before Zack returned. A violent bang of the street door announced his entry into the passage—a confused clattering and stumbling marked his progress upstairs—a shrill crash, a heavy thump, and a shout of laughter indicated his arrival on the landing. Mat ran out directly, and found him prostrate on the floor, with the yellow pie-dish in halves at the bottom of the stairs, and dozens of oyster-shells scattered about him in every direction.

"Hurt?" inquired Mat, pulling him up by the collar, and dragging him into the room.

"Not a bit of it," answered Zack. "I've woke Blyth, though (worse luck!), and spoiled our shot with the oyster, haven't I? Oh, Lord! how he stares!"

Valentine certainly did stare. He was standing up, leaning against the wall, and looking about him in a wofully dazed condition. Either his nap, or the alarming manner in which he had been awakened from it, had produced a decided change for the worse in him. As he slowly recovered what little sense he had left to make use of, all his talkativeness and cordiality seemed to desert him. He shook his head mournfully; refused to eat or drink anything; declared, with sullen solemnity, that his digestion was "a perfect wreck in consequence of his keeping drunken society;" and insisted on going home directly, in spite of everything that Zack could say to him. The landlord, who had been brought from his shop below by the noise, and who thought it very desirable to take the first opportunity that offered of breaking up the party before any more grog was consumed, officiously ran downstairs and called a cab—the result of this maneuver proving, in the sequel, to be what the tobacconist desired. The moment the sound of wheels was heard at the door, Mr. Blyth clamored peremptorily for his hat and coat; and, after some little demur, was at last helped into the cab in the most friendly and attentive manner by Mat himself.

"Just see the lights out upstairs, and the young 'un in bed, will ye?" said Mat to his landlord, as they stood together on the doorstep. "I'm going to blow some of the smoke out of me by taking a turn in the fresh air."

He walked away briskly, as he said the last words; but when he got to the end of the street, instead of proceeding northward toward the country, and the cool night-breeze that was blowing from it, he perversely turned southward toward the filthiest little lanes and courts in the whole neighborhood.

Stepping along at a rapid pace, he directed his course toward that particular row of small and vile houses which he had already visited early in the day, and stopped, as before, at the second-hand iron shop. It was shut up for the night, but a dim light, as of one farthing candle, glimmered through the circular holes in the tops of the shutters; and when Mat knocked at the door with his knuckles, it was opened immediately by the same humpbacked shopman with whom he had conferred in the morning.

"Got it?" asked the hunchback, in a cracked, querulous voice, the moment the door was ajar.

"All right," answered Mat, in his gruffest bass tones, handing to the little man the tin tobacco-box.

"We said to-morrow evening, didn't we?" continued the squalid shopman.

"Not later than six," added Mat.

"Not later than six," repeated the other, shutting the door softly as his customer walked away —northward this time—to seek the fresh air in good earnest.

CHAPTER XI.

THE GARDEN DOOR.

"HIT or miss, I'll chance it to-night." Those words were the first that issued from Mat's lips on the morning after Mr. Blyth's visit, as he stood alone amid the festive relics of the past evening, in the front room at Kirk Street. "To-night," he repeated to himself, as he pulled off his coat and prepared to make his toilet for the day in a pail of cold water, with the assistance of a short bar of wholesome yellow soap.

Though it was still early, his mind had been employed for some hours past in considering how the second and only difficulty, which now stood between him and the possession of the hair bracelet, might best be overcome. Having already procured the first requisite for executing his design, how was he next to profit by what he had gained? Knowing that the false key would be placed in his hands that evening, how was he to open Mr. Blyth's bureau without risking discovery by the owner, or by some other person in the house?

To this important question he had as yet found no better answer than was involved in the words he had just whispered to himself, while preparing for his morning ablutions. As for any definite plan by which to guide himself, he was desperately resigned to trust for the discovery of it to the first lucky chance which might be brought about by the events of the day. "I should like though to have one good look by daylight round that place they call the painting-room," thought Mat, plunging his face into two handfuls of hissing soapsuds.

He was still vigorously engaged over the pail of cold water, when a loud yawn, which died away gradually into a dreary howl, sounded from the next room, and announced that Zack was awake. In another minute the young gen-

tleman appeared gloomily, in his nightgown, at
the folding-doors by which the two rooms communicated. His eyes looked red-rimmed and
blinking, his cheeks mottled and sodden, his
hair tangled and dirty. He had one hand to
his forehead, and groaning, with the corners of
his mouth lamentably drawn down, exhibited
a shocking and salutary picture of the consequences of excessive conviviality.

"Oh Lord, Mat!" he moaned, "my head's
coming in two."

"Souse it in a pail of cold water and walk off
what you can't get rid of, after that, along with
me," suggested his friend.

Zack wisely took this advice. As they left
Kirk Street for their walk, Mat managed that
they should shape their course so as to pass Valentine's house on their way to the fields. As he
had anticipated, young Thorpe proposed to call
in for a minute, to see how Mr. Blyth was after
the festivities of the past night, and to ascertain
if he still remained in the same mind about making the drawing of Mat's arms that evening.

"I suspect you didn't brew the Squaw's Mixture half as weak as you told us you did," said
Zack, slyly, when they rang at the bell. "It
wasn't a bad joke for once in a way. But
really, Blyth is such a good kind-hearted fellow, it seems too bad—in short, don't let's do it
next time, that's all!"

Mat gruffly repudiated the slightest intention
of deceiving their guest as to the strength of the
liquor he had drunk. They went into the paint-

ing-room and found Mr. Blyth there, pale and penitent, but manfully preparing to varnish "The Golden Age," with a very trembling hand, and a very headachy contraction of the eyebrows.

"Ah, Zack, Zack! I ought to lecture you about last night," said Valentine; "but I have no right to say a word, for I was much the worst of the two. I'm wretchedly ill this morning, which is just what I deserve, and heartily ashamed of myself, which is only what I ought to be. Look at my hand! It's all in a tremble, like an old man's. Not a thimbleful of spirits shall ever pass my lips again: I'll stick to lemonade and tea for the rest of my life. No more Squaw's Mixture for *me!* Not, my dear sir," continued Valentine, addressing Mat, who had been quietly stealing a glance at the bureau while the painter was speaking to young Thorpe; "not, my dear sir, that I think of blaming you, or doubt for a moment that the drink you kindly mixed for me would have been considered quite weak and harmless by people with stronger heads than mine. It was all my own fault, my own want of proper thoughtfulness and caution. If I misconducted myself last night, as I am afraid I did, pray make allowances—"

"Nonsense!" cried Zack, seeing that Mat was beginning to fidget away from Valentine, instead of returning an answer. "Nonsense! you were glorious company. We were three choice spirits, and you were Number One of the social Trio. Away with melancholy! Do you still keep in the same mind about drawing Mat's arms? He

will be delighted to come, and so shall I; and
we'll all get virtuously uproarious this time on
toast-and-water and tea.''

"Of course I keep in the same mind,'' returned
Mr. Blyth. "I had my senses about me, at any
rate, when I invited you and your friend here
to-night. Not that I shall be able to do much,
I am afraid, in the way of drawing—for a letter
has come this morning to hurry me into the country. Another portrait-job has turned up, and I
shall have to start to-morrow. However, I can
get in the outline of your friend's arms to-night,
and leave the rest to be done when I come back.—
Shall I take that sketch down for you, my dear
sir, to look at close?'' continued Valentine, suddenly raising his voice and addressing himself
to Mat. "I venture to think it one of my most
conscientious studies from actual Nature.''

While Mr. Blyth and Zack had been whispering together, Mat had walked away from them
quietly toward one end of the room, and was
now standing close to a door lined inside with
sheet-iron, having bolts at top and bottom, and
leading down a flight of steps from the studio
into the back garden. Above this door hung a
large chalk sketch of an old five-barred gate, being the identical study from Nature which, as
Valentine imagined, was at that moment the
special object of interest to Mat.

"No, no! don't trouble to get the sketch now,''
said Zack, once more answering for his friend.
"We are going out to get freshened up by a
long walk, and can't stop. Now, then, Mat,

what on earth are you staring at—the garden door, or the sketch of the five-barred gate?"

"The picter, in course," answered Mat, with unusual quickness and irritability.

"It shall be taken down for you to look at close to-night," said Mr. Blyth, delighted by the impression which the five-barred gate seemed to have produced on the new visitor.

On leaving Mr. Blyth's, young Thorpe and his companion turned down a lane partially built over, which led past Valentine's back garden wall. This was their nearest way to the fields and to the high-road into the country beyond. Before they had taken six steps down the lane, Mat, who had been incomprehensibly stolid and taciturn inside the house, became just as incomprehensibly curious and talkative all on a sudden outside it.

In the first place, he insisted on mounting some planks lying under Valentine's wall (to be used for the new houses that were being built in the lane), and peeping over to see what sort of garden the painter had. Zack summarily pulled him down from his elevation by the coat-tails, but not before his quick eye had traveled over the garden; had ascended the steps leading from it to the studio; and had risen above them as high as the brass handle of the door by which they were approached from the painting-room.

In the second place, when he had been prevailed on to start fairly for the walk, Mat began to ask questions with the same pertinacious inquisitiveness which he had already displayed on

the day of the picture-show. He set out with
wanting to know whether there were to be any
strange visitors at Mr. Blyth's that evening;
and then, on being reminded that Valentine
had expressly said at parting: "Nobody but
ourselves," asked if they were likely to see the
painter's wife downstairs. After the inquiry
had of necessity been answered in the negative,
he went on to a third question, and desired to
know whether "the young woman" (as he persisted in calling Madonna) might be expected to
stay upstairs with Mrs. Blyth, or to show herself
occasionally in the painting-room. Zack answered this inquiry also in the negative—with
a running accompaniment of bad jokes, as usual.
Madonna, except under extraordinary circumstances, never came down into the studio in the
evening when Mr. Blyth had company there.

Satisfied on these points, Mat now wanted to
know at what time Mr. Blyth and his family
were accustomed to go to bed; and explained,
when Zack expressed astonishment at the inquiry, that he had only asked this question in
order to find out the hour at which it would be
proper to take leave of their host that night. On
hearing this, young Thorpe answered as readily
and carelessly as usual that the painter's family
were early people, who went to bed before eleven
o'clock; adding that it was, of course, particularly necessary to leave the studio in good time
on the occasion referred to, because Valentine
would most probably start for the country next
day by one of the morning trains.

Mat's next question was preceded by a silence of a few minutes. Possibly he was thinking in what terms he might best put it. If this were the case, he certainly decided on using the briefest possible form of expression, for when he spoke again, he asked in so many words what sort of a woman the painter's wife was.

Zack characteristically answered the inquiry by a torrent of his most superlative eulogies on Mrs. Blyth; and then, passing from the lady herself to the chamber that she inhabited, wound up with a magnificent and exaggerated description of the splendor of her room.

Mat listened to him attentively; then said he supposed Mrs. Blyth must be fond of curiosities, and all sorts of "knickknack things from foreign parts." Young Thorpe not only answered the question in the affirmative, but added, as a private expression of his own opinion, that he believed these said curiosities and "knickknacks" had helped, in their way, to keep her alive by keeping her amused. From this, he digressed to a long narrative of poor Mrs. Blyth's first illness; and having exhausted that sad subject at last, ended by calling on his friend to change the conversation to some less mournful topic.

But just at this point it seemed that Mat was perversely determined to let himself lapse into another silent fit. He not only made no attempt to change the conversation, but entirely ceased asking questions; and, indeed, hardly uttered another word of any kind, good or bad. Zack, after vainly trying to rally him into talking lit a cigar in despair, and the two walked on together silently—Mat having his hands in his pockets, keeping his eyes bent on the ground, and altogether burying himself, as it were, from the outer world, in the innermost recesses of a deep brown study.

As they returned and got near Kirk Street, Mat gradually began to talk again, but only on indifferent subjects; asking no more questions about Mr. Blyth, or any one else. They arrived at their lodgings at half-past five o'clock. Zack went into the bedroom to wash his hands. While he was thus engaged, Mat opened that leather bag of his which has been already described as lying in the corner with the bear-skins, and taking out the feather-fan and the Indian tobacco-pouch, wrapped them up separately in paper. Having done this, he called to Zack; and, saying that he was about to step over to the shaving-shop to get his face scraped clean before going to Mr. Blyth's, left the house with his two packages in his hand.

"If the worst comes to the worst, I'll chance it to-night with the garden door," said Mat to himself, as he took the first turning that led toward the second-hand iron-shop. "This will do to get rid of the painter-man with. And this will send Zack after him," he added, putting first the fan and then the tobacco-pouch into separate pockets of his coat. A cunning smile hovered about his lips for a moment, as he disposed of his two packages in this manner; but it passed away again almost immediately, and was succeeded by a curious contraction and twitching of the upper part of his face. He began muttering once again that name of "Mary," which had been often on his lips lately; and quickened his pace mechanically, as it was always his habit to do when anything vexed or disturbed him.

When he reached the shop, the hunchback was at the door, with the tin tobacco-box in his hand. On this occasion, not a single word was exchanged between the two. The squalid shopman, as the customer approached, rattled something significantly inside the box, and then handed it to Mat; and Mat put his finger and thumb into his waistcoat-pocket, winked, nodded, and handed some money to the squalid shopman. The brief ceremony of giving and taking thus completed, these two originals turned away from each other without a word of farewell; the hunchback returning to the counter, and his customer proceeding to the shaving-shop.

Mat opened the box for an instant on his way to the barber's; and, taking out the false key (which, though made of baser metal, was almost as bright as the original), put it carefully into his waistcoat-pocket. He then stopped at an oil and candle shop and bought a wax-taper and a box of matches. "The garden door's safest: I'll chance it with the garden door," thought Mat, as he sat down in the shaving-shop chair and ordered the barber to operate on his chin.

Punctually at seven o'clock Mr. Blyth's visitors rang at his bell.

When they entered the studio, they found

Valentine all ready for them, with his drawing-board at his side, and his cartoon-sketch for
the proposed new picture of "Hercules bringing
to King Eurystheus the Erymanthian Boar" lying rolled up at his feet. He said he had got
rid of his headache, and felt perfectly well now;
but Zack observed that he was not in his usual
good spirits. Mat, on his side, observed nothing
but the garden door, toward which he lounged
carelessly as soon as the first salutations were over.

"This way, my dear sir," said Valentine,
walking after him. "I have taken down the
drawing you were so good as to admire this
morning, as I said I would. Here it is on this
painting-stand, if you would like to look at it."

Mat, whose first glance at the garden door had
assured him that it was bolted and locked for the
night, wheeled round immediately; and, to Mr.
Blyth's great delight, inspected the sketch of the
old five-barred gate with the most extraordinary
and flattering attention. "Wants doing up, don't
it?" said Mat, referring to the picturesquely-
ruinous original of the gate represented. "Yes,
indeed," answered Valentine, thinking he spoke
of the creased and ragged condition of the paper
on which the sketch was made; "a morsel of
paste and a sheet of fresh paper to stretch it on
would make quite another thing of it." Mat
stared.   "Paste and paper for a five-barred
gate? A nice carpenter *you* would make!" he
felt inclined to say. Zack, however, spoke at
that moment; so he left the sketch, and wisely
held his tongue.

"Now, then, Mat, strip to your chest, and put your arms in any position Blyth tells you. Remember, you are going to be drawn as Hercules; and mind you look as if you were bringing the Erymanthian boar to King Eurystheus for the rest of the evening," said young Thorpe, composedly warming himself at the fire.

While Mat awkwardly, and with many expressions of astonishment at the strange piece of service required from him by his host, divested himself of his upper garments, Valentine unrolled on the floor the paper cartoon of his classical composition; and, having refreshed his memory from it, put his model forthwith into the position of Hercules, with a chair to hold instead of an Erymanthian boar, and Zack to look at as the only available representative of King Eurystheus. This done, Mr. Blyth wasted some little time, as usual, before he began to work, in looking for his drawing materials. In the course of his search over the littered studio table, he accidentally laid his hand on two envelopes with inclosures, which, after examining the addresses, he gave immediately to young Thorpe.

"Here, Zack," he said, "these belong to you. "The large envelope contains your permission to draw at the British Museum. The small one has a letter of introduction inside, presenting you, with my best recommendations, to my friend, Mr. Strather. a very pleasing artist, and the Curator of an excellent private Drawing Academy. You had better call to-morrow before eleven. Mr. Strather will go with you to the Museum, and show you how to begin, and will introduce you to his drawing academy the same evening. Pray, pray, Zack, be steady and careful. Remember all you have promised your mother and me; and show us that you are now really determined to study the Art in good earnest.''

Zack expressed great gratitude for his friend's kindness, and declared, with the utmost fervor of voice and manner, that he would repair all his past faults by unflagging future industry as a student of Art. After a little longer delay, Valentine at last collected his drawing materials and fairly began to work; Mat displaying from the first the most extraordinary and admirable steadiness as a model. But while the work of the studio thus proceeded with all the smoothness and expedition that could be desired, the incidental conversation by no means kept pace with it. In spite of all that young Thorpe could say or do, the talk lagged more and more, and grew duller and duller. Valentine was evidently out of spirits, and the Hercules of the evening had stolidly abandoned himself to the most inveterate silence. At length Zack gave up all further effort to be sociable and left the painting-room to go upstairs and visit the ladies. Mat looked after him as he quitted the studio, and seemed about to speak—then glancing aside at the bureau, checked himself suddenly, and did not utter a word.

Mr. Blyth's present depression of spirits was not entirely attributable to a certain ominous reluctance to leave home, which he had been vainly trying to shake off since the morning. He had a secret reason for his uneasiness which happened to be intimately connected with the model, whose Herculean chest and arms he was now busily engaged in drawing.

The plain fact was, that Mr. Blyth's tender conscience smote him sorely, when he remembered the trust Mrs. Thorpe placed in his promised supervision over her son, and when he afterward reflected that he still knew as little of Zack's strange companion as Zack did himself. His visit to Kirk Street, undertaken for the express purpose of guarding the lad's best interests by definitely ascertaining who Mr. Matthew Marksman really was, had ended in—what he was now ashamed to dwell over, or even to call to mind. "Dear, dear me!" thought Mr. Blyth, while he worked away silently at the outline of his drawing, "I ought to find out whether this very friendly, good-natured, and useful man is fit to be trusted with Zack; and now the lad is out of the room, I might very well do it. Might? I will!" And, acting immediately on this conscientious resolve, simple-hearted Mr. Blyth actually set himself to ask Mat the important question of who he really was!

Mat was candor itself in answering all inquiries that related to his wanderings over the American continent. He confessed with the utmost frankness that he had been sent to sea, as a wild boy whom it was impossible to keep steady at home; and he quite readily admitted that he had not introduced himself to Zack under

his real name. But at this point his communicativeness stopped. He did not quibble or pre-
varicate; he just bluntly and simply declared
that he would tell nothing more than he had told
already.

"I said to the young 'un," concluded Mat,
"when we first come together, 'I haven't heard
the sound of my own name for better than
twenty year past; and I don't care if I never
hear it again.' That's what I said to *him*.
That's what I say to *you*. I'm a rough 'un, I
know; but I haven't broke out of prison, or
cheated the gallows—"

"My dear sir," interposed Valentine, eagerly
and alarmedly, "pray don't imagine any such
offensive ideas ever entered my head! I might
perhaps have thought that family troubles—"

"That's it," Mat broke in quickly. "Family
troubles. Drop it there; and you'll leave it
right."

Before Mr. Blyth could make any attempt to
shift the conversation to some less delicate topic,
he was interrupted (to his own great relief) by
the return of young Thorpe to the studio.

Zack announced the approaching arrival of
the supper-tray, and warned "Hercules" to cover
up his neck and shoulders immediately, unless
he wished to frighten the housemaid out of her
wits. At this hint Mr. Blyth laid aside his
drawing-board, and Mat put on his flannel
waistcoat; not listening the while to one word
of the many fervent expressions of gratitude addressed to him by the painter, but appearing to

be in a violent hurry to array himself in his coat again. As soon as he had got it on, he put his hand in one of the pockets, and looked hard at Valentine. Just then, however, the servant came in with the tray; upon which he turned round impatiently, and walked away once again to the lower end of the room.

When the door had closed on the departing housemaid, he returned to Mr. Blyth with the feather fan in his hand; and saying, in his usual downright way, that he had heard from Zack of Mrs. Blyth's invalid condition, and of her fondness for curiosities, bluntly asked the painter if he thought his wife would like such a fan as that now produced.

"I got this plaything for a woman in the Old Country, many a long year ago," said Mat, pressing the fan roughly into Mr. Blyth's hands. "When I come back, and thought for to give it her, she was dead and gone. There's not another woman in England as cares about me, or knows about me. If you're too proud to let your wife have the thing, throw it into the fire. I haven't got nobody to give it to; and I can't keep it by me, and won't keep it by me, no longer."

In the utterance of these words there was a certain rough pathos and bitter reference to past calamity which touched Valentine in one of his tender places. His generous instincts overcame his prudent doubts in a moment; and moved him, not merely to accept the present, but also to predict warmly that Mrs. Blyth would be delighted with it.

"Zack," he said, speaking in an undertone to young Thorpe, who had been listening to Mat's last speech, and observing his production of the fan, in silent curiosity and surprise—"Zack, I'll run upstairs with the fan to Lavvie at once, so as not to seem careless about your friend's gift. Mind you do the honors of the supper-table with the proper hospitality while I am away."

Speaking these words, Mr. Blyth bustled out of the room as nimbly as usual. A minute or two after his departure, Mat put his hand into his pocket once more; mysteriously approached young Thorpe, and opened before him the paper containing the Indian tobacco-pouch, which was made of scarlet cloth, and was very prettily decorated with colored beads.

"Do you think the young woman would fancy this for a kind of plaything?" he asked.

Zack, with a shout of laughter, snatched the pouch out of his hands, and began to rally his friend more unmercifully than ever. For the first time Mat seemed to be irritated by the boisterous merriment of which he was made the object, and cut his tormentor short quite fiercely with a frown and an oath.

"Don't lose your temper, you amorous old savage!" cried Zack, with incorrigible levity. "I'll take your pouch upstairs to the Beloved Object; and, if Blyth will let her have it, I'll bring her down here to thank you for it herself!" Saying this, young Thorpe ran laughing out of the room with the scarlet pouch in his hand.

Mat listened intently till the sound of Zack's

rapid footsteps died away upstairs—then walked quickly and softly down the studio to the garden door—gently unlocked it—gently drew the bolts back—gently opened it, and ascertained that it could also be opened from without merely by turning the handle — then, quietly closing it again, left it, to all appearance, as fast for the night as before; provided no one went near enough, or had sufficiently sharp eyes, to observe that it was neither bolted nor locked.

"Now for the big chest!" thought Mat, taking the false key out of his pocket and hastening back to the bureau. "If Zack or the painter-man come down before I've time to get at the drawer inside, I've made sure of my second chance with the garden door."

He had the key in the lock of the bureau as this thought passed through his mind. He was just about to turn it, when the sound of rapidly-descending footsteps upon the stairs struck on his quick ear.

"Too late!" muttered Mat. "I must chance it, after all, with the garden door."

Putting the key into his pocket again as he said this, he walked back to the fireplace. The moment after he got there Mr. Blyth entered the studio.

"I am quite shocked that you should have been so unceremoniously left alone," said Valentine, whose naturally courteous nature prompted him to be just as scrupulously polite in his behavior to his rough guest, as if Mat had been a civilized gentleman of the most refined feeling

and the most exalted rank. "I am so sorry you
should have been left, through Zack's carelessness, without anybody to ask you to take a little
supper," continued Valentine, turning to the
table. "Mrs. Blyth, my dear sir (do take a
sandwich!), desires me to express her best
thanks for your very pretty present (that is the
brandy in the bottle next to you). She admires
the design (sponge-cake? Ah! you don't care
about sweets), and thinks the color of the center
feathers—"

At this moment the door opened, and Mr.
Blyth, abruptly closing his lips, looked toward
it with an expression of the blankest astonishment; for he beheld Madonna entering the painting-room in company with Zack.

Valentine had been persuaded to let the deaf
and dumb girl accept the scarlet pouch by his
wife; but neither she nor Zack had said a word
before him upstairs about taking Madonna into
the studio. When the painter was well out of
ear-shot, young Thorpe had confided to Mrs.
Blyth the new freak in which he wanted to engage; and, signing unscrupulously to Madonna
that she was wanted in the studio, to be presented to the "generous man who had given her
the tobacco-pouch," took her out of the room
without stopping to hear to the end the somewhat faint remonstrance by which his proposition was met. To confess the truth, Mrs. Blyth
—seeing no great impropriety in the girl's being
introduced to the stranger, while Valentine was
present in the room, and having, moreover, a

very strong curiosity to hear all she could about Zack's odd companion—was secretly anxious to ascertain what impressions Madonna would bring away of Mat's personal appearance and manners. And thus it was that Zack, by seizing his opportunity at the right moment, and exerting a little of that cool assurance in which he was never very deficient, now actually entered the painting-room in a glow of mischievous triumph with Madonna on his arm.

Valentine gave him a look as he entered which he found it convenient not to appear to see. The painter felt strongly inclined, at that moment, to send his adopted child upstairs again directly; but he restrained himself out of a feeling of delicacy toward his guest—for Mat had not only seen Madonna, but had hesitatingly advanced a step or two to meet her, the instant she came into the room.

Few social tests for analyzing female human nature can be more safely relied on than that which the moral investigator may easily apply, by observing how a woman conducts herself toward a man who shows symptoms of confusion on approaching her for the first time. If she has nothing at all in her, she awkwardly forgets the advantage of her sex, and grows more confused than he is. If she has nothing but brains in her, she cruelly abuses the advantage, and treats him with quiet contempt. If she has plenty of heart in her, she instinctively turns the advantage to its right use, and forthwith sets him at his ease by the timely charity of a word or the mute encouragement of a look.

Now Madonna, perceiving that the stranger showed evident signs, on approaching her, of what appeared like confusion to her apprehension, quietly drew her arm out of Zack's, and, to his unmeasured astonishment, stepped forward in front of him—looked up brightly into the grim, scarred face of Mat—dropped her usual courtesy —wrote a line hurriedly on her slate—then offered it to him with a smile and a nod, to read if he pleased, and to write on in return.

"Who would ever have thought it?" cried Zack, giving vent to his amazement; "she has taken to old Rough and Tough, and made him a prime favorite at first sight!"

Valentine was standing near, but he did not appear to hear this speech. He was watching the scene before him closely and curiously. Accustomed as he was to the innocent candor with which the deaf and dumb girl always showed her approval or dislike of strangers at a first interview—as also to her apparent perversity in often displaying a decided liking for the very people whose looks and manners had been previously considered certain to displease her—he was now almost as much surprised as Zack, when he witnessed her reception of Mat. It was an infallible sign of Madonna's approval if she followed up an introduction by handing her slate of her own accord to a stranger. When she was presented to people whom she disliked, she invariably kept it by her side until it was formally asked for.

Eccentric in everything else, Mat was consistently eccentric even in his confusion. Some men who are bashful in a young lady's presence show it by blushing. Mat's color sank instead of rising. Other men, similarly affected, betray their burdensome modesty by fidgeting incessantly. Mat was as still as a statue. His eyes wandered heavily and vacantly over the girl, beginning with her soft brown hair, then resting for a moment on her face, then descending to the gay pink ribbon on her breast, and to her crisp black silk apron with its smart lace pockets—then dropping at last to her neat little shoes, and to the thin bright line of white stocking that just separated them from the hem of her favorite gray dress. He only looked up again when she touched his hand and put her slate-pencil into it. At that signal he raised his eyes once more, read the line she had written to thank him for the scarlet pouch, and tried to write something in return. But his hand shook, and his thoughts seemed to fail him. He gave her back the slate and pencil, looking her full in the eyes as he did so. A curious change came over his face at the same time—a change like that which had altered him so remarkably in the hosier's shop at Dibbledean.

"Zack might, after all, have made many a worse friend than this man," thought Mr. Blyth, still attentively observing Mat. "Vagabonds don't behave in the presence of young girls as he is behaving now."

With this idea in his mind, Valentine advanced to help his guest by showing Mat how to communicate with Madonna. The painter was interrupted, however, by young Thorpe, who, the moment he recovered from his first sensations of surprise, began to talk nonsense again at the top of his voice, with the mischievous intention of increasing Mat's embarrassment.

While Mr. Blyth was attempting to silence Zack by leading him to the supper-table, Madonna was trying her best to reassure the great bulky sun-burned man, who seemed to be absolutely afraid of her! She moved to a stool, which stood near a second table in a corner by the fireplace; and sitting down, produced the scarlet pouch, intimating by a gesture that Mat was to look at what she was now doing. She then laid the pouch open on her lap, and put into it several little work-box toys, a Tonbridge silk-reel, an ivory needle-case, a silver thimble with an enameled rim, a tiny pair of scissors, and other things of the same kind—which she took first from one pocket of her apron and then from another. While she was engaged in filling the pouch, Zack, standing at the supper-table, drummed on the floor with his foot to attract her attention, and interrogatively held up a decanter of wine and a glass. She started as the sound struck on her delicate nerves; and, looking at young Thorpe directly, signed that she did not wish for any wine. The sudden movement of her body thus occasioned, shook off her lap a little mother-of-pearl bodkin case, which lay more than half out of one of the pockets of her apron. The bodkin-case rolled under the stool without her seeing it, for she was looking toward the supper-table: without being observed by Mat, for his eyes were following the direction of hers: without being heard by Mr. Blyth, for Zack was, as usual, chattering and making a noise.

When she had put two other little toys that remained in her pockets into the pouch, she drew the mouth of it tight, passed the loops of the loose thongs that fastened it over one of her arms, and then, rising to her feet, pointed to it, and looked at Mat with a very significant nod. The action expressed the idea she wished to communicate, plainly enough: "See," it seemed to say, "see what a pretty work-bag I can make of your tobacco-pouch!"

But Mat, to all appearance, was not able to find out the meaning of one of her gestures, easy as they were to interpret. His senses seemed to grow more and more perturbed the longer he looked at her. As she courtesied to him again, and moved away in despair, he stepped forward a little, and suddenly and awkwardly held out his hand. "The big man seems to be getting a little less afraid of me," thought Madonna, turning directly, and meeting his clumsy advance toward her with a smile. But the instant he took her hand, her lips closed, and she shivered through her whole body as if dead fingers had touched her. "Oh!" she thought now, "how cold his hand is! how cold his hand is!"

"If I hadn't felt her warm to touch, I should have been dreaming to-night that I'd seen Mary's ghost." This was the grim fancy which darkly

troubled Mat's mind, at the very same moment
when Madonna was thinking how cold his hand
was. He turned away impatiently from some
wine offered to him just then by Zack; and,
looking vacantly into the fire, drew his coat-cuff
several times over his eyes and forehead.

The chill from the strange man's hand still
lingered icily about Madonna's fingers, and made
her anxious, though she hardly knew why, to
leave the room. She advanced hastily to Valentine, and made the sign which indicated Mrs.
Blyth, by laying her hand on her heart; she then
pointed upstairs. Valentine, understanding what
she wanted, gave her leave directly to return to
his wife's room. Before Zack could make even
a gesture to detain her, she had slipped out of
the studio, after not having remained in it much
longer than five minutes.

"Zack," whispered Mr. Blyth, as the door
closed, "I am anything but pleased with you
for bringing Madonna downstairs. You have
broken through all rule in doing so; and, besides that, you have confused your friend by
introducing her to him without any warning
or preparation."

"Oh, that doesn't matter," interrupted young
Thorpe. "He's not the sort of man to want
warning about anything. I apologize for breaking rules; but as for Mat—why, hang it, Blyth,
it's plain enough what has been wrong with him
since supper came in! He's fairly knocked up
with doing Hercules for you. You have kept
the poor old Guy for near two hours standing in

one position, without a rag on his back; and then you wonder—"

"Bless my soul! that never occurred to me, I'm afraid you're right," exclaimed Valentine. "Do let us make him take something hot and comfortable! Dear, dear me! how ought one to mix grog?"

Mr. Blyth had been for some little time past trying his best to compound a species of fiery and potential Squaw's Mixture for Mat. He had begun the attempt some minutes before Madonna left the studio, having found it useless to offer any explanations to his inattentive guest of the meaning of the girl's signs and gestures with the slate and tobacco-pouch. He had presevered in his hospitable endeavor all through the whispered dialogue which had just passed between Zack and himself; and he had now filled the glass nearly to the brim, when it suddenly occurred to him that he had put sherry in at the top of the tumbler, after having begun with brandy at the bottom; also that he had altogether forgotten some important ingredient which he was, just then, perfectly incapable of calling to mind.

"Here, Mat!" cried Zack. "Come and mix yourself something hot. Blyth's been trying to do it for you, and can't."

Mat, who had been staring more and more vacantly into the fire all this time, turned round again at last toward his friends at the supper-table. He started a little when he saw that Madonna was no longer in the room—then looked

aside from the door by which she had departed
to the bureau. He had been pretty obstinately
determined to get possession of the hair bracelet
from the first; but he was doubly and trebly
determined now.

"It's no use looking about for the young lady,"
said Zack; "you behaved so clumsily and queerly
that you frightened her out of the room."

"No! no! nothing of the sort," interposed
Valentine, good-naturedly. "Pray take something to warm you. I am quite ashamed of my
want of consideration in keeping you standing
so long, when I ought to have remembered that
you were not used to being a painter's model.
I hope I have not given you cold—"

"Given me cold?" repeated Mat, amazedly.
He seemed about to add a sufficiently indignant
assertion of his superiority to any such civilized
bodily weakness as a liability to catch cold—but
just as the words were on his lips, he looked fixedly
at Mr. Blyth and checked himself.

"I am afraid you must be tired with the long
sitting you have so kindly given me," added
Valentine.

"No," answered Mat, after a moment's consideration; "not tired. Only sleepy. I'd best
go home. What's o'clock?"

A reference to young Thorpe's watch showed
that it was ten minutes past ten. Mat held out
his hand directly to take leave; but Valentine
positively refused to let him depart until he had
helped himself to something from the supper-
table. Hearing this, he poured out a glass of

brandy and drank it off, then held out his hand once more and said good-night.

"Well, I won't press you to stay against your will," said Mr. Blyth, rather mournfully. "I will only thank you most heartily for your kindness in sitting to me, and say that I hope to see you again when I return from the country. Goodby, Zack. I shall start in the morning by an early train. Pray, my dear boy, be steady, and remember your mother and your promises, and call on Mr. Strather in good time to-morrow, and stick to your work, Zack—for all our sakes, stick to your work!"

As they left the studio, Mat cast one parting glance at the garden door. Would the servant, who had most likely bolted and locked it early in the evening, go near it again before she went to bed? Would Mr. Blyth walk to the bottom of the room to see that the door was safe, after he had raked the fire out? Important questions these, which only the events of the night could answer.

A little way down Kirk Street, at the end by which Zack and his friend entered it on returning from Mr. Blyth's, stood the local theater— all ablaze with dazzling gas, and all astir with loitering blackguards. Young Thorpe stopped, as he and his companion passed under the portico, on the way to their lodgings further up the street.

"It's only half-past ten now," he said. "I shall drop in here, and see the last scenes of the pantomime. Won't you come, too?"

"No," said Mat; "I'm too sleepy.   I shall go on home."

They separated.   While Zack entered the theater, Mat proceeded steadily in the direction of the tobacco-shop.   As soon, however, as he was well out of the glare of gas from the theater door, he crossed the street; and, returning quickly by the opposite side of the way, took the road that led him back to Valentine's house.

CHAPTER XII.

THE HAIR BRACELET.

Mr. Blyth's spirits sank apace, as he bolted and locked the front door, when his guests had left him.   He actually sighed as he now took a turn or two alone up and down the studio.

Three times did he approach close to the garden door, as he walked slowly from end to end of the room.   But he never once looked up at it. His thoughts were wandering after Zack, and Zack's friend, and his attention was keeping them company.   "Whoever this mysterious Mat may be," mused Valentine, stopping at the fourth turn, and walking up to the fireplace; "I don't believe there's anything bad about him; and so I shall tell Mrs. Thorpe the next time I see her."

He set himself to rake out the fire, leaving only a few red embers and tiny morsels of coal to flame up fitfully from time to time in the bottom of the grate.   Having done this, he stood

and warmed himself for a little while, and tried
to whistle a favorite tune. The attempt was a
total failure. He broke down at the third bar,
and ended lamentably in another sigh.

"What can be the matter with me? I never
felt so miserable about going away from home
before." Puzzling himself uselessly with such
reflections as these, he went to the supper-table
and drank a glass of wine, picked a bit of a sandwich, and unnecessarily spoiled the appearance
of two sponge-cakes by absently breaking a small
piece off each of them. He was in no better
humor for eating or drinking than for whistling;
so he wisely determined to light his candle forthwith and go to bed.

After extinguishing the lights that had been
burning on the supper-table, he cast a parting
glance all round the room, and was then about
to leave it, when the drawing of the old five-
barred gate, which he had taken down for Mat
to look at and had placed on a painting-stand at
the lower end of the studio, caught his eye. He
advanced toward it directly—stopped half-way
—hesitated—yawned—shivered a little—thought
to himself that it was not worth while to trouble
about hanging the drawing up over the garden
door that night—and so, yawning again, turned
on his heel and left the studio.

Mr. Blyth's two servants slept upstairs. About
ten minutes after their master had ascended to
his bedroom, they left the kitchen for their dormi-
tory on the garret-floor. Patty, the housemaid,
stopped as she passed the painting-room, to look

in, and see that the lights were out and the fire safe for the night. Polly, the cook, went on with the bedroom candle; and, after having ascended the stairs as far as the first landing from the hall, discreetly bethought herself of the garden door, the general care and superintendence of which was properly attached to her department in the household.

"I say, did you lock the garden door?" said Polly to Patty through the banisters.

"Yes; I did it when I took up master's tea," said Patty to Polly, appearing lazily in the hall, after one sleepy look round the fast-darkening studio.

"Hadn't you better see to it again, to make sure?" suggested the cautious cook.

"Hadn't *you?* It's *your* place," retorted the careless housemaid.

"Hush!" whispered Valentine, suddenly appearing on the landing above Polly, from his bedroom, arrayed in his flannel dressing-gown and nightcap. "Don't talk here, or you'll disturb your mistress. Go up to bed, and talk there. Good-night!"

"Good-night, sir," answered together the two faithful female dependents of the house of Blyth, obeying their master's order with simpering docility, and deferring to a future opportunity all further considerations connected with the garden door.

The fire was fading out fast in the studio grate. Now and then, at long intervals, a thin tongue of flame leaped up faintly against the ever-invading gloom, flickered for an instant over the brighter and more prominent objects in the room, then dropped back again into darkness. The profound silence was only interrupted by those weird house-noises which live in the death of night and die in the life of day; by that sudden crackling in the wall, by that mysterious creaking in the furniture, by those still small ghostly sounds from inanimate bodies, which we have all been startled by, over and over again, while lingering at our book after the rest of the family are asleep in bed, while waiting up for a friend who is out late, or while watching alone through the dark hours in a sick-chamber. Excepting such occasional night-noises as these, so familiar, yet always so strange, the perfect tranquillity of the studio remained undisturbed for nearly an hour after Mr. Blyth had left it. No neighbors came home in cabs, no bawling drunken men wandered into the remote country fastnesses of the new suburb. The night-breeze, blowing in from the fields, was too light to be audible. The watchdog in the nurseryman's garden hard by was as quiet on this particular night as if he had actually barked himself dumb at last. Outside the house, as well as inside, the drowsy reign of old primeval Quiet was undisturbed by the innovating vagaries of the rebel, Noise.

Undisturbed, till the clock in the hall pointed to a quarter past eleven. Then there came softly and slowly up the iron stairs that led from the back garden to the studio a sound of footsteps.

When these ceased, the door at the lower end of the room was opened gently from outside, and the black, bulky figure of Mat appeared on the threshold, lowering out gloomily against a background of starry sky.

He stepped into the painting-room and closed the door quietly behind him; stood listening anxiously in the darkness for a moment or two; then pulling from his pocket the wax-taper and the matches which he had bought that afternoon, immediately provided himself with a light.

While the wick of the taper was burning up, he listened again. Except the sound of his own heavy breathing, all was quiet around him. He advanced at once to the bureau, starting involuntarily as he brushed by Mr. Blyth's lay figure with the Spanish hat and the Roman toga; and cursing it under his breath for standing in his way, as if it had been a living creature. The door leading from the studio into the passage of the house was not quite closed; but he never noticed this as he passed to the bureau, though it stood close to the chink left between the door and the post. He had the false key in his hand; he knew that he should be in possession of the hair bracelet in another moment; and, his impatience for once getting the better of his cunning, he pounced on the bureau, without looking aside first either to the right or the left.

He had unlocked it, had pulled open the inner drawer, had taken out the hair bracelet, and was just examining it closely by the light of his taper (after having locked the bureau again)—when a faint sound on the staircase of the house caught his ear.

At the same instant, a thin streak of candle-light flashed on him through the narrow chink between the hardly-closed door and the door-post. It increased rapidly in intensity, as the sound of softly-advancing footsteps now grew more and more distinct from the stone passage leading to the interior of the house.

He had the presence of mind to extinguish his taper, to thrust the hair bracelet into his pocket, and to move across softly from the bureau (which stood against the lock-side door-post) to the wall (which was by the hinge-side door-post); so that the door itself might open back upon him, and thus keep him concealed from the view of any person entering the room. He had the presence of mind to take these precautions instantly; but he had not self-control enough to suppress the in-voluntary exclamation which burst from his lips at the moment when the thin streak of candle-light first flashed into his eyes. A violent spas-modic action contracted the muscles of his throat. He clinched his fist in a fury of sup-pressed rage against himself, as he felt that his own voice had turned traitor and betrayed him.

The light came close: the door opened—opened gently, till it just touched him as he stood with his back against the wall.

For one instant his heart stopped; the next, it burst into action again with a heave, and the blood rushed hotly through every vein all over him, as his wrought-up nerves of mind and body

relaxed together under a sense of ineffable relief.
He was saved almost by a miracle from the in-
evitable consequence of the rash exclamation
that had escaped him. It was Madonna who
had opened the door—it was the deaf and dumb
girl whom he saw walking into the studio.

She had been taking her working materials
out of the tobacco-pouch in her own room before
going to bed, and had then missed her mother-
of-pearl bodkin-case. Suspecting immediately
that she must have dropped it in the studio, and
fearing that it might be trodden on and crushed
if she left it there until the next morning, she
had now stolen downstairs by herself to look for
it. Her hair, not yet put up for the night, was
combed back from her face, and hung lightly
down in long silky folds over her shoulders.
Her complexion looked more exquisitely clear
and pure than ever, set off as it was by the
white dressing-gown which now clothed her.
She had a pretty little red-and-blue china candlestick, given to her by Mrs. Blyth, in her
hand; and, holding the light above her, advanced slowly from the studio doorway, with
her eyes bent on the ground, searching anxiously
for the missing bodkin-case.

Mat's resolution was taken the moment he
caught sight of her. He never stirred an inch
from his place of concealment until she had advanced three or four paces into the room, and
had her back turned full upon him. Then
quietly stepping a little forward from the door,
but still keeping well behind her, he blew out

her candle just as she was raising it over her head and looking down intently on the floor in front of her.

He had calculated, rightly enough, on being able to execute this maneuver with impunity from discovery, knowing that she was incapable of hearing the sound of his breath when he blew her candle out, and that the darkness would afterward not only effectually shield him from detection, but also oblige her to leave him alone in the room again while she went to get another light. He had not calculated, however, on the serious effect which the success of his stratagem would have upon her nerves, for he knew nothing of the horror which the loss of her sense of hearing caused her always to feel when she was left in darkness; and he had not stopped to consider that, by depriving her of her light, he was depriving her of that all-important guiding sense of sight, the loss of which she could not supply in the dark, as others could, by the exercise of the ear.

The instant he blew her candle out, she dropped the china candlestick, in a paroxysm of terror. It fell, and broke, with a deadened sound, on one of the many portfolios lying on the floor about her. He had hardly time to hear this happen, before the dumb moaning, the inarticulate cry of fear which was all that the poor panic-stricken girl could utter, rose low, shuddering, and ceaseless, in the darkness—so close at his ear that he fancied he could feel her breath palpitating quick and warm on his cheek.

If she should touch him? If she should be sensible of the motion of *his* foot on the floor, as she had been sensible of the motion of Zack's when young Thorpe offered her the glass of wine at supper-time? It was a risk to remain still—it was a risk to move! He stood as helpless even as the helpless creature near him. That low, ceaseless, dumb moaning smote so painfully on his heart, roused up so fearfully the rude superstitious fancies lying in wait within him, in connection with the lost and dead Mary Grice, that the sweat broke out on his face, the coldness of sharp mental suffering seized on his limbs, the fever of unutterable expectation parched up his throat, and mouth, and lips; and for the first time, perhaps, in his existence, he felt the chillness of mortal dread running through him to his very soul—he, who amid perils of seas and wildernesses, and horrors of hunger and thirst, had played familiarly with his own life for more than twenty years past, as a child plays familiarly with an old toy.

He knew not how long it was before the dumb moaning seemed to grow fainter; to be less fearfully close to him; to change into what sounded, at one moment, like a shivering of her whole body; at another, like a rustling of her garments; at a third, like a slow scraping of her hands over the table on the other side of her, and of her feet over the floor. She had summoned courage enough at last to move, and to grope her way out—he knew it as he listened. He heard her touch the edge of the half-opened

KEEPING WELL BEHIND HER, HE BLEW OUT HER CANDLE JUST AS
SHE WAS RAISING IT OVER HER HEAD AND LOOKING INTENTLY ON THE
FLOOR IN FRONT OF HER.—HIDE-AND-SEEK, Vol. XI., page 495.

door; he heard the still sound of her first footfall on the stone passage outside; then the noise of her hand drawn along the wall; then the lessening gasps of her affrighted breathing as she gained the stairs.

When she was gone, and the change and comfort of silence and solitude stole over him, his power of thinking, his cunning and resolution began to return. Listening yet a little while, and hearing no sound of any disturbance among the sleepers in the house, he ventured to light one of his matches; and, by the brief flicker that it afforded, picked his way noiselessly through the lumber in the studio and gained the garden door. In a minute he was out again in the open air. In a minute more, he had got over the garden wall, and was walking freely along the lonely road of the new suburb, with the hair bracelet safe in his pocket.

At first he did not attempt to take it out and examine it. He had not felt the slightest scruple beforehand; he did not feel the slightest remorse now, in connection with the bracelet, and with his manner of obtaining possession of it. Callous, however, as he was in this direction, he was sensitive in another. There was both regret and repentance in him, as he thought of the deaf and dumb girl, and of the paroxysm of terror he had caused her. How patiently and prettily she had tried to explain to him her gratitude for his gift, and the use she meant to put it to; and how cruelly he had made her suffer in return! "I wish I hadn't frightened her so," said Mat to himself, thinking of this in his own rough way, as he walked rapidly homeward. "I wish I hadn't frightened her so."

But his impatience to examine the bracelet got the better of his repentance, as it had already got the better of every other thought and feeling in him. He stopped under a gas lamp and drew his prize out of his pocket. He could see that it was made of two kinds of hair, and that something was engraved on the flat gold of the clasp. But his hand shook, his eyes were dimmer than usual, the light was too high above him, and try as he might he could make out nothing clearly.

He put the bracelet into his pocket again, and, muttering to himself impatiently, made for Kirk Street at his utmost speed. His landlord's wife happened to be in the passage when he opened the door. Without the ceremony of a single preliminary word, he astonished her by taking her candle out of her hand and instantly disappearing upstairs with it. Zack had not come from the theater—he had the lodgings to himself—he could examine the hair bracelet in perfect freedom.

His first look was at the clasp. By holding it close to the flame of the candle, he succeeded in reading the letters engraved on it.

"M. G.   In memory of S. G."

"*Mary Grice.   In memory of Susan Grice.*" Mat's hand closed fast on the bracelet—and dropped heavily on his knee, as he uttered those words.

*   *   *   *   *   *   *

The pantomime which Zack had gone to see was so lengthened out by encores of incidental songs and dances, that it was not over till close on midnight. When he left the theater, the physical consequences of breathing a vitiated atmosphere made themselves felt immediately in the regions of his mouth, throat, and stomach. Those ardent aspirations in the direction of shell-fish and malt liquor, which it is especially the mission of the English drama to create, over-came him as he issued into the fresh air, and took him to the local oyster-shop for refreshment and change of scene.

Having the immediate prospect of the private Drawing Academy vividly and menacingly pres-ent before his eyes, Zack thought of the future for once in his life, and astonished the minister-ing vassals of the oyster-shop (with all of whom he was on terms of intimate friendship), by en-joying himself with exemplary moderation at the festive board. When he had done supper, and was on his way to bed at the tobacconist's across the road, it is actually not too much to say that he was sober and subdued enough to have borne inspection by the President and Council of the Royal Academy as a model stu-dent of the Fine Arts.

It was rather a surprise to him not to hear his friend snoring when he let himself into the pas-sage, but his surprise rose to blank astonishment when he entered the front room, and saw the employment on which his fellow-lodger was engaged.

Mat was sitting by the table, with his rifle laid across his knees, and was scouring the barrel bright with a piece of sand-paper. By his side was an unsnuffed candle, an empty bottle, and a tumbler with a little raw brandy left in the bottom of it. His face, when he looked up, showed that he had been drinking hard. There was a stare in his eyes that was at once fierce and vacant, and a hard, fixed, unnatural smile on his lips which Zack did not at all like to see.

"Why, Mat. old boy!" he said, soothingly, "you look a little out of sorts. What's wrong?"

Mat scoured away at the barrel of the gun harder than ever, and gave no answer.

"What in the name of wonder can you be scouring your rifle for to-night?" continued young Thorpe. "You have never yet touched it since you brought it into the house. What can you possibly want with it now? We don't shoot birds in England with rifle-bullets."

"A rifle-bullet will do for *my* game, if I put it up," said Mat, suddenly and fiercely fixing his eyes on Zack.

"What game does he mean?" thought young Thorpe. "He's been drinking himself pretty nearly drunk. Can anything have happened to him since we parted company at the theater?—I should like to find out; but he's such an old savage when the brandy's in his head that I don't half like to question him—"

Here Zack's reflections were interrpted by the voice of his eccentric friend.

"Did you ever meet with a man of the name

of Carr?'' asked Mat. He looked away from
young Thorpe, keeping his eyes steadily on the
rifle, and rubbing hard at the barrel as he put
this question.

"No," said Zack. "Not that I can remember.''

Mat left off cleaning the gun and began to
fumble awkwardly in one of his pockets. After
some little time, he produced what appeared to
Zack to be an inordinately long letter, written in
a cramped hand, and superscribed apparently
with two long lines of inscription, instead of an
ordinary address. Opening this strange-looking
document, Mat guided himself a little way down
the lines on the first page with a very unsteady
forefinger—stopped, and read somewhat anxiously and with evident difficulty—then put the
letter back in his pocket, dropped his eyes once
more on the gun in his lap, and said, with a
strong emphasis on the Christian name,

"*Arthur* Carr?''

"No," returned Zack. "I never met with a
man of that name. Is he a friend of yours?''

Mat went on scouring the rifle-barrel.

Young Thorpe said nothing more. He had
been a little puzzled early in the evening, when
his friend had exhibited the fan and tobacco-
pouch (neither of which had been produced before), and had mentioned to Mr. Blyth that they
were once intended for "a woman" who was
now dead. Zack had thought this conduct rather
odd at the time; but now, when it was followed
by these strangely abrupt references to the name

of Carr, by this mysterious scouring of the rifle
and desperate brandy-drinking in solitude, he
began to feel perplexed in the last degree about
Mat's behavior. "Is this about Arthur Carr a
secret of the old boy's?" Zack asked himself
with a sort of bewildered curiosity. "Is he letting out more than he ought, I wonder, now he's
a little in liquor?"

While young Thorpe was pondering thus, Mat
was still industriously scouring the barrel of his
rifle. After the silence in the room had lasted
some minutes, he suddenly threw away his morsel of sand-paper, and spoke again.

"Zack," he said, familiarly smacking the
stock of his rifle, "me and you had some talk
once about going away to the wild country over
the waters together. I'm ready to sail when you
are, if—" He had glanced up at young Thorpe
with his vacant bloodshot eyes as he spoke the
last words. But he checked himself almost at
the same moment and looked away again quickly
at the gun.

"If what?" asked Zack.

"If I can lay my hands first on Arthur Carr,"
answered Mat, with very unusual lowness of
tone. "Only let me do that, and I shall be game
to tramp it at an hour's notice. He may be dead
and buried for anything I know—"

"Then what's the use of looking after him?"
interposed Zack.

"The use is, I've got it into my head that he's
alive, and that I shall find him," returned Mat.

"Well?" said young Thorpe, eagerly.

Mat became silent again. His head drooped slowly forward, and his body followed it till he rested his elbows on the gun. Sitting in this crouched-up position, he abstractedly began to amuse himself by snapping the lock of the rifle. Zack, suspecting that the brandy he had swallowed was beginning to stupefy him, determined, with characteristic recklessness, to rouse him into talking at any hazard.

"What the devil is all this mystery about?" he cried boldly. "Ever since you pulled out that feather-fan and tobacco-pouch at Blyth's—"

"Well, what of them?" interrupted Mat, looking up instantly with a fierce, suspicious stare.

"Nothing particular," pursued Zack, undauntedly, "except that it's odd you never brought them out before; and odder still that you should tell Blyth, and never say a word here to me, about getting them for a woman—"

"What of *her?*" broke out Mat, rising to his feet with flushed face and threatening eyes, and making the room ring again as he grounded his rifle on the floor.

"Nothing but what a friend ought to say," replied Zack, feeling that, in Mat's present condition, he had ventured a little too far. "I'm sorry, for your sake, that she never lived to have the presents you meant for her. There's no offense, I hope, in saying that much, or in asking (after what you yourself told Blyth) whether her death happened lately, or—"

"It happened afore ever you was born."

He gave this answer, which amazed Zack, in

a curiously smothered, abstracted tone, as if he were talking to himself: laying aside the rifle suddenly as he spoke, sitting down by the table again, and resting his head on his hand. Young Thorpe took a chair near him, but wisely refrained from saying anything just at that moment. Silence seemed to favor the change that was taking place for the better in Mat's temper. He looked up, after a while, and regarded Zack with a rough wistfulness and anxiety working in his swarthy face.

"I like you, Zack," he said, laying one hand on the lad's arm and mechanically stroking down the cloth of his sleeve—"I like you. Don't let us two part company. Let's always pull together as brotherly and pleasant as we can." He paused. His hand tightened round young Thorpe's arm; and the hot, dry, tearless look in his eyes began to soften as he added, "I take it kind in you, Zack, saying you were sorry for her just now. She died afore ever you was born." His hand relaxed its grasp; and when he had repeated those last words, he turned a little away, and said no more.

Astonishment and curiosity impelled young Thorpe to hazard another question.

"Was she a sweetheart of yours?" he asked, unconsciously sinking his voice to a whisper, "or a relation, or—"

"Kin to me. Kin to me," said Mat quickly, yet not impatiently; reaching out his hand again to Zack's arm, but without looking up.

"Was she your mother?"

"No."

"Sister?"

"Yes."

For a minute or two Zack was silent after this answer. As soon as he began to speak again, his companion shook his arm—a little impatiently this time—and stopped him.

"Drop it," said Mat, peremptorily. "Don't let's talk no more; my head—"

"Anything wrong with your head?" asked Zack.

Mat rose to his feet again. A change began to appear in his face. The flush that had tinged it from the first deepened palpably, and spread up to the very rim of his black skull-cap. A confusion and dimness seemed to be stealing over his eyes, a thickness and heaviness to be impeding his articulation when he spoke again.

"I've overdone it with the brandy," he said; "my head's getting hot under the place where they scalped me. Give me holt of my hat, and show me a light, Zack. I can't stop indoors no longer. Don't talk! Let me out of the house at once."

Young Thorpe took up the candle directly; and leading the way downstairs, let him out into the street by the private door, not venturing to irritate him by saying anything, but waiting on the doorstep, and watching him with great curiosity as he started for his walk. He was just getting out of sight, when Zack heard him stop and strike his stick on the pavement. In less than a minute he had turned and was back again at the door of the tobacconist's shop.

"Zack," he whispered, "you ask about among your friends if any of 'em ever knowed a man with that name I told you of."

"Do you mean the '*Arthur Carr*' you were talking about just now?" inquired young Thorpe.

"Yes; *Arthur Carr*," said Mat, very earnestly.

Then, turning away before Zack could ask him any more questions, he disappeared rapidly this time in the darkness of the street.

CHAPTER XIII.

THE SEARCH FOR ARTHUR CARR.

MR. BLYTH was astir betimes on the morning after Mat and young Thorpe had visited him in the studio. Manfully determined not to give way an inch to his own continued reluctance to leave home, he packed up his brushes and colors, and started on his portrait-painting tour by the early train which he had originally settled to travel by.

Although he had every chance of spending his time, during his absence, agreeably as well as profitably, his inexplicable sense of uneasiness at being away from home remained with him even on the railway; defying all the exhilarating influences of rapid motion and change of scene, and oppressing him as inveterately as it had oppressed him the night before. Bad, however, as his spirits now were, they would have been much worse if he had known of two remarkable domestic events which it had been the policy of his household to keep strictly concealed from him on the day of his departure.

When Mr. Blyth's cook descended the first thing in the morning to air the studio in the usual way, by opening the garden door, she was not a little amazed and alarmed to find that, although it was closed, it was neither bolted nor locked. She communicated this circumstance (reproachfully, of course) to the housemaid, who answered (indignantly, as was only natural) by reiterating her assertion of the past night, that she had secured the door properly at six o'clock in the evening. Polly, appealing to contradictory visible fact, rejoined that the thing was impossible. Patty, holding fast to affirmatory personal knowledge, retorted that the thing had been done. Upon this, the two had a violent quarrel—followed by a sulky silence—succeeded by an affectionate reconciliation—terminated by a politic resolution to say nothing more about the matter, and especially to abstain from breathing a word in connection with it to the ruling authorities above stairs. Thus it happened that neither Valentine nor his wife knew anything of the suspicious appearance presented that morning by the garden door.

But, though Mrs. Blyth was ignorant on this point, she was well enough informed on another of equal, if not greater, domestic importance. While her husband was downstairs taking his early breakfast, Madonna came into her room; and communicated confidentially all the particulars of the terrible fright that she had suffered, while looking for her bodkin-case in the studio, on the night before. How her candle could possibly have gone out, as it did in an instant, she could not say. She was quite sure that nobody was in the room when she entered it; and quite sure that she felt no draught of wind in any direction—in short, she knew nothing of her own experience, but that her candle suddenly went out; that she remained for a little time, half dead with fright, in the darkness; and that she then managed to grope her way back to her bedroom, in which a night-light was always burning.

Mrs. Blyth followed the progress of this strange story on Madonna's fingers with great interest to the end; and then—after suggesting that the candle might have gone out through some defect in the make of it, or might really have been extinguished by a puff of air which the girl was too much occupied in looking for her bodkin-case to attend to—earnestly charged her not to say a word on the subject of her adventure to Valentine, when she went to help him in packing up his painting materials. "He is nervous and uncomfortable enough all ready, poor fellow, at the idea of leaving home," thought Mrs. Blyth; "and if he heard the story about the candle going out, it would only make him more uneasy still." To explain this consideration to Madonna was to insure her discretion. She accordingly kept her adventure in the studio so profound a secret from Mr. Blyth that he no more suspected what had happened to her than he suspected what had happened to the hair bracelet, when he hastily assured himself that he was leaving his bureau properly locked, by trying the lid of it the last thing before going away.

Such were the circumstances under which Valentine left home.   He was not, however, the only traveler of the reader's acquaintance whose departure from London took place on the morning after the mysterious extinguishing of Madonna's light in the painting - room.   By a whimsical coincidence, it so happened that, at the very same hour when Mr. Blyth was journeying in one direction, to paint portraits, Mr. Matthew Marksman (now, perhaps, also recognizable as Mr. Matthew Grice), was journeying in another, to pay a second visit to Dibbledean.

Not a visit of pleasure by any means, but a visit of business—business, which, in every particular, Mat had especially intended to keep secret from Zack; but some inkling of which he had nevertheless allowed to escape him during his past night's conversation with the lad in Kirk Street.

When young Thorpe and he met on the morning after that conversation, he was sufficiently aware of the fact that his overdose of brandy had set him talking in a very unguarded manner; and desired Zack, as bluntly as usual, to repeat to him all that he had let out while the liquor was in his head.   After this request had been complied with, he volunteered no additional

confidences. He simply said that what had slipped
from his tongue was no more than the truth; but
that he could add nothing to it, and explain nothing about it, until he had discovered whether
"Arthur Carr" were alive or dead. On being
asked how, and when, he intended to discover
this, he answered that he was going into the
country to make the attempt that very morning;
and that, if he succeeded, he would, on his return, tell his fellow-lodger unreservedly all that
the latter might wish to know. Favored with
this additional promise, Zack was left alone in
Kirk Street, to quiet his curiosity as well as he
could, with the reflection that he might hear
something more about his friend's secrets when
Mat returned from his trip to the country.

In order to collect a little more information on
the subject of these secrets than was at present
possessed by Zack, it will be necessary to return
for a moment to the lodgings in Kirk Street, at
that particular period of the night when Mr.
Marksman was sitting alone in the front room,
and was holding the hair bracelet crumpled up
tight in one of his hands.

His first glance at the letters engraved on the
clasp not only showed him to whom the bracelet
had once belonged, but set at rest in his mind
all further doubt as to the identity of the young
woman whose face had so startled and impressed
him in Mr. Blyth's studio. He was neither logical enough nor legal enough in his mode of reasoning to see that, although he had found his
sister's bracelet in Valentine's bureau, it did not

actually follow as a matter of proof—though it might as a matter of suspicion—that he had also found his sister's child in Valentine's house. No such objection as this occurred to him. He was now perfectly satisfied that Madonna was what he had suspected her to be from the first—Mary's child.

But to the next questions that he asked himself, concerning the girl's unknown father, the answers were not so easy to be found:—Who was Arthur Carr? Where was he? Was he still alive?

His first hasty suspicion that Valentine might have assumed the name of Arthur Carr, and might therefore be the man himself, was set at rest immediately by another look at the bracelet. He knew that the lightest in color, of the two kinds of hair of which it was made, was Carr's hair, because it exactly resembled the surplus lock sent back by the jeweler, and inclosed in Jane Holdsworth's letter. He made the comparison, and discovered the resemblance at a glance. The evidence of his own eyesight, which was enough for this, was also enough to satisfy him immediately that Arthur Carr's hair was, in color, as nearly as possible the exact opposite of Mr. Blyth's hair.

Still, though the painter was assuredly not the father, might he not know who the father was, or had been? How could he otherwise have got possession of Mary Grice's bracelet and Mary Grice's child?

These two questions suggested a third in Mat's mind. Should he discover himself at once to Mr.

Blyth; and compel him, by fair means or foul, to solve all doubts, and disclose what he knew?

No: not at once. That would be playing, at the outset, a desperate and dangerous move in the game, which had best be reserved to the last. Besides, it was useless to think of questioning Mr. Blyth just now—except by the uncertain and indiscreet process of following him into the country—for he had settled to take his departure from London early the next morning.

But it was now impossible to rest, after what had been already discovered, without beginning, in one direction or another, the attempt to find out Arthur Carr. Mat's purpose of doing this sprang from the strongest of all resolutions—a vindictive resolution. That dangerous part of the man's nature which his life among the savages and his wanderings in the wild places of the earth had been stealthily nurturing for many a long year past, was beginning to assert itself, now that he had succeeded in penetrating the mystery of Madonna's parentage by the mother's side. Placed in his position, the tender thought of their sister's child would, at this particular crisis, have been uppermost in many men's hearts. The one deadly thought of the villain who had been Mary's ruin was uppermost in Mat's.

He pondered but a little while on the course that he should pursue, before the idea of returning to Dibbledean, and compelling Joanna Grice to tell more than she had told at their last interview, occurred to him. He disbelieved the passage in her narrative which stated that she had

seen and heard nothing of Arthur Carr in all the
years that had elapsed since the flight and death
of her niece: he had his own conviction, or rather
his own presentiment (which he had mentioned
to Zack), that the man was still alive somewhere;
and he felt confident that he had it in his power,
as a last resource, to awe the old woman into
confessing everything that she knew. To Dibbledean, therefore, in the first instance, he resolved
to go.

If he failed there in finding any clew to the
object of his inquiry, he determined to repair
next to Rubbleford, and to address himself boldly
to Mrs. Peckover. He remembered that, when
Zack had first mentioned her extraordinary behavior about the hair bracelet in Mr. Blyth's hall,
he had prefaced his words by saying, that she
knew apparently as much of Madonna's history
as the painter did himself, and that she kept that
knowledge just as close and secret. This woman,
therefore, doubtless possessed information which
she might be either entrapped or forced into communicating. There would be no difficulty about
finding out where she lived; for, on the evening
when he had mimicked her, young Thorpe had
said that she kept a dairy and muffin-shop at
Rubbleford. To that town, then, he proposed to
journey, in the event of failing in his purpose at
Dibbledean.

And if, by any evil chance, he should end in
ascertaining no more from Mrs. Peckover than
from Joanna Grice, what course should he take
next? There would be nothing to be done then

but to return to London—to try the last great
hazard—to discover himself to Mr. Blyth, come
what might, with the hair bracelet to vouch for
him in his hand.

These were his thoughts, as he sat alone in the
lodging in Kirk Street.   At night, they had ended
in the fatal consolation of the brandy-bottle—in
the desperate and solitary excess, which had so
cheated him of his self-control that the lurking
taint which his life among the savages had left
in his disposition, and the deadly rancor which
his recent discovery of his sister's fate had stored
up in his heart, escaped from concealment, and
betrayed themselves in that half-drunken, half-
sober occupation of scouring the rifle-barrel,
which it had so greatly amazed Zack to witness,
and which the lad had so suddenly and strangely
suspended by his few chance words of sympathizing reference to Mary's death.

But in the morning Mat's head was clear, and
his dangerous instincts were held once more under cunning control.   In the morning, therefore,
he declined explaining himself to young Thorpe,
and started quietly for the country by the first
train.

On being set down at the Dibbledean Station,
Mat lingered a little and looked about him, just
as he had lingered and looked on the occasion of
his first visit.   He subsequently took the same
road to the town which he had then taken; and,
on gaining the church, stopped, as he had formerly stopped, at the churchyard gate.

This time, however, he seemed to have no intention of passing the entrance—no intention, indeed, of doing anything, unless standing vacantly by the gate, and mechanically swinging it backward and forward with both his hands, can be considered in the light of an occupation. As for the churchyard, he hardly looked at it now. There were two or three people, at a little distance, walking about among the graves, who it might have been thought would have attracted his attention; but he never took the smallest notice of them. He was evidently meditating about something, for he soon began to talk to himself —being, like most men who have passed much of their time in solitude, unconsciously in the habit of thinking aloud.

"I wonder how many year ago it is since she and me used to swing back'ard and for'ard on this," he said, still pushing the gate slowly to and fro. "The hinges used to creak then. They go smooth enough now. Oiled, I suppose." As he said this, he moved his hands from the bar on which they rested and turned away to go on to the town; but stopped, and walking back to the gate, looked attentively at its hinges. "Ah," he said, "not oiled. New."

"New," he repeated, walking slowly toward the High Street—"new since my time, like everything else here. I wish I'd never come back—I wish to God I'd never come back!"

On getting into the town, he stopped at the same place where he had halted on his first visit to Dibbledean, to look up again, as he had looked then, at the hosier's shop which had once belonged

to Joshua Grice.   Here those visible and tangible
signs and tokens which he required to stimulate
his sluggish memory were not very easy to recognize.   Though the general form of his father's
old house was still preserved, the re-painting and
renovating of the whole front had somewhat altered it, in its individual parts, to his eyes.   He
looked up and down at the gables, and all along
from window to window, and shook his head
discontentedly.

"New again here," he said.   "I can't make
out for certain which winder it was Mary and
me broke between us, when I come away from
school, the year afore I went to sea.   Whether
it was Mary that broke the winder, and me that
took the blame," he continued, slowly pursuing
his way—"or whether it was her that took the
blame, and me that broke the winder, I can't
rightly call to mind.   And no great wonder
neither, if I've forgot such a thing as that,
when I can't even fix it for certain, yet, whether
she used to wear her hair bracelet or not, while
I was at home."

Communing with himself in this way, he
reached the turning that led to Joanna Grice's
cottage.

His thoughts had thus far been straying away
idly and uninterruptedly to the past.   They were
now recalled abruptly to present emergencies by
certain unexpected appearances which met his
eye, the moment he looked down the lane along
which he was walking.

He remembered this place as having struck

him by its silence and its loneliness, on the occasion of his first visit to Dibbledean. He now observed with some surprise that it was astir with human beings, and noisy with the clamor of gossiping tongues. All the inhabitants of the cottages on either side of the road were out in their front gardens. All the towns-people, who ought to have been walking about the principal streets, seemed to be incomprehensibly congregated in this one narrow little lane. What were they assembled here to do? What subject was it that men and women—and even children as well—were all eagerly talking about?

Without waiting to hear, without questioning anybody, without appearing to notice that he was stared at (as indeed all strangers are in rural England), as if he were walking about among a breeched and petticoated people in the character of a savage with nothing but war paint on him, Mat steadily and rapidly pursued his way down the lane to Joanna Grice's cottage. "Time enough," thought he, "to find out what all this means when I've got quietly into the house I'm bound for." As he approached the cottage, he saw, standing at the gate, what looked, to his eyes, like two coaches—one, very strange in form : both very remarkable in color. All about the coaches stood solemn - looking gentlemen; and all about the solemn-looking gentlemen circled inquisitively and excitably the whole vagabond boy-and-girl population of Dibbledean.

Amazed, and even bewildered (though he hardly knew why) by what he saw, Mat hast-

ened on to the cottage. Just as he arrived at
the garden paling, the door opened, and from
the inside of the dwelling there protruded slowly
into the open air a coffin carried on four men's
shoulders, and covered with a magnificent black
velvet pall.

Mat stopped the moment he saw the coffin,
and struck his hand violently on the paling
by his side. "Dead!" he exclaimed under his
breath.

"A friend of the late Miss Grice's?" asked a
gently inquisitive voice near him.

He did not hear. All his attention was fixed
on the coffin, as it was borne slowly over the
garden path. Behind it walked two gentlemen,
mournfully arrayed in black cloaks and hat-
bands. They carried white handkerchiefs in
their hands, and used them to wipe—not their
eyes—but their lips, on which the balmy dews
of recent wine-drinking glistened gently.

"Dix and Nawby—the medical attendant of the
deceased and the solicitor who is her sole executor," said the voice near Mat, in tones which
had ceased to be gently inquisitive, and had become complacently explanatory instead. "That's
Millbury the undertaker, and the other is Gutteridge of the White Hart Inn, his brother-in-
law, who supplies the refreshments, which in
my opinion makes a regular job of it," continued
the voice, as two red-faced gentlemen followed
the doctor and the lawyer. "Something like a
funeral, this! Not a half-penny less than forty
pound, I should say, when it's all paid for. Beau-

tiful, ain't it?" concluded the voice, becoming
gently inquisitive again.

Still Mat kept his eyes fixed on the funeral
proceedings in front, and took not the smallest
notice of the pertinacious speaker behind him.

The coffin was placed in the hearse. Dr. Dix
and Mr. Nawby entered the mourning-coach provided for them. The snug human vultures who
prey commercially on the civilized dead arranged
themselves, with black wands, in solemn Under-
takers' order of procession on either side of the
funeral vehicles. Those clumsy pomps of feathers
and velvet, of strutting horses and marching
mutes, which are still permitted among us to
desecrate with grotesquely-shocking fiction the
solemn fact of death, fluttered out in their black-
est state grandeur and showed their most woful
state paces, as the procession started magnifi-
cently with its meager offering of one dead body
more to the bare and awful grave.

When Mary Grice died, a fugitive and an outcast, the clown's wife and the Irish girl who
rode in the circus wept for her, stranger though
she was, as they followed her coffin to the poor-
corner of the churchyard. When Joanna Grice
died in the place of her birth, among the towns-
people with whom her whole existence had been
passed, every eye was tearless that looked on her
funeral procession; the two strangers who made
part of it gossiped pleasantly as they rode after
the hearse about the news of the morning; and
the sole surviving member of her family, whom
chance had brought to her door on her burial-day,

stood aloof from the hired mourners and moved not a step to follow her to the grave.

No: not a step. The hearse rolled on slowly toward the churchyard, and the sightseers in the lane followed it; but Matthew Grice stood by the garden paling, at the place where he had halted from the first. What was her death to him? Nothing but the loss of his first chance of tracing Arthur Carr. Tearlessly and pitilessly she had left it to strangers to bury her brother's daughter; and now, tearlessly and pitilessly, there stood her brother's son, leaving it to strangers to bury *her*.

"Don't you mean to follow to the churchyard and see the last of her?" inquired the same inquisitive voice which had twice already endeavored to attract Mat's attention.

He turned round this time to look at the speaker, and confronted a wizen, flaxen-haired, sharp-faced man, dressed in a jaunty shooting-jacket, carrying a riding-cane in his hand, and having a thoroughbred black-and-tan terrier in attendance at his heels.

"Excuse me asking the question," said the wizen man; "but I noticed how dumfounded you were when you saw the coffin come out. 'A friend of the deceased,' I thought to myself directly—"

"Well," interrupted Mat, gruffly, "suppose I am; what then?"

"Will you oblige me by putting this in your pocket?" asked the wizen man, giving Mat a card. "My name's Tatt, and I've recently started in practice here as a solicitor. I don't want to ask any improper questions, but, being a friend of the deceased, you may perhaps have some claim on the estate; in which case, I should feel proud to take care of your interests. It isn't strictly professional, I know, to be touting for the chance of a client in this way; but I'm obliged to do it in self-defense. Dix, Nawby, Millbury and Gutteridge all play into one another's hands, and want to monopolize among 'em the whole Doctoring, Lawyering, Undertaking and Licensed Victualing business of Dibbledean. I've made up my mind to break down Nawby's monopoly and keep as much business out of his office as I can. That's why I take time by the forelock, and give you my card." Here Mr. Tatt left off explaining and began to play with his terrier.

Max looked up thoughtfully at Joanna Grice's cottage. Might she not, in all probability, have left some important letters behind her? And, if he mentioned who he was, could not the wizen man by his side help him to get at them?

"A good deal of mystery about the late Miss Grice," resumed Mr. Tatt, still playing with the terrier. "Nobody but Dix and Nawby can tell exactly when she died, or how she's left her money. Queer family altogether. (Rats, Pincher! where are the rats?) There's a son of old Grice's who has never, they say, been properly accounted for. (Hie, boy! there's a cat! hie after her, Pincher!) If he was only to turn up now, I believe, between ourselves, it would put such a spoke in Nawby's wheel—"

"I may have a question or two to ask you one of these days," interposed Mat, turning away from the garden paling at last. While his new acquaintance had been speaking, he had been making up his mind that he should best serve his purpose of tracing Arthur Carr by endeavoring forthwith to get all the information that Mrs. Peckover might be able to afford him. In the event of this resource proving useless there would be plenty of time to return to Dibbledean, discover himself to Mr. Tatt, and ascertain whether the law would not give Joshua Grice's son the right of examining Joanna Grice's papers.

"Come to my office," cried Mr. Tatt, enthusiastically. "I can give you a prime bit of Stilton, and as good a glass of bitter beer as ever you drank in your life."

Mat declined this hospitable invitation peremptorily, and set forth at once on his return to the station. All Mr. Tatt's efforts to engage him for an "early day," and an "appointed hour," failed. He would only repeat, doggedly, that at some future time he might have a question or two to ask about a matter of law, and that his new acquaintance should then be the man to whom he would apply for information.

They wished each other "good-morning" at the entrance of the lane, Mr. Tatt lounging slowly up the High Street, with his terrier at his heels, and Mat walking rapidly in the contrary direction, on his way back to the railway station.

As he passed the churchyard, the funeral procession had just arrived at its destination, and the bearers were carrying the coffin from the hearse to the church door. He stopped a little by the road-side to see it go in. "She was no good to anybody about her all her lifetime," he thought bitterly, as the last heavy fold of the velvet pall was lost to view in the darkness of the church entrance. "But if she'd only lived a day or two longer, she might have been of some good to *me*. There's more of what I wanted to know nailed down along with her in that coffin than ever I'm likely to find out anywhere else. It's a long hunt of mine, this is—a long hunt on a dull scent; and *her* death has made it duller." With this farewell thought, he turned from the church.

As he pursued his way back to the railroad, he took Jane Holdsworth's letter out of his pocket, and looked at the hair inclosed in it. It was the fourth or fifth time he had done this during the few hours that had passed since he had possessed himself of Mary's bracelet. From that period there had grown within him a vague conviction that the possession of Carr's hair might in some way lead to the discovery of Carr himself. He knew perfectly well that there was not the slightest present or practical use in examining this hair, and yet there was something that seemed to strengthen him afresh in his purpose, to encourage him anew after his unexpected check at Dibbledean, merely in the act of looking at it. "If I can't track him no other way," he muttered, replacing the hair in his pocket, "I've got the notion into my head, somehow, that I shall track him by this."

Mat found it no very easy business to reach Rubbleford. He had to go back a little way on the Dibbledean line, then to diverge by a branch line, and then to get upon another main line, and travel along it some distance before he reached his destination. It was dark by the time he reached Rubbleford. However, by inquiring of one or two people, he easily found the dairy and muffin-shop when he was once in the town; and saw, to his great delight, that it was not shut up for the night. He looked in at the window, under a plaster-cast of a cow, and observed by the light of one tallow-candle burning inside, a chubby buxom girl sitting at the counter, and either drawing or writing something on a slate. Entering the shop, after a moment or two of hesitation, he asked if he could see Mrs. Peckover.

"Mother went away, sir, three days ago, to nurse Uncle Bob at Bangbury," answered the girl.

(Here was a second check—a second obstacle to defer the tracing of Arthur Carr! It seemed like a fatality!)

"When do you expect her back?" asked Mat.

"Not for a week or ten days, sir," answered the girl. "Mother said she wouldn't have gone, but for Uncle Bob being her only brother, and not having wife or child to look after him at Bangbury."

(*Bangbury!*—Where had he heard that name before?)

"Father's up at the Rectory, sir," continued the girl, observing that the stranger looked both disappointed and puzzled. "If it's dairy business you come upon, I can attend to it; but if it's anything about accounts to settle, mother said they were to be sent on to her."

"Maybe I shall have a letter to send your mother," said Mat, after a moment's consideration. "Can you write me down on a bit of paper where she is?"

"Oh, yes, sir." And the girl very civilly and readily wrote in her best round hand, on a slip of bill-paper, this address: "Martha Peckover, at Rob. Randle, 2 Dawson's Buildings, Bangbury."

Mat absently took the slip of paper from her and put it into his pocket; then thanked the girl, and went out. While he was inside the shop, he had been trying in vain to call to mind where he had heard the name of Bangbury before: the moment he was in the street, the lost remembrance came back to him. Surely, Bangbury was the place where Joanna Grice had told him that Mary was buried!

After walking a few paces, he came to a large linen-draper's shop, with plenty of light in the window. Stopping here, he hastily drew from his pocket the manuscript containing the old woman's "Justification" of her conduct; for he wished to be certain about the accuracy of his recollection, and he had an idea that the part of the Narrative which mentioned Mary's death would help to decide him in his present doubt.

Yes! on turning to the last page, there it was written in so many words: "I sent, by a person I could depend on, money enough to bury her decently in Bangbury churchyard."

"I'll go there to-night," said Mat to himself, thrusting the letter into his pocket, and taking the way back to the railway station immediately.

CHAPTER XIV.

MARY'S GRAVE.

MATTHEW GRICE was a resolute traveler; but no resolution is powerful enough to alter the laws of inexorable Time-tables to suit the convenience of individual passengers. Although Mat left Rubbleford in less than an hour after he had arrived there, he only succeeded in getting halfway to Bangbury, before he had to stop for the night, and wait at an intermediate station for the first morning train on what was termed the Trunk Line. By this main railroad he reached his destination early in the forenoon, and went at once to Dawson's Buildings.

"Mrs. Peckover has just stepped out, sir—Mr. Randle being a little better this morning—for a mouthful of fresh air. She'll be in again in half an hour," said the maid-of-all-work who opened Mr. Randle's door.

Mat began to suspect that something more

than mere accident was concerned in keeping
Mrs. Peckover and himself asunder. "I'll come
again in half an hour," he said—then added,
just as the servant was about to shut the door,
"Which is my way to the church?"

Bangbury church was close at hand, and the
directions he received for finding it were easy to
follow. But when he entered the churchyard,
and looked about him anxiously to see where he
should begin searching for his sister's grave, his
head grew confused, and his heart began to fail
him. Bangbury was a large town, and rows
and rows of tombstones seemed to fill the churchyard bewilderingly in every visible direction.

At a little distance a man was at work opening a grave, and to him Mat applied for help;
describing his sister as a stranger who had been
buried somewhere in the churchyard better than
twenty years ago. The man was both stupid
and surly, and would give no advice, except that
it was useless to look near where he was digging,
for they were all respectable towns-people buried
about there.

Mat walked round to the other side of the
church. Here the graves were thicker than
ever; for here the poor were buried. He went
on slowly through them, with his eyes fixed on
the ground, toward some trees which marked the
limits of the churchyard; looking out for a
place to begin his search in, where the graves
might be comparatively few, and where his head
might not get confused at the outset. Such a
place he found at last, in a damp corner under

the trees. About this spot the thin grass languished; the mud distilled into tiny water-pools; and the brambles, briers, and dead leaves lay thickly and foully between a few ragged turf-mounds. Could they have laid her here? Could this be the last refuge to which Mary ran after she fled from home?

A few of the mounds had stained mouldering tombstones at their heads. He looked at these first; and finding only strange names on them, turned next to the mounds marked out by cross-boards of wood. At one of the graves the cross-board had been torn, or had rotted away, from its upright supports, and lay on the ground weather-stained and split, but still faintly showing that it had once had a few letters cut in it. He examined this board to begin with, and was trying to make out what the letters were, when the sound of some one approaching disturbed him. He looked up, and saw a woman walking slowly toward the place where he was standing.

It was Mrs. Peckover herself! She had taken a prescription for her sick brother to the chemist's—had bought him one or two little things he wanted in the High Street—and had now, before resuming her place at his bedside, stolen a few minutes to go and look at the grave of Madonna's mother. It was many, many years since Mrs. Peckover had last paid a visit to Bangbury churchyard.

She stopped and hesitated when she first caught sight of Mat; but, after a moment or two, not being a woman easily balked in anything when she had once undertaken to do it, continued to advance, and never paused for the second time until she had come close to the grave by which Mat stood, and was looking him steadily in the face, exactly across it.

He was the first to speak. "Do you know whose grave this is?" he asked.

"Yes, sir," answered Mrs. Peckover, glancing indignantly at the broken board and the mud and brambles all about it. "Yes, sir, I *do* know; and, what's more, I know that it's a disgrace to the parish. Money has been paid twice over to keep it decent; and look what a state it's left in!"

"I asked you whose grave it was," repeated Mat, impatiently.

"A poor, unfortunate, forsaken creature's, who's gone to Heaven if ever an afflicted, repenting woman went there yet!" answered Mrs. Peckover, warmly.

"Forsaken? Afflicted? A woman, too?" Mat repeated to himself, thoughtfully.

"Yes, forsaken and afflicted," cried Mrs. Peckover, overhearing him. "Don't you say no ill of her, whoever you are. She shan't be spoken unkindly of in my hearing, poor soul!"

Mat looked up suddenly and eagerly. "What's your name?" he inquired.

"My name's Peckover, and I'm not ashamed of it," was the prompt reply. "And now, if I may make so bold, what's yours?"

Mat took from his pocket the hair bracelet, and, fixing his eyes intently on her face, held it up across the grave, for her to look at. "Do you know this?" he said.

Mrs. Peckover stooped forward, and closely inspected the bracelet for a minute or two. "Lord save us!" she exclaimed, recognizing it, and confronting him with cheeks that had suddenly become colorless, and eyes that stared in terror and astonishment. "Lord save us! how did you come by that? And who for mercy's sake are you?"

"My name's Matthew Grice," he answered, quickly and sternly. "This bracelet belonged to my sister, Mary Grice. She run away from home, and died, and was buried in Bangbury churchyard. If you know her grave, tell me in plain words—is it here?"

Breathless as she was with astonishment, Mrs. Peckover managed to stammer a faint answer in the affirmative, and to add that the initials, "M. G.," would be found somewhere on the broken board lying at their feet. She then tried to ask a question or two in her turn; but the words died away in faint exclamations of surprise. "To think of me and you meeting together!" was all she could say; "her own brother, too! Oh! to think of that!—only to think of that!"

Mat looked down at the mud, the brambles, and the rotting grass that lay over what had once been a living and loving human creature. The dangerous brightness glittered in his eyes, the cold change spread fast over his cheeks, and the scars of the arrow-wounds began to burn redly and more redly, as he whispered to himself, "I'll be even yet, Mary, with the man who laid you here!"

"Does Mr. Blyth know who you are, sir?" asked Mrs. Peckover, hesitating and trembling as she put this question. "Did he give you the bracelet?"

She stopped. Mat was not listening to her. His eyes were fastened on the grave: he was still talking to himself in quick, whispering tones.

"Her bracelet was hid from me in another man's chest," he said—"I've found her bracelet. Her child was hid from me in another man's house—I've found her child. Her grave was hid from me in a strange churchyard—I've found her grave. The man who laid her in it is hid from me still—I shall find *him!*"

"Please do listen to me, sir, for one moment," pleaded Mrs. Peckover, more nervously than before. "*Does* Mr. Blyth know about you? And little Mary—oh, sir, whatever you do, pray, pray don't take her away from where she is now! You can't mean to do that, sir, though you are her own mother's brother? You can't surely?"

He looked up at her so quickly, with such a fierce, steady, serpent-glitter in his light-gray eyes, that she recoiled a step or two; still pleading, however, with desperate perseverance for an answer to her last question.

"Only tell me, sir, that you don't mean to take little Mary away, and I won't ask you to say so much as another word! You'll leave her with Mr. and Mrs. Blyth, won't you, sir? For your sister's sake, you'll leave her with the poor bed-ridden lady that's been like a mother to her for so many years past?—for your dear, lost sister's sake, that I was with when she died—"

"Tell me about her." He said those few words with surprising gentleness, as Mrs. Peck-over thought, for such a rough-looking man.

"Yes, yes, all you want to know," she answered. "But I can't stop here. There's my brother—I've got such a turn with seeing you, it's almost put him out of my head—there's my brother, that I must go back to, and see if he's asleep still. You just please to come along with me, and wait in the parlor—it's close by—while I step upstairs—" (Here she stopped in great confusion. It seemed like running some desperate risk to ask this strange, stern-featured relation of Mary Grice's into her brother's house.) "And yet," thought Mrs. Peckover, "if I can only soften his heart by telling him about his poor unfortunate sister, it may make him all the readier to leave little Mary—"

At this point her perplexities were cut short by Matthew himself, who said, shortly, that he had been to Dawson's Buildings already to look after her. On hearing this, she hesitated no longer. It was too late to question the propriety or impropriety of admitting him now.

"Come away, then," she said; "don't let's wait no longer. And don't fret about the infamous state they've left things in here," she added, thinking to propitiate him, as she saw his eyes turn once more, at parting, on the broken board and the brambles around the grave. "I know where to go, and who to speak to—"

"Go nowhere, and speak to nobody," he broke in sternly, to her great astonishment. "All what's got to be done to it, I mean to do my-self."

"You!"

"Yes, me. It was little enough I ever did for her while she was alive; and it's little enough now, only to make things look decent about the place where she's buried. But I mean to do that much for her; and no other man shall stir a fin-ger to help me."

Roughly as it was spoken, this speech made Mrs. Peckover feel easier about Madonna's pros-pects. The hard-featured man was, after all, not so hard-hearted as she had thought him at first. She even ventured to begin questioning him again, as they walked together toward Dawson's Buildings.

He varied very much in his manner of receiving her inquiries, replying to some promptly enough, and gruffly refusing, in the plainest terms, to give a word of answer to others.

He was quite willing, for example, to admit that he had procured her temporary address at Bangbury from her daughter at Rubbleford; but he flatly declined to inform her how he had first found out that she lived at Rubbleford at all. Again, he readily admitted that neither Ma-donna nor Mr. Blyth knew who he really was; but he refused to say why he had not disclosed himself to them, or when he intended—if he ever

intended at all—to inform them that he was the
brother of Mary Grice. As to getting him to
confess in what manner he had become possessed
of the hair bracelet, Mrs. Peckover's first question about it, although only answered by a look,
was received in such a manner as to show her
that any further efforts on her part in that
direction would be perfectly fruitless.

On one side of the door, at Dawson's Buildings, was Mr. Randle's shop; and on the other
was Mr. Randle's little dining parlor. In this
room Mrs. Peckover left Mat while she went upstairs to see if her sick brother wanted anything.
Finding that he was still quietly sleeping, she
only waited to arrange the bed-clothes comfortably about him, and to put a hand-bell easily
within his reach in case he should awake, and
then went downstairs again immediately.

She found Mat sitting with his elbows on the
one little table in the dining-parlor, his head
resting on his hands. Upon the table, lying by
the side of the bracelet, was the lock of hair out
of Jane Holdsworth's letter, which he had yet
once more taken from his pocket to look at.

"Why, mercy on me!" cried Mrs. Peckover,
glancing at it, "surely it's the same hair that's
worked into the bracelet! Wherever, for goodness' sake, did you get that?"

"Never mind where I got it. Do you know
whose hair it is? Look a little closer. The
man this hair belonged to was the man she
trusted in—and he laid her in the churchyard
for her pains."

"Oh! who was he? who was he?" asked Mrs. Peckover, eagerly.

"Who was he?" repeated Matthew, sternly. "What do you mean by asking me that?"

"I only mean that I never heard a word about the villain—I don't so much as know his name."

"You don't?" He fastened his eyes suspiciously on her as he said those two words.

"No; as true as I stand here, I don't. Why, I didn't even know that your poor dear sister's name was Grice till you told me."

His look of suspicion began to change to a look of amazement as he heard this. He hurriedly gathered up the bracelet and the lock of hair and put them into his pocket again.

"Let's hear first how you met with her," he said. "I'll have a word or two about the other matter afterward."

Mrs. Peckover sat down near him, and began to relate the mournful story which she had told to Valentine and Doctor and Mrs. Joyce, now many years ago, in the Rectory dining-room. But on this occasion she was not allowed to go through her narrative uninterruptedly. While she was speaking the few simple words which told how she had sat down by the roadside and suckled the half-starved infant of the forsaken and dying Mary Grice, Mat suddenly reached out his heavy, trembling hand, and took fast hold of hers. He griped it with such force that, stout-hearted and hardy as she was, she cried out in alarm and pain: "Oh, don't! you hurt me— you hurt me!"

SHE FOUND MAT SITTING WITH HIS ELBOWS ON THE ONE LITTLE
TABLE IN THE DINING-PARLOR, HIS HEAD RESTING ON HIS HANDS.
—HIDE-AND-SEEK, Vol. XI., page 535.

He dropped her hand directly, and turned his face away from her; his breath quickening painfully, his fingers fastening on the side of his chair as if some great pang of oppression were trying him to the quick. She rose and asked anxiously what ailed him; but, even as the words passed her lips, he mastered himself with that iron resolution of his which few trials could bend, and none break, and motioned to her to sit down again.

"Don't mind me," he said; "I'm old and tough-hearted with being battered about in the world, and I can't give myself vent nohow with talking or crying like the rest of you. Never mind; it's all over now. Go on."

She complied, a little nervously at first; but he did not interrupt her again. He listened while she proceeded, looking straight at her; not speaking or moving—except when he winced once or twice, as a man winces under unexpected pain, while Mary's death-bed words were repeated to him. Having reached this stage of her narrative, Mrs. Peckover added a little more; only saying, in conclusion, "I took care of the poor soul's child, as I said I would; and did my best to behave like a mother to her till she got to be ten year old; then I give her up—because it was for her own good—to Mr. Blyth."

He did not seem to notice the close of the narrative. The image of the forsaken girl, sitting alone by the roadside, with her child's natural sustenance dried up within her — travel-worn, friendless and desperate—was still uppermost in

his mind; and when he next spoke, gratitude for
the help that had been given to Mary in her last
sore distress was the one predominant emotion,
which strove roughly to express itself to Mrs.
Peckover in these words:

"Is there any living soul you care about that
a trifle of money would do a little good to?" he
asked, with such abrupt eagerness that she was
quite startled by it.

"Lord bless me!" she exclaimed, "what do
you mean? What has that got to do with your
poor sister, or Mr. Blyth?"

"It's got this to do," burst out Matthew, starting to his feet as the struggling gratitude within
him stirred body and soul both together; "you
turned to and helped Mary when she hadn't nobody else in the world to stand by her. She was
always father's darling—but father couldn't help
her then; and I was away on the wrong side of
the sea, and couldn't be no good to her neither.
But I'm on the right side now; and if there's any
friends of yours, north, south, east, or west, as
would be happier for a trifle of money, here's all
mine; catch it, and give it 'em." (He tossed
his beaver-skin roll, with the banknotes in it,
into Mrs. Peckover's lap.) "Here's my two
hands, that I durstn't take a holt of yours with,
for fear of hurting you again; here's my two
hands that can work along with any man's.
Only give 'em something to do for you, that's
all! Give 'em something to make or mend, I
don't care what—"

"Hush! hush!" interposed Mrs. Peckover;

"don't be so dreadful noisy, there's a good man! or you'll wake my brother upstairs. And, besides, where's the use to make such a stir about what I done for your sister? Anybody else would have took as kindly to her as I did, seeing what distress she was in, poor soul! Here," she continued, handing him back the beaver-skin roll; "here's your money, and thank you for the offer of it. Put it up safe in your pocket again. We manage to keep our heads above water, thank God! and don't want to do no better than that. Put it up in your pocket again, and then I'll make bold to ask you for something else."

"For what?" inquired Mat, looking her eagerly in the face.

"Just for this: that you'll promise not to take little Mary away from Mr. Blyth. Do, pray do promise me you won't."

"I never thought to take her away," he answered. "Where should I take her to? What can a lonesome old vagabond like me do for her? If she's happy where she is—let her stop where she is."

"Lord bless you for saying that!" fervently exclaimed Mrs. Peckover, smiling for the first time, and smoothing out her gown over her knees with an air of inexpressible relief. "I'm rid of my grand fright now, and getting to breathe again freely, which I haven't once yet been able to do since I first set eyes on you. Ah! you're rough to look at; but you've got your feelings like the rest of us. Talk away now as much as you like. Ask me about anything you please—"

"What's the good?" he broke in, gloomily. "You don't know what I wanted you to know. I come down here for to find out the man as once owned this"—he pulled the lock of hair out of his pocket again—"and you can't help me. I didn't believe it when you first said so, but I do now."

"Well, thank you for saying that much; though you might have put it civiler—"

"His name was Arthur Carr. Did you never hear tell of anybody with the name of Arthur Carr?"

"No; never—never till this very moment."

"The painter-man will know," continued Mat, talking more to himself than to Mrs. Peckover. "I must go back and chance it with the painter-man, after all."

"Painter - man?" repeated Mrs. Peckover. "Painter? Surely you don't mean Mr. Blyth?"

"Yes, I do."

"Why, what in the name of fortune can you be thinking of! How should Mr. Blyth know more than me? He never set eyes on little Mary till she was ten year old; and he knows nothing about her poor unfortunate mother except what I told him."

These words seemed at first to stupefy Mat: they burst upon him in the shape of a revelation for which he was totally unprepared. It had never once occurred to him to doubt that Valentine was secretly informed of all that he most wished to know. He had looked forward to what the painter might be persuaded—or, in the last

resort, forced—to tell him, as the one certainty
on which he might finally depend; and here
was this fancied security exposed, in a moment,
as the wildest delusion that ever man trusted in!
What resource was left? To return to Dibbledean, and, by the legal help of Mr. Tatt, to possess himself of any fragments of evidence which
Joanna Grice might have left behind her in writing? This seemed but a broken reed to depend
on; and yet nothing else now remained.

"I shall find him! I don't care where he's hid
away from me, I shall find him yet," thought
Mat, still holding with dogged and desperate obstinacy to his first superstition, in spite of every
fresh sign that appeared to confute it.

"Why worrit yourself about finding Arthur
Carr at all?" pursued Mrs. Peckover, noticing
his perplexed and mortified expression. "The
wretch is dead, most likely, by this time—"

"I'm not dead!" retorted Mat, fiercely; "and
you're not dead; and you and me are as old as
him. Don't tell me he's dead again! I say he's
alive; and, by God, I'll be even with him!"

"Oh, don't talk so, don't! It's shocking to
hear you and see you," said Mrs. Peckover, recoiling from the expression of his eye at that moment, just as she had recoiled from it already
over Mary's grave. "Suppose he is alive, why
should you go taking vengeance into your own
hands after all these years? Your poor sister's
happy in heaven; and her child's took care of by
the kindest people, I do believe, that ever drew
breath in this world. Why should you want to

be even with him now? If he hasn't been punished already, I'll answer for it, he will be—in the next world, if not in this. Don't talk about it, or think about it any more, that's a good man! Let's be friendly and pleasant together again—like we were just now—for Mary's sake. Tell me where you've been to all these years. How is it you've never turned up before? Come! tell me, do."

She ended by speaking to him in much the same tone which she would have made use of to soothe a fractious child. But her instinct as a woman guided her truly: in venturing on that little reference to "Mary," she had not ventured in vain. It quieted him, and turned aside the current of his thoughts into the better and smoother direction. "Didn't she never talk to you about having a brother as was away aboard ship?" he asked, anxiously.

"No. She wouldn't say a word about any of her friends, and she didn't say a word about you. But how did you come to be so long away?—that's what I want to know," said Mrs. Peckover, pertinaciously repeating her question, partly out of curiosity, partly out of the desire to keep him from returning to the dangerous subject of Arthur Carr.

"I was alway a bitter bad 'un, *I* was," said Matthew, meditatively. "There was no keeping of me straight, try it anyhow you like. I bolted from home, I bolted from school, I bolted from aboard ship—"

"Why? What for?"

"Partly because I was a bitter bad 'un, and

partly because of a letter I picked up in port, at
the Brazils, at the end of a long cruise. Here's
the letter—but it's no good showing it to you:
the paper's so grimed and tore about, you can't
read it."

"Who wrote it? Mary?"

"No: father—saying what had happened to
Mary, and telling me not to come back home till
things was pulled straight again. Here—here's
what he said—under the big grease-spot: 'If you
can get continued employment anywhere abroad,
accept it instead of coming back. Better for you,
at your age, to be spared the sight of such sorrow
as we are now suffering.' Do you see that?"

"Yes, yes, I see. Ah! poor man! he couldn't
give no kinder nor better advice; and you—"

"Deserted from my ship. The devil was in
me to be off on the tramp, and father's letter
did the rest. I got wild and desperate with the
thought of what had happened to Mary, and
with knowing they were ashamed to see me
back again at home. So the night afore the
ship sailed for England I slipped into a shore-
boat and turned my back on salt-junk and the
boatswain's mate for the rest of my life."

"You don't mean to say you've done nothing
but wander about in foreign parts from that time
to this?"

"I do, though! I'd a notion I should be shot
for a deserter if I turned up too soon in my own
country. That kep' me away for ever so long,
to begin with. Then tramps' fever got into my
head; and there was an end of it."

"Tramps' fever! Mercy on me! what do you mean?"

"I mean this: when a man turns gypsy on his own account, as I did, and tramps about through cold and hot, and winter and summer, not caring where he goes or what becomes of him, that sort of life ends by getting into his head, just like liquor does—except that it don't get out again. I got it into my head. It's in it now. Tramps' fever kep' me away in the wild country. Tramps' fever will take me back there afore long. Tramps' fever will lay me down, some day, in the lonesome places, with my hand on my rifle and my face to the sky; and I shan't get up again till the crows and vultures come and carry me off piecemeal."

"Lord bless us! how can you talk about yourself in that way?" cried Mrs. Peckover, shuddering at the grim image which Mat's last words suggested. "You're trying to make yourself out worse than you are. Surely you must have thought of your father and sister sometimes—didn't you?"

"Think of them? Of course I did! But, mind ye, there come a time when I as good as forgot them altogether. They seemed to get smeared out of my head—like we used to smear old sums off our slates at school."

"More shame for you! Whatever else you forgot you oughtn't to have forgotten—"

"Wait a bit. Father's letter told me—I'd show you the place only I know you couldn't read it—that he was a-going to look after Mary

R—11

and bring her back home and forgive her. He'd done that twice for *me*, when *I* run away; so I didn't doubt but what he'd do it just the same for *her*. She'll pull through her scrape with her father just as I used to pull through mine—was what I thought. And so she would if her own kin hadn't turned against her; if her father's own sister hadn't—" He stopped; the frown gathered on his brow and the oath burst from his lips, as he thought of Joanna Grice's share in preventing Mary's restoration to her home.

"There! there!" interposed Mrs. Peckover, soothingly. "Talk about something pleasanter. Let's hear how you come back to England."

"I can't rightly fix it when Mary first begun to drop out of my head like," Mat continued, abstractedly pursuing his previous train of recollections. "I used to think of her often enough when I started for my run in the wild country. That was the time, mind ye, when I had clear notions about coming back home. I got her a scarlet pouch and another feather plaything then, knowing she was fond of knickknacks, and making it out in my own mind that we two was sure to meet together again. It must have been a longish while after that afore I got ashamed to go home. But I did get ashamed. Thinks I, 'I haven't a rap in my pocket to show father, after being away all this time. I'm getting summit of a savage to look at already; and Mary would be more frighted than pleased to see me as I am now. I'll wait a bit,' says I, 'and see if I can't keep from tramping about, and try and get a little money by doing some decent sort of work afore I go home.' I was nigh about a good ten days' march then from any seaport where honest work could be got for such as me; but I'd fixed to try, and I did try, and got work in a shipbuilder's yard. It wasn't no good. Tramps' fever was in my head; and in two days more I was off again to the wild country, with my gun over my shoulder, just as d—d a vagabond as ever.''

Mrs. Peckover held up her hands in mute amazement. Matthew, without taking notice of the action, went on, speaking partly to her and partly to himself.

"It must have been about that time when Mary and father, and all what had to do with them, begun to drop out of my head. But I kep' them two knickknacks, which was once meant for presents for her—long after I'd lost all clear notion of ever going back home again, I kep' 'em—from first to last I kep' 'em—I can't hardly say why, unless it was that I'd got so used to keeping of them that I hadn't the heart to let 'em go. Not, mind ye, but what they mightn't now and then have set me thinking of father and Mary at home—at times, you know, when I changed 'em from one bag to another, or took and blew the dust off of 'em, for to keep 'em as nice as I could. But the older I got, the worse I got at calling anything to mind in a clear way about Mary and the old country. There seemed to be a sort of fog rolling up betwixt us now. I couldn't see her face clear, in my own mind, no longer. It come upon me once or twice in dreams, when I nodded alone over my fire after a tough day's march—it come upon me at such times so clear, that it startled me up, all in a cold sweat, wild and puzzled with not knowing at first whether the stars was shimmering down at me in father's paddock at Dibbledean, or in the lonesome places over the sea, hundreds of miles away from any living soul. But that was only dreams, you know. Waking, I was all astray now, whenever I fell a-thinking about father or her. The longer I tramped it over the lonesome places, the thicker that fog got which seemed to have rose up in my mind between me and them I'd left at home. At last it come to darken in altogether, and never lifted no more, that I can remember, till I crossed the seas again and got back to my own country."

"But how did you ever think of coming back, after all those years?" asked Mrs. Peckover.

"Well, I got a good heap of money, for once in a way, with digging for gold in California," he answered; "and my mate that I worked with, he says to me one day: 'I don't see my way to how we are to spend our money, now we've got it, if we stop here. What can we treat ourselves to in this place, excepting bad brandy and cards? Let's go over to the Old Country, where there ain't nothing we want that we can't get for our money; and, when it's all gone, let's turn tail again and work for more.' He wrought upon me, like that, till I went back with him. We quarreled aboard ship; and when we got into port, he went his way and I went mine.

Not, mind ye, that I started off at once for the old place as soon as I was ashore. That fog in my mind, I told you of, seemed to lift a little when I heard my own language, and saw my own country-people's faces about me again. And then there come a sort of fear over me—a fear of going back home at all, after the time I'd been away. I got over it, though, and went in a day or two. When I first laid my hand on the churchyard gate that Mary and me used to swing on, and when I looked up at the old house, with the gable-ends just what they used to be (though the front was new painted, and strange names was over the shop door)—then all my time in the wild country seem to shrivel up somehow, and better than twenty year ago begun to be a'most like yesterday. I'd seen father's name in the churchyard—which was no more than I looked for; but when they told me Mary had never been brought back, when they said she'd died many a year ago among strange people, they cut me to the quick."

"Ah! no wonder, no wonder!"

"It was a wonder to *me*, though. I should have laughed at any man, if he'd told me I should be took so at hearing what I heard about her, after all the time I'd been away. I couldn't make it out then, and I can't now. I didn't feel like my own man, when I first set eyes on the old place. And then to hear she was dead—it cut me, as I told you. It cut me deeper still when I come to tumble over the things she'd left behind her in her box. Twenty years ago got

nigher and nigher to yesterday, with every fresh
thing belonging to her that I laid a hand on.
There was a arbor in father's garden she used to
be fond of working in of evenings. I'd lost all
thought of that place for more years than I can
reckon up. I called it to mind again—and
called *her* to mind again, too, sitting and working and singing in the arbor—only with laying
holt of a bit of patch-work stuff in the bottom of
her box, with her needle and thread left sticking
in it."

"Ah, dear, dear!" sighed Mrs. Peckover, "I
wish I'd seen her then! She was as happy, I
dare say, as the bird on the tree. But there's
one thing I can't exactly make out yet," she
added—"how did you first come to know all
about Mary's child?"

"All? There wasn't no *all* in it, till I see the
child herself. Except knowing that the poor
creeter's baby had been born alive, I knowed
nothing when I first come away from the old
place in the country. Child! I hadn't nothing
of the sort in my mind when I got back to London. It was how to track the man as was Mary's
death, that I puzzled and worrited about in my
head at that time—"

"Yes, yes," said Mrs. Peckover, interposing
to keep him away from the dangerous subject,
as she heard his voice change and saw his eyes
begin to brighten again. "Yes, yes—but how
did you come to see the child? Tell me that."

"Zack took me into the painter-man's big
room—"

"Zack! Why, good gracious heavens! do you mean Master Zachary Thorpe?"

"I see a young woman standing among a lot of people as was all a-staring at her," continued Mat, without noticing the interruption. "I see her just as close to, and as plain, as I see you. I see her look up, all of a sudden, front face to front face with me. A creeping and a crawling went through me; and I says to myself, 'Mary's child has lived to grow up, and that's her.'"

"But, do pray tell me, however you come to know Master Zack?"

"I says to myself, 'That's her,'" repeated Mat, his rough voice sinking lower and lower, his attention wandering further and further away from Mrs. Peckover's interruptions. "Twenty year ago had got to be like yesterday, when I was down at the old place; and things I hadn't called to mind for long times past, I called to mind when I come to the churchyard gate, and see father's house. But there was looks Mary had with her eyes, turns Mary had with her head, bits of twitches Mary had with her eyebrows when she looked up at you, that I'd clean forgot. They all come back to me together, as soon as ever I see that young woman's face."

"And do you really never mean to let your sister's child know who you are? You may tell me that, surely—though you won't speak a word about Master Zack."

"Let her know who I am? Mayhap I'll let her know that much, before long. When I'm going back to the wild country, I may say to her: 'Rough as I am to look at, I'm your mother's brother, and you're the only bit of my own flesh and blood I've got left to cotton to in all the world. Give us a shake of your hand, and a kiss for mother's sake, and I won't trouble you no more.' I *may* say that, afore I go back, and lose sight of her for good and all."

"Oh, but you won't go back. Only you tell Mr. Blyth you don't want to take her away, and then say to him, 'I'm Mr. Grice, and—'"

"Stop! Don't you get a-talking about Mr. Grice."

"Why not? It's your lawful name, isn't it?"

"Lawful enough, I dare say. But I don't like the sound of it, though it *is* mine. Father as good as said he was ashamed to own it, when he wrote me that letter; and I was afraid to own it, when I deserted from my ship. Bad luck has followed the name from first to last. I ended with it years ago, and I won't take up with it again now. Call me 'Mat.' Take it as easy with me as if I was kin to you."

"Well, then—Mat," said Mrs. Peckover, with a smile. "I've got such a-many things to ask you still—"

"I wish you could make it out to ask them to-morrow," rejoined Matthew. "I've overdone myself already, with more talking than I'm used to. I want to be quiet with my tongue, and get to work with my hands for the rest of the day. You don't happen to have a foot-rule in the house, do you?"

On being asked to explain what motive could induce him to make this extraordinary demand for a foot-rule, Mat answered that he was anxious to proceed at once to the renewal of the cross-board at the head of his sister's grave.   He wanted the rule to measure the dimensions of the old board : he desired to be directed to a timber-merchant's, where he could buy a new piece of wood; and, after that, he would worry Mrs. Peckover about nothing more.   Extraordinary as his present caprice appeared to her, the good woman saw that it had taken complete possession of him, and wisely and willingly set herself to humor it.   She procured for him the rule, and the address of a timber-merchant; and then they parted, Mat promising to call again in the evening at Dawson's Buildings.

When he presented himself at the timber-merchant's, after having carefully measured the old board in the churchyard, he came in no humor to be easily satisfied.   Never was any fine lady more difficult to decide about the texture, pattern, and color to be chosen for a new dress than Mat was when he arrived at the timber-merchant's, about the grain, thickness, and kind of wood to be chosen for the cross-board at the head of Mary's grave.   At last he selected a piece of walnut-wood; and, having paid the price demanded for it, without any haggling, inquired next for a carpenter, of whom he might hire a set of tools.   A man who has money to spare has all things at his command.   Before evening, Mat had a complete set of tools, a dry shed to use them in, and a comfortable living-room at a public-house near, all at his own sole disposal.

Being skillful enough at all carpenter's work of an ordinary kind, he would, under most circumstances, have completed in a day or two such an employment as he had now undertaken. But a strange fastidiousness, a most uncharacteristic anxiety about the smallest matters, delayed him through every stage of his present undertaking. Mrs. Peckover, who came every morning to see how he was getting on, was amazed at the slowness of his progress. He was, from the first, morbidly scrupulous in keeping the board smooth and clean. After he had shaped it, and fitted it to its upright supports; after he had cut in it (by Mrs. Peckover's advice) the same inscription which had been placed on the old board—the simple initials "M. G.," with the year of Mary's death, "1828"—after he had done these things, he was seized with an unreasonable, obstinate fancy for decorating the board at the sides. In spite of all that Mrs. Peckover could say to prevent him, he carved an anchor at one side and a tomahawk at the other—these being the objects with which he was most familiar, and therefore the objects which he chose to represent. But even when the carving of his extraordinary ornaments had been completed, he could not be prevailed on to set the new cross-board up in its proper place. Fondly as artists or authors linger over their last loving touches to the picture or the book, did Mat now linger, day after day, over the poor monument to his sister's memory, which his own rough hands had made. He smoothed it carefully with bits of sand-paper, he rubbed it industriously with leather, he polished it anxiously with oil, until, at last, Mrs. Peckover lost all patience; and, trusting in the influence she had already gained over him, fairly insisted on his bringing his work to a close. Even while obeying her, he was still true to his first resolution. He had said that no man's hand should help in the labor he had now undertaken; and he was as good as his word, for he carried the cross-board himself to the churchyard.

All this time he never once looked at that lock of hair which he had been accustomed to take so frequently from his pocket but a few days back. Perhaps there was nothing in common between the thought of tracing Arthur Carr, and the thoughts of Mary that came to him while he was at work on the walnut-wood plank.

But when the cross-board had been set up; when he had cleared away the mud and brambles about the mound, and had made a smooth little path round it; when he had looked at his work from all points of view, and had satisfied himself that he could do nothing more to perfect it, the active, restless, and violent elements in his nature seemed to awake, as it were, on a sudden. His fingers began to search again in his pocket for the fatal lock of hair; and when he and Mrs. Peckover next met, the first words he addressed to her announced his immediate departure for Dibbledean.

She had strengthened her hold on his gratitude

by getting him permission, through the rector of
Bangbury, to occupy himself, without molesta-
tion, in the work of repairing his sister's grave.
She had persuaded him to confide to her many
of the particulars concerning himself which he
had refused to communicate at their first interview. But when she tried, at parting, to fathom
what his ultimate intentions really were, now
that he was leaving Bangbury with the avowed
purpose of discovering Arthur Carr, she failed
to extract from him a single sentence of explanation, or even so much as a word of reply. When
he took his farewell, he charged her not to communicate their meeting to Mr. Blyth till she
heard from him or saw him again; and he tried
once more to thank her in as fit words as he
could command, for the pity and kindness she
had shown toward Mary Grice; but, to the very
last, he closed his lips resolutely on the ominous
subject of Arthur Carr.

He had been a fortnight absent from London,
when he set forth once more for Dibbledean, to
try that last chance of tracing out the hidden
man, which might be afforded him by a search
among the papers of Joanna Grice.

The astonishment and delight of Mr. Tatt
when Matthew, appearing in the character of a
client at the desolate office door, actually announced himself as the sole surviving son of old
Joshua Grice, flowed out in such a torrent of
congratulatory words, that Mat was at first literally overwhelmed by them. He soon recovered himself, however; and while Mr. Tatt was

still haranguing fluently about proving his client's identity, and securing his client's right of inheritance, silenced the solicitor, by declaring as bluntly as usual, that he had not come to Dibbledean to be helped to get hold of money, but to be helped to get hold of Joanna's Grice's papers. This extraordinary announcement produced a long explanation and a still longer discussion, in the middle of which Mat lost his patience, and declared that he would set aside all legal obstacles and delays forthwith, by going to Mr. Nawby's office, and demanding of that gentleman, as the official guardian of the late Miss Grice's papers, permission to look over the different documents which the old woman might have left behind her.

It was to no earthly purpose that Mr. Tatt represented this course of proceeding as unprofessional, injudicious, against etiquette, and utterly ruinous, looked at from any point of view. While he was still expostulating, Matthew was stepping out at the door; and Mr. Tatt, who could not afford to lose even this most outrageous and unmanageable of clients, had no other alternative but to make the best of it, and run out after him.

Mr. Nawby was a remarkably lofty, solemn, and ceremonious gentleman, feeling as bitter a hatred and scorn for Mr. Tatt as it is well possible for one legal human being to entertain toward another. There is no doubt that he would have received the irregular visit of which he was now the object with the most chilling contempt, if he had only been allowed time to assert his own dignity. But before he could utter a single word, Matthew, in defiance of all that Mr. Tatt could say to silence him, first announced himself in his proper character; and then, after premising that he came to worry nobody about money matters, coolly added that he wanted to look over the late Joanna Grice's letters and papers directly, for a purpose which was not of the smallest consequence to any one but himself.

Under ordinary circumstances, Mr. Nawby would have simply declined to hold any communication with Mat, until his identity had been legally proved. But the prosperous solicitor of Dibbledean had a grudge against the audacious adventurer who had set up in practice against him; and he therefore resolved to depart a little on this occasion from the strictly professional course, for the express purpose of depriving Mr. Tatt of as many prospective six-and-eight-pences as possible. Waving his hand solemnly, when Mat had done speaking, he said: "Wait a moment, sir," then rang a bell and ordered in his head clerk.

"Now, Mr. Scutt," said Mr. Nawby, loftily addressing the clerk, "have the goodness to be a witness, in the first place, that I protest against this visit on Mr. Tatt's part as being indecorous, unprofessional, and unbusiness-like. In the second place, be a witness, also, that I do not admit the identity of this party" (pointing to Mat), "and that what I am now about to say to him I

say under protest, and denying *pro formâ* that
he is the party he represents himself to be.   You
thoroughly understand, Mr. Scutt?"

Mr. Scutt bowed reverently.   Mr. Nawby
went on.

"If your business connection, sir, with that
party," he said, addressing Matthew and in-
dicating Mr. Tatt, "was only entered into to
forward the purpose you have just mentioned
to me, I beg to inform you (denying, you will
understand, at the same time, your right to ask
for such information) that you may wind up
matters with your solicitor whenever you please.
The late Miss Grice has left neither letters nor
papers.   I destroyed them all, by her own wish,
in her own presence and under her own written
authority, during her last illness.   My head clerk
here, who was present to assist me, will corrobo-
rate the statement, if you wish it."

Mat listened attentively to these words, but
listened to nothing more.   A sturdy legal alter-
cation immediately ensued between the two solici-
tors—but it hardly reached his ears.   Mr. Tatt
took his arm and led him out, talking more
fluently than ever; but he had not the poorest
trifle of attention to bestow on Mr. Tatt.   All
his faculties together seemed to be absorbed by
this one momentous consideration: Had he really
and truly lost the last chance of tracing Arthur
Carr?

When they got into the High Street, his mind
somewhat recovered its freedom of action, and
he began to feel the necessity of deciding at once

on his future movements.   Now that his final resource had failed him, what should he do next?
It was useless to go back to Bangbury, useless to
remain at Dibbledean.   Yet the fit was on him
to be moving again somewhere—better even to
return to Kirk Street than to remain irresolute
and inactive on the scene of his defeat.

He stopped suddenly; and saying: "It's no
good waiting here now—I shall go back to London," impatiently shook himself free of Mr. Tatt's
arm in a moment.   He found it by no means so
easy, however, to shake himself free of Mr. Tatt's
legal services.   "Depend on my zeal," cried this
energetic solicitor, following Matthew pertinaciously on his way to the station.   "If there's
law in England, your identity shall be proved,
and your rights respected. .I intend to throw
myself into this case, heart and soul.   Money,
Justice, Law, Morality, are all concerned— One
moment, my dear sir!   If you must really go
back to London, oblige me, at any rate, with
your address, and just state in a cursory way
whether you were christened or not at Dibbledean church.   I want nothing more to begin
with—absolutely nothing more, on my word of
honor as a professional man."

Willing in his present mood to say or do anything to get rid of his volunteer solicitor, Mat
mentioned his address in Kirk Street, and the
name by which he was known there; impatiently said "Yes," to the inquiry as to whether
he had been christened at Dibbledean church;
and then abruptly turning away, left Mr. Tatt

standing in the middle of the high-road, excitably making a note of the evidence just collected in a new legal memorandum-book.

As soon as Mat was alone, the ominous question suggested itself to him again: Had he lost the last chance of tracing Arthur Carr? Although inexorable facts seemed now to prove past contradiction that he had—even yet he held to his old superstition more doggedly and desperately than ever. Once more, on his way to the station, he pulled out the lock of hair and obstinately pondered over it. Once more, while he journeyed to London, that strange conviction upheld him which had already supported him under previous checks. "I shall find him," thought Mat, whirling along in the train. "I don't care where he's hid away from me, I shall find him yet!"

CHAPTER XV.

THE DISCOVERY OF ARTHUR CARR.

WHILE Matthew Grice was traveling backward and forward between town and town in the midland counties, the life led by his young friend and comrade in the metropolis was by no means devoid of incident and change. Zack had met with his adventures as well as Mat; one of them, in particular, being of such a nature, or, rather, leading to such results, as materially altered the domestic aspect of the lodgings in Kirk Street.

562 WORKS OF WILKIE COLLINS.

True to his promise to Valentine, Zack, on the morning of his friend's departure for the country, presented himself at Mr. Strather's house, with his letter of introduction, punctually at eleven o'clock; and was fairly started in life by that gentleman before noon on the same day as a student of the Classic beau-ideal in the statue-halls of the British Museum. He worked away resolutely enough till the rooms were closed; and then returned to Kirk Street, not by any means enthusiastically devoted to his new occupation; but determined to persevere in it, because he was determined to keep to his word.

His new profession wore, however, a much more encouraging aspect when Mr. Strather introduced him, in the evening, to the private Academy. Here live people were the models to study from. Here he was free to use the palette, and to mix up the pinkest possible flesh tints with brand-new brushes. Here were high-spirited students of the fine arts, easy in manners and picturesque in personal appearance, with whom he contrived to become intimate directly. And here, to crown all, was a Model, sitting for the chest and arms, who had been a great prize-fighter, and with whom Zack joyfully cemented the bonds of an eternal (pugilistic) friendship on the first night of his admission to Mr. Strather's Academy.

All through the second day of his probation as a student he labored at his drawing with immense resolution and infinitesimal progress. All through the evening he daubed away indus-

triously under Mr. Strather's supervision, until
the Academy sitting was suspended. It would
have been well for him if he had gone home as
soon as he laid down his brushes. But in an
evil hour he lingered after the studies of the
evening were over, to have a gossip with the
prize-fighting Model; and in an indiscreet moment he consented to officiate as one of the
patrons at an exhibition of sparring, to be held
that night in a neighboring tavern, for the ex-
pugilist's benefit.

After being conducted in an orderly manner
enough for some little time, the pugilistic proceedings of the evening were suddenly interrupted
by one of the Patrons present (who was also a
student at the Drawing Academy), declaring
that his pocket had been picked, and insisting
that the room door should be closed and the police
summoned immediately. Great confusion and
disturbance ensued, amid which Zack supported
the demand of his fellow-student—perhaps a little
too warmly. At any rate, a gentleman sitting
opposite to him with a patch over one eye and a
nose broken in three places, swore that young
Thorpe had personally insulted him by implying
that he was the thief; and vindicated his moral
character by throwing a cheese-plate at Zack's
head. The missile struck the mark (at the side,
however, instead of in front), and breaking when
it struck, inflicted what appeared to every unprofessional eye that looked at the injury like a very
extensive and dangerous wound.

The chemist to whom Zack was taken in the

first instance to be bandaged, thought little of
the hurt; but the local doctor who was called in,
after the lad's removal to Kirk Street, did not
take so re-assuring a view of the patient's case.
The wound was certainly not situated in a very
dangerous part of the head; but it had been
inflicted at a time when Zack's naturally full-
blooded constitution was in a very unhealthy
condition from the effects of much more ardent
spirit-drinking than was at all good for him.
Bad fever symptoms set in immediately, and
appearances became visible in the neighborhood
of the wound at which the medical head shook
ominously. In short, Zack was now confined
to his bed with the worst illness he had ever had
in his life, and with no friend to look after him
except the landlady of the house.

Fortunately for him, his doctor was a man of
skill and energy, who knew how to make the
most of all the advantages which the patient's
youth and strength could offer to assist the medical treatment. In ten days' time young Thorpe
was out of danger of any of the serious inflam-
matory results which had been apprehended from
the injury to his head.

Wretchedly weak and reduced—unwilling to
alarm his mother by informing her of his illness
—without Valentine to console him, or Mat to
amuse him, Zack's spirits now sank to a far
lower ebb than they had ever fallen to before.
In his present state of depression, feebleness and
solitude there were moments when he doubted
of his own recovery, in spite of all that the doc-

tor could tell him. While in this frame of mind the remembrance of the last sad report he had heard of his father's health affected him very painfully, and he bitterly condemned himself for never having written so much as a line to ask Mr. Thorpe's pardon since he had left home. He was too weak to use the pen himself; but the tobacconist's wife—a slovenly, showy, kind-hearted woman—was always ready to do anything to serve him; and he determined to make his mind a little easier by asking her to write a few penitent lines for him, and by having the letter dispatched immediately to his father's address in Baregrove Square. His landlady had long since been made the confidante of all his domestic tribulations (for he freely communicated them to everybody with whom he was brought much in contact); and she showed, therefore, no surprise, but on the contrary expressed great satisfaction, when his request was preferred to her. This was the letter which Zack, with tearful eyes and faltering voice, dictated to the tobacconist's wife:

"My dear Father—I am truly sorry for never having written to ask you to forgive me before. I write now, and beg your pardon with all my heart, for I am indeed very penitent, and ashamed of myself. If you will only let me have another trial, and will not be too hard upon me at first, I will do my best never to give you any more trouble. Therefore, pray write to me at 14 Kirk Street, Wendover Market, where I am now living with a friend who has been very kind to me. Please give my dear love to mother, and believe me your truly penitent son,

"Z. THORPE, Jun."

Having got through this letter pretty easily, and finding that the tobacconist's wife was quite ready to write another for him if he pleased, Zack resolved to send a line to Mr. Blyth, who, as well as he could calculate, might now be expected to return from the country every day. On the evening when he had been brought home with the wound in his head he had entreated that this accident might be kept a secret from Mrs. Blyth (who knew his address), in case she should send after him. This preliminary word of caution was not uselessly spoken. Only three days later a note was brought from Mrs. Blyth, upbraiding him for never having been near the house during Valentine's absence, and asking him to come and drink tea that evening. The messenger, who waited for an answer, was sent back with the most artful verbal excuse which the landlady could provide for the emergency, and no more notes had been delivered since. Mrs. Blyth was doubtless not overwell satisfied with the cool manner in which her invitation had been received.

In his present condition of spirits Zack's conscience upbraided him soundly for having thought of deceiving Valentine by keeping him in ignorance of what had happened. Now that Mat seemed, by his long absence, to have deserted

Kirk Street forever, there was a double attraction and hope for the weary and heart-sick Zack in the prospect of seeing the painter's genial face by his bedside. To this oldest, kindest, and most merciful of friends, therefore, he determined to confess what he dare not so much as hint to his own father.

The note which, by the assistance of the tobacconist's wife, he now addressed to Valentine, was as characteristically boyish, and even childish in tone, as the note which he had sent to his father. It ran thus:

"MY DEAR BLYTH—I begin to wish I had never been born; for I have got into another scrape—having been knocked on the head by a prize-fighter with a cheese-plate. It was wrong in me to go where I did, I know. But I went to Mr. Strather, just as you told me, and stuck to my drawing—I did, indeed! Pray do come, as soon as ever you get back—I send this letter to make sure of getting you at once. I am so miserable and lonely, and too weak still to get out of bed.

"My landlady is very good and kind to me; but, as for that old vagabond, Mat, he has been away in the country, I don't know how long, and has never written to me. Please, please do come! and don't blow me up much if you can help it, for I am so weak I can hardly keep from crying when I think of what has happened. Ever yours,   Z. THORPE, Jun.

"P.S.—If you have got any of my money left

by you, I should be very glad if you would bring it. I haven't a farthing, and there are several little things I ought to pay for."

This letter and the letter to Mr. Thorpe, after being duly sealed and directed, were confided for delivery to a private messenger. They were written on the same day which had been occupied by Matthew Grice in visiting Mr. Tatt and Mr. Nawby, at Dibbledean. And the coincidences of time so ordered it that while Zack's letters were proceeding to their destinations, in the hand of the messenger, Zack's fellow-lodger was also proceeding to his destination in Kirk Street by the fast London train.

Baregrove Square was nearer to the messenger than Valentine's house, so the first letter that he delivered was that all-important petition for the paternal pardon, on the favorable reception of which depended Zack's last chance of reconciliation with home.

Mr. Thorpe sat alone in his dining-parlor—the same dining-parlor in which, so many weary years ago, he had argued with old Mr. Goodworth about his son's education. Mrs. Thorpe, being confined to her room by a severe cold, was unable to keep him company—the doctor had just taken leave of him—friends in general were forbidden, on medical authority, to excite him by visits—he was left lonely, and he had the prospect of remaining lonely for the rest of the day. That total prostration of the nervous system, from which the doctor had declared him to be now suffering, showed itself painfully from time to time in his actions as well as his looks —in his sudden startings when an unexpected noise occurred in the house, in the trembling of his wan, yellowish-white hand whenever he lifted it from the table, in the transparent paleness of his cheeks, in the anxious uncertainty of his ever-wandering eyes.

His attention was just now directed on an open letter lying near him—a letter fitted to encourage and console him, if any earthly hopes could still speak of happiness to his heart, or any earthly solace still administer repose to his mind.

But a few days back his wife's entreaties and the doctor's advice had at length prevailed on him to increase his chances of recovery by resigning the post of secretary to one of the Religious Societies to which he belonged. The letter he was now looking at had been written officially to inform him that the members of the Society accepted his resignation with the deepest regret, and to prepare him for a visit on the morrow from a deputation charged to present him with an address and testimonial—both of which had been unanimously voted by the Society "in grateful and affectionate recognition of his high character and eminent services while acting as their secretary." He had not been able to resist the temptation of showing this letter to the doctor; and he could not refrain from reading it once again now before he put it back in his desk. It was, in his eyes, the great reward and the great distinction of his life.

He was still lingering thoughtfully over the last sentence when Zack's letter was brought in to him. It was only for a moment that he had dared to taste again the sweetness of a well-worn triumph; but even in that moment there mingled with it the poisoning bitter of every past association that could pain him most! With a heavy sigh, he put away the letter from the friends who honored him, and prepared to answer the letter from the son who had deserted him.

There was grief, but no anger, in his face, as he read it over for the second time. He sat thinking for a little while—then drew toward him his inkstand and paper—hesitated—wrote a few lines—and paused again, putting down the pen this time, and covering his eyes with his thin, trembling hand. After sitting thus for some minutes, he seemed to despair of being able to collect his thoughts immediately, and to resolve on giving his mind full time to compose itself. He shut up his son's letter and his own unfinished reply together in the paper case. But there was some re-assuring promise for Zack's future prospects contained even in the little that he had already written; and the letter suggested forgiveness at the very outset; for it began with, "My dear Zachary."

On delivering Zack's second note at Valentine's house, the messenger was informed that Mr. Blyth was expected back on the next day, or on the day after that at the latest. Having a

discretionary power to deal as she pleased with
her husband's correspondence when he was away
from home, Mrs. Blyth opened the letter as soon
as it was taken up to her. Madonna was in the
room at the time, with her bonnet and shawl on,
just ready to go out for her usual daily walk,
with Patty the housemaid for a companion, in
Valentine's absence.

"Oh, that wretched, wretched Zack!" exclaimed Mrs. Blyth, looking seriously distressed
and alarmed the moment her eyes fell on the
first lines of the letter. "He must be ill indeed," she added, looking closely at the handwriting; "for he has evidently not written this
himself."

Madonna could not hear these words, but she
could see the expression which accompanied their
utterance, and could indicate by a sign her anxiety to know what had happened. Mrs. Blyth
ran her eye quickly over the letter, and ascertaining that there was nothing in it which Madonna might not be allowed to read, beckoned to
the girl to look over her shoulder, as the easiest
and shortest way of explaining what was the
matter.

"How distressed Valentine will be to hear of
this!" thought Mrs. Blyth, summoning Patty
upstairs by a pull at her bell-rope, while Madonna was eagerly reading the letter. The
housemaid appeared immediately, and was
charged by her mistress to go to Kirk Street at
once; and after inquiring of the landlady about
Zack's health, to get a written list of any com-

forts he might want, and bring it back as soon as possible. "And mind you leave a message," pursued Mrs. Blyth, in conclusion, "to say that he need not trouble himself about money matters, for your master will come back from the country either to-morrow or next day."

Here her attention was suddenly arrested by Madonna, who was eagerly and even impatiently signing on her fingers, "What are you saying to Patty? Oh! do let me know what you are saying to Patty?"

Mrs. Blyth repeated, by means of the deaf-and-dumb alphabet, the instructions which she had just given to the servant; and added—observing the paleness and agitation of Madonna's face—"Let us not frighten ourselves unnecessarily, my dear, about Zack; he may turn out to be much better than we think him from reading his letter."

"May I go with Patty?" rejoined Madonna, her eyes sparkling with anxiety, her fingers trembling as they rapidly formed these words. "Let me take my walk with Patty just as if nothing had happened. Let me go! pray, let me go!"

"She can't be of any use, poor child," thought Mrs. Blyth; "but if I keep her here, she will only be fretting herself into one of her violent headaches. Besides, she may as well have her walk now, for I shan't be able to spare Patty later in the day." Influenced by these considerations, Mrs. Blyth, by a nod, intimated to her adopted child that she might accompany the housemaid to Kirk Street. Madonna, the moment this permission was granted, led the way out of the room; but stopped as soon as she and Patty were alone on the staircase, and, making a sign that she would be back directly, ran up to her own bed-chamber.

When she entered the room, she unlocked a little dressing-case that Valentine had given to her; and emptying out of one of the trays four sovereigns and some silver, all her savings from her own pocket-money, wrapped them up hastily in a piece of paper and ran downstairs again to Patty. Zack was ill, and-lonely, and miserable; longing for a friend to sit by his bedside and comfort him—and she could not be that friend! But Zack was also poor; she had read it in his letter; there were many little things he wanted to pay for; he needed money; and in that need she might secretly be a friend to him, for she had money of her own to give away.

"My four golden sovereigns shall be the first he has," thought Madonna, nervously taking the housemaid's offered arm at the house door. "I will put them in some place where he is sure to find them, and never to know who they come from. And Zack shall be rich again—rich with all the money I have got to give him." Four sovereigns represented quite a little fortune in Madonna's eyes. It had taken her a long, long time to save them out of her small allowance of pocket-money.

When they knocked at the private door of the tobacco-shop, it was opened by the landlady,

who, after hearing what their errand was from
Patty, and answering some preliminary inquiries
after Zack, politely invited them to walk into
her back parlor. But Madonna seemed—quite
incomprehensibly to the servant—to be bent on
remaining in the passage till she had finished
writing some lines which she had just then begun to trace on her slate. When they were
completed, she showed them to Patty, who read
with considerable astonishment these words:
"Ask where his sitting-room is, and if I can go
into it. I want to leave something for him there
with my own hands, if the room is empty."

After looking at her young mistress's eager
face in great amazement for a moment or two,
Patty asked the required questions; prefacing
them with some words of explanation which
drew from the tobacconist's wife many voluble
expressions of sympathy and admiration for Madonna. At last these came to an end; and the
desired answers to the questions on the slate
were readily given enough, and duly, though
rather slowly, written down by Patty for her
young lady's benefit. The sitting-room belonging to Mr. Thorpe and the other gentleman was
the front room on the first floor. Nobody was in
it now. Would the lady like to be shown—

Here Madonna arrested the servant's further
progress with the slate-pencil—nodded to indicate that she understood what had been written
—and then, with her little packet of money ready
in her hand, lightly ran up the first flight of
stairs; ascending them so quickly that she was

on the landing before Patty and the landlady had settled which of the two ought to have officially preceded her.

The front room was indeed empty when she entered it, but one of the folding-doors leading into the back room had been left ajar; and when she looked toward the opening thus made, she also looked, from the particular point of view she then occupied, toward the head of the bed on which Zack lay, and saw his face turned toward her, hushed in deep, still, breathless sleep.

She started violently—trembled a little—then stood motionless, looking toward him through the door; the tears standing thick in her eyes, the color gone from her cheeks, the yearning pulses of grief and pity beating faster and faster in her heart. Ah! how pale and wan and piteously still he lay there, with the ghastly white bandages round his head, and one helpless, languid hand hanging over the bedside! How changed from that glorious creature, all youth, health, strength, and exulting activity, whom it had so long been her innocent idolatry to worship in secret! How fearfully like what might be the image of him in death, was the present image of him as he lay in his hushed and awful sleep! She shuddered as the thought crossed her mind, and drying the tears that obscured her sight, turned a little away from him and looked round the room. Her quick feminine eyes detected at a glance all its squalid disorder, all its deplorable defects of comfort, all its repulsive unfitness as a habitation for the suffering and the sick. Surely a little money might help Zack to a better place to recover in! Surely *her* money might be made to minister in this way to his comfort, his happiness, and even his restoration to health!

Full of this idea, she advanced a step or two, and sought for a proper place on the one table in the room in which she might put her packet of money.

While she was thus engaged, an old newspaper, with some hair lying in it, caught her eye. The hair was Zack's, and was left to be thrown away; having been cut off that very morning by the doctor, who thought that enough had not been removed from the neighborhood of the wound by the barber originally employed to clear the hair from the injured side of the patient's head. Madonna had hardly looked at the newspaper before she recognized the hair in it as Zack's by its light-brown color, and by the faint golden tinge running through it. One little curly lock, lying rather apart from the rest, especially allured her eyes; she longed to take it as a keepsake—a keepsake which Zack would never know that she possessed! For a moment she hesitated, and in that moment the longing became an irresistible temptation. After glancing over her shoulder to assure herself that no one had followed her upstairs, she took the lock of hair, and quickly hid it away in her bosom.

Her eyes had assured her that there was no one in the room; but, if she had not been deprived of the sense of hearing, she would have known that persons were approaching it, by the sound of voices on the stairs—a man's voice being among them. Necessarily ignorant, however, of this, she advanced unconcernedly, after taking the lock of hair, from the table to the chimney-piece, which it struck her might be the safest place to leave the money on. She had just put it down there, when she felt the slight concussion caused by the opening and closing of the door behind her; and turning round instantly, confronted Patty, the landlady, and the strange swarthy-faced friend of Zack's who had made her a present of the scarlet tobacco-pouch.

Terror and confusion almost overpowered her, as she saw him advance to the chimney-piece and take up the packet she had just placed there. He had evidently opened the room door in time to see her put it down; and he was now deliberately unfolding the paper and examining the money inside.

While he was thus occupied, Patty came close up to her, and, with rather a confused and agitated face, began writing on her slate, much faster and much less correctly than usual. She gathered, however, from the few crooked lines scrawled by the servant, that Patty had been very much startled by the sudden entrance of the landlady's rough lodger, who had let himself in from the street, just as she was about to follow her young mistress up to the sitting-room, and had uncivilly stood in her way on the stairs, while he listened to what the good woman of the house had to tell him about young Mr.

Thorpe's illness. Confused as the writing was on the slate, Madonna contrived to interpret it thus far, and would have gone on interpreting more, if she had not felt a heavy hand laid on her arm, and had not, on looking round, seen Zack's friend making signs to her, with her money loose in his hand.

She felt confused, but not frightened now; for his eyes, as she looked into them, expressed neither suspicion nor anger. They rested on her face kindly and sadly, while he first pointed to the money in his hand, and then to her. She felt that her color was rising, and that it was a hard matter to acknowledge the gold and silver as being her own property; but she did so acknowledge it. He then pointed to himself; and when she shook her head, pointed through the folding-doors into Zack's room. Her cheeks began to burn, and she grew suddenly afraid to look at him; but it was no harder trial to confess the truth than shamelessly to deny it by making a false sign. So she looked up at him again, and bravely nodded her head.

His eyes seemed to grow clearer and softer as they still rested kindly on her; but he made her take back the money immediately, and, holding her hand as he did so, detained it for a moment with a curious, awkward gentleness. Then, after first pointing again to Zack's room, he began to search in the breast-pocket of his coat, took from it at one rough grasp some letters tied together loosely, and a clumsy-looking rolled-up strip of fur, put the letters aside on the table be-

hind him, and, unrolling the fur, showed her
that there were bank-notes in it. She understood him directly—he had money of his own
for Zack's service, and wanted none from her.

After he had replaced the strip of fur in his
pocket, he took up the letters from the table, to
be put back also. As he reached them toward
him, a lock of hair, which seemed to have accidentally got between them, fell out on the floor
just at her feet. She stooped to pick it up for
him; and was surprised, as she did so, to see
that it exactly resembled in color the lock of
Zack's hair which she had taken from the old
newspaper, and had hidden in her bosom.

She was surprised at this; and she was more
than surprised, when he angrily and abruptly
snatched up the lock of hair just as she touched
it. Did he think that she wanted to take it
away from him? If he did, it was easy to show
him that a lock of Zack's hair was just now no
such rarity that people need quarrel about the
possession of it. She reached her hand to the
table behind, and, taking some of the hair from
the old newspaper, held it up to him with a
smile just as he was on the point of putting his
own lock of hair back in his pocket.

For a moment he did not seem to comprehend
what her action meant; then the resemblance
between the hair in her hand and the hair in his
own struck him suddenly.

The whole expression of his face changed in
an instant—changed so darkly that she recoiled
from him in terror and put back the hair into

the newspaper. He pounced on it directly; and, crunching it up in his hand, turned his grim, threatening face and fiercely-questioning eyes on the landlady. While she was answering his inquiry, Madonna saw him look toward Zack's bed; and, as he looked, another change passed over his face—the darkness faded from it, and the red scars on his cheek deepened in color. He moved back slowly to the further corner of the room from the folding-doors; his restless eyes fixed in a vacant stare, one of his hands clutched round the old newspaper, the other motioning clumsily and impatiently to the astonished and alarmed women to leave him.

Madonna had felt Patty's hand pulling at her arm more than once during the last minute or two. She was now quite as anxious as her companion to quit the house. They went out quickly, not venturing to look at Mat again; and the landlady followed them. She and Patty had a long talk together at the street door—evidently, judging by the expression of their faces, about the conduct of the rough lodger upstairs. But Madonna felt no desire to be informed particularly of what they were saying to each other. Much as Matthew's strange behavior had surprised and startled her, he was not the uppermost subject in her mind just then. It was the discovery of her secret, the failure of her little plan for helping Zack with her own money, that she was now thinking of with equal confusion and dismay. She had not been in the front room at Kirk Street much more than five minutes altogether—yet what a succession of untoward events had passed in that short space of time!

For a long while after the women had left him, Mat stood motionless in the furthest corner of the room from the folding-doors, looking vacantly toward Zack's bed-chamber. His first surprise on finding a stranger talking in the passage, when he let himself in from the street; his first vexation on hearing of Zack's accident from the landlady; his momentary impulse to discover himself to Mary's child, when he saw Madonna standing in his room, and again when he knew that she had come there with her little offering for the one kind purpose of helping the sick lad in his distress—all these sensations were now gone from his memory as well as from his heart; absorbed in the one predominant emotion with which the discovery of the resemblance between Zack's hair and the hair from Jane Holdsworth's letter now filled him. No ordinary shocks could strike Mat's mind hard enough to make it lose its balance—*this* shock prostrated it in an instant.

In proportion as he gradually recovered his self-possession, so did the desire strengthen in him to ascertain the resemblance between the two kinds of hair once more—but in such a manner as it had not been ascertained yet. He stole gently to the folding-doors and looked into young Thorpe's room. Zack was still asleep.

After pausing for a moment and shaking his head sorrowfully as he noticed how pale and wasted the lad's face looked, he approached the pillow and laid the lock of Arthur Carr's hair upon it, close to the uninjured side of Zack's head.   It was then late in the afternoon, but not dusk yet.   No blind hung over the bedroom window, and all the light in the sky streamed full on to the pillow as Mat's eyes fastened on it.

The similarity between the sleeper's hair and the hair of Arthur Carr was perfect!   Both were of the same light-brown color, and both had running through that color the same delicate golden tinge, brightly visible in the light, hardly to be detected at all in the shade.

Why had this extraordinary resemblance never struck him before?   Perhaps because he had never examined Arthur Carr's hair with attention until he had possessed himself of Mary's bracelet, and had gone away to the country. Perhaps, also, because he had never yet taken notice enough of Zack's hair to care to look close at it.   And now the resemblance was traced, to what conclusion did it point?   Plainly, from Zack's youth, to none in connection with *him*. But what elder relatives had he? and which of them was he most like?

Did he take after his father?

Mat was looking down at the sleeper just then; something in the lad's face troubled him, and kept his mind from pursuing that last thought. He took the lock of hair from the pillow and went into the front room.   There was anxiety and almost dread in his face, as he thought of the fatally decisive question in relation to the momentous discovery he had just made, which must be addressed to Zack when he awoke. He had never really known how fond he was of his fellow-lodger until now, when he was conscious of a dull, numbing sensation of dismay at the prospect of addressing that question to the friend who had lived as a brother with him since the day when they first met.

As the evening closed in Zack woke. It was a relief to Mat, as he went to the bedside, to know that his face could not now be clearly seen. The burden of that terrible question pressed heavily on his heart while he held his comrade's feeble hand; while he answered as considerately, yet as briefly as he could, the many inquiries addressed to him; and while he listened patiently and silently to the sufferer's long, wandering, faintly-uttered narrative of the accident that had befallen him. Toward the close of that narrative Zack himself unconsciously led the way to the fatal question which Mat longed, yet dreaded, to ask him.

"Well, old fellow," he said, turning feebly on his pillow so as to face Matthew, "something like what you call the 'horrors' has been taking hold of me. And this morning, in particular, I was so wretched and lonely that I asked the landlady to write for me to my father, begging his pardon, and all that. I haven't behaved as well as I ought; and, somehow, when a fellow's ill and lonely he gets homesick—"

His voice began to grow faint, and he left the sentence unfinished.

"Zack," said Mat, turning his face away from

the bed while he spoke, though it was now quite dark—"Zack, what sort of a man is your father?"

"What sort of a man! How do you mean?"

"To look at. Are you like him in the face?"

"Lord help you, Mat! as little like as possible. My father's face is all wrinkled and marked."

"Ay, ay, like other old men's faces. His hair's gray, I suppose?"

"Quite white. By-the-by—talking of that—there *is* one point I'm like him in—at least, like what he *was* when he was a young man."

"What's that?"

"What we've been speaking of—his hair. I've heard my mother say, when she first married him—just shake up my pillow a bit, will you, Mat?"

"Yes, yes. And what did you hear your mother say?"

"Oh, nothing particular. Only that when he was a young man his hair was exactly like what mine is now."

As those momentous words were spoken, the landlady knocked at the door and announced that she was waiting outside with candles and a nice cup of tea for the invalid. Mat let her into the bed-chamber, then immediately walked out of it into the front room, and closed the folding-doors behind him. Brave as he was, he was afraid at that moment to let Zack see his face.

He walked to the fireplace and rested his head and arm on the chimney-piece—reflected for a little while — then stood upright again — and searching in his pocket, drew from it once more that fatal lock of hair, which he had examined so anxiously and so often during his past fortnight in the country.

"*Your* work's done," he said, looking at it for a moment, as it lay in his hand, then throwing it into the dull red fire which was now burning low in the grate. "*Your* work's done; and mine won't be long a-doing." He rested his head and arm again wearily on the chimneypiece, and added:

"I'm brothers with Zack — there's the hard part of it!—I'm brothers with Zack."

CHAPTER XVI.

THE DAY OF RECKONING.

ON the forenoon of the day that followed Mat's return to Kirk Street, the ordinarily dull aspect of Baregrove Square was enlivened by a procession of three handsome private carriages which stopped at Mr. Thorpe's door.

From each carriage there descended gentlemen of highly respectable appearance, clothed in shining black garments, and wearing, for the most part, white cravats. One of these gentlemen carried in his hands a handsome silver inkstand, and another gentleman who followed him bore a roll of glossy paper, tied round with a broad ribbon of sober purple hue. The roll contained an Address to Mr. Thorpe, eulogizing his character in very affectionate terms; the inkstand

was a Testimonial to be presented after the Address; and the gentlemen who occupied the three
private carriages were all eminent members of
the religious society which Mr. Thorpe had served
in the capacity of Secretary, and from which he
was now obliged to secede in consequence of the
precarious state of his health.

A small and orderly assembly of idle people
had collected on the pavement to see the gentlemen light, to watch them go into the house, to
stare at the inkstand, to wonder at the Address,
to observe that Mr. Thorpe's page wore his best
livery, and that Mr. Thorpe's housemaid had on
new cap-ribbons and her Sunday gown. After
the street door had been closed, and these various
objects for popular admiration had disappeared,
there still remained an attraction outside in the
square which addressed itself to the general ear.
One of the footmen in attendance on the carriages had collected many interesting particulars
about the Deputation and the Testimonial; and
while he related them in regular order to another
footman anxious for information the small and
orderly public of idlers stood round about and
eagerly caught up any stray words explanatory
of the ceremonies then in progress inside the
house which fell in their way.

One of the most attentive of these listeners
was a swarthy-complexioned man with bristling
whiskers and a scarred face, who had made one
of the assembly on the pavement from the moment of its first congregating. He had been almost as much stared at by the people about him

as the Deputation itself; and had been set down among them generally as a foreigner of the most outlandish kind: but, in plain truth, he was English to the backbone, being no other than Matthew Grice.

Mat's look, as he stood listening among his neighbors, was now just as quietly vigilant, his manner just as gruffly self-possessed, as usual. But it had cost him a hard struggle that morning, in the solitude of one of his longest and loneliest walks, to compose himself—or, in his favorite phrase, to "get to be his own man again."

From the moment when he had thrown the lock of hair into the fire to the moment when he was now loitering at Mr. Thorpe's door, *he* had never doubted, whatever others might have done, that the man who had been the ruin of his sister and the man who was the nearest blood-relation of the comrade who shared his roof, and lay sick at that moment in his bed, were one and the same. Though he stood now, amid the casual street spectators, apparently as indolently curious as the most careless among them, looking at what they looked at, listening to what they listened to, and leaving the square when they left it, he was resolved all the time to watch his first opportunity of entering Mr. Thorpe's house that very day; resolved to investigate, through all its ramifications, the secret which he had first discovered when the fragments of Zack's hair were playfully held up for him to look at in the deaf and dumb girl's hand.

The dispersion of the idlers on the pavement

was accelerated, and the footman's imaginary description of the proceedings then in progress at Mr. Thorpe's was cut short, by the falling of a heavy shower. The frost, after breaking up, had been succeeded that year by prematurely mild spring weather—April seemed to have come a month before its time.

Regardless of the rain, Mat walked slowly up and down the streets round Baregrove Square, peering every now and then from afar off, through the misty shower, to see if the carriages were still drawn up at Mr. Thorpe's door. The ceremony of presenting the Testimonial was evidently a protracted one; for the vehicles were long kept waiting for their owners. The rain had passed away—the sun had re-appeared—fresh clouds had gathered, and it was threatening a second shower before the Deputation from the great Religious Society re-entered their vehicles and drove out of the square.

When they had quitted it, Mat advanced and knocked at Mr. Thorpe's door. The clouds rolled up darkly over the sun, and the first warning drops of the new shower began to fall as the door opened.

The servant hesitated about admitting him. He had anticipated that this sort of obstacle would be thrown in his way at the outset, and had provided against it in his own mind beforehand. "Tell your master," he said, "that his son is ill, and I've come to speak to him about it."

This message was delivered, and had the desired effect. Mat was admitted into the drawing-room immediately.

The chairs occupied by the members of the Deputation had not been moved away—the handsome silver inkstand was on the table—the Address, beautifully written on the fairest white paper, lay by it. Mr. Thorpe stood before the fireplace, and bending over toward the table, mechanically examined, for the second time, the signatures attached to the Address, while his strange visitor was being ushered upstairs.

Mat's arrival had interrupted him just at the moment when he was going to Mrs. Thorpe's room to describe to her the Presentation ceremony which she had not been well enough to attend. He had stopped immediately, and the faint smile that was on his face had vanished from it, when the news of his son's illness reached him through the servant. But the hectic flush of triumph and pleasure which his interview with the Deputation had called into his cheeks still colored them as brightly as ever when Matthew Grice entered the room.

"You have come, sir," Mr. Thorpe began, "to tell me—"

He hesitated, stammered out another word or two, then stopped. Something in the expression of the dark and strange face that he saw lowering at him under the black velvet skull-cap suspended the words on his lips. In his present nervous, enfeebled state, any sudden emotions of doubt or surprise, no matter how slight and temporary in their nature, always proved too

powerful for his self - control, and betrayed
themselves in his speech and manner painfully.

Mat said not a word to break the ominous silence. Was he at that moment, in very truth,
standing face to face with Arthur Carr? Could
this man—so frail and meager, with the narrow
chest, the drooping figure, the effeminate pink
tinge on his wan, wrinkled cheeks—be indeed
the man who had driven Mary to that last refuge, where the brambles and weeds grew thick,
and the foul mud-pools stagnated in the forgotten
corner of the churchyard?

"You have come, sir," resumed Mr. Thorpe,
controlling himself by an effort which deepened
the flush on his face, "to tell me news of my
son, which I am not entirely unprepared for. I
heard from him yesterday; and, though it did
not strike me at first, I noticed, on referring to
his letter afterward, that it was not in his own
handwriting. My nerves are not very strong,
and they have been tried — pleasurably, most
pleasurably tried — already this morning, by
such testimonies of kindness and sympathy as
it does not fall to the lot of many men to earn.
May I beg you, if your news should be of an
alarming nature (which God forbid!), to communicate it as gently—"

"My news is this," Mat broke in: "Your
son's been hurt in the head, but he's got over
the worst of it now. He lives with me; I like
him; and I mean to take care of him till he gets
on his legs again. That's my news about your

son. But that's not all I've got to say. I bring you news of somebody else."

"Will you take a seat, and be good enough to explain yourself?"

They sat down at opposite sides of the table, with the Testimonial and the Address lying between them. The shower outside was beginning to fall at its heaviest. The splashing noise of the rain and sound of running footsteps as the few foot-passengers in the square made for shelter at the top of their speed, penetrated into the room during the pause of silence which ensued after they had taken their seats. Mr. Thorpe spoke first.

"May I inquire your name?" he said, in his lowest and calmest tones.

Mat did not seem to hear the question. He took up the Address from the table, looked at the list of signatures, and turned to Mr. Thorpe.

"I've been hearing about this," he said. "Are all of them names there the names of friends of yours?"

Mr. Thorpe looked a little astonished; but he answered, after a moment's hesitation:

"Certainly; the most valued friends I have in the world."

"Friends," pursued Mat, reading to himself the introductory sentence in the address, "*who have put the most affectionate trust in you.*"

Mr. Thorpe began to look rather offended, as well as rather astonished. "Will you excuse me," he said, coldly, "if I beg you to proceed to the business that has brought you here."

Mat placed the Address on the table again, immediately in front of him; and took a pencil from a tray with writing materials in it, which stood near at hand. "Friends '*who have put the most affectionate trust in you,*'" he repeated. "The name of one of them friends isn't here. It ought to be; and I mean to put it down."

As the point of his pencil touched the paper of the Address, Mr. Thorpe started from his chair.

"What am I to understand, sir, by this conduct?" he began, haughtily, stretching out his hand to possess himself of the Address.

Mat looked up with the serpent-glitter in his eyes and the angry red tinge glowing in the scars on his cheek. "Sit down," he said; "I'm not quick at writing. Sit down, and wait till I'm done."

Mr. Thorpe's face began to look a little agitated. He took a step toward the fireplace, intending to ring the bell.

"Sit down and wait," Mat reiterated, in quick, fierce, quietly uttered tones of command, rising from his own chair, and pointing peremptorily to the seat just vacated by the master of the house.

A sudden doubt crossed Mr. Thorpe's mind, and made him pause before he touched the bell. Could this man be in his right senses? His actions were entirely unaccountable—his words, and his way of uttering them, were alike strange—his scarred, scowling face looked hardly human at that moment. Would it be well to sum-

mon help? No; worse than useless. Except
the page, who was a mere boy, there were none
but women-servants in the house. When he remembered this, he sat down again, and at the
same moment Mat began, clumsily and slowly,
to write on the blank space beneath the last sig-
nature attached to the Address.

The sky was still darkening apace, the rain
was falling heavily and more heavily, as he
traced the final letter and then handed the paper
to Mr. Thorpe, bearing inscribed on it the name
of MARY GRICE.

"Read that name," said Mat.

Mr. Thorpe looked at the characters traced by
the pencil. His face changed instantly—he sank
down into the chair—one faint cry burst from
his lips—then he was silent.

Low, stifled, momentary as it was, that cry
proclaimed him to be the man. He was self-
denounced by it even before he cowered down,
shuddering in the chair, with both his hands
pressed convulsively over his face.

Mat rose to his feet and spoke, eying him pitilessly from head to foot.

"Not a friend of all of 'em," he said, pointing
down at the Address, "put such affectionate
trust in you as she did. When first I see her
grave in the strange churchyard, I said I'd be
even with the man who laid her in it. I'm here
to-day to be even with *you*. Carr or Thorpe,
whichever you call yourself, I know how you
used her from first to last! *Her* father was *my*
father; *her* name is *my* name: you were *her*

worst enemy three-and-twenty year ago; you are *my* worst enemy now. I'm her brother, Matthew Grice!"

The hands of the shuddering figure beneath him suddenly dropped—the ghastly uncovered face looked up at him, with such a panic stare in the eyes, such a fearful quivering and distortion of all the features, that it tried even his firmness of nerve to look at it steadily. In spite of himself, he went back to his chair, and sat down doggedly by the table, and was silent.

A low murmuring and moaning, amid which a few disconnected words made themselves faintly distinguishable, caused him to look round again. He saw that the ghastly face was once more hidden. He heard the disconnected words reiterated, always in the same stifled wailing tones. Now and then, a half-finished phrase was audible from behind the withered hands, still clasped over the face. He heard such fragments of sentences as these: "Have pity on my wife"—"Accept the remorse of many years"—"Spare me the disgrace—"

After those four last words, Mat listened for no more. The merciless spirit was roused in him again the moment he heard them.

"Spare you the disgrace?" he repeated, starting to his feet. "Did you spare *her?*—Not you!"

Once more the hands dropped; once more the ghastly face slowly and horribly confronte⁻ him. But this time he never recoiled from it. There was no mercy in him—none in his looks, none in his tones—as he went on.

"What! it would disgrace you, would it? Then disgraced you shall be! You've kep' it a secret, have you? You shall tell that secret to every soul that comes about the house! You shall own Mary's disgrace, Mary's death, and Mary's child before every man who's put his name down on that bit of· paper!—You shall, as soon as· to-morrow, if I like! You shall, if I have to bring your child with me to make you; if I have to stand up, hand in hand along with her, here on your own hearth-stone."

He stopped. The cowering figure was struggling upward from the chair: one of the withered hands, slowly raised, was stretching itself out toward him; the panic-stricken eyes were growing less vacant, and were staring straight into his with a fearful meaning in their look; the pale lips were muttering rapidly—at first he could not tell what; then he succeeded in catching the two words, "Mary's child?" quickly, faintly, incessantly reiterated, until he spoke again.

"Yes," he said, pitiless as ever. "Yes: Mary's child. Your child. Haven't you seen her? Is it *that* you're staring and trembling about? Go and look at her: she lives within gunshot of you. Ask Zack's friend, the painter-man, to show you the deaf and dumb girl he picked up among the horse-riders. Look here—look at this bracelet! Do you remember your own hair in it? The hands that brought up Mary's child took that bracelet from Mary's pocket. Look at it again! Look at it as close as you like—"

Once more he stopped.   The frail figure, which had been feebly rising out of the chair while he held up the hair bracelet, suddenly and heavily sank back in it—he saw the eyelids half close, and a great stillness pass over the face—he heard one deep-drawn breath: but no cry now, no moaning, no murmuring—no sound whatever, except the steady splash of the fast-falling rain on the pavement outside.

Dead?

A thought of Zack welled up into his heart, and troubled it.

He hesitated for a moment, then bent over the chair, and put his hand on the bosom of the deathly figure reclining in it.   A faint fluttering was still to be felt; and the pulse, when he tried that next, was beating feebly.   It was not death he looked on now, but the swoon that is near neighbor to it.

For a minute or two he stood with his eyes fixed on the white, calm face beneath him, thinking.   "If me and Zack," he whispered to himself, "hadn't been brothers together—"   He left the sentence unfinished, took his hat quickly, and quitted the room.

In the passage downstairs, he met one of the female servants, who opened the street door for him.

"Your master wants you," he said, with an effort.   He spoke those words, passed by her, and left the house.

CHAPTER XVII.

MATTHEW GRICE'S REVENGE.

NEITHER looking to the right nor the left, neither knowing nor caring whither he went, Matthew Grice took the first turning he came to which led him out of Baregrove Square. It happened to be the street communicating with the long suburban road, at the remote extremity of which Mr. Blyth lived. Mat followed this road mechanically, not casting a glance at the painter's abode when he passed it, and taking no notice of a cab, with luggage on the roof, which drew up, as he walked by, at the garden gate. If he had only looked round at the vehicle for a moment, he must have seen Valentine sitting inside it, and counting out the money for his fare.

But he still went on—straight on, looking aside at nothing. He fronted the wind and the clearing quarter of the sky, as he walked. The shower was now fast subsiding; and the first rays of returning sunlight, as they streamed through mist and cloud, fell tenderly and warmly on his face.

Though he did not show it outwardly, there was strife and trouble within him. The name of Zack was often on his lips, and he varied constantly in his rate of walking; now quickening, now slackening his pace at irregular intervals. It was evening before he turned back toward home—night, before he sat down again in the chair by young Thorpe's bedside.

"I'm a deal better to-night, Mat," said Zack, answering his first inquiries. "That good fellow, Blyth, has come back: he's been sitting here with me a couple of hours or more. Where have you been to all day, you restless old Rough and Tough?" he continued, with something of his natural light-hearted manner returning already. "There's a letter come for you, by-the-by. The landlady said she would put it on the table in the front room."

Matthew found and opened the letter, which proved to contain two inclosures. One was addressed to Mr. Blyth; the other had no direction. The handwriting in the letter being strange to him, Mat looked first for the name at the end, and found that it was *Thorpe*. "Wait a bit," he said, as Zack spoke again just then, "I want to read my letter. We'll talk after."

This is what he read:

"Some hours have passed since you left my house. I have had time to collect a little strength and composure, and have received such assistance and advice as have enabled me to profit by that time. Now I know that I can write calmly, I send you this letter.

"My object is not to ask how you became possessed of the guilty secret which I had kept from every one—even from my wife—but to offer you such explanation and confession as you have a right to demand from me. I do not cavil about that right—I admit that you possess it, without desiring further proof than your actions, your merciless words, and the bracelet in your possession, have afforded me.

"It is fit you should first be told that the assumed name by which I was known at Dibbledean merely originated in a foolish jest—in a wager that certain companions of my own age, who were accustomed to ridicule my fondness for botanical pursuits, and often to follow and disturb me when I went in search of botanical specimens, would not be able to trace and discover me in my country retreat. I went to Dibbledean, because the neighborhood was famous for specimens of rare ferns, which I desired to possess; and I took my assumed name before I went, to help in keeping me from being traced and disturbed by my companions. My father alone was in the secret, and came to see me once or twice in my retirement. I have no excuse to offer for continuing to preserve my false name at the time when I was bound to be candid about myself and my station in life. My conduct was as unpardonably criminal in this, as it was in greater things.

"My stay at the cottage I had taken lasted much longer than my father would have permitted, if I had not deceived him, and if he had not been much harassed at that time by unforeseen difficulties in his business as a foreign merchant. These difficulties arrived at last at a climax, and his health broke down under them. His presence, or the presence of a properly qualified person to represent him, was absolutely required in Germany, where one of his business houses, conducted by an agent, was established. I was his only son; he had taken me as a partner into his London house; and had allowed me, on the plea of delicate health, to absent myself from my duties for months and months together, and to follow my favorite botanical pursuits just as I pleased. When, therefore, he wrote me word that great part of his property, and great part, consequently, of my sisters' fortunes, depended on my going to Germany (his own health not permitting him to take the journey), I had no choice but to place myself at his disposal immediately.

"I went away, being assured beforehand that my absence would not last more than three or four months at the most.

"While I was abroad, I wrote to your sister constantly. I had treated her dishonorably and wickedly, but no thought of abandoning her had ever entered my heart: my dearest hope, at that time, was the hope of seeing her again. Not one of my letters was answered. I was detained in Germany beyond the time during which I had consented to remain there; and in the excess of my anxiety, I even ventured to write twice to your father. Those letters also remained unanswered. When I at last got back to England, I immediately sent a person on whom I could rely to Dibbledean, to make the inquiries which I dreaded to make myself. My messenger was turned from your doors, with the fearful news of your sister's flight from home and of her death.

"It was then I first suspected that my letters had been tampered with. It was then, too, when the violence of my grief and despair had a little abated, that the news of your sister's flight inspired me, for the first time, with a suspicion of the consequence which had followed the commission of my sin. You may think it strange that this suspicion should not have occurred to me before. It would seem so no longer, perhaps, if I detailed to you the peculiar system of home education by which my father, strictly and conscientiously, endeavored to preserve me—as other young men are not usually preserved—from the moral contaminations of the world. But it would be useless to dwell on this now. No explanations can alter the events of the guilty and miserable past.

"Anxiously—though privately, and in fear and trembling—I caused such inquiries to be made as I hoped might decide the question whether the child existed or not. They were long persevered in, but they were useless—useless, perhaps, as I now think with bitter sorrow, because I trusted them to others, and had not the courage to make them openly myself.

"Two years after that time I married, under circumstances not of an ordinary kind—what circumstances you have no claim to know. *That* part of my life is my secret and my wife's, and belongs to us alone.

"I have now dwelt long enough for your information on my own guilty share in the events of the Past. As to the Present and the Future, I have still a word or two left to say.

"You have declared that I shall expiate, by the exposure of my shameful secret before all my friends, the wrong your sister suffered at my hands. My life has been one long expiation for that wrong. My broken health, my altered character, my weary secret sorrows, unpartaken and unconsoled, have punished me for many years past more heavily than you think. Do you desire to see me visited by more poignant sufferings than these? If it be so, you may enjoy the vindictive triumph of having already inflicted them. Your threats will force me, in a few hours, from the friends I have lived with, at the very time when the affection shown to me, and the honor conferred on me by those friends, have made their society most precious to my heart. You force me from this, and from more —for you force me from my home, at the moment when my son has affectionately entreated me to take him back to my fireside.

"These trials, heavy as they are, I am ready to endure, if, by accepting them humbly, I may be deemed to have made some atonement for my sin. But more I have not the fortitude to meet. I cannot face the exposure with which you are resolved to overwhelm me. The anxiety—perhaps I ought to say the weakness—of my life has been to win and keep the respect of others. You are about, by disclosing the crime which dishonored my youth, to deprive me of my good fame. I can let it go without a struggle, as part of the punishment that I have deserved; but I have not the courage to wait and see you take it from me. My own sensations tell me that I have not long to live; my own convictions assure me that I cannot fitly prepare myself for death, until I am far removed from worldly interests and worldly terrors—in a word, from the horror of an exposure, which I have deserved, but which, at the end of my weary life, is more than I can endure. We have seen the last of each other in this world. To-night I shall be beyond the reach of your retaliation; for to-night I shall be journeying to the retreat in which the short remainder of my life will be hidden from you and from all men.

"It now only remains for me to advert to the two inclosures contained in this letter.

"The first is addressed to Mr. Blyth. I leave it to reach his hands through you, because I am ashamed to communicate with him directly, as from myself. If what you said about my child be the truth—and I cannot dispute it—then, in my ignorance of her identity, in my estrangement from the house of her protector since she first entered it, I have unconsciously committed such an offense against Mr. Blyth as no contrition can ever adequately atone for. Now indeed I feel how presumptuously merciless my bitter conviction of the turpitude of my own sin has made me toward what I deemed like sins in others. Now also I know that, unless you have spoken falsely, I have been guilty of casting the

shame of my own deserted child in the teeth
of the very man who had nobly and tenderly
given her an asylum in his own home. The unutterable anguish which only the bare suspicion
of this has inflicted on me might well have been
my death. I marvel even now at my own recovery from it.

"You are free to look at the letter to Mr. Blyth
which I now intrust to you. Besides the expression of my shame, my sorrow, and my sincere
repentance, it contains some questions to which
Mr. Blyth, in his Christian kindness, will, I
doubt not, readily write answers. The questions only refer to the matter of the child's identity; and the address I have written down at the
end is that of the house of business of my lawyer
and agent in London. He will forward the document to me, and will then arrange with Mr.
Blyth the manner in which a fit provision from
my property may be best secured to his adopted
child. He has deserved her love, and to him I
gratefully and humbly leave her. For myself,
I am not worthy even to look upon her face.

"The second inclosure is meant for my son;
and is to be delivered in the event of your having already disclosed to him the secret of his
father's guilt. But, if you have not done this
—if any mercy toward me has entered into your
heart, and pleads with it for pardon and for silence—then destroy the letter, and tell him that
he will find a communication waiting for him
at the house of my agent. He wrote to ask my
pardon—he has it freely. Freely, in my turn,

I hope to have his forgiveness for severities exercised toward him, which were honestly meant to preserve him betimes from ever falling as his father fell, but which I now fear were persevered in too hardly and too long. I have suffered for this error, as for others, heavily—more heavily, when he abandoned his home, than I should ever wish him to know. You said he lived with you, and that you were fond of him. Be gentle with him, now that he is ill, for his mother's sake.

"My hand grows weaker and weaker: I can write no more. Let me close this letter by entreating your pardon. If you ever grant it me, then I also ask your prayers."

With this the letter ended.

Matthew sat holding it open in his hand for a little while. He looked round once or twice at the inclosed letter from Mr. Thorpe to his son, which lay close by on the table—but did not destroy it; did not so much as touch it even.

Zack spoke to him before long from the inner room.

"I'm sure you must have done reading your letter by this time, Mat. I've been thinking, old fellow, of the talk we used to have about going back to America together and trying a little buffalo-hunting and roaming about in the wilds. If my father takes me into favor again, and can be got to say Yes, I should so like to go with you, Mat. Not for too long, you know, because of my mother and my friends over here. But a sea-voyage, and a little scouring about in what you call the lonesome places, would do me such good! I don't feel as if I should ever settle properly to anything till I've had my fling. I wonder whether my father would let me go?"

"I know he would, Zack."

"You! How?"

"I'll tell you how another time. You shall have your run, Zack—you shall have your heart's content along with me." As he said this, he looked again at Mr. Thorpe's letter to his son, and took it up in his hand this time.

"Oh! how I wish I was strong enough to start! Come in here, Mat, and let's talk about it."

"Wait a bit and I will." Pronouncing those words, he rose from his chair. "For your sake, Zack," he said, and dropped the letter into the fire.

"What can you be about all this time?" asked young Thorpe.

"Do you call to mind," said Mat, going into the bedroom and sitting down by the lad's pillow—"Do you call to mind me saying that I'd be brothers with you when first us two come together? Well, Zack, I've only been trying to be as good as my word."

"Trying? What do you mean? I don't understand, old fellow."

"Never mind: you'll make it out better some day. Let's talk about getting aboard ship and going a buffalo-hunting, now."

They discussed the projected expedition until Zack grew sleepy. As he fell off into a pleasant doze Mat went back into the front room, and, taking from the table Mr. Thorpe's letter to Mr. Blyth, left Kirk Street immediately for the painter's house.

It had occurred to Valentine to unlock his bureau twice since his return from the country, but on neither occasion had he found it necessary to open that long narrow drawer at the back in which he had secreted the hair bracelet years ago. He was consequently still totally ignorant that it had been taken away from him when Matthew Grice entered the painting-room and quietly put it into his hand.

Consternation and amazement so thoroughly overpowered him that he suffered his visitor to lock the door against all intruders, and then to lead him peremptorily to a chair without uttering a single word of inquiry or expostulation. All through the narrative, on which Mat now entered, he sat totally speechless, until Mr. Thorpe's letter was placed in his hands and he was informed that Madonna was still to be left entirely under his own care. Then, for the first time, his cheeks showed symptoms of returning to their natural color, and he exclaimed fervently: "Thank God! I shan't lose her after all! I only wish you had begun by telling me of that the moment you came into the room!"

Saying this, he began to read Mr. Thorpe's letter. When he had finished it and looked up at Mat, the tears were in his eyes.

"I can't help it," said the simple-hearted

painter. "It would even affect *you*, Mr. Grice, to be addressed in such terms of humiliation as these. How can he doubt my forgiving him when he has a right to my everlasting gratitude for not asking me to part with our darling child? They never met—he has never, never seen her face," continued Valentine, in lower and fainter tones. "She always wore her veil down, by my wish, when we went out; and our walks were generally into the country, instead of town way. I only once remember seeing him coming toward us; and then I crossed the road with her, knowing we were not on terms. There's something shocking in father and daughter living so near each other, yet being—if one may say so—so far, so very far apart. It is dreadful to think of that. It is far more dreadful to think of its having been *her* hand which held up the hair for you to look at, and *her* little innocent action which led to the discovery of who her father really was!"

"Do you ever mean to let her know as much about it as we do?" asked Matthew.

The look of dismay began to appear again in Valentine's face. "Have you told Zack yet?" he inquired, nervously and eagerly.

"No," said Mat; "and don't *you!* When Zack's on his legs again he's going to take a voyage, and get a season's hunting along with me in the wild country over the water. I'm as fond of the lad as if he was a bit of my own flesh and blood. I cottoned to him when he hit out so hearty for me at the singing-shop—and

we've been brothers together ever since. You
mightn't think it, to look at me; but I've spared
Zack's father for Zack's sake; and I don't ask
no more reward for it than to take the lad a-hunt-
ing for a season or two along with me. When
he comes back home again and we say Good-by,
I'll tell him all what's happened; but I won't
risk bringing so much as a cross look into his
eyes now by dropping a word to him of what's
passed betwixt his father and me."

Although this speech excited no little surprise
and interest in Valentine's mind, it did not succeed in suspending the anxieties which had been
awakened in him by Matthew's preceding question, and which he now began to feel the necessity of confiding to Mrs. Blyth—his grand counselor in all difficulties and unfailing comforter
in all troubles.

"Do you mind waiting here," he said, "while
I go upstairs and break the news to my wife?
Without her advice, I don't know what to do
about communicating our discovery to the poor
dear child. Do you mind waiting?"

No: Matthew would willingly wait. Hearing
this, Mr. Blyth left the room directly.

He remained away a long time. When he
came back his face did not seem to have gained
in composure during his absence.

"My wife has told me of another discovery,"
he said, "which her motherly love for our adopted
daughter enabled her to make some time since.
I have been sadly surprised and distressed at
hearing of it. But I need say no more on the

subject to you than that Mrs. Blyth has at once decided me to confide nothing to Madonna—to Mary, I ought to say—until Zack has got well again, and has left England. When I heard just now, from you, of his projected voyage, I must confess I saw many objections to it. They have all been removed by what my wife has told me. I heartily agree with her that the best thing Zack can do is to make the trip he proposes. You are willing to take care of him; and I honestly believe that we may safely trust him with you.''

A serious difficulty being thus disposed of, Valentine found leisure to pay some attention to minor things. Among other questions which he now asked was one relating to the hair bracelet, and to the manner in which Matthew had become possessed of it. He was answered by the frankest confession, a confession which tried even *his* kindly and forbearing disposition to the utmost as he listened to it; and which drew from him, when it was ended, some of the strongest terms of reproach that had ever passed his lips.

Mat listened till he had done; then, taking his hat to go, muttered a few words of rough apology, which Valentine's good-nature induced him to accept, almost as soon as they were spoken. ''We must let by-gones be by-gones,'' said the painter. ''You have been candid with me at last, at any rate; and, in recognition of that candor, I say, 'Good-night, Mr. Grice,' as a friend of yours still.''

When Mat returned to Kirk Street, the landlady came out of her little parlor to tell him of a visitor who had been to the lodgings in his absence. An elderly lady, looking very pale and ill, had asked to see young Mr. Thorpe, and had prefaced the request by saying that she was his mother. Zack was then asleep, but the lady had been taken upstairs to see him in bed — had stooped over him and kissed him—and had then gone away again, hastily, and in tears. Matthew's face grew grave as he listened, but he said nothing when the landlady had done, except a word or two charging her not to mention to Zack what had happened when he woke. It was plain that Mrs. Thorpe had been told her husband's secret, and that she had lovingly devoted herself to him as comforter and companion to the last.

When the doctor paid his regular visit to the invalid the next morning he was called on immediately for an answer to the important question of when Zack would be fit to travel. After due consideration and careful inspection of the injured side of the patient's head, he replied that in a month's time the lad might safely go on board ship; and that the sea-voyage proposed would do more toward restoring him to perfect health and strength than all the tonic medicines that all the doctors in England could prescribe.

Matthew might have found the month's inaction to which he was now obliged to submit for Zack's sake rather tedious, but for the opportune arrival in Kirk Street of a professional visitor from Dibbledean.

Though his client had ungratefully and en-

tirely forgotten him, Mr. Tatt had not by any
means forgotten his client, but had, on the contrary, attended to his interests with unremitting
resolution and assiduity. He had discovered
that Mat was entitled, under his father's will,
to no less a sum than two thousand pounds, if
his identity could be properly established. To
effect this result was now, therefore, the grand
object of Mr. Tatt's ambition. He had the prospect not only of making a little money, but of
establishing a reputation in Dibbledean if he
succeeded — and, by dint of perseverance, he
ultimately did succeed. He carried Mat about
to all sorts of places, insisted on his signing all
sorts of papers and making all sorts of declarations, and ended by accumulating such a mass
of evidence before the month was out that Mr.
Nawby, as executor to "the late Joshua Grice,"
declared himself convinced of the claimant's
identity.

On being informed of this result, Mat ordered
the lawyer, after first deducting the amount of
his bill from the forthcoming legacy, to draw
him out such a legal form as might enable him
to settle his property forthwith on another person. When Mr. Tatt asked to be furnished with
the name of this person, he was told to write
"Martha Peckover."

"Mary's child has got you to look after her,
and money enough from her father to keep her,"
said Mat, as he put the signed instrument into
Valentine's hands. "When Martha Peckover's
old and past her work she may want a banknote
or two to fall back on. Give her this when I'm
gone—and say she earned it from Mary's brother
the day she stopped and suckled Mary's child by
the roadside."

The day of departure drew near. Zack rallied
so rapidly that he was able, a week before it
arrived, to go himself and fetch the letter from

his father which was waiting for him at the agent's office. It assured him, briefly, but very kindly, of the forgiveness which he had written to ask—referred him to the man of business for particulars of the allowance granted to him while he pursued his studies in the Art, or otherwise occupied himself—urged him always to look on Mr. Blyth as the best friend and counselor that he could ever have—and ended by engaging him to write often about himself and his employments to his mother; sending his letters to be forwarded through the agent. When Zack, hearing from this gentleman that his father had left the house in Baregrove Square, desired to know what had occasioned the change of residence, he was only informed that the state of Mr. Thorpe's health had obliged him to seek perfect retirement and repose: and that there were reasons at present for not mentioning the place of his retreat to any one, which it was not deemed expedient for his son to become acquainted with.

The day of departure arrived.

In the morning, by Valentine's advice, Zack wrote to his mother; only telling her, in reference to his proposed trip, that he was about to travel to improve and amuse himself, in the company of a friend, of whom Mr. Blyth approved. While he was thus engaged the painter had a private interview with Matthew Grice, and very earnestly charged him to remember his responsibilities toward his young companion. Mat answered briefly and characteristically: "I told you I was as fond of him as if he was a bit of my own flesh and blood. If you don't believe I shall take care of him, after that—I can't say nothing to make you."

Both the travelers were taken up into Mrs. Blyth's room to say Farewell. It was a sad parting. Zack's spirits had not been so good as usual since the day of his visit to the agent's—

and the other persons assembled were all more
or less affected in an unusual degree by the approaching separation. Madonna had looked ill
and anxious—though she would not own to having anything the matter with her—for some days
past. But now, when she saw the parting looks
exchanged around her, the poor girl's agitation
got beyond her control, and became so painfully
evident that Zack wisely and considerately hurried over the farewell scene. He went out first.
Matthew followed him to the landing — then
stopped—and suddenly retraced his steps.

He entered the room again and took his sister's child by the hand once more; bent over her
as she stood pale and in tears before him, and
kissed her on the cheek. "Tell her some day
that me and her mother was playmates together,"
he said to Mrs. Blyth as he turned away to join
Zack on the stairs.

Valentine accompanied them to the ship.
When they shook hands together, he said to
Matthew: "Zack has engaged to come back
in a year's time. Shall we see *you* again with
him?"

Mat took the painter aside, without directly
answering him.

"If ever you go to Bangbury," he whispered,
"look into the churchyard, in the dark corner
among the trees. There's a bit of walnut-wood
planking put up now at the place where she's
buried; and it would be a comfort to me to know
that it was kep' clean and neat. I should take
it kind of you if you'd give it a brush or two
with your hand when you're near it—for I never
hope to see the place myself no more."

*   *   *   *   *   *   *

Sadly and thoughtfully Valentine returned
alone to his own house. He went up at once
to his wife's room.

As he opened the door, he started, and stopped on the threshold. Madonna was sitting on the couch by her adopted mother, with her face hidden on Mrs. Blyth's bosom and her arms clasped tight round Mrs. Blyth's neck.

"Have you ventured to tell her all, Lavvie?" he asked.

Mrs. Blyth was not able to speak in answer—she looked at him with tearful eyes and bowed her head.

Valentine lingered at the door for a moment—then softly closed it and left them together.

CLOSING CHAPTER

A YEAR AND A HALF AFTERWARD.

It is sunset after a fine day in August, and Mr. Blyth is enjoying the evening breeze in the invalid-room.

Besides the painter and his wife and Madonna, two visitors are present, who occupy both the spare beds in the house. One is Mrs. Thorpe, the other Mrs. Peckover; and they have been asked to become Valentine's guests to assist at the joyful ceremony of welcoming Zack to England on his return from the wilds of America. He has outstayed his year's leave of absence by nearly six months; and his appearance at Mr. Blyth's has become an event of daily, or more properly, of hourly expectation.

There is a sad and significant change in Mrs. Thorpe's dress. She wears the widow's cap and weeds. It is nearly seven months since her husband died, in the remote Welsh village to which he retired on leaving London. With him, as with many other confirmed invalids, Nature drooped to her final decay gradually and wearily; but his death was painless, and his mental powers remained unimpaired to the end. One of the last names that lingered lovingly on his lips—after he had bade his wife farewell—was the name of his absent son.

Mrs. Thorpe sits close to Mrs. Blyth, and talks to her in low, gentle tones. The kind black eyes of the painter's wife are brighter than they have been for many a long year past, and the clear tones of her voice—cheerful always—have a joyous sound in them now. Ever since the first days of the Spring season, she has been gaining so greatly in health and strength that the "favorable turn" has taken place in her malady, which was spoken of as "possible" by the doctors long ago, at the time of her first sufferings. She has several times, for the last fortnight, been moved from her couch for a few hours to a comfortable seat near the window; and if the fine weather still continues, she is to be taken out, in a day or two, for an airing in an invalid-chair.

The prospect of this happy event, and the pleasant expectation of Zack's return, have made Valentine more gayly talkative and more nimbly restless than ever. As he skips discursively about the room at this moment, talking of all sorts of subjects, and managing to mix Art up with every one of them; dressed in the old jaunty frock-coat with the short tails, he looks, if possible, younger, plumper, rosier, and brisker than when he was first introduced to the reader. It is wonderful, when people are really youthful at heart, to see how easily the Girdle of Venus fits them, and how long they contrive to keep it on, without ever wearing it out.

Mrs. Peckover, arrayed in festively-flaring cap-ribbons, sits close to the window to get all the air she can, and tries to make more of it by fanning herself with the invariable red cotton

pocket-handkerchief to which she has been all
her life attached. In bodily circumference she
has not lost an inch of rotundity; suffers, in
consequence, considerably, from the heat; and
talks to Mr. Blyth with parenthetical pantings,
which reflect little credit on the cooling influence
of the breeze, or the ventilating properties of the
pocket-handkerchief fan.

Madonna sits opposite to her at the window—
as cool and pretty a contrast as can be imagined,
in her white muslin dress, and light rose-colored
ribbons. She is looking at Mrs. Peckover, and
smiling every now and then at the comically
languishing faces made by that excellent woman
to express to "little Mary" the extremity of her
sufferings from the heat. The whole length of
the window-sill is occupied by an Æolian harp—
one of the many presents which Valentine's portrait-painting expeditions have enabled him to
offer to his wife. Madonna's hand is resting
lightly on the box of the harp; for by touching
it in this way, she becomes sensible to the influence of its louder and higher notes when the rising breeze draws them out. This is the only
pleasure she can derive from music; and it is
always, during the summer and autumn evenings, one of the amusements that she enjoys in
Mrs. Blyth's room.

Mrs. Thorpe, in the course of her conversation
with Mrs. Blyth, has been reminded of a letter
to one of her sisters, which she has not yet completed, and goes to her own room to finish it—
Valentine running to open the door for her, with
the nimblest juvenile gallantry, then returning
to the window and addressing Mrs. Peckover.

"Hot as ever, eh? Shall I get you one of
Lavvie's fans?" says Mr. Blyth.

"No, thank'ee, sir; I ain't quite melted yet,"
answers Mrs. Peckover. "But I'll tell you what
I wish you would do for me. I wish you would

read me Master Zack's last letter. You promised, you know, sir."

"And I would have performed my promise
before, Mrs. Peckover, if Mrs. Thorpe had not
been in the room. There are passages in the
letter which it might revive very painful remem-
brances in her to hear. Now she has left us, I
have not the least objection to read, if you are
ready to listen."

Saying this, Valentine takes a letter from his
pocket. Madonna recognizing it, asks by a sign
if she may look over his shoulder and read it for
the second time. The request is granted immediately. Mr. Blyth makes her sit on his knee,
puts his arm round her waist, and begins to read
aloud as follows:

"MY DEAR VALENTINE—Although I am writing to you to announce my return, I cannot say
that I take up my pen in good spirits. It is not
so long since I picked up my last letters from
England that told me of my father's death. But
besides that, I have had a heavy trial to bear, in
hearing the dreadful secret, which you all kept
from me when it was discovered; and afterward
in parting from Matthew Grice.

"What I felt when I knew the secret, and
heard why Mat and all of you had kept it from
me, I may be able to tell you—but I cannot and
dare not write about it. You may be interested to
hear how my parting with Matthew happened;
and I will relate it to you, as well as I can.

"You know, from my other letters, all the glorious hunting and riding we have had, and the
thousands of miles of country we have been
over, and the wonderful places we have seen.
Well, Bahia (the place I now write from) has
been the end of our travels. It was here I told
Mat of my father's death; and he directly agreed
with me that it was my duty to go home, and

comfort my poor dear mother, by the first ship that sailed for England. After we had settled that, he said he had something serious to tell me, and asked me to go with him, northward, half a day's march along the sea-coast; saying we could talk together quietly as we went along. I saw that he had got his rifle over his shoulder and his baggage at his back; and thought it odd —but he stopped me from asking any questions by telling me, from beginning to end, all that you and he knew about my father, before we left England. I was at first so shocked and amazed by what I heard, and then had so much to say to him about it, that our half-day's march, by the time we had got to the end of it, seemed to me to have hardly lasted as long as an hour.

"He stopped, though, at the place he had fixed on; and held out his hand to me, and said these words: 'I've done my duty by you, Zack, as brother should by brother. The time's come at last for us two to say Good-by. You're going back over the sea to your friends, and I'm going inland by myself on the tramp.' I had heard him talk of our parting in this way before, but had never thought it would really take place; and I tried hard, as you may imagine, to make him change his mind, and sail for England with me. But it was useless.

"'No, Zack,' he said, 'I doubt if I'm fit for the life you're going back to lead. I've given it a trial, and a hard and bitter one it's been to me. I began life on the tramp; and on the tramp I shall end it. Good-by, Zack. I shall think of you when I light my fire and cook my bit of victuals without you, in the lonesome places to-night.'

"I tried to control myself, Valentine; but my eyes got dim, and I caught fast hold of him by the arm. 'Mat,' I said, 'I can't part with you in this dreary, hopeless way. Don't shut the future up from both of us forever. We have been eighteen months together, let another year and a half pass if you like; and then give yourself, and give me, another chance. Say you'll meet me, when that time is past, in New York; or say, at least, you'll let me hear where you are?' His face work and quivered, and he only shook his head. 'Come, Mat,' I said, as cheerfully as I could, 'if I am ready to cross the sea again, for your sake, you can't refuse to do what I ask you, for mine?' 'Will it make the parting easier to you, my lad?' he asked kindly. 'Yes, indeed it will,' I answered. 'Well, then, Zack,' he said, 'you shall have your way. Don't let's say no more, now. Come, let's cut it as short as we can, or we shan't part as men should. God bless you, lad, and all of them you're going back to see.' Those were his last words.

"After he had walked a few yards inland, he turned round and waved his hand—then went on, and never turned again. I sat down on the sand-hillock where we had said Good-by, and burst out crying. What with the dreadful secret he had been telling me as we came along, and then the parting when I didn't expect it, all I had of the man about me gave way somehow in a moment. And I sat alone, crying and sobbing on the sand-hillock, with the surf roaring miles out at sea behind me, and the great plain before, with Matthew walking over it alone on his way to the mountains beyond.

"When I had had time to get ashamed of myself for crying, and had got my eye-sight clear again, he was already far away from me. I ran to the top of the highest hillock, and watched him over the plain—a desert, without a shrub to break the miles and miles of flat ground spreading away to the mountains. I watched him, as he got smaller and smaller—I watched till he got a mere black speck—till I was doubtful

HE STOPPED, THOUGH, AT THE PLACE HE HAD FIXED ON, AND HELD
OUT HIS HAND TO ME, AND SAID THESE WORDS: "I'VE DONE MY DUTY
BY YOU, ZACK, AS BROTHER SHOULD BY BROTHER. THE TIME'S COME
AT LAST FOR US TWO TO SAY GOOD-BY."

—HIDE-AND-SEEK, Vol. XI., page 619.

whether I still saw him or not—till I was certain, at last, that the great vacancy of the plain had swallowed him up from sight.

"My heart was very heavy, Valentine, as I went back to the town by myself. It is sometimes heavy still; for though I think much of my mother, and of my sister—whom you have been so kind a father to, and whose affection it is such a new happiness to me to have the prospect of soon returning—I think occasionally of dear old Mat, too, and have my melancholy moments when I remember that he and I are not going back together.

"I hope you will think me improved by my long trip—I mean in behavior, as well as health. I have seen much, and learned much, and thought much—and I hope I have really profited and altered for the better during my absence. It is such a pleasure to think I am really going home—"

Here Mr. Blyth stops abruptly and closes the letter, for Mrs. Thorpe re-enters the room. "The rest is only about when he expects to be back," whispers Valentine to Mrs. Peckover. "By my calculations," he continues, raising his voice and turning toward Mrs. Thorpe; "by my calculations (which, not having a mathematical head, I don't boast of, mind, as being infallibly correct), Zack is likely, I should say, to be here in about—"

"Hush! hush! hush!" cries Mrs. Peckover, jumping up with incredible agility at the window, and clapping her hands in a violent state of excitement. "Don't talk about when he will be here—*here he is!* He's come in a cab—he's got out into the garden—he sees me. Welcome back, Master Zack, welcome back! Hooray! hooray!" Here Mrs. Peckover forgets her company-manners, and waves the red cotton hand-

kerchief out of the window in an irrepressible
burst of triumph.

Zack's hearty laugh is heard outside—then his
quick step on the stairs—then the door opens,
and he comes in with his beaming sun-burned
face healthier and heartier than ever. His first
embrace is for his mother, his second for Madonna; and, after he has greeted every one else
cordially, he goes back to those two, and Mr.
Blyth is glad to see that he sits down between
them and takes their hands gently and affectionately in his.

Matthew Grice is in all their memories, when
the first greetings are over. Valentine and Madonna look at each other—and the girl's fingers
sign hesitatingly the letters of Matthew's name.

"She is thinking of the comrade you have
lost," says the painter, addressing himself, a little sadly, to Zack.

"The only living soul that's kin to her now by
her mother's side," adds Mrs. Peckover. "It's
like her pretty ways to be thinking of him kindly,
for her mother's sake."

"Are you really determined, Zack, to take
that second voyage?" asks Valentine. "Are
you determined to go back to America, on the
one faint chance of seeing Mat once more?"

"If I am a living man eighteen months
hence," Zack answers resolutely, "nothing shall
prevent my taking the voyage. Matthew Grice
loved me like a brother. And, like a brother, I
will yet bring him back—if he lives to keep his
promise and meet me, when the time comes."

The time came; and on either side, the two
comrades of former days—in years so far apart,
in sympathies so close together—lived to look
each other in the face again. The solitude
which had once hardened Matthew Grice had
wrought on him, in his riper age, to better and
higher ends. In all his later roamings, the tie

which had bound him to those sacred human interests in which we live and move and have our being—the tie which he himself believed that he had broken—held fast to him still. His grim, scarred face softened, his heavy hand trembled in the friendly grasp that held it, as Zack pleaded with him once more; and, this time, pleaded not in vain.

"I've never been my own man again," said Mat, "since you and me wished each other good-by on the sand-hills. The lonesome places have got strange to me—and my rifle's heavier in hand than ever I knew it before. There's some part of myself that seems left behind-like, between Mary's grave and Mary's child. Must I cross the seas again to find it? Give us hold of your hand, Zack—and take the leavings of me back, along with you."

So the noble nature of the man unconsciously asserted itself in his simple words. So the two returned to the old land together. The first kiss with which his dead sister's child welcomed him back cooled the Tramp's Fever forever; and the Man of many Wanderings rested at last among the friends who loved him, to wander no more.

END OF VOLUME ELEVEN.